A Light in the Window

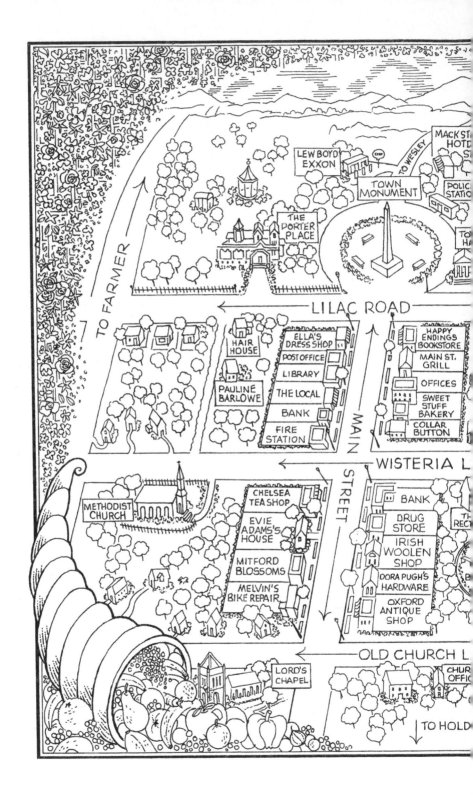

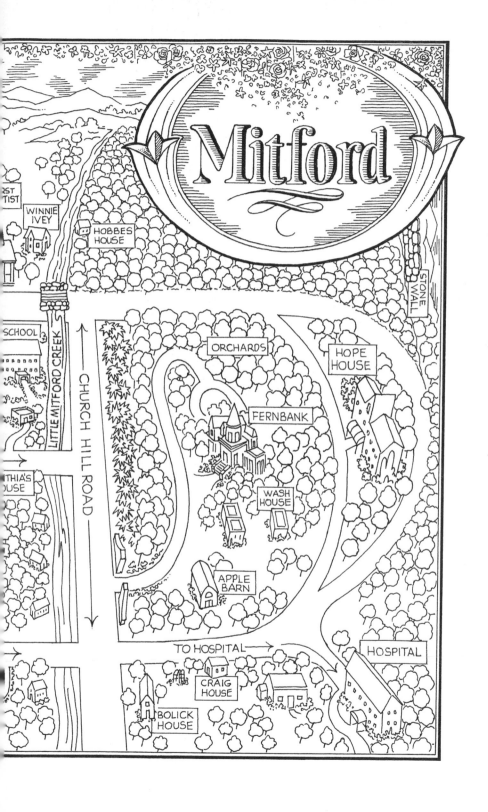

Other Mitford Books by Jan Karon

AT HOME IN MITFORD

THESE HIGH, GREEN HILLS

OUT TO CANAAN

The Mitford Years

A Light
in the
Window

JAN KARON

Viking

VIKING
Published by the Penguin Group
Penguin Putnam Inc., 375 Hudson Street,
New York, New York 10014, U.S.A.
Penguin Books Ltd, 27 Wrights Lane, London W8 5TZ, England
Penguin Books Australia Ltd, Ringwood, Victoria, Australia
Penguin Books Canada Ltd, 10 Alcorn Avenue, Toronto, Ontario, Canada M4V 3B2
Penguin Books (N.Z.) Ltd, 182–190 Wairau Road,
Auckland 10, New Zealand
Penguin India, 210 Chiranjiv Tower, 43 Nehru Place,
New Delhi 11009, India

Penguin Books Ltd, Registered Offices:
Harmondsworth, Middlesex, England

Published in 1998 by Viking Penguin,
a member of Penguin Putnam Inc.

1   3   5   7   9   10   8   6   4   2

Illustrations by George Ulrich
Map by Hal Just. Copyright © Penguin Books USA Inc., 1997

Publisher's Note
This is a work of fiction. Names, characters, places, and incidents either are
the product of the author's imagination or are used fictitiously, and any
resemblance to actual persons, living or dead, events, or locales is entirely
coincidental.

LIBRARY OF CONGRESS CATALOGING IN PUBLICATION DATA
Karon, Jan, date.
A light in the window / Jan Karon.
p.   cm. — (The Mitford years)
ISBN 0-670-88226-7
1. City and town life—United States—Fiction.   2. Clergy—North Carolina—Fiction.
3. Christian fiction, American.   4. Domestic fiction, American.
5. Mitford (N.C. : Imaginary place)—Fiction.
I. Title.   II. Series: Karon, Jan, date   Mitford years.
PS3561.A678L54   1998
813'.54—dc21   98-21317

This book is printed on acid-free paper.

Printed in the United States of America
Set in Adobe Garamond
Designed by Francesca Belanger

For my mother,
Wanda Setzer,
an encourager

Acknowledgments

My warmest thanks to Buck Waddell; Derald West; Murray Whisnant; Joyce Alexander; Mitford's attending physician, Dr. Bunky Davant; Mitford's attorney, Tony DiSanti; my editor, Dave Toht; my brother and friend, Barry Setzer; my sister and pal, Brenda Furman; my brother, Randy Setzer, who gave me my writing shirt; Father Jack Podsiadlo; Gina and Allan Morehead; Laura Watts; The Singing Boys of Beacon; and all the book-sellers whose enthusiasm for Mitford is greatly appreciated. Thanks, also, to my readers, to whom I lovingly give a small town—and a big family—to call your very own.

Contents

A Light in the Window

CHAPTER ONE

Close Encounters

Serious thinking and crossing the street, he once said, shouldn't be attempted simultaneously.

The red pickup truck was nearly upon him when he saw it. The shock of seeing it bear down with such ferocious speed sent him reeling backward to the curb, where he crashed in a sitting position. He caught a fleeting glance of the driver, talking on a telephone, as the truck careened around the corner.

"Father Tim! Are you all right?"

Winnie Ivey's expression was so grieved he felt certain he was badly hurt. He let Winnie help him up, feeling a numb shock where he'd slammed onto the curb.

Winnie's broad face was flushed with anger. "That maniac! Who was that fool, anyway?"

"I don't know. Perhaps I'm the fool for not looking where I was going." He laughed weakly.

"You're no such thing! I saw the light, it was still yellow, you had plenty of time to cross, and here comes this truck roarin' down on you like a freight train, and somebody in it talkin' on a phone."

She turned to the small crowd that had rushed out of the Main Street Grill. "A phone in a truck!" she said with disgust. "Can you believe it? I should have got his license number."

"Thank you, Winnie." He put his arm around the sturdy shoulders of the Sweet Stuff Bakery owner. "You've got a special talent for being in the right place at the right time."

Percy Mosely, who owned the Grill, ran out with his spatula in his hand. "If I was you, I'd ask th' good Lord to kick that feller's butt plumb to Wesley. Them poached eggs you eat are now scrambled."

The rector patted his pockets for the heavy office key and checked his wallet. All there. "No harm done," he assured his friends. The incident had simply been a regrettably dramatic way to begin his first week home from Ireland.

Though he'd spent the summer in Sligo, he found on returning that he hadn't, after all, missed summer in Mitford. His roses bloomed on, the grass lay like velvet under the network of village sprinklers, and parishioners were still leaving baskets of tomatoes on his porch.

As he came up the walk to the rectory, he heard a booming bark from the garage. It was the greeting he had missed every livelong day of his sojourn across the pond.

Since returning home less than a week ago, he had awakened each morning to see Barnabas standing by the bed, staring at him soberly. The inquiry in the eyes of his black Bouvier-cum-sheepdog companion was simple: Are you home to stay, or is this a joke?

He walked through the kitchen and opened the garage door, as Barnabas, who had grown as vast as a bear during his absence, rushed at him with joy. Laying his front paws on the rector's shoulders, he gazed dolefully into the eyes of his master, whose glasses fogged at once.

"Come now, old fellow. Slack off!"

Barnabas leapt backward, danced for a moment on his hind legs, and lunged forward to give the rector a great lick on the face that sent a shower of saliva into his left ear.

The victim dodged toward his parked Buick and crashed onto the hood with his elbow. " 'Sing and make music in your hearts,' " he recited loudly from a psalm, " 'always giving thanks to the Father for everything'!"

Barnabas sat down at once and gazed at him, mopping the garage floor with his tail.

His dog was the only living creature he knew who was unfailingly disciplined by the hearing of the Word. It was a phenomenon that Walter had told over the whole of Ireland's West Country.

"Let's have a treat, pal. And you," he said to Dooley's rabbit, Jack, "will have beet tops." The Flemish giant regarded him with eyes the color of peat.

The house was silent. It wasn't one of Puny's days to work, and Dooley was at football practice. He had missed the boy terribly, reading and rereading the one scrawled message he had received in two long months:

I am fine. Barnabus is fine. Im ridin the hair off that horse.

He had missed the old rectory, too, with its clamor and quiet, its sunshine and shadow. Never before in his life as a rector had he found a home so welcoming or comfortable—a home that seemed, somehow, like a friend.

He spied the thing on his counter at once. It was Edith Mallory's signature blue casserole dish.

He was afraid of that.

Emma had written to Sligo to say that Pat Mallory had died soon after he left for Ireland. Heart attack. No warning. Pat, she said, had felt a wrenching chest pain, had sat down on the top step outside his bedroom, and after dropping dead sitting up, had toppled to the foot of the stairs, where the Mallorys' maid of thirty years had found him just before dinner.

"Oh, Mr. Mallory," she was reported to have said, "you shouldn't have gone and done that. We're havin' lasagna."

Sitting there on the farmhouse window seat, reading Emma's five-page letter, he had known that Edith Mallory would not waste any time when he returned.

Long before Pat's death, he'd been profoundly unsteadied when she had slipped her hand into his or let her fingers run along his arm. At one point, she began winking at him during sermons, which distracted him to such a degree that he resumed his old habit of preaching over the heads of the congregation, literally.

So far, he had escaped her random snares but had once dreamed he was locked with her in the parish-hall coat closet, pounding desperately on the door and pleading with the sexton to let him out.

Now Pat, good soul, was cold in the grave, and Edith's casserole was hot on his counter.

Casseroles! Their seduction had long been used on men of the cloth, often with rewarding results for the cook.

Casseroles, after all, were a gesture that on the surface could not be mistaken for anything other than righteous goodwill. And, once one had consumed and exclaimed over the initial offering, along would come another on its very heels, until the bachelor curate ended up a married curate or the divorced deacon a fellow so skillfully ensnared that he never knew what hit him.

In the language of food, there were casseroles, and there were casseroles. Most were used to comfort the sick or inspire the down-hearted. But certain others, in his long experience, were so filled with allure and innuendo that they ceased to be Broccoli Cheese Delight intended for the stomach and became arrows aimed straight for the heart.

In any case, there was always the problem of what to do with the dish. Decent people returned it full of something else. Which meant that the person to whom you returned it would be required, at some point, to give you another food item, all of which produced a cycle that was unimaginably tedious.

Clergy, of course, were never required to fill the dish before returning it, but either way, it had to be returned. And there, clearly, was the rub.

He approached the unwelcome surprise as if a snake might have been coiled inside. His note of thanks, which he would send over to-morrow by Puny, would be short and to the point:

Dear Edith: Suffice it to say that you remain one of the finest cooks in the county. That was no lie; it was undeniably true.

Your way with (blank, blank) is exceeded only by your graciousness. A thousand thanks. In His peace, Fr Tim.

There.

He lifted the lid. Instantly, his mouth began to water, and his heart gave a small leap of joy.

Crab cobbler! One of his favorites. He stared with wonder at the dozen flaky homemade biscuits poised on the bed of fresh crabmeat and fragrant sauce.

Perhaps, he thought with sudden abandon, he should give Edith Mallory a ring this very moment and express his thanks.

As he reached for the phone, he realized what he was doing—he was placing his foot squarely in a bear trap.

He hastily clamped the lid on the steaming dish. "You see?" he muttered darkly. "That's the way it happens."

Where casseroles were concerned, one must constantly be on guard.

"Edith Mallory's lookin' to give you th' big whang-do," said Emma.

Until this inappropriate remark, there had been a resonant peace in the small office. The windows were open to morning air embroidered with birdsong. His sermon notes were going at a pace. And the familiar comfort of his old swivel chair was sheer bliss.

"And what, exactly, is that supposed to mean?"

His part-time church secretary glanced up from her ledger. "It means she's going to cook your goose."

He did not like her language. "I am sixty-one years old and a life-long bachelor. Why anyone would want to give me a whang . . . why anyone would . . . it's unthinkable," he said flatly.

"I can tell she thinks about it all th' time. Besides, remember Father Appel who got married when he was sixty-five, right after his social security kicked in? And that deacon who was fifty-nine, who married th' redheaded woman who owned the taxi company in Wesley? Then, there was that salesman who worked at the Collar Button . . ."

"Spare me the details," he said curtly, opening his drawer and looking for the Wite-Out.

Emma peered at him over her glasses. "Just remember," she muttered.

"Remember what?"

"Forearmed is forewarned."

"No, Emma. Forewarned is forearmed."

"Peedaddle. I never do get that right. But if I were you, I'd duck when I see her comin'."

I've been ducking when I see her coming for twelve years, he thought.

"One thing in her favor," said Emma, recording another check, "is she's a great hostess. As you have surely learned from doin' your parties, a rector needs that. Some preachers' wives don't do pea-turkey, if you ask me. Of course, if anything's goin' to happen with your neighbor, and Lord knows, I hope it will—you ought to just go on and give 'er a nice engagement ring—then Edith would have to jump on some-body else."

"Emma," he said, ripping the cover off the typewriter, "I have finally got a handle on the most important sermon I've written in a year . . ."

"Don't say I didn't warn you," she replied, pressing her lips to-gether in that way he loathed.

At noon, Ron Malcolm appeared at the door, wearing boots caked with dried mud and a red baseball cap.

Being away for two months had given everyone the rector knew, and Mitford as well, a fresh, almost poignant, reality. He had scarcely ever noticed that Ron Malcolm was a man of such cheering vigor. Then again, perhaps it was the retired contractor's involvement in the nursing-home project that had done something for the color in his face and put a gleam in his eyes.

"Well, Father, we're off and running. Jacobs has sent their job superintendent over. He's having a trailer installed on the site today." He shook the rector's hand with great feeling.

"I can hardly believe it's finally happening."

"Five million bucks!" Ron said. "This nursing home is the biggest thing to happen around here since the Wesley furniture factory. Have you met Leeper?"

"Leeper?"

"Buck Leeper. The job superintendent. We talked about him be-fore you left for Ireland. He said he'd try to get by your office."

"I haven't met him. I'll have to walk up—maybe Wednesday afternoon."

Ron sat down on the visitors' bench and removed his cap. "Emma around?"

"Gone to the post office."

"I think it's only fair that I talk to you straight about Buck Leeper. A few months ago, I told you he's hardheaded, rough. I know I don't have to worry about you, but he's the kind who can make you lose your religion."

"Aha."

"His daddy was Fane Leeper, so called because a preacher once said he was the most profane man he'd ever met. Fane Leeper was also the best job superintendent on the East Coast. He made three contractors rich men, and then alcohol got 'im, as they say.

"You need to know that Buck is just like his daddy. He learned contractin', cussin', and drinkin' from Fane, and the only way he could get out from under the shadow of his father was to outdo him in all three categories."

Ron paused, as if to let that information sink in.

"Buck's on this job because he'll save us money—and a lot of grief. He'll bring it in on time and on budget, and you can count on it. Out of respect to you, Father, I talked to Jacobs about sending us another man, but they won't send anybody but Buck on a job this size." He stood up and zipped his jacket. "We'll probably hate Jacobs for this, but before it's over, we'll thank him."

"I trust your judgment."

Ron opened the door and was backing out with his hat in his hand.

"You might look softhearted, Father, but I've seen you operate a time or two, and I know you can handle Buck. Just give 'im his rein."

The rector looked out at the maple across the street, which had taken on a tinge of russet since yesterday. "I can't imagine that Mr. Leeper will be any problem at all," he said.

"Timothy?"

It was Cynthia, his neighbor, peering through the screened door of the kitchen, her hands cupped on either side of her eyes. She was wearing a white blouse and blue denim skirt and a bandanna around her blond hair.

"You look like Heidi!" he said to his neighbor. Though she admitted to being fiftysomething, there were times when she looked like a girl. Again he was struck by the fresh, living way in which he saw people, as if he had lately risen from the dead.

She walked past him, unfurling the faintest scent of wisteria on the air. "You said to think of something we could do to celebrate your return."

She went to the stove and lifted the lid on the pot of soup he was making. "Yum," she said, inhaling. Then, she turned to him and smiled. Her eyes were like sapphires, smoky and deep with that nearly violet hue that always caught him off-guard.

"And have you thought about it?" he asked, afraid he might croak like a frog when he spoke.

"They say walls have ears. I'd better whisper it."

He had completely forgotten how easily she fit into his arms.

Going to a town council meeting was decidedly not what he wanted to do with his evening. After two months away, he hardly knew what was going on. And he was still feeling oddly jet-lagged, shaking his head vigorously on occasion with some hope of clearing it. But he would go; it might put him back in the swing of things, and frankly, he was curious why the mayor, Esther Cunningham, had called an unofficial meeting and why it might concern him.

"Don't eat," Esther told him on the phone. "Ray's bringin' baked beans, cole slaw, and ribs from home. Been cookin' all day."

"Hallelujah," he said with feeling.

There was a quickening in the air of the mayor's office. Ray was setting out his home-cooked supper on the vast desktop, overlooked by pictures of their twenty-three grandchildren at the far end.

"Mayor," said Leonard Bostick, "it's a cryin' shame you cain't cook as good as Ray."

"I've got better things to do," she snapped. "I did the cookin' for forty years. Now it's his turn."

Ray grinned. "You tell 'em, honey."

"Whooee!" said Paul Hartley. "Baby backs! Get over here, Father, and give us a blessin'."

"Come on!" shouted the mayor to the group lingering in the hall. "It's blessin' time!"

Esther Cunningham held out her hands, and the group eagerly formed a circle.

"Our Lord," said the rector, "we're grateful for the gift of friends and neighbors and those willing to lend their hand to the welfare of this place. We thank you for the peace of this village and for your grace to do the work that lies ahead. We thank you, too, for this food and ask a special blessing on the one who prepared it. In Jesus' name."

"Amen!" said the assembly.

The mayor was the first in line. "You're goin' t' get a blessing, all right," she told her husband. "Just look at this sauce! You've done it again, sweet face."

Ray winked at the rector. There, thought the rector, is a happy man if I ever saw one.

"How's your diabetes, Father?"

"It won't tolerate the torque you've put under the hood of that pot, I regret to say."

"Take doubles on m' slaw, then," said Ray, heaping the rector's plate.

"You know what we're here to talk about," said the mayor.

Everybody nodded, except the rector.

"I don't want it to come up in a town meetin', and I don't want it officially voted on, vetoed, or otherwise messed with. We're just goin' to seek agreement here tonight like a family and let it go at that."

She looked at their faces and leaned forward. "Got it?"

Linder Hayes stood up slowly, thin as a strip of baling wire. He placed his hands carefully behind his back, peered at his shoes, and cleared his throat.

"Here goes," said Joe Ivey, nudging the rector.

"Your honor," said Linder.

"You don't have t' 'your honor' me. This is an unofficial meetin'."

"Your honor," said Linder, who was a lawyer and preferred the formalities, "I'd like to speak for the merchants of this town who have to make a livin' out of the day-to-day run of things.

"Now, we know that an old woman dressed up in party hats and gumboots, directin' traffic around the monument, is not a fit sight for tourists, especially with leaf season comin' on.

"You say she's harmless, but that, in fact, is not the point. With her infamous snaggle tooth and those old army decorations, think what she'd look like if she came flyin' out of th' fog wavin' at cars. She'd clean th' tourists out of here so fast it'd make your head swim."

"And good riddance," said the mayor testily.

"Madam Mayor, we've fought this tourist battle for years. We've all moved over to give you plenty of room to do your job, and you've done it. Your faithful defense of what is good and right and true to the character of this town has been a strong deterrent to the rape and plunder of senseless development and reckless growth.

"But . . ." Linder gave a long pause and looked around the room. "Two Model Village awards will not suffice our merchants for cold, hard cash. That ol' woman is enough to make babies squall and grown men tuck tail and run. Clearly, I don't have to make a livin' off tourists, but my wife does—and so, incidentally, do half your grandchildren."

"We're in for it," muttered Joe Ivey. "I should've carried a bed roll and a blanket."

"Linder," said Esther Cunningham, "sit down and take a load off your feet."

"Your honor . . ."

"Thank you, Linder," the mayor said, measuring each word.

Linder appeared to waver for a moment, like a leaf caught in a breeze. Then, he sat down.

"I'd like us to look at a couple of things before we open for a brief discussion," said the mayor. "First, let's look at my platform. There is no such thing in it as a middle plank, a left plank, or a right plank. It's just one straight platform. Period. Joe, why don't you remind us what it is?"

Joe stood up. "Mitford takes care of its own!" He sat down again, flushed with pride.

"Mitford . . . takes . . . care . . . of . . . its . . . own. That's been my platform for fourteen years, and as long as I'm mayor, it will continue to be th' platform. Number one. Miss Rose Watson may be snaggle-toothed and she may be crazy, but she's our own. Number two. Based on that, we're goin' to take care of 'er.

"Number three. Directin' traffic around the monument is the best thing that's happened to her since she was a little girl, as normal as you and me. Uncle Billy says she sleeps like a baby now, instead of ramblin' through that old house all night, and she's turned nice as you please to him. Directin' traffic is a genuine responsibility to her. She takes pride in it."

"She does a real good job," said Ernestine Ivory, who colored beet red at the sound of her own voice.

"What's that, Ernestine?" asked the mayor.

"Miss Rose does a real good job of directing traffic. 'Course that's just me . . ."

"That's just you and a lot of other people who think the same thing. She's very professional. I don't know where in th' world she learned it.

"Now, here's what I propose, and I ask you to consider it in your hearts. Every day from noon to one o'clock, traffic drops off and Mitford eats lunch. My stomach starts growlin' right on th' button, like th' rest of this crowd.

"I propose we let Miss Rose direct traffic five days a week, from noon 'til one, which'll give her just enough cars to keep her happy.

"Now, Linder, I have to hand it to you about those cocktail hats and funny clothes, so I propose we give 'er a uniform. Navy hat, skirt, and jacket from my old days in th' Waves. Be a perfect fit. I was skinny as a rail, wasn't I, doll?"

Ray gave the mayor a thumbs-up.

"Ernestine, I want you to go with me to dress her in th' mornin' at ten o'clock, and Joe, how about you givin' her a nice haircut. We'll bring 'er up to your shop about eleven."

"Be glad to."

"Father, I wish you'd make it your business to pray about this."

"You have my word," he said.

"And Linder, honey, I really appreciate the way you're lookin' after the merchants. God knows, somebody needs to. Any questions?"

Before anyone could respond, the mayor pounded her desk with a gavel. "Meeting adjourned. All in favor say aye."

"I declare," said the rector, walking home with Joe Ivey, "every time I go to a meeting with Esther Cunningham, I feel like somebody's screwed my head around backwards."

You'll be coming home to a new Dooley, Marge had written just before he left Ireland. When he read that, his heart sank. He had managed to grow fond of the old Dooley.

He's actually learning to speak English, his friend wrote from Meadowgate Farm. *Just wait; you'll be thrilled.*

He couldn't say he had been thrilled, exactly, on seeing his twelve-year-old charge again. First, the cowlick had miraculously disappeared. When he left for Sligo in July, it had been shooting up like a geyser; now, it simply wasn't there, and frankly, he missed it. Then, he noticed that Dooley's freckles appeared to be fading, an upshot that he especially regretted.

He also found a new resoluteness in the boy that he'd only fleetingly glimpsed before, not to mention the fact that he was putting the top back on the catsup and the mayonnaise. How could so much change have taken place in two short months?

"I refuse to take credit," Marge told him on the phone from Meadowgate the morning after his return. "It's all that wonderful spade work you'd already done, laced with a strong dose of cow manure and fresh air. Last weekend, he helped Hal deliver a colt, which was like a shot of Miracle-Gro to his self-confidence. Furthermore, I'm crushed to tell you that Rebecca Jane took her first step to . . . guess who? Uncle Dools!"

I have planted, Apollos watered, but God gave the increase, the rector mused as he approached the rectory from the council meeting. Joe Ivcy had offered him "a taste of brandy" if he cared to walk up the stairs to the barber shop, but he declined. He could hardly wait to get home and into the old burgundy bathrobe he'd sorely missed in Ireland.

After a quick trip with Barnabas to the Baxter Park hedge, he took a bottle of mineral water from the cabinet, and the two of them climbed the stairs.

"Dooley!"

"Yessir?"

Yessir? He walked down the hall to the boy's room and found him sitting against the head of his bed, reading and absently scratching his big toe. The room seemed remarkably well-ordered.

"How's it going?"

Dooley looked up. "Great."

"Terrific." He stood in the doorway, feeling an awkward joy. "What's the book?"

"Dynamics of Veterinary Medicine."

"Aha."

"See this?" Dooley held the book toward him. "It's a picture of a colt being born. That's jis' the way it happened last weekend. It's the neatest thing I ever done . . . did. I want t' be a vet. Doc Owen said I could be one."

"Of course you can. You can be whatever you want to be." He stepped into the room.

"I never wanted to be anything before."

"Maybe you never saw any choices before."

"I never wanted to be an astronaut or a rock star or anything, like Buster Austin wants t' be."

"That's OK. Why rush into wanting to be something?" He sat down on the bed.

"That's what I thought." Dooley went back to his book, ignoring him but somehow comfortable with the fact that he was there.

"So, how's Buster?" Only months ago, he and Buster Austin had been the darkest adversaries, with Dooley whipping the tar out of him twice.

"Cool. We swapped lunches today. He likes 'at old meatloaf you make. I got 'is baloney."

"Done your homework?"

"Yessir."

Yessir. It rang in his ears like some foreign language. "How's the science project coming? Are we finishing it up Sunday evening?"

"Yep. You'll like it. It's neat."

Since he came home from Ireland, he'd been peering into Dooley's face, searching it out. Something was different. A wound had healed, perhaps; he was looking more like a boy instead of someone who'd grown old before his time.

It had been nearly a year since Russell Jacks, the church sexton and Dooley's grandfather, had come down with pneumonia and was rushed into emergency treatment. The boy had come home with him from the hospital, and he'd been here ever since.

One of the best things he had ever done was bring Dooley Barlowe home. Yes, he'd been trouble and calamity and plenty of it—but worth it and then some.

"I hear you went to see your grandpa every week. Good medicine."

"Yep."

"How is he?"

"That woman that's lookin' after 'im, she says he's doing good, but he ain't had any livermush since you left . . ."

"Uh-oh."

"And he was riled about it."

"We'll take him some. And I'll see you at breakfast. Has Jenny been around?"

"I ain't into 'at ol' poop, n' more."

The rector grinned. There! he thought. There's my old Dooley.

In his room, Barnabas leapt onto the blanket at the foot of the bed, then lay down with a yawn as the rector stepped into the shower. While the raftered room in the Sligo farmhouse had been perfectly comfortable, the long passage down the hall to the finicky shower was another story entirely. As far as he could see, it might be months before the thrill of his own bathroom, *en suite,* began to wane.

He felt as mindless and contented as a steamed clam as he sat on the bed and dialed his neighbor.

"Hello?"

"Hello, yourself."

"Timothy!" said Cynthia. "I was just thinking of you."

"Surely you have something better to do."

"I was thinking that my idea of how to celebrate was too silly."

"Silly, yes, but not too silly," he said. "In fact, I was wondering—when are we going to do it?"

"Ummmm . . ."

"Saturday night?" he asked, hoping.

"Oh, rats. My nephew's coming. I mean, I'm delighted he's coming. You must meet him. He's very dear. Saturday would have been so perfect. Could we do it Monday evening?"

"Vestry meeting," he said.

"Tuesday I have to finish an illustration and FedEx it first thing Wednesday morning. Could you do it Wednesday around six-thirty?"

"Building committee at seven."

"Darn."

"I could do it Friday," he said.

"Great!"

"No. No, wait, there's something on Friday," he said, extending the phone cord to the dresser where he opened his black engagement book. "Yes, that's it. The hospital is having a staff dinner for Hoppy, and I'm giving the invocation. Would you come?"

"Dinner in a hospital? That's suicide! Besides, I can't stand hospitals. I nearly died in one, you know."

"No, I didn't know."

"And I don't know how you ever will know these things unless we can figure out a way to see each other. What about Sunday evening? That's usually a relaxing time for you. Sunday might be lovely."

"I'm helping Dooley finish his science project. He has to hand it in Monday morning." A nameless despair was robbing him of any contentment he had just felt.

"I could meet you on the bench by your German roses at six o'clock tomorrow. We could do it there and get it over with."

But he didn't want to do it and get it over with. He wanted to linger over it, to savor it.

"You're sighing," she said.

"It's just that there's so much going on after being away for two months."

"I understand," she said simply.

"You do? Do you really?"

"Of course I do."

"I'll call you tomorrow. Let's not waste it on the garden bench."

"All that lumpy, wet moss," she said, laughing.

"All that cold, damp concrete," he said forlornly.

"I hope you sleep well." He could hear a tenderness in her voice. "Jet lag really does persist for days."

"Yes. Well. So," he said, feeling immeasurably foolish, "blink your bedroom lights good night."

"I will if you will."

"Cynthia?"

"Yes?"

"I . . ." He cleared his throat. "You . . ."

"Spit it out," she said.

He had started to croak; he couldn't have uttered another word if his life depended on it.

"I'm not going to worry anymore about being too silly. It's you, Timothy, who are far too silly!"

His heart pounded as he hung up the phone. He had nearly told her he loved her, that she was wonderful; he had nearly gone over the edge of the cliff, with no ledges to break his fall.

He went to the window and looked down upon her tiny house. He saw the lights blink twice through the windows of her bedroom under the eaves. He raced around the bed and flipped his own light switch off, then on again, and off.

"Good Lord," he said, breathlessly, standing there in the dark. "Who is the twelve-year-old in this house, anyway?"

When he called at noon, her answering machine emitted a long series of beeps followed by a dial tone.

He had just hung up when the phone rang.

"Father!" It was Absalom Greer, the country preacher.

"Brother Greer! I was going to call you this very afternoon."

"Well, sir, how bad a mess did I leave for you to clean up?"

"People are still telling me how much they enjoyed your supply preaching at Lord's Chapel. We caught them off-guard, you know. I hope it didn't go too hard for you in the beginning."

"The first Sunday was mighty lean. Your flock didn't mind you too good about throwin' their support to an old revival preacher. Then the next Sunday, about half-full, I'd say. Third Sunday, full up. On and on like that 'til they were standin' on the steps.

"If you hadn't come home s' soon, we'd have had an altar call. It was all I could do t' hold it back toward the end."

Father Tim laughed. "You're going to be a tough act to follow, my friend."

"I tried to hold back on the brimstone, too, but I didn't always succeed. 'Repent and be saved!' said John. 'Repent and be saved!' said Jesus. There's the gist of it. If you don't repent, you don't get saved. So, you're lookin' at the alternative, and people don't want to hear that nowadays."

"You'd better prepare your crowd for me when I come out to the country."

Absalom laughed heartily. "That might be askin' the impossible!" He could see the faces of his rural Baptist congregation when they got a load of a preacher in a long dress.

"I've got something for you," said the rector. "I'd like to bring it out one day and hear what another man saw from the backside of my pulpit."

"Just let us know when you're comin'. We'll lay on a big feed."

"I'll do it! And God bless you for all the effort you gave us here. It counted for something. Ron Malcolm said you were as plain as the bark on a tree in delivering the Gospel."

"A man has to stand out of the way of the Gospel, and that keeps us plain if we let it."

The rector sat smiling after he hung up. There was nothing, in fact, plain about the old man with the craggy brows and mane of silver hair. His tall, lean frame made a stunning sight in the pulpit, Cynthia said, with his blue eyes blazing like flint striking rock and a sprig of laurel in his buttonhole.

Greer, he wrote on the calendar for the third week of October.

He was walking home from the office in a misting rain when the heavens erupted in a downpour.

Drenched at once, he raced to the wool shop and stood under the awning that was drumming with rain, pondering what to do. Hazel Bailey waved to him from the back of the shop, signaling that he should come in and take refuge. Already soaked, he decided he would make a run for it.

He lifted his newspaper over his head and was ready to dash toward the next awning when he heard a car horn. It was Edith Mallory's black Lincoln, which was approximately the size of a condominium.

The window slipped down as if oiled, and her driver leaned across the seat. "Father Tim," Ed Coffey yelled, "Miz Mallory says get in. We'll carry you home."

The water was already running along the curb in a torrent.

He got in.

Edith Mallory might have been Cleopatra on her barge, for all the swath of silk raincoat that flowed against the cushiony leather and the mahogany bar that appeared from the arm rest.

"Sherry?" she said, smiling in that enigmatic way that made his adrenalin pump. It was, however, his flight adrenalin.

"No, thanks!" he exclaimed, trying to do something with the sodden newspaper. A veritable cloud of perfume hung in the air of the warm interior; he felt instantly woozy, drugged, like a child of four going down for a nap.

That's the way it was with Edith; one's guard weakened when needed most.

"Dreadful weather, and you above all must mind your health . . ."

Why above all, he wondered, irritated.

". . . Because you're our shepherd, of course, and your little flock needs you to take care of us." Edith looked at him with the large brown eyes that overpowered her sharp features, rather like, he thought, one of those urchin children in paintings done on velvet.

"Well, yes, you have a point," he said stiffly. He saw Ed Coffey's eyes in the rearview mirror; the corners appeared to be crinkling, as if he were grinning hugely.

"We want you to stay strong," she crooned, "for all your widows and orphans."

He looked out the window mindlessly, not noticing that they had passed his street. The awning over the Grill had come loose on one corner, and the rain was gushing onto the sidewalk like a waterfall.

"You might have just the weensiest sherry," she said, filling a small glass from a decanter that sat in the mahogany bar like an egg in a nest.

"I really don't think . . . ," he said, feeling the glass already in his hand.

"There, now!" she said. "That will hit the nail on the jackpot!" When she smiled, her wide mouth pushed her cheeks into a series of tiny wrinkles like those in crepe paper. Some people actually found her attractive, he reminded himself—why couldn't he?

He gulped the sherry and returned the glass to her, feeling like a child who had taken his croup medicine.

"Good boy," she said.

Where were they, anyway? The windows were streaming with rain, and the lights of the car didn't penetrate far enough to give him any idea of their whereabouts. They had just passed the Grill, but he couldn't remember turning at the corner. Perhaps they had driven by the monument and were on their way to Wesley.

"Why ah, haven't we gone to the rectory?" He felt a mild panic.

"We're going in just the weensiest minute," she said, blinking at him. He could not believe that her hand snaked across the seat toward his. He remembered the dream about the coat closet, and how he had pounded on the door and shouted for Russell Jacks.

He drew his hand away, quite unobtrusively, he thought, and scratched his nose. The sherry had turned on a small light in a far corner of his mind. Perhaps she imagined he'd be after her money for the Sunday school rooms and willing to do a little hand-holding to get it. It was going to take a cool two hundred thousand to turn that sprawling airstrip of an attic into the Sunday school Josiah Baxter had envisioned. But his own hand would most certainly not milk it forth. On his visitation meeting with the vestry, he had gone over a list of wouldn'ts, so no one would be aggrieved down the road.

He wouldn't, for example, participate in fund-raising efforts outside the pulpit. Period. He would not personally court, cajole, preach to, sweet-talk, or exhort anyone for money to build anything.

"Ah, Timothy," sighed Edith Mallory, rubbing the tweed of his sleeve as if it were a cat, "Ireland has done wonders for you, I can tell." She moved closer. "It's so lonely being a widow," she said, sniffing. "I sometimes just . . . ache all over."

When he was finally delivered to the rectory, nearly soaked to the skin, Puny was getting ready to leave. She stared at him with alarm as she put on her coat.

"You look like you been through somethin' awful!"

"Hell!" he exclaimed.

She was shocked to hear him use such language.

There was a red pickup truck parked in front of the office when he arrived on Monday. Someone inside appeared to be talking on a car phone.

The rector fished the key from his pocket as the man got out of the truck and slammed the door. He flipped a cigarette to the sidewalk and ground it out with a quick turn of his heel.

He was big, beefy, and heavy, wearing chinos stuffed into high boots, a flannel shirt under a quilted vest, and a hard hat.

"You the father?"

"Yes. What can I do for you?"

The man took a package of Lucky Strikes from his shirt pocket, shook a cigarette out, lit it, and inhaled deeply.

"Buck Leeper," he said, walking to the rector and extending his hand. The handshake lasted only an instant, but in that instant, the rector felt an odd shock. The hand seemed hugely swollen and red, as if the flesh might burst suddenly from the skin.

"I'm glad to meet you," he lied, hearing the words automatically form and speak themselves. Yet, in a way, he was glad to meet him; the deed was done. "Come in, Mr. Leeper, and have a cup of coffee."

"No coffee," he said, wedging through the door ahead of the rector. The rector hung his jacket on the peg, noticing how the man's presence had made the room suddenly smaller.

"Malcolm said to ask you about the garden statues."

"Garden statues?"

"Lyin' up there on the site. We dozed 'em up. Maybe a dozen pieces, some broke, some not. I don't have time to mess with it." He exhaled a fume of smoke.

"How extraordinary. Of course. I'll be right up. Give me an hour."

The superintendent took a quick, deep drag off his cigarette. "At fifty smackers an hour for dozers, I don't have an hour."

"Well, then. What would you suggest I do?"

Leeper's tone was insolent and hard. "Tell me I can doze that crap off the side of the mountain."

The rector felt ice water in his veins. "I'd appreciate it," he said evenly, "if you'd put your cigarette out. This small room doesn't tolerate smoke."

The superintendent looked at him for a long moment, dropped his cigarette on the floor, and ground it out with a turn of his heel.

He opened the door. "I don't have time to run errands for your building committee. If you want th' statues, come and get 'em," he said and was gone.

"Good grief," moaned Ron Malcolm, hanging his head.

"Well, I can't say you didn't warn me."

"Yes, but I guess there's no warning that really prepares you for Buck Leeper. I insisted he come down here, say hello, introduce himself, ask you about the statues. I thought you'd want to keep them, but I didn't know. I guess I'm to blame. I should have handled it."

"No. Stop right there. There's no blame now and there's not going to be. If this morning was any indication, we're in for a rough ride. The man is clearly a walking time bomb. All I want to do is stay out of the way and let him get his job done."

"Fine," said Ron.

His building-committee chairman looked so despondent the rector put an arm around his shoulders. "Buck up," he said, without thinking.

They were still laughing when Ron pulled away from the curb in his blue pickup, headed for Lord's Chapel with the load of statuary.

"Whang-do," said Emma sourly, handing him the phone.

"I've invited the building committee to meet here on Wednesday evening." Edith Mallory sounded pleased with herself. "Of course, they loved the idea. Magdolen will do her famous spoonbread, but I'll do the tenderloin."

Tenderloin!

"I know how you enjoy a tenderloin. I've had it sent from New York."

"That's very generous of you. Of course, there's really no need to impose for a dinner meeting . . ."

"But life is so short," she said, sniffing. "Why have a dull meeting when you can have a dinner party?"

He didn't know why. Why, indeed?

"You can see the trump lloyd I had painted in the study. It looks just like old books on a shelf."

"Aha."

"I'll have Ed pick you up at a quarter 'til," she said. He could hear the little sucking noise that came from dragging on that blasted cigarette.

"No!" he nearly shouted. His car was still sitting in the garage with a dead battery. "Ah, no thanks. I'll come with Ron. We have a lot to discuss . . ."

"Of course, but Ron is coming with Tad Sherrill, he said, because his pickup . . . what did he say . . . blew a gasket, I think."

"Well, then, I'll just squeeze in with them. And thank you, Edith. It's more than good of you." He hung up at once, not surprised to find his forehead slightly damp.

"June," said Puny.

"No," sighed the rector.

"The fourteenth."

"But how will I get along without you? I've been dreading this."

"You don't have t' git along without me," she said. "After our honeymoon, I'm comin' back. I told you I would."

"Yes, but shouldn't you and Joe Joe move ahead with having children or . . . something?"

"Not right this minute, if you don't mind," she said archly, setting the mop bucket in the middle of the floor. He thought he had never seen his house help look more enchanting. Her red hair appeared suffused with a kind of glow; her very being radiated happiness. It was like having a wonderful lamp turned on around the place, and he certainly did not want the light to go out.

"Of course," she said, dipping the scrub brush in the soapy water, "we won't leave you hangin'. They'll git somebody else to look after things while I'm gone."

"I don't want anybody else," he said, feeling petulant.

"Oh, poop, eat your carrots. I made 'em th' way my grandpa liked 'em, with butter and a little brown sugar. And that's all the sweets you can have today."

"Thank you, Puny," he said. He couldn't help but notice that when she sassed him these days, she smiled. Looking at her on her hands and knees on the kitchen floor, in that earnest subjection he could hardly bear to see, he thought how he'd learned to love Puny Bradshaw like his own blood.

He wondered if she'd gotten the illustration finished, the one that had to be rushed to her publisher. When he called, he got only the last of her voice recording, ". . . the beep, thanks," and a sort of static that sounded like a transfer truck rolling along the highway.

When he hung up, he sat for a moment, looking at the rain lashing the office windows. He realized he hadn't wanted to talk with her, exactly. It was more like he had a longing to see her.

He skulked toward the rectory in a raincoat and rain hat, vowing to have Lew Boyd come and jump his battery tomorrow morning, first thing. Before going to his own door, he knocked on Cynthia's.

The roof over the shallow back stoop was hardly any protection. The wind and rain gusted around him violently.

"Cynthia!" he called through the roar. She had locked the screen, he knew, to keep the wind from catching it and tearing it off its hinges.

He shouted her name again. Only a dim light glowed in the direction of the stairs.

He rattled the screen door and pounded as hard as he could. He saw Violet leap onto the kitchen counter and peer at him as if he were the garbage collector.

"Madness!" he muttered at last, fleeing through the drenched hedge to the warm kitchen next door.

Magdolen greeted them at Clear Day, the Mallorys' vast contemporary house astride a ridge overlooking the valley. "Oh, good! Here's the father!" she said happily, helping him out of his raincoat. "We're so glad you're back from Ireland. You can never be too sure of your life over there. It's just tragic."

Tad and Ron left their dripping slickers in the foyer and went toward the library, where their hostess was serving canapés.

"We sure missed you during all the . . . well, you know," Magdolen sighed. "Miss Edith took it so hard and no children to comfort her. I thought you might like to see where I found Mr. Pat." She led him to the staircase.

"Right there," she said, pointing to the third step from the bottom. "He had landed there, half sitting up with his back against the banister. When I came into the hall, his eyes were wide open, staring straight at me. I thought he looked kind of off-color. So I said, 'Mr. Pat, I made you a nice, big dish of lasagna, so come and sit down before it gets cold.'"

She shuddered and held tight to his arm. "That's when he . . . rolled down the rest of the way."

"Magdolen!" Edith Mallory said sharply, taking the rector by the other arm and drawing him toward the library. Five damp committee members huddled around a fire that snapped and crackled on the grate.

"Mud and more mud," Ron Malcolm was saying. "Rivers of mud."

Tad Sherrill grunted. "Oceans of mud."

"And more mud coming, if the forecast holds," announced Winona Presley, thumping her secretarial pad with her ballpoint pen.

Warmed by a cabernet from the Mallory cellar, the diners avidly discussed weather disasters they had known.

"I worked on a job in Kentucky one time," said Ron, "where the rain didn't stop for twenty-one days." He was pleased to see he could cut the tenderloin with a fork. "Had four big Cats sittin' in mud up to the cab doors when it was over."

"What I hope I never see again," said Tad, "is a mud slide. Have you ever seen mud slide? It's as bad as lava out of a volcano. I've seen it cover houses above the roof line . . ."

"You know what I like about the French?" asked their hostess.

All eyes turned toward her in the great pause she designed to follow this question.

"When they dine, they talk only of food. The meal in front of them is the topic of their most earnest conversation. They would never think of ruining their digestion by talking of politics, and certainly not . . . mud," she said icily.

"But Edith, honey," said Tad, "mud is one of the things this meetin' is about."

Father Tim thought the look she gave her affable guest was needlessly patronizing. "This," their hostess informed them, "is dinner. The meeting about mud will be held in the library by the fire, with a glass of brandy." She drummed her fingers lightly on the table and smiled.

The rector could not avoid the thought that presented itself for consideration. It was that Pat Mallory probably threw himself down the stairs.

After the dessert of orange mocha cake with fresh cream, which, to the disappointment of their hostess, he feasted on with his eyes only, he excused himself to check his sugar. Diabetes was the sorriest of infirmities to drag to a dinner party.

In the guest powder room, awash with berry-colored chintz and black marble, he did what he had to do, then lowered the commode seat and sat there, wearily. To tell the truth, he would have preferred a meeting in the parish hall, with everyone drinking coffee out of Styrofoam cups.

What if the rain drew on for another week? Worse yet, for another two or three weeks? It had been known to happen in Mitford, which had its own exclusive weather system. Since nothing could go forward on the nursing-home site, did they want to put Buck Leeper's crew to work in the attic?

This would mean a good deal of money up front, entirely separate from the construction budget for Hope House, and so far, not one cent had been raised for that effort. Also, the rain could stop, the crew would go back up the hill, and there the attic job would sit, leaving the sanctuary covered with a fine film of dust.

Beginning on the Sunday school now was untimely, he thought. Yes, his mind was definitely clearing on the issue. Mud was not a sound reason to initiate the attic project.

He got up and went into the hall and headed toward the library. Under the pounding of the rain on the skylights, there was an odd silence in the house.

"Where is everybody?" he asked Edith, who came to meet him.

"They thought they should go before it started pouring again, which of course it did. I told them to go ahead—Ed would take you home."

"I thought we were all going to see your trompe l'oeil in the study."

He felt as if a noose had slipped around his neck. Desperate, he looked for Magdolen. Hadn't she been standing near the dining room door when he came down the hall? If so, she had vanished.

Edith drew him along by the arm. "We'll see it later, just the two of us."

The fire gleamed brightly on the hearth. He saw that someone had pulled the sofa closer to the fire and that the little table where he'd left his notebook now held a silver tray, two glasses, and a crystal decanter.

Dead meat. That's what Dooley would call him.

That she asked for counseling because it was his job was one thing. That she was holding him against his will was another.

As she moved closer to him on the sofa, he leapt to his feet and began pacing the floor. He couldn't emphasize enough, he told her, how some involvement with others would help her regain balance. The Children's Hospital in Wesley might be the best of outlets for her time and energy; he had supported it for years. They were currently anxious for funds to build a cancer unit, and he knew for a fact it was a responsible organization, capable of giving back the truest satisfaction.

But why should she get involved with sick children, she sniffed, which would only make her feel depressed? Besides, where would she find the time? She recited a stunning list of real estate that Pat Mallory had left in her care, including the Shoe Barn and the surrounding property on the highway, not to mention the building that housed the Main Street Grill.

He stood at last in front of the fire, so drowsy and exhausted from the long day, the heavy dinner, Edith's tearful monologue, and the warmth of the room, that he had to steel himself against dropping down prostrate.

At eleven o'clock, Ed Coffey appeared, hat in hand, reporting the car was stalled and it would be awhile before he could get it going. It seemed rain had got under the hood, somehow.

A likely story, he thought miserably. Now it was too late to call
Dooley and say he'd been detained. Of course, the boy had the Mallorys' number in case he was worried. But chances were, Dooley was
sleeping soundly, emitting that light, whiffling snore that he hoped
was not a case of adenoids gone haywire.

The rain was still rattling the skylights as if a full batallion were
marching over them. He would be lost out there in the storm, his umbrella ripped out of his hand and tossed into a tree, and no light to
see by for miles. If, by grace, he made it to town, he might as well go
straight to the hospital and check into the emergency room, as he
would shortly be dying of pneumonia.

He sat on the sofa, defeated, only to have Edith grasp his knee.
Would this never end?

"Edith," he said firmly, in the voice he knew Emma hated, "it's
been a long day, and we both need rest. I think I'll just move to the
armchair and have a nap while Ed works on the car."

"Don't you want to see my trump lloyd?" she asked piteously.

In reply, he stalked to the armchair and sat down, folding his arms
across his chest as tight as armor plating. Just in case, he also crossed
his legs and squeezed his eyes shut.

He deserved this. He had asked for it. He might as well have gotten down on his hands and knees and begged for it. Why hadn't he
asked Lew to charge the battery the day after he got home, so he could
have driven here under his own steam?

If she laid a hand on him, what could he do besides run for it? Perhaps a coma, if worse came to worst. If he remembered correctly, one
simply blanked out and fell down. That, however, could be the most
compromising position he could put himself into.

If he ever got out of this one, he would . . . what? He would tell
Cynthia he would like to go steady.

There it was. The thought that had been waiting to be revealed,
waiting to take him by surprise. And yet, he wasn't surprised.

Instead, he was struck by the irrevocable understanding that Cynthia Coppersmith was a rare find, indeed. Her sweetness, her candor,
her joie de vivre and fresh beauty—why had he been so long in appre-
ciating it? And why not enjoy the unexpected gift of happiness that
her companionship would surely bring?

He felt a relieved smile spreading over his face and something like
freedom in his heart.

Edith sat down on the arm of his chair. "Ummmm," she crooned, "you look cozy."

Enveloped at once by the smell of perfume and stale tobacco, he refused to open his eyes. "I am not cozy," he said through clenched teeth. "I am wanting my bed and a decent night's sleep."

"And you shall soon have it!" she snapped. "When will you ever loosen up?"

He drove toward home with a haggard Ed Coffey at daylight, neither of them speaking. The rain had subsided to a wan drizzle.

What if someone saw him bowling along in Edith Mallory's car at five o'clock in the morning? He slid so far down into the leather that he was sitting on his spine.

What if they passed Percy Mosely, who often arrived at the Grill at five o'clock to do his bookkeeping and load the coffeepots?

Or what if Winnie Ivey spied him on her way to the bakery?

When they pulled to the curb at the rectory, all that could be seen of him was the top of his head, covered by a tweed cap. The five-minute drive had felt like the better part of a day.

Ed turned around as the rector opened the door. The message in the eyes of the exhausted chauffeur was clear: I'm sorry. I didn't mean for this to happen.

He took Ed's hand. "God bless you," he said with feeling.

As he started around the side of the house to the back door, he saw something pink in the hedge. It was Cynthia, in a robe and gown with her hair full of curlers. She stared at him as Ed Coffey pulled quietly away from the curb.

He stared back for one agonizing moment, seeing a certain message in her eyes, as well. She was holding a dripping Violet, who had very likely stayed out all night.

He raised one hand, as if to salute his neighbor, but she turned and dashed through the hedge, the robe flying behind like a coronation mantle. Standing there in the drizzling rain, he heard her back door slam.

His lunch with Miss Sadie and Louella made him feel as if he'd really come home.

He realized he had taken a positive shine to their white bread, and even the processed cheese seemed to possess a certain delicacy.

"I never got Olivia Davenport's hats to her," Miss Sadie confessed. "Two whole months of good intentions and nothing more! But Louella and I are going up to the attic this very week and bring them down, aren't we, Louella?"

Over the pineapple sherbet, his hostess said she wanted to have a meeting with him before too long. Not today, she said, but soon. He remembered other meetings with Miss Sadie and how something major always resulted. In this faded house among the ferns, a bright idea was inevitably taking form.

He told her about the garden statuary, about the moss-covered St. Francis with the missing arm, the seated Virgin with the child, the figure of Jesus carrying a lamb, and the host of wingless cherubs. "Beautiful pieces! A round dozen in all. We'll see to having them restored and put in the church gardens."

"I can't seem to remember them," she said. "We never returned to the churchyard after the fire. It was as if there had been a terrible death, and we never spoke of it. We never even glanced that way when we went down the road.

"But for years, when I looked out my window to the hill where the steeple used to stand against the sky, there was an awful emptiness there, as if something had been stolen from the heavens."

Louella looked at him and shook her head. "Honey, it was mournful."

"Louella, do you think you ought to call the father honey?"

"I think she should," said the rector.

"Well, then," said Miss Sadie. "Papa did everything he could to get the new church going, and we were having services before the roof was even on. Remember, Louella, we used to sit in canvas chairs like you take to a horse event, with just the framing around us. That was a beautiful time, a healing time—the fresh lumber, the new beginning. I remember the way our hymns sounded, out in the open like that, with nothing but grass and trees to catch the music. It was sweet and simple, like the early settlers must have worshiped.

"I remember Absalom came around one Sunday morning. He stood in the back holding his hat and his Bible, and afterward, he walked out front and said to us, 'I'm so sorry.' He was meaning the fire, of course, and everything else.

"You know, Father, I would give anything if I could have fallen in love with Absalom Greer."

Something had to be done, but he couldn't figure out what.

He had called over and over, only to get some odd scrap of message from her answering machine. He had pounded on her door in a thunderstorm but couldn't find her. He had promised to make good on that silly wish but had done absolutely nothing about it. And now, this.

Flowers. He would send flowers.

He couldn't remember sending flowers to anyone before, save his own cut roses. On the other hand, how would it look to tumble out of some woman's car at daylight, only to send flowers to the woman who caught you red-handed? It didn't seem smart.

He would write a note, then. He was fairly decent at penning his thoughts, after all. *Dear Cynthia.*

He stood and stared out the office window.

Dearest Cynthia.

My dear Cynthia.

Cynthia.

He could go on like this for hours. Perhaps even days. Blast!

"You need a haircut," said Emma. He had forgotten she was in the room.

"What else?" he asked sarcastically.

"You need to be seein' more of your neighbor."

He was walking home in a thick fog, wondering when the crisp, blue skies of autumn might appear. He would go to the country, then, perhaps to the very same place he had sat with Cynthia on the quilt, and let Barnabas run until he fell over with joy.

Dearest Cynthia, I remember the day on the quilt . . .

He could feel his face grow warm. That opening seemed too direct. Yet, faint heart never won fair lady.

. . . I remember the day on the quilt, and it's a memory I will always cherish.

How could he not always remember the way she had lain on her back like a girl, looking up at the clouds and seeing Andrew Jackson, and the way she laughed at him when the bull turned and skulked away? And certainly he could never forget the way she had leaned against him, so soft and supple, as he stroked her cheek. They had talked about not letting the path through the hedge grow over; he had said they mustn't let it happen. But how many times had he used that path since he came home a full ten days ago? Just once, as he fled homeward in a downpour.

But he was getting off the point. The point was that he had been remiss and that he was sorry and wanted to make it right. He especially wanted to say that what she'd seen was misleading—he could explain everything.

Dearest Cynthia . . .

He realized he had walked past his corner and was standing helplessly in front of the Main Street Grill. This very thing was only one of the reasons why he had never wanted to lose his heart to anyone.

If Homeless Hobbes had lived in town, the rector was certain he couldn't have confided a word of what he had on his mind. That his friend lived in the woods on Little Mitford Creek, however, was different.

He didn't have the wits to refuse the cup of coffee Homeless brewed at five o'clock in the afternoon. He watched him fill the cup as if he were seeing it happen to someone else.

Homeless was barefoot and wearing a new pair of burgundy pants with galluses. He snapped one brace against his undershirt. "Good as new! Fresh out of th' dumpster."

"That's where Miss Rose does most of her shopping."

"See these pants? I never wanted two pairs, Now I got two pairs. They was layin' right there with th' galluses. I couldn't turn 'em down."

"A new look for fall."

"I hope m' britches don't go to my head."

"I never heard of that particular thing happening to anyone, so I wouldn't worry about it."

"They's somethin' worryin' you, I vow."

The rector raised his cup in a salute. "You've got a good eye."

"I don't know if it's th' eye as much as th' gut. Right here." Homeless thumped himself below the ribs.

"There is something worrying me. I hate to admit it."

"You can admit what you need to back here on the creek."

How in heaven's name was he supposed to talk about it? In all his years as a priest, there had been only one friend to whom he could pour out his innermost conflicts. That friend was now his bishop, and he didn't want to trouble Stuart Cullen with what could seem a triviality.

He sat looking at the steaming black coffee, wondering how long it could keep him awake. Well past Thanksgiving, he decided, taking a reckless swallow.

He was grateful that Homeless didn't urge him on to confession but sat quietly himself. The stove door stood open to reveal a low fire, made with a few sticks of wood to cheer the place against the eternal drumming of rain on the roof.

It wouldn't stay light forever, and walking home along the dark creek in the rain was nothing to look forward to.

He felt as if he were stepping off a cliff when he spoke. "It's a woman," he said.

Homeless looked at him without blinking. "Lord, have mercy."

CHAPTER TWO

Lost

"But who would have sent me a microwave?" he wanted to know.

Puny threw up her hands. "Don't ask me."

"And who am I to ask, for heaven's sake? Weren't you here when it was delivered?"

She shrugged.

"Come on, Puny. Who did this low thing?"

"They was goin' to give you a VCR," she said, "so I told 'em t' send a microwave."

"I won't have it in my kitchen. I knew this would happen someday. It's insidious the way these things take over people's lives."

"How can it take over your dern life if you don't even use it? Who does most of th' cookin' around here, anyway? If I want to heat up some soup for your lunch, I can do it while you're comin' through th' door. If Dooley wants a hamburger, whap, in it goes, out it comes, instead of me slavin' over a hot stove to feed that bottomless pit."

"You don't have to touch it. You don't have to lay a finger on it. I'll cover it with a sheet when I leave of an evenin' if that'll suit you any better."

"Who?" he asked darkly.

"Those vestry people."

"Them again," he said.

"They were jis' tryin' to be helpful."

Helpful! Since when did a vestry have the right to violate a man's kitchen? Was nothing sacred?

"I hope you don't mind my sayin' this . . ."

He knew he would mind.

"You prob'ly ought to take you a laxative."

In all the years of his priesthood, he had pastored the needs of others. Now, he found himself pastoring others to meet his own needs.

He didn't go to encourage Miss Rose in her civic duties because he thought it would be decent of him. He went because he needed what she had to offer, which, although strange, was comforting and familiar.

He walked up the street at noon and stood on the sidewalk while she waved cars around the monument. Well done!

He was astounded by her appearance. No cocktail hat, no military decorations, no trench coat actually worn in the trenches. Just Esther Cunningham's old Waves uniform with a spiffy hat over a new haircut. That she was still sporting her unlaced saddle oxfords hardly mattered. One thing at a time, and be glad for it.

When there was a lull, he called to her and threw up his hand.

She looked at him menacingly.

"I like your uniform!" he said.

"Regulation!" she snapped and turned her back on him.

"Uncle Billy," he said at the Grill, "Miss Rose acted like she didn't know me. I haven't been gone that long, have I?"

"Oh, she knowed you, all right. It's just she don't mix business with pleasure. Keeps 'er mind on 'er work, don't you know. Wants to do 'er best."

The old man was wearing one of his dead brother-in-law's suits, and a tie Father Tim recognized as having been one of his own.

"It's a blessin' if I ever seen it. She's wore out after doin' her job, comes in meek as any lamb, eats her somethin', and sleeps 'til dinner. We have us a nice bite, then we watch the news an' all, an' go to bed. It's th' most peace I can recollect."

"I'm goin' to buy you a hamburger to celebrate."

"If you was to tip in some fries, I'd be much obliged."

Velma wiped off the table. "You ought to get th' special," she advised the rector. "It's a one-day-only deal."

"What is it?" he asked cautiously.

"Beef kidneys."

"Beef kidneys? What got into Percy to cook beef kidneys?"

"Avis had a big run of kidneys and let 'em go cheap. You ought to give 'em a go," she said, poised with her order book.

"Did you give 'em a go?"

"Well . . ."

"Did Percy give 'em a go?"

"He don't eat organ meat."

Uncle Billy looked pale. "You keep talkin' like that, you won't have t' bring me nothin'. I won't be able t' keep it down."

"Bring my friend a hamburger all the way and a large order of fries," said the rector. "I'll have the chicken-salad plate."

"I hope you don't regret it," she said sulkily, walking away. "We'll probably never have these again."

"We dodged a bullet, Uncle Billy."

"Have you seen the drawin's of Willard's statue?"

"No, I haven't. I've got to get by the mayor's office. What do you think?"

"The one a-settin' down is dead-on, if you ask me. Even Rose likes it, but she's stickin' with th' one a-standin', says it makes 'im more dignified."

"You're liking your new apartment? It's good and warm?"

"Oh, it's th' most comfort you'd ever want."

"Nice, dry roof?"

"Not a leak in th' place."

"Well, then, sitting or standing, who cares?"

Uncle Billy laughed, his gold tooth flashing. "Could be a-standin' on 'is head for all I care, when th' hot air comes out of th' vents!"

He was wanting to see Russell Jacks, too, and Betty, and Olivia, and Hoppy. And, of course, Marge and Hal and Rebecca Jane. But most of all, he wanted to see . . .

Dear . . . Dearest Cynthia.

Why could he get no further than this?

When he walked home at four-thirty, he was planning to go to his study, sit down, and force himself to write the letter explaining everything.

Instead, he marched through the hedge and up her back steps and hammered on the door. He knew she was in there; her Mazda was parked in the garage.

Not a sound. He might have been pounding on the door of a tomb.

He felt certain someone was watching him. She was probably looking out the bathroom window, chuckling to herself. Or worse, she'd gone to the club with Andrew Gregory and was doing the tango with the new social director who reputedly looked like Tyrone Power.

Blast!

He stomped through the hedge. Maybe he'd go for a ride on his motor scooter. Maybe he'd open it up on that flat road to Farmer and see, for once, just what it could do. He must remember not to hit the brake too hard; it would lock the rear wheel and lay the bike down. He'd have to hurry if he wanted to get back by six o'clock to feed Dooley who was at football practice.

As he opened the back door, a marvelous aroma greeted him. There was a pot on the stove, a casserole in the oven, and a note on the counter.

Turn the oven off at 5 30, not a minit after. I hope you like it. plese share ¹/₂ the stew with your neighbor. yours sincerely, Puny.

There it was. A perfect excuse to call and say he was coming over with hot, homemade stew.

"Hello," her answering machine said brightly, "I'm sorry I can't talk to you in person, but Violet and I are in New York for awhile. Please leave a message and I'll get back to you. Thanks!"

His heart pounded as he hung up the receiver.

In New York?

Not right next door, where he might have gone and had a talk with her and arranged a time for them to do the simple thing she asked.

In New York.

He felt an awful emptiness. Even the quality of the afternoon light seemed suddenly flat and dull.

He heard Barnabas in the garage barking to go out, but he sat down on his stool at the counter and stared at the morning mail, not seeing it.

When he stopped in to see the mayor and the renderings of the statue, she looked him up and down.

"You're antsy," she said. "You ought to get you a chew of tobacco to work on. That's what Ray does, an' it helps him every time."

Get a haircut!

See your neighbor!

Loosen up!

Take a laxative!

Chew tobacco!

Women were forever trying to tell him what to do. What he needed was the company of other men. Perhaps he should go hunting. But then, he'd never been hunting in his life.

He saw himself stalking something through the woods, possibly a deer, which made him feel nauseated. Then he saw himself tripping over the gun and blowing his head off.

No, he was not outfitted for stalking anything. And no wonder. His father had not only refused to take him hunting and fishing but refused to let him go with anyone else. He had ended up with his nose stuck in a book when he might have been bagging a few quail with Tommy Noles.

The truth was if he wanted male camaraderie, he'd have to get it in his private club—that finest of institutions known as the Main Street Grill.

In the meantime, he would pour himself into his work as he hadn't done in years. And, he would mind his health with more spirit than ever. No, he was not ready to retire. Stuart had seen all along something he couldn't see. He had many more years left to serve, and that was what he wanted to do, desperately. If nothing else came of his feelings for Cynthia, he had realized, at last, that he wanted to go on, with more stamina and conviction than ever.

He needed to look into Olivia's Bible-reading group, which had become so popular that other churches in the diocese had requested bookings.

He needed to make time for a Youth Choir supper and ferret out his final Bane and Blessing contribution, perhaps that lace cloth bought so long ago for the rectory by the old bishop's wife, which should fetch a nice sum.

There was the visit to Absalom Greer coming up, the final touches required to pull together the Men's Prayer Breakfast, the slide show of his Ireland trip for the ECW and the choir, and the Francis of Assisi observance that would be held in the church gardens. He needed to prepare some remarks for the presentation of the fountain to be installed near the memorial roses.

He needed, also, to get by and see Miss Pattie, and he absolutely had to check on Russell Jacks, their church sexton and Dooley's grandfather.

Though it wasn't on his list of church matters, Dooley Barlowe must have clothes—at once. That meant an evening sorting through Dooley's closet, followed by an afternoon in Wesley.

On top of everything else, of course, were the upcoming sermons. The one he preached on returning from Ireland had been like a crude raft launched upon the ocean; he had nearly swamped himself. That he could have gotten so rusty after two short months was astounding to him.

"Why don't you use one you already done? Did?" Dooley had asked.

Sermons, like manna, he replied, must be fresh. He'd once heard a priest say that he prepared his sermons up to a year in advance! He'd been incredulous.

For him, making a sermon was like getting dressed in the mornings. As the Spirit moved, one put on what one felt like wearing that particular day. After all, who could preach effectively from a prepared sermon on joy when he might be feeling as dull as a post? No, he would not be tempted by prepared sermons any more than he might be tempted by the meatloaf Puny made eight days ago, sitting in the refrigerator in Saran Wrap.

Soon, he wanted to preach on personal, as compared to institutional, salvation. Confessing Christ before others was an act of institutional salvation that most churchgoers had done long ago. He wanted to get at something more compelling, more life-changing—the process of personal confession, of personal relationship with Christ. He also wanted to point out that being a priest no more assured him of heaven than being a chipmunk would assure him of nuts for winter.

He realized he hadn't felt so strong in nearly a year. He would go home, put on his jogging suit, and take Barnabas for a run up Church Hill if the blasted rain would hold off long enough. Yesterday, the sun shone until everything he beheld revealed its dazzle. Then, today, the gray clouds stretched across the heavens like a canopy of steel.

He had turned the corner toward the rectory when he saw it.

A moving van was backed within inches of Cynthia's front door, barely missing the bushes she had so proudly twined last year with strings of Christmas lights.

"Wait up!" he called, running. He reached the van just as two men came out with her drawing board.

"What are you doing?" he asked hoarsely, feeling his heart thunder in his ears.

"We're loadin' this van," said the man with a tattoo on his arm.

"What for? Why are you loading this van when someone lives here? This is a permanent residence!"

"Coppersmith. We're movin' a Coppersmith. And if we're goin' to make time, we gotta haul butt outta here."

"Where? Where are you moving Miss Coppersmith?" He was afraid to hear the answer.

"New York City," they said in unison, disappearing into the van with the drawing board.

"Eat you some grits," said Percy.

"Eat! Eat! Is that all anyone can think of? I'm not here to eat." He came closer to cursing than he had come in years. It was right there, waiting to be spoken, but he turned from it, ashen.

"Dadgum," said Percy quietly.

He sat frozen in the booth, thankful that Emma was out with a toothache. If he had been trapped today in that minuscule office with Emma Newland, he couldn't have hacked it. He felt stripped, exposed, not wanting anyone to speak to him.

Eat. Well, if that's not what he came here to do, what was he doing here? The tea looked insipid to him. He went to the counter and took his mug off the rack.

"I'll have coffee. Half decaf."

Percy filled the mug without a word.

"Sorry."

Percy nodded. He would make it up to him, the rector thought. He had no right to bite the head off one of his staunchest friends. He felt humiliated. Was this what life was going to be like because things hadn't gone to suit him?

The salty old evangelist, Vance Havner, once preached at his mother's church and told a story he'd never forgotten. "How're you?" the preacher had asked one of his congregation. "Oh, pretty good, under the circumstances," was the reply. "What I want to know," said Havner, peering intently at his audience, "is what is a Christian doing under the circumstances?"

What, indeed, was he doing under the circumstances?'

Straighten me out, Lord, he prayed, before I become an embarrassment to you and everybody else.

"Only the mediocre man is always at his best," Somerset Maugham had said.

Aha, he thought, hoping to find some consolation in this.

He did not find any.

"Have you started on the family research?" his cousin Walter wanted to know when he called from New Jersey.

"Haven't touched it," he said. "Too much going on."

"Like what?"

He reeled off his list dutifully, thinking it sounded pretty flat after all. He needed a big wedding, perhaps, or a baptism. He always loved celebrations that filled the church with flowers and relatives and that little hum of excitement and love that gave special witness to the Holy Spirit.

"What about your neighbor?"

"What about her?"

"Blast, Timothy! You know what I mean. Tell all, or I'll put Katherine on. *She'll* be unmerciful."

Lord knows, that was the truth. "She moved to New York."

"What?" Why did his cousin sound so personally affronted? What was it to him that she moved to New York? "Why?"

"I don't have the particulars."

"Well, if you don't have the particulars, who does?"

"Walter . . ."

"You let her slip away, didn't you, old boy? Right through your fingers. As if you could afford such a thing . . ."

"What do you mean, as if I could afford . . ."

"How many men your age, in your income bracket, would be pursued by a good-looking woman with all her wits about her? She sounded like a prize to me, but if you're so hell-bent on growing old alone, with no one to . . ."

"Walter," he said sternly, "put Katherine on."

"Hello, Teds!" She had called him by this silly nickname for twenty years, which she had thankfully shortened from the early version, "Teddy Bear."

"You wicked girl, how are you?"

"Oh, fine, I suppose, as long as Walter goes into the city. But he's been home for days with a runny nose. You'd think it was terminal. I've fetched and carried like a slave."

"There's a good wife."

"Speaking of wife, how's your neighbor?" She had never owned the slightest streak of discretion.

"Moved to New York!" He was surprised to hear himself say this almost gaily, with a certain enthusiasm. There. That was the solution right there. Just toss it off as if it were nothing. A couple of times, and he'd have it down pat.

"Timothy!" she exclaimed. "How could you?"

"Katherine, I refuse to discuss it, and that's that. The whole thing has been beyond me, is beyond me, and promises to stay beyond me. So, please. Back off."

"Back off! Ha! You forget who you're talking to. This is me, Teds, who does not believe that life consists of backing off but of forging ahead! Did you have a fight?"

"We did not. I hardly even saw her after I came home."

"Well, you big dope, that's the problem right there."

He felt weary of all this, as if he'd like to fall prostrate on the carpet and not bother getting up.

The sun had been shining brilliantly for days, and the intense blue sky he'd looked for was there, cloudless, perfect.

Up on the hill, where the ruins of the old church had lain for so many years, something new, something restorative was going on. He could hear engines gunning, hammers ringing, voices shouting back and forth. It was not a clamor. It was, instead, the sound of excitement, even of happiness.

He remembered the summer he and Tommy Noles had hung over the fence surrounding a gaping hole that, in the spring, became the First National Bank. As much as he loved baseball, he had wanted nothing more than to watch the sober gray edifice being constructed, stone upon stone. The sight of an entire building coming together before their very eyes was awesome, better than a movie, better than a hundred movies.

He would have given anything, anything he owned or would ever own, to get in the cab of one of those cranes and muscle something around, something huge, something gigantic.

He would visit Russell and Betty tomorrow, then he'd walk up to the job site and take a look. That he'd steer clear of Leeper went without saying.

Betty Craig looked ten years younger and had lost weight into the bargain.

"Betty! You look like a girl. What's your secret? I demand to be told."

"I don't know!" she said, blushing. "I guess it's that Mr. Jacks is bein' such a help around here. I can't imagine what I ever did without him."

"You can't mean it."

"Oh, but I do! Just look at these shelves he built in the hall."

Putting Russell Jacks into Betty Craig's care had been a brilliant move. It had also kept him from going back to his derelict house in the scrap yard and taking Dooley with him.

Betty took the rector by the arm and led him along the little hallway. "And look here in my room how he made that nice headboard I always wanted and built me a little round table to go by the bed."

Betty's clock radio and a Bible were sitting on the table the old sexton had built. Amazing!

"And see," she said, leading him to the window, "how he's made those nice beds with the pansies for me to look at of a mornin'!"

"A beautiful sight! He's completely well, then, is he?"

"Oh, yes, sir, and I just hate it, I just hate it! Don't tell a soul I said so, but once he goes, they'll want me to nurse Miss Pattie, and I don't believe I'm up to that, oh, Father . . ." Betty was wringing her hands. She had gone from blithe to mournful in only moments.

"Let's cross that bridge when we get to it," he said.

"Do you know the latest on Miss Pattie?"

How could Emma have skipped over that one? "What's the latest?"

"Naked on the roof."

"No."

"Oh, yes. Used to crawl out on the roof in that little pink wrapper, but not anymore. No sirree, now it's her birthday suit."

He put his arm around her shoulder as they walked up the hall.

He was as anxious as Betty for Russell to stay in this sunny home with the starched curtains. Something would have to be done to keep him from going back to the scrap yard, but he didn't know what.

She sighed. "Well, come and see him. He'll want to see you. Oh, dear, you didn't bring the livermush. He's nearly had a fit for livermush since you left."

"I confess I forgot. Two months without livermush is a stretch. Of course, you could have asked Puny to bring some from Wesley. She would have done it gladly."

"Well, he'll be happy to get it when it comes. You know, Father, it's good to do without something that means a lot to you."

"Is it, Betty?" he asked, sincerely wanting to know.

"Oh, yes. Then when you get it again, you appreciate it more."

But he didn't know if he would ever get it again, if he'd ever have the chance to appreciate it more.

"Are you all right?" she asked.

"I am," he said and smiled.

"Got 'er runnin' like a top," said Lew Boyd, wiping his hands on a rag. "You want t' sell 'er, I'll make you an offer."

Lew Boyd no more wanted to buy his Buick than he wanted to go bungee jumping in Wesley. He always said that to his customers. He felt it was part of his service to make them feel good about the vehicle he'd just worked on.

"What would you give me for it, Lew?" He assumed what might be taken for his pulpit look.

"Well," said Lew, "I'd . . . ah, have to think about it."
He tried not to laugh until he got around the monument.

The weather was turning colder, the flame of autumn had torched the red maples along Lilac Road, and now and again he caught the scent of wood smoke. It was his favorite perfume, right up there with horse manure and new-mown hay. And where would he get wood to make his own smoke this year? Parishioners were good about supplying everything from produce for his table to bulbs for his garden, but wood was not something that often came his way. As smart as Avis was about finding a load of corn, surely he'd know where to get a load of wood.

He was barely winded when he turned onto Church Hill Drive from Lilac Road and headed toward Fernbank.

Louella had called and asked him to come. Was Miss Sadie sick? Something worse than sick, Louella said ominously.

When Louella answered the door, she didn't speak but shook her head as if words could not suffice.

In Miss Sadie's upstairs bedroom, he saw hats piled on the bed and hatboxes stacked in the corners and on the dresser. Miss Sadie was sitting in the wing chair where she had told him the last tragic episode of her love story. He was surprised to realize her feet did not touch the floor; she might have been a doll sitting there. Like Louella, she didn't speak.

She handed him a yellowed certificate, and he sat down in the wing chair across from hers.

This certifies that Lydia Anne, child of Father (unknown) and Mother, Rachel Amelia Livingstone, was born in Arbourville, Jackson County, North Carolina, on the 14th day of March, 1901, and that the birth is recorded as Certificate No. 5417.

He looked up slowly to meet her eyes, but she was looking out the window.

He found he didn't wish to speak, either. Three people in one household had been struck dumb by the appearance of a piece of paper, a piece of plain truth. Rachel Livingstone was the maiden name of Miss Sadie's mother.

Clearly, she had sent for him so that he might come and do something, but he could do nothing. He looked at her face in profile, in the unforgiving autumn light, and saw a strange peace. Indeed, the room seemed wrapped in a peace that he began to enter.

They sat for a long time in a silence that he found deeply comforting. He could not remember ever sitting like this with someone, except following a death. Perhaps this hard thing was for her a type of death; the mother whom she had adored as a saint had at last revealed the secret of her illegitimate child. It had been a family of secrets, a life of secrets.

"We went up in the attic yesterday, looking for Mama's hats. I said, 'Louella, let's look in this old dresser. We never really went through Mama's things.' We found the birth certificate folded up in a handkerchief bag with a little pair of socks.

"Last night when I couldn't sleep, I remembered Mama going out with her basket for the poor. Twice a week, every week, she went and always came back so sad, so sad. Finally, I quit begging to go with her. She was going to see my older sister," she said, looking at him in amazement. "Just think . . . I had a sister."

He smiled, sensing an odd happiness welling up in her, even though tears began to roll down her cheeks. She did not try to stop them nor turn her face away but let them come freely.

"All those years I might have known her! Might have skipped rope with her, or let her braid my hair, or told her my dreams! If I might just have seen her or touched her, my own flesh. There she was, all I'd ever wanted, yet God kept her from me . . . and replaced her with China Mae and Louella." She laughed through her tears.

"Two for one," he said gently.

"I have to believe He knew what He was doing."

"You can count on it."

"I had a great aunt in Arbourville. Maybe that's why Mama had the child there. A year and a half later, she married Papa . . . I don't suppose he ever knew . . . In another year and a half, she had me." Her breath caught. "Oh, I so wish I could have known my sister!"

"I so wish she could have known you, Miss Sadie." He stood up and went to her and drew her from the chair and put his arms around her and held her like a child. "I love you," he said simply.

She looked up at him, the tears shining in her eyes. "We're going to make the best of this thing."

She pulled a handkerchief from her pocket and blew her nose. "Now, let's move on to what started all this in the first place. You are going to help me take these hats to Olivia Davenport, aren't you, Father?"

"Absolutely."

"Just think of the joy we'll have when we see her wearing them! You do think she'll wear them, don't you?"

"I haven't the slightest doubt."

"Can we take them this week?"

"I'll have to see about renting a U-Haul," he said, grinning.

"Pshaw! We can get them all in my Plymouth. I have a trunk as big as a bathtub, and you'll do the driving."

"Deal!"

"I'm so glad to have a priest who minds me," she said.

He turned left out of the Fernbank driveway and walked toward the construction site. Church Hill literally vibrated under his feet with the churn and tumult of heavy equipment, which at last had fair weather for operating.

It was a wonder to him that the street wasn't thronged with on-lookers, field trips from schools, and chartered buses from every point in the county. For there, under a perfectly blue and cloudless sky, lay an open wound in the earth, with more spectacular vehicles crawling upon it than one could count.

He felt light as air. And no wonder—it was the first time in his life that he'd worn tennis shoes with his tab collar, though that was all the rage with Father Roland and his crowd in New Orleans. He'd been accustomed to running a few years behind the rest of the world, but he was going to make an effort to change that. He was tired of bringing up the rear in the march of civilization.

The equipment crawled over the site like ants on a hill, except for two thundering yellow Cats, stationed at either end of a vast excavation. His attention was instantly riveted by their great maws that dipped into the earth and came up again, overfed with red clay. The arms of the machines swung around and dumped their loads onto a pile.

A man pulled onto the site in a truck, got out, and threw up his hand. It was Ron Malcolm's boy, who had driven from Colorado to work on this job. Though Ed Malcolm was walking hurriedly toward the trailer, the rector caught up with him.

"Ed, how's it going?" They shook hands.

"Great, Father, just great. We're glad to have the good weather."

"And we're glad to have you on this job."

"Thanks, I appreciate that." Ed glanced anxiously at the trailer and then sprinted away. "See you around," he called over his shoulder.

He'd take a look in the hole before he walked to the Grill for lunch. Recalling the plans, he knew the basement would house the kitchen, a composting drum, storage, a ten-bed infirmary, and a small pharmacy.

If he'd worn a hat, he would have removed it respectfully at the rim of the crater. The vast excavation appeared to penetrate Beijing, dug in clay that ranged in layers of color from blood red to purple to black to ochre. Were those layers like the rings of a tree, telling the age of this ancient hill?

"You sonofa . . ." was all he heard as the arm of the machine thundered up from the hole, and he was jerked backward by his left shoulder.

He stumbled, but before he could fall, he was spun around and Buck Leeper grabbed him by his lapel. His face was so close that he could feel the man's spittle when he shouted.

"Do that again, Mister, and you'll *eat* my dirt. Got it? I got enough trouble without some fool lookin' to fall in my excavation. Now, leave my men alone and stay off my site."

Leeper cursed and shoved him roughly away, then stalked toward the trailer.

The rector had felt the man's raw power, as if he were part of the heavy equipment, some extension of it in human form. He stood rooted to the spot, shaken.

"You look like you seen a ghost," said Percy.

"I wish," he muttered. It had been years since anyone had muscled him around like Buck Leeper had just done.

"They's a paper in your booth. J.C. come early and left it for you, said look on page five."

Percy peered intently at him. "Page . . . five . . ." He said this slowly, as if speaking to someone deaf as a stone.

Sitting in the booth, he stirred his unsweetened tea as if it were poison. He couldn't think of anything he detested more than a glass of tea without a few spoonfuls of sugar.

He glanced at the paper on the table but couldn't concentrate. He was remembering Louella's face when she stopped him at the front door.

"We goan tell her 'bout Miss Olivia?"

He had thought for a moment. "No. Something tells me we ought to wait."

"If she fin' out I been knowin' all my days 'bout Miss Olivia bein' her kin, she goan be plenty mad and hurt. Law!" Louella had turned an odd, gray color.

"Let's keep our peace," he had said. "And whatever you do, don't worry. It's going to work out."

Frankly, he wasn't so sure.

He continued to stir his tea, as if there might be something in there to stir.

How would Miss Sadie feel toward Louella, knowing she had hidden that ancient secret about her mother? And what if they told Miss Sadie it was her own great-niece who'd be wearing those hats?

"You seen it yet?"

The *Muse* editor tossed his battered briefcase on the seat and sat down heavily.

"Seen what?"

"Page five. Dadgummit, I told Percy to tell you to look on page five." He stared at the rector, disgruntled, until page five was located.

"You probably know this, already, bein' her neighbor, but I wanted you to see how I wrote it up."

The story appeared under a picture of Fancy Skinner's new beauty shop, the Hair House.

J.C. tapped the headline with his stubby finger. "Right here," he said, "Local Woman Wins Critical Acclaim."

He read the article silently.

Cynthia Coppersmith, a local author and illustrator of children's books, has been praised by reviewers for her new release, *The Mouse in the Manger*.

Mrs. Coppersmoth, who lives on Wisteria Lane in the house that once belonged to her uncle, Joe Hadleigh, has been writing and drawing since she was ten years old, according to a news report released to the Mitford library.

Mrs. Copermoth's story about a mouse who attended the

birth of the baby Jesus was called "a rare jewel" by one library journal, and another called it "a tiny masterpiece." Our library volunteers say, "This could be another medal winner."

Avette Harris, our local library head, says the book is great for story hour, any time of year. "The only trouble," says Avette, "is that both our copies already have jam or something on the covers and we could do with a new batch."

Mrs. Coppersmitj's book, *Violet Goes Abroad*, won a Davant medal five years ago. It is just one in a series of books about her white cat, Violet, who also lives on Wistoria Lane. According to the titles of the books, this cat has been to school, learned to play a piano and speak French, not to mention has visited the queen. The entire collection is at the library, so hurry on over.

As the rector put the paper down, the editor leaned forward, obviously pleased. "I tried to give it a personal touch. What do you think?"

Think? He couldn't think. His mind felt like it had been stirred with his teaspoon. "Great," he said, feebly. "Terrific. What else did the story at the library say?"

"Said she liked to walk in the rain and eat peanut-butter-and-banana sandwiches. Said somethin' else, too, ah . . . let's see, oh, she likes to dance the rhumba, I thought all that was a little weird, so I left it out."

"Good idea." His heart felt leaden.

"I tried to call her for an interview, but th' machine said she was in . . ."

"New York."

"Right. Well, I gotta get outta here. The Presbyterians have a big story brewin'."

The rector didn't look up.

"Don't you want to know what it is?" asked J.C. wiping his face with the ever-present handkerchief.

"Sure I do."

"They're givin' away a Cadillac," said J.C.

He was dumbfounded. "Doing what?"

"Adios, hasta la vista," said J.C. creaking out of the vinyl seat with his bulging briefcase. "See you in the funny papers."

If there was anything J.C. loved, it was going around town telling half a story to make sure somebody bought his newspaper.

"Don't that beat all?" said Percy, who had heard J.C.'s announcement. "I never knew the Lord was in the car business."

He went at once to the library and gave an astonished Avette Harris two twenty-dollar bills.

"My!" she said, looking at him with admiration.

"This is to replace those *Mouse in the Manger* books," he said.

"I declare, we have tried and tried to clean those book covers. It's something just like jam, but it won't come off. We don't know what it is. You should see the things that happen to children's books, sometimes. We found a dead cricket the other day in *Little Women*, and it looked like lasagna in *The Hungry Caterpillar*."

He nodded.

"Isn't that Miss Coppersmith something? We're so proud of her, we could just bust."

He smiled.

"Of course, this is way too much money. Two little books don't cost forty dollars! Not yet, anyway."

"If there's anything left," he said, "buy a box of candy and pass it around to the volunteers."

He was on the sidewalk, headed toward the post office, when Avette caught up with him.

"Oh, Father, when someone gives a book, we like to put a little book plate in the front that says who it's given by. What would you like yours to say?"

He thought for a moment.

"Just say, 'Given by Miss Coppersmith's neighbor.'"

Peanut-butter-and-banana sandwiches? That had been Tommy Noles's favorite food. Tommy had subsisted on that very fare from fourth grade through high school, with an occasional side of grape jelly. Tommy liked his on white bread, with the bananas mashed flat into the peanut butter. He wondered how she liked hers.

Barnabas stopped to sniff a rock.

The rhumba! What an extraordinary thought. He would have thought the fox trot, if he had ever thought about it at all.

He was struck by the endless number of things he hadn't thought about concerning Cynthia. Why had he never been more curious about her life, about her work? Where had she gone to school, for heaven's sake? And why hadn't he found out why she nearly died in a hospital? He'd even lacked the courtesy to ask lately about her nephew, who was as cherished as a son. It seemed a small thing to wonder, but what was his last name? He didn't even know what kind of work he did.

She had asked him to pose for a wise man in *The Mouse in the Manger*, yet he'd never inquired about the finished book. Worse, he had never once read anything she had written.

He had treated her, he realized, as if she didn't really exist.

That realization was overwhelming to him. He'd believed what his parishioners had told him, that he was caring and nurturing. Yet, it was a lie. He wasn't really either of those things. The truth was, he was unutterably selfish and self-seeking, going his own way, doing his own pious thing. It was disgusting to him.

How had he come this far without seeing himself for what he really was? How had God let him get away with this loathsome deception for so long?

Barnabas lifted his leg against a tulip poplar.

He believed he had never married because he was married to his calling. The truth was, he had a complete lack of the equipment demanded for truly loving.

Perhaps he was like his father, after all, though he'd believed all these years that he had his mother's disposition. He had believed the friends and relatives and old Bishop Slade who had said, "Kind like his mother! Patient like his mother! Easygoing like his mother!"

Yet, underneath all that show of sop and decency was a man utterly fixed on himself, on his own concerns. And underneath some shallow layer of seeming warmth and caring was a cold stratum of granite.

The very last place he wanted to be day after tomorrow was in the pulpit. It was all a joke, and the joke was on him.

CHAPTER THREE

Found

You ought to let fancy give you a haircut," said Mule Skinner over breakfast at the Grill. "Get you somethin' new goin'."

"I've got enough going, thank you," said the rector, who was scheduled for two meetings, a noon invocation at the Rotary Club, a livermush delivery to Russell Jacks, and a visit to the construction site with Ron Malcolm.

"You could take a little more off the sides, if you ask me," said Mule.

"They ain't anybody askin' you," said Percy, handing a plate of toast to J.C.

J.C. grabbed the toast and sopped his egg yolk. "If you promoted your real-estate business like you're promotin' your wife's beauty shop, you'd be a millionaire."

"Besides," said the rector, "I've been with Joe for thirteen going on fourteen years."

"Well, that's the trouble," said Mule. "A man needs a change."

Percy poured another round of coffee. "I hope you can look Joe Ivey in th' eye, th' way you're tryin' to rob 'im of his business."

"Anyway," said J.C., "why would a man want to get a haircut from a woman?"

"I guess you never heard of unisex," said Mule. "Fancy runs a unisex shop. That means she cuts anybody's hair, one sex as well as the other. You ought to let 'er have a go at you, in the meantime."

"Where is she set up?" the rector inquired.

"In th' basement where we had that big blow-out for our twenty-fifth. You ought to see it now—completely redecorated wall to wall, new pink carpet, you name it. Put in two sinks, in case she adds on a stylist."

"Your neighbor still got that dog tied up next door?" Percy called from the grill.

"That dog'll never let anybody near your basement," said J.C. "When it starts lungin' at somebody gettin' out of their car, that'll be enough right there to curl their hair."

"That dog died," said Mule, scowling.

"They'll probably get another one just like it," said J.C. "That's what usually happens."

The rector checked his wristwatch. "Tell Fancy I wish her well. If Joe goes down with the flu this winter, I might consider it. I've got to get out of here. Catch you tomorrow."

"I declare," said Mule as the local priest went out the door, "a little excitement starin' him right in the face, and he won't even spring for it."

"You won't believe this," said Ron Malcolm, "but they've hit rock on the hill. Twelve feet of rock."

"What does that mean?"

"It means Buck Leeper is calling in a dynamite man. This'll set us back. They'll have to drill into the rock and set the dynamite at intervals. It'll be a series of explosions—blam, blam, blam—probably going on for more than a week."

"Not good."

"Once the rock is busted up, they'll have to excavate it out of there with a back hoe and a grab bucket. That's more time."

"And more money."

"By the way," said Ron, as if reading his mind, "Buck is in Wesley today. I guess you won't be brokenhearted."

He had decided not to tell Ron that the superintendent had shoved him around the other day; it was hardly worth repeating.

The architect met them in the trailer. "I've been rethinking a couple of things, Father. I feel the chapel ceiling is too bland, to . . . uninspired. With your blessing, I'd like to enrich the vault. Here's what could happen."

He unrolled a drawing and spread it out on a metal table.

"What if we come in here with a herringbone pattern using V-joint tongue-and-groove fir? Fir is native to these mountains, and the pattern would add to the overall beauty without being a visual distraction. Then we'd come in with a deep fir molding around the base of the vault. What do you think?"

"I like it," said the rector.

"Ditto," said Ron. "And we know a man and his son who could do an outstanding job of it, real native artisans."

"Great! Native workmanship can add a lot of aesthetic value. Terrific."

The architect was clearly excited about the new plan and shook hands gratefully with both men.

"How's Buck working out for you?"

"Couldn't be better," said Ron, eyeing the rector.

"Tough break about striking rock. Well, I'm going to walk over the job and see what's happened since last week. Want to come?"

"You go," said Father Tim. "I've got to make a call."

The two men went out, letting a blast of stinging air into the trailer. He shivered as he sat down at the desk in Buck Leeper's ravaged swivel chair.

"Hello, Avis? I'm running late. Could you put together a few things for me to pick up before you close? A pound of ground sirloin. Right. A gallon of milk. A pack of buns. No, not the whole wheat. Dooley won't eat anything brown." He still felt the blast of cold air along his shoulders.

"While I'm at it, do you know where I can get a load of wood for the winter? Sure, I'll hold."

While Avis laid the receiver down to help a customer, his eyes wandered to the desk blotter that contained a large calendar. He blinked.

In each square that represented the day until today, October the nineteenth, was an exquisite pen-and-ink drawing. Each was intensely thoughtful and rendered with infinite detail. There was a mollusk, an owl, a brick wall, a mountain, a bridge, a chambered nautilus, an ornate staircase, whorls, spirals, hieroglyphs, a pyramid. All so intricate and perfect they might have been mechanically printed.

Nothing was written in any of the squares, no appointments, no schedules, no reminders. The heavy pressure of the pen made each line appear engraved.

There was something jarring about the perfection and precise control, as if these characteristics combined to speak through the drawings with one loud voice. But what was the voice saying?

The thought came to him instantly and clearly. It was saying, Help.

"Right this way," said Mrs. Kershaw. "Miss Olivia has cleared a great big spot in her dressing room."

He could barely see over the stack of hatboxes he was carrying. Trooping behind him like a string of ducks were Miss Sadie, clutching the ribbons of a hatbox in each hand, and Louella, with a hatbox in the crook of each arm.

"Oh, my, I hope that's all," said the housekeeper.

"It certainly is not all," Miss Sadie said. "We'll have to make two more trips to the car!"

They went down the hall to Olivia's bed and dressing room, where she came in from the terrace to greet them. The rector thought she had never looked more beautifully eager and alive, yet only months ago, they had carried her from this room, near death.

"Just put them here for now," she said, rushing to kiss every cheek. "I'm so excited! After lunch, we'll have a hat show. Hoppy is coming over, and we're all going to model!"

"I pass," said Father Tim.

She laughed, giving him a fervent hug. "Oh, I'm so glad to see you all. What a blessing."

"We'll have to make two more trips to the car," Miss Sadie said proudly.

"We'll all help," Olivia insisted. "Lunch is on the terrace, but it's covered, so no bumblebees will land in the salad."

"Ladies, I'm taking charge here. Go sit on the terrace and soak up this unexpected sunshine. I'll fetch the hats."

"But . . ." said Olivia.

"Mind your priest, dear," said Miss Sadie, looking at the large, sunny room with appreciation.

Lunch under an umbrella, in the warm sunshine, surrounded by autumn color and a lawn splashed with the first of the fallen leaves. He was so removed from his daily rounds he felt as if he might be in a foreign country.

Hoppy arrived precisely as Mrs. Kershaw set the dessert tray on the skirted table.

"Wonderful timing, old fellow!" The rector loved the sight of his doctor and friend, who had put on weight and improved in color. Only the wild tangle of his graying hair seemed unchanged. It was a different man who, only a year ago, was still grieving over his dead wife and cursing God.

Hoppy embraced each guest with warmth, saving Olivia until last. He went and stood by her side, his arm around her slender waist. Their happiness was palpable; like the pulsing shimmer of a humming-bird, it seemed to radiate the very air.

He felt an odd piercing of his heart. "My friend, who's your doctor these days? You look positively remade."

"Doctor Davenport is attending me," Hoppy said, grinning. "She's a heart specialist, you know."

When the women went in to get ready for the hat show, Hoppy peered at him intently. "You look a little peaked."

"I'm fine. Top-notch. Stop drumming up business."

"Let me see you next week. I haven't looked at you since Ireland."

"If you insist."

"I saw the story about your neighbor."

The rector gazed at him steadily and smiled.

"So, what's the scoop?" Hoppy asked.

"The scoop? If there's any scoop, J.C. already got it."

"You know what I mean. Are you seeing her?"

"A bit difficult since she's living in New York."

The doctor ran his fingers through his hair. "Rats," he said with feeling.

They heard the first shattering boom on the hill, as if a jet had just broken the sound barrier.

"What an opening!" said Hoppy, as the slender, dark-haired Olivia appeared on the terrace in a swirl of cream-colored chiffon.

"Ta-daaaa!" She was wearing a wide-brimmed hat that tied under her chin with a sash of limp organdy. The hat, once white, had turned a soft ivory color and was adorned with velvet roses. "This fetching number," she announced, "was worn to country picnics and often graced lawn parties at Fernbank."

Hoppy stood and applauded. "Bravo!" he crowed.

"And now," said Olivia, gesturing toward the French doors, "Miss Sadie Baxter, wearing a scarlet felt with leghorn feathers, so perfect for motoring to Wesley in one's town car . . ."

Another thundering boom as Miss Sadie strolled happily onto the terrace, wearing a hat that engulfed her head and left only her mouth and chin visible.

Cheered on by the applause, Miss Sadie bowed low, sending her hat rolling into a perennial border.

"And now," she said in her warbly voice, "Louella, my best friend and lifelong companion, in a smart panama straw, which Mama wore to summer services at Lord's Chapel!"

Louella called loudly from the bedroom, "Miss Sadie, do I have t' do this foolishness?"

"You most certainly do, Louella! It's the entertainment!"

Clutching her handbag, Louella stomped out in a hat smothered with silk lilacs, which were mashed flat with decades of lying in a box.

"Slavery done been over all these years," she grumbled to the rector, "an' some folks act like it still goin' on."

"Poshtosh," said Hoppy. "You should see yourself. You look terrific." He nudged the rector for a comment.

"Sharp as a tack!" he blurted.

"You mean it?"

"Would we lie to you?"

"Well," Louella said thoughtfully and broke into one of her huge smiles.

"More! More!" Hoppy shouted, beating on his tea glass with a spoon. Six more hats were exhibited before the models began to protest and thumped down in chairs in Olivia's bedroom.

After Hoppy left, they sat and talked, the conversation punctuated by explosions on the hill.

"I hope the noise won't be too much for you, Miss Sadie," said the rector. "It's mighty close to Fernbank."

"Oh, no! I like a little something going on for a change." She sighed contentedly. "I don't know when I've had such a good time. Certainly not since Father had his dinner party last spring."

Olivia went to the double closet behind her chaise and pulled out a garment bag.

"While I was rearranging my closets to make room for your mother's wonderful hats, I came across something precious to me, something I'd like to share with just the three of you. It was my grandmother's."

She unzipped the bag and took out a child's red velvet coat with white fur collar and cuffs. A white fur muff, stuffed with tissue paper, was tied around the neck of the padded hanger. Smiling, she held it up for all to see.

An odd sound escaped Miss Sadie; perhaps it was only the word, "Oh."

Louella sank into a chair by the bed, as if her knees had given way.

"Long ago, an aunt told me that my grandmother was born out of wedlock. She never lived with her mother. She grew up in the home of a very kind woman. But her mother visited her each week, never letting it be known who she was. She always brought lovely things, I'm told, and this little coat was one of them. Isn't it beautiful? My aunt said Grandmother treasured it more than anything else.

"I've just finished going through Mother's things, where I found it. So many years have gone by, I feel at peace about sharing this old family secret with friends."

Miss Sadie gave a shuddering sigh, while Louella sat frozen in the chair.

"Miss Sadie, are you all right?" Olivia went to the old woman, who had closed her eyes.

"Father," said Miss Sadie, "could you come and hold my hand?"

He pulled the vanity bench close and did as she asked.

"It's done, now," moaned Louella, who had turned an odd, gray color.

Miss Sadie's eyes remained closed. Then, she spoke slowly, as if something inside were winding down.

"What . . . was your grandmother's name?"

"Lydia Anne. But that's all I know. We've never talked about it in the family all these years. My aunt said I should never discuss it. But it's all so long ago that surely . . ."

Miss Sadie opened her eyes and looked at Olivia. "I've seen that little coat before, my dear. I found it in a box under my mother's bed and thought she had bought it for me. It was a trifle large, and I remember thinking I would grow into it. It was the prettiest thing I ever saw. Several times, I took it out of the box and put it on when Mama was out of the house."

There was a long silence in the room. Olivia looked stricken.

"Christmas came and went," said Miss Sadie, "and the little red coat did not appear. I crawled under her bed to look for it, but it was gone."

The rector held her hand and prayed silently.

"Olivia, dear," said the old woman, "I have every reason to believe your grandmother was my half-sister . . . and that you are my grand-niece."

Olivia sat down beside the rector on the vanity bench, clutching the coat. "I'm so sorry if I said . . . if I did . . ."

Miss Sadie's voice trembled. "I've just learned that my mother had a little girl named Lydia Anne before she married my father. Every week for many years, I watched her go out with her basket for the poor and come home brokenhearted. How strange that I should find this out while collecting her hats to bring to you."

"Oh, Miss Sadie!" Olivia slipped from the bench and knelt by the old woman's knees, weeping with remorse and surprised joy.

Miss Sadie gave Olivia her other hand. "It's all right, my dear. Just wait until you see Mama's picture. You'll think you're looking in a mirror."

"I can't believe the little coat has given me what I long for most—family!"

"Family!" said Miss Sadie, letting her own tears come. "The sweetest treasure on earth. If I hadn't had Louella . . ." Louella came and stood by Miss Sadie, touching her shoulder.

In the room splashed with golden autumn light, they had drawn together, as close as eggs in a nest.

He was no wimp. Instead of writing, he would call her.

That he miserably dreaded the coldness he might hear in her voice was beside the point. The point was to establish contact, to see whether the path through the hedge might be cleared again for passage.

So what if she were cold to him? Hadn't he faced glacial vestries and stony congregations?

He had always managed, somehow, to follow a canonized saint when he was called to a parish, someone who had worn a halo and been surrounded by seraphim, even when walking to the corner for a newspaper.

In his first parish, it had taken a full year to be forgiven his green innocence in the wake of a priest who, mellowed by age, was wise and all-knowing, not to mention full of truth and light.

Though he was again and again the leading choice among the candidates, the frost inevitably came as his congregations sized him up.

One parish had chosen him because he was unmarried but later wished he were married with children.

Another liked him because he was unaffected but decided he needed more charisma.

One search committee thought that being slightly under five feet nine inches in his sock feet was a characteristic that lent spiritual humility but changed their minds and wished he were taller.

What had he to fear, after all?

Absolutely nothing, of course. There was only one problem—he didn't know where to call her.

He walked quickly to the library after lunch and looked up one of the Violet books. He sat down in the reading room and tucked it behind Tuesday's *Wall Street Journal*.

Violet Visits the Queen was filled with watercolors of the irrepressible Violet trying to make friends with garden rabbits under the queen's rosebushes, leaping from a drawing room mantel onto a bird cage, and sending terrified corgis fleeing along dim passageways.

Violet only wanted a friend, read one of the pages in the picture book. *But every time she tried to have one, she did something that chased them away.*

He found the name of the publisher and entered it in his black address book.

He walked to the office, hearing a series of shuddering booms from the hill. His heart beat dully at the very thought of what he was about to do.

He sat in his swivel chair and prayed as simply as he knew how. Lord, if this friendship is not meant to grow, please close the door. If it pleases you, throw the door open wide, and give me the courage to walk through it.

"Bardzvark," someone said at the other end of the line.

"I beg your pardon?"

"Moment, pliz."

He was instantly dumped into the voice mail of someone who suggested he either leave a message or press star for the operator. He had no message to leave and could not, for the life of him, find a star on the telephone keys. He located what appeared to be an asterisk, which produced only an empty silence that he was paying for.

He hung up.

Perhaps he would humiliate himself and Cynthia, to boot. But he would go straight to the publisher, the president, the editor-in-chief, the blasted top.

"Bardzvark."

"The president!" he said, reckless with anxiety.

Pitched into voice mail, he got a recording. "You have reached the office of Helen Boatwright. At the sound of the tone, please leave a message, or dial star for the operator."

He hung up and dialed again.

"Bardzvarkholdpliz."

He was nearly deafened by the music that came pouring out of the telephone. Mozart. Or was it Vivaldi? What a perilous thing it was to try and reach someone in the outside world.

"Who're you holding for, pliz?"

He was glad he had never been troubled with high blood pressure. "The boss of the children's book section, the publisher, the main . . ."

The line seemed to go dead for a moment. "Argonaut."

"May I please speak with the publisher?" he said through his teeth.

"Of which division?"

"Children. Juvenile. Young people."

"This is the children's division."

"I'm trying to find one of your authors."

"I'm sorry, we don't give whereabouts or addresses of our authors. You'll have to write a letter."

"I am this person's neighbor," he said ominously, "and it is imperative that I locate her."

"You may send a letter to our group office and we'll forward it to her. Thank you for calling."

He pounded his fist on the desk. The door appeared not only to have closed but to have slammed in his face.

"How sweet, how passing sweet, is solitude."

"Cowper."

"A man cain't hardly be a hermit n' more," said Homeless.

"Why's that?" the rector asked, moving closer to the glowing wood stove. The door of the stove stood open, and shadows flickered over the walls of a dwelling that was smaller than the rectory kitchen.

"When I moved here a few years ago, I was about th' only one on th' creek. Now th' place is crawlin' with house trailers and squirmin' with little doodad houses. You got dope and alcohol, wife beatin', shootin' and stabbin', you name it. Back along th' creek is th' same as everywhere else . . . namely, th' devil walks to and fro upon the earth . . ."

". . . seeking whom he may devour."

"You know my Wednesday night soup deal has got so it draws upwards of thirty or more at a time. The Local is still givin' me good provender for my pot, an' that bank account from th' reward money I got f'r findin' Barnabas, it squeezes out a pair of shoes here, a pair of britches there. Last week, we got a little kid outfitted with glasses. You ought to seen 'er. She was a doll in them glasses, eyes big as saucers. But you know what we really need in here?"

"What's that?"

"We're gettin' so we need a preacher. You'll not get this bunch to church, no sir, but they need to hear somethin' solid. To my mind, preachin' is like soup. They want a little chunk of meat in it, an' they like it seasoned good. Don't hold back on th' pepper, don't be scant with th' salt, and make sure it ain't watery. They'll turn it down if it's watery, even on an empty stomach."

Father Tim looked into his cocoa. Could this call be for him?

"To tell th' truth, I think you're a mite too educated f'r this bunch. No offense, but that wouldn't be soup, that'd be consommé, if you know what I mean."

The rector nodded.

"We need some gloriously saved sinner that's got the fire of God in 'im, somebody who'd stand on that stump out yonder and say what's what and no bones about it. 'Course, in th' winter, it's goin' to be mighty tight filin' a horde of people through this little shoebox, much less a preacher. Maybe ought to just have summer preachin'."

"Wouldn't hurt to have some music."

"No sir, it wouldn't."

"Let me think about it. Let's pray about it."

"I'll go along with that," said Homeless, taking the lid off a black iron skillet. "Now, how about a dipper of mush?"

"I wouldn't miss it."

"Yeah, but ain't you got some ol' meetin' or somethin'? I seen, saw it on your calendar."

"I won't go to the meeting. There are more important things in life than meetings."

"Really?"

"Really. Are you fellows going to do any good against Wesley?"

Dooley grinned. "We're gonna whip 'em s' bad they'll bawl like sissies."

He looked handsome in his uniform, thought the rector. Very handsome, very healthy, very whole. He put his arm around the boy's padded shoulders. An offensive tackle. A miracle!

"You know what?"

"What's 'at?"

"You're one heck of a guy. I'm proud of you."

Dooley colored slightly and dropped his head.

What he really wanted to say was, "I love you, pal." Why couldn't he say it? He was, after all, in the business of love.

On the way to Absalom Greer's country store, Barnabas sat in the front seat with his eyes fixed on the road, as if he wanted to do a good job of riding in the car.

"I say, old man, you're taking this too seriously. Why don't you loosen up and smudge the windows I've just washed or lean over here and fog my glasses? No, no. Erase that! Too simple. Why not give the collar of my clean shirt a good licking or drool on my jacket?"

Barnabas continued to stare ahead, but one ear flickered.

The rector reached over and put his hand on the dog's neck. Right here was as solid a friend as he'd ever had, with the possible exceptions of Tommy Noles and Stuart Cullen, with Walter thrown in for good measure.

Why didn't he do this more often? Go driving in the country and talk to his dog? It was the simplest of refreshments and didn't cost a dime.

Indian summer was a glad fifth season that didn't come every year. It stepped in without warning, as an inexpressibly welcome bonus, a gift that made limbs lighter, minds clearer, steps quicker.

Absalom Greer bounded from behind the counter of his country store as if all the bonuses of the season resided in him.

They shook hands warmly and embraced. "Preacher Greer has sent his son to greet me," said the rector.

The old man laughed. "You're a fine one to talk, seein' as Ireland knocked a decade or two off your own years."

"What's that wondrous smell? Wait! Don't tell me. Fried chicken!"

"Sure as you're born. Crisp and brown, with a mess of green beans and a bowl of mashed potatoes and gravy. We won't even talk about the biscuits stacked up on our best china platter, already buttered."

"Hallelujah and four amens," said the rector, who refused to consider the lethal consequences of that particular menu on his diabetes.

"Lottie has cooked all morning, and don't be sayin' you wish she hadn't gone to any trouble. It's my sister's joy to go to trouble when the town priest is comin'. Did you bring your dog?"

"I did. In the car."

"Our cat's off on a toot, so bring him in. We'll give him a home-cooked dinner."

Absalom put the handwritten *Closed* sign on the knob of the front door, and all three of them walked the length of the creaking floor to the back rooms. Though the rector had been here but once before, he felt instantly at home.

After the meal the Greers called dinner and the rector called lunch, Lottie went to the garden to clean out the vegetable beds, and Barnabas lay with his head on Absalom's foot.

The rector sipped the strong, black coffee that had been brewed on the stove. "Have they let you retire yet?"

"Law, it's like weanin' babies. They don't want to let me go, but it's got to be done. Next Sunday, I'll be preaching to my last little handful at Sandy Creek, and then it's over—I'll be just a twig broom standin' in the corner."

"I may have a pulpit for you, if the Lord so moves."

Absalom Greer threw back his head and laughed. "You're always looking to put me in the traces! A poor ol' gray-headed country preacher can't get a mite of rest and peace."

"This is a special congregation."

"They're all special."

"This one meets on Wednesday evening, leaving Sunday free to supply one of your little handfuls, if the need arises."

The old man took an apple out of the basket on the table and began to peel it.

"It would be a summer pulpit," the rector said. "You'd be preaching from a hickory stump. Winter along the creek is too hard. You wouldn't be able to get around in there."

"Eighty-nine years old this November, and they won't let me be . . ."

"Of course, the little band at Mitford Creek is very different from the one at Sandy Creek."

"How's that?" He cut a slice of the apple and passed it to the rector on the point of his knife.

"They're not seasoned in the Word of God. They're unchurched. Once a week, they come together to eat a pot of soup made with scraps, but you could give them a banquet, my brother."

"I thought you drove down here in a Buick," said Absalom Greer, "but it looks like you've come drivin' a hard bargain."

"Tasty apple," said the rector.

"I'll talk to th' Lord about it," said the country preacher.

His mail was stacked on the desk in his study.

Dear Father,

They've moved me from the laundry to the mess hall, where I set up and clean up. The boiling temperatures in the laundry took some weight off, so I've been looking like a display in anatomy class. Prison life is not for the fainthearted . . .

He would never forget the look on the faces of his congregation when, just as he was beginning his sermon last spring, the pull-down stairs behind the pulpit lowered. His heart had thundered like a jack hammer when the jewel thief who had hidden for months behind the bells in the church attic came down and confessed his crime.

George Gaynor had been little more than a skeleton even then, living as he had on pilfered coffee-hour provender, Sunday school juice, canned vegetables from the basement, and an occasional carton of half and half. Not to mention, of course, Esther Bolick's marmalade cake, which he had snatched out of its container during a lay readers' meeting.

> . . . *Thank you for* My Utmost for His Highest, *which also is not for the fainthearted. I find it as compelling as anything I've read, apart from the Bible.*
>
> *Chambers talks about substituting credal belief for personal belief. He says that's why so many are devoted to causes and so few devoted to Christ. This struck a deep chord with me, and I wish we could sit and talk about it. I grew up on credal belief, and it never worked. It's a dangerous masquerade that's seldom found out until it's too late.*
>
> *Pete came twice while you were away. A visit with him always has a bonus—it's like a visit with you . . .*

He looked up from the letter and realized he was smiling. No, beaming would be a better word for it. While he had prayed that day in the nave with Pete Jamison, George Gaynor had, quite unknown to them, joined them in prayer in his hiding place in the attic.

Two for one, George had called the simple prayer of salvation that had set the lives of both men on vastly different courses.

> . . . *Please tell Mrs. Bolick that I have dreamed about her marmalade cake on several occasions . . .*

He laughed. Esther Bolick's legendary cake had become a warm memory for a convicted criminal, had been devoured at a baptism ceremony in a police station, and had sent him into a diabetic coma that almost took him out. "To die for!" Emma had once said, and hadn't he nearly proved it?

A postcard from Pete Jamison:

My territory has been expanded to six states. I'm praying and it's working. Saw George. Call you soon. God bless.

He didn't recognize the handwriting on the mauve envelope. There was no return address, but the stamps and postmark were Irish. Before opening it, he grudgingly used the microwave to heat a cup of cocoa, then sat at the kitchen counter.

Dear Cousin Timothy,

It was lovely to meet you at Erin Donovan's tea. I had heard for years of the Cousin Tim who was a priest in America and never dreamed we might tip a glass together. I found you terribly clever and charming and so like Great-aunt Fiona that I could scarcely tell the difference except for your trousers.

My scheme is to see your country, as you have seen mine, and to settle for a bit among the people.

It was sweet of you to suggest that I come 'round whenever I'm in America.

Yours very truly,
Meg Patrick

There had been dozens of cousins at Erin Donovan's tea, and he couldn't say that he remembered anyone named Meg Patrick.

There had been Patricks on his grandmother's side, but if there were any left, he didn't know of it. Good of her to write, although he was frankly puzzled by her comparison of his likeness to the famed Great-aunt Fiona, whom he'd always found to be astonishingly attractive in the old photographs in his father's desk.

He glanced up from the letter and studied his reflection in the glass panel of the cabinet door. Perhaps he did have his ancestor's broad forehead and large eyes.

It seemed odd to consider such a connection after so many years of feeling those family connections severed. His father's lifelong reticence about ancestry had caused his paternal side to appear like a nearly blank sheet of paper, with only Walter occupying a space.

The trip, however, had stirred something in him, rather like yeast beginning to work in dough.

He knew little, except for the photographs in his father's desk and a bundle of letters he had read as a child with great avidity in secret. He knew that his grandfather had come over from Ireland at the age of fourteen and went on to make a small fortune as the owner of a box factory. Some rift between his father and grandfather, and later between his father and uncle, had served to slam the door on Ireland.

No wonder he had burrowed so deeply into his mother's small, closely-knit family with their strong Baptist traditions. It had been warm in that burrow, and one always got the straight of things, full force, yet tempered with love.

His mother's family had been shocked at the worst and saddened at the least when he announced his plans to become an Episcopal priest. Perhaps to this day he had never completely understood that decision himself. Though it made no rational sense, he felt it was a way to minister to his Episcopalian father, to his frozen spirit and aloof disdain, though his father would die even before he left seminary.

He had also felt, without being able to express it, that this course could somehow heal their lifelong rift. But more than that, more than anything, he had wanted to serve God and His people—and he had never looked back.

Clearly, Ireland had given him a sense of wholeness he'd longed for, and the mass gatherings at Erin's of near and distant cousins had been a high point. The Irish were known to grumble about the hordes of Americans who stumbled through parish graveyards, rubbing stones, trampling flowers, looking for their roots. But once connected, it was a different story—one was taken in and cosseted like the biblical prodigal.

Yet, if the cousins had been a high point, one event had been higher still—the day he'd taken the rented car with Katherine and Walter and the picnic basket with the rhubarb tart. The landlady had wrapped the tart, hot from the oven, and for miles they salivated as the aroma crept out of the basket and filled the car.

With a sudden screech of tires, Katherine had pulled off the narrow road and looked them dead in the eye. "I can't wait another minute," she said. Excited as children, they peeled the tea towel from around the still-warm delicacy and devoured every crumb.

"There!" Katherine had said, recklessly wiping her mouth on the hem of her dress. "That's how I want to live for the rest of my life!"

He remembered that Katherine had gone up the steep knoll ahead of him, pushing along with the aid of a walking stick. Walter was farther ahead, at the crest of the hill, when they heard his voice echoing off the endless green hills and ancient stone walls, "Look! We've found it! You won't believe it!"

He nearly killed himself climbing to the top to stand there panting with his companions in utter astonishment. "By George!" he had said hoarsely.

The remains of the family castle lay along the top of the facing hill, a shattered toy abandoned to solitude and mist.

Without speaking, he and Walter gazed in wonder at the ruin that bound them together as one blood, until heaven.

Leaning into the wind, he walked to Fernbank for tea, wearing his down jacket for the first time, a muffler, and gloves.

Boom. He could feel the ground shake beneath his feet. According to Ron, the explosions would end today, and he thought how he'd grown accustomed to them.

Much against Miss Sadie's will, Louella had made an effort to remove the crusts from their sandwiches.

"Waste not, want not!" Miss Sadie reminded her friend for the thousandth time in their long life together.

"Miss Sadie, if it's jus' you an' me, don't matter 'bout leavin' on th' crust, but this is *comp'ny.*"

Miss Sadie looked unconvinced.

"This is a *preacher!*" said Louella.

Miss Sadie furrowed her brow.

Louella pulled out her last stop. "Would yo' mama want you servin' san'wiches with *crusts?*" She said the word with such loathing she might have been discussing snakes.

Miss Sadie sniffed and dropped the tea bags into the pot. That was the end of that discussion, thought Louella, who garnished her crustless sandwiches with a stem of parsley.

They sat in Miss Sadie's yellow bedroom, which had lately become a favorite spot to entertain. "It's so she don' have to look at them rain buckets in th' parlor," Louella had told him. "We jus' let 'em get full, then pour it down th' toilet. Miss Sadie call it a free flush."

Louella removed her apron and sat on the vanity bench, as they took their accustomed places in the wing chairs.

His hostess sighed. "I've gone through all Papa's money, you know."

"Yes, I know." She had freely given five million dollars to build Hope House, an ambitious nursing-care facility that promised to be state-of-the-art. Would its benefactor be among its poorest residents? Perhaps he should offer something out of the Lord's Chapel discretionary funds.

"So," she said, brightening, "now we'll start on Mama's money. It's not nearly as much as Papa's, I hate to admit. I could have done so much better, been a much better steward. But when I did so well with Papa's by staying tight as a corset all those years, I decided I'd experiment with Mama's."

"Aha."

She looked at her hands in her lap. "That was a mistake. I conducted a very unfortunate experiment in 1954 and again in 1977." She shook her head, then looked up, smiling again. "But I forgave myself and asked the Lord to do the same. Let bygones be bygones!"

"That's the spirit."

"I'm ashamed to say I'm nearly cleaned out . . ."

"I'm sorry." What a sad irony!

". . . I've got just a little over a million left."

He hoped his face didn't register his shock and amusement, but only the admiration he felt.

"So," she said, "what we need to do is start spending it . . . and I think we should start with Dooley."

"With Dooley?"

"That boy needs to go away to school, Father, to get the kind of education that will make the most of what the good Lord put in him. Mitford School is a fine school, but at best, it can only try to *make up* for his deprivations. We need something that will *overcome* them! Don't you see?"

"Yes. I do see. And you've put it very well."

"Louella and I agree on this a hundred percent."

"Aha."

"He'll be in the eighth grade next year, and if we want to get him in the right school, something needs to be done right away. He may even need tutoring, especially for his English! Now, how do we get started?" There it was again—something he'd seen before; it was the girl in Sadie Baxter.

"I . . . don't exactly know how to start."

"Father," she said a bit sharply, "if I'm going to do my part, you must do yours. It's up to you to find out how to start!"

Boom went the last of the dynamite, rattling the cups on their saucers.

He was sitting at his desk in the study when he happened to glance up and look out the window. There, perched on the window box with her nose glued to the other side of the glass, was Violet. He froze.

Violet studied him like a fish in a tank.

He studied her in return.

He had never noticed that her eyes were so green or that they perfectly matched her collar. She sat like a statue, white against the approaching dusk, unblinking.

Or was it Violet?

Absolutely, he decided. There was something about Violet, after all. And why shouldn't there be? She had been to visit the queen, for Pete's sake, not to mention learned to play the piano.

He didn't want his neighbor's straying cat to be startled and leave. He wanted her to sit right there until he could get his hands on her. Because what he wanted to do, he realized, was find her.

Yes! Violet had run away, but he had found her, and he would return her to her distraught owner, safe and sound, and gain the opening he had hoped for. Perfect.

He moved like a cat, himself, easing out of the chair and gliding across the creaking floor. Violet's eyes followed him as if he were a minnow in a pool.

When he reached the kitchen, he bounded to the back door, threw it open, and looked out at the window box. Violet had vanished.

Blast!

Then he felt something at his ankles.

As he dashed through the hedge with the squirming cat, he saw a red welt on his hand, with blood oozing through. Even better, he thought with satisfaction.

Cynthia opened the door and glared. Somehow, he knew exactly what she was going to say. "Violet, you wretch!"

She grabbed the errant cat from his arms. "I found her!" he exclaimed, displaying his bleeding hand as evidence.

But she closed the door abruptly, and he heard footsteps retreating down the hall.

He was trembling when he reached his back stoop and opened the kitchen door. He was feeling something he didn't like to acknowledge, something he had run from feeling most of his life. It was fury.

How could she close the door in his face without even a thank you or a by-your-leave? What had he done, after all, to deserve her ingratitude and hostility? Nothing!

Hadn't he tried and tried to call her, and pounded on her door in a driving rain, and brought her a Waterford goblet from Ireland even if she hadn't seen it yet, thinking of her always during the entire two months?

Hadn't he written her twice from Sligo?

Hadn't he been perfectly innocent in the Edith Mallory escapade?

Hadn't he rung that blasted publisher's phone off the hook trying to reach her and composed endless letters of contrition in his mind?

He was sick of Dear Cynthia this and Dearest Cynthia that and the whole mess of feelings that erupted in him like a volcano every time he so much as thought of her and which lately had been settling like ash on everyone in his vicinity.

No, he would not write and he would not call. He would not swing this way and that until he was fairly churned to butter over his Pecksniff neighbor. He would march over there right now and pound on her door and demand to be heard. And let the chips fall where they may.

Ulcers! he thought, feeling the wrench in his stomach. He knew that if he backed off for one moment, he would be done for—he would wimp along with her until the cows came home. It was now or never, and the sweat that broke out on his forehead proved it.

There was just one thing he needed:

Prayer.

But where could he turn for it? He dialed Walter. Answering machine. Blast.

Marge Owen. He wouldn't need to say anything more than "Pray for me," and it would be done at once. No answer. Didn't anybody stay home these days?

It came to him so suddenly and with such force, he didn't hesitate. He dialed the phone and when she answered, he said:

"Cynthia, I'm coming over to see you. Pray for me."

He did his own praying as he dodged through the hedge.

The back door was standing open, presumably so he didn't have to be formally greeted.

"Cynthia!"

"I'm in here," she said from the studio. What did he hear in her voice? Iron. Steel. Sheetrock. Knives.

He walked in and saw her sitting on the floor, piling books into a carton. She brushed her hair back and looked at him. He felt he had been slammed across the chest when he saw her eyes. They were the most extraordinary eyes he had ever seen. Why did he always feel he was seeing them for the first time? "Cynthia . . ."

"Timothy." She stared at him, cool and removed.

"Listen to me."

He sat on the floor across from her, and Violet slithered into his lap.

"I'm cursed with an orderly mind," he said, "so let's begin some-where vaguely at the beginning." There! He was not croaking, and he was not going to croak. He had the voice of Moses on the mount. It might have shattered the glasses in her cupboard.

"I tried to call you again and again, but your machine . . ."

"What about my machine?"

"It made noises like a truck on a highway."

She gave him a stupefying look.

"I knocked one day," he continued, "but it was raining."

"Raining. Oh, my," she said, looking bored.

"And I don't know what you were thinking the morning I came home in Edith Mallory's car . . ."

"Thinking? I didn't think. My mind felt like oat bran stirred with a spoon."

He plunged ahead. "There is absolutely nothing between Edith and me. She held me at her house against my will."

"Really," she said in a voice encrusted with ice.

"It was raining. Tad and Ron went ahead without me. Ed Coffey was going to bring me home, but the car flooded. I slept in a chair. It was a miserable experience."

"Caring about you has been a miserable experience."

He noted the past tense. "Cynthia, I'm sorry. That's what I really came over here to say. If you could know the letters I've written to you . . ."

"I never got them."

"I wrote them in my mind."

"Oh, *those* letters!"

"I tried to call you in New York. I rang your publisher and they wouldn't give me your address." Something was going wrong here. Why was he pleading and explaining?

He tacked into the wind. "Listen," he said firmly, "why didn't you tell me you were moving? Why just go off like that without a word?"

"Without a word? I had hardly had a word from you in months! Two letters that might have been written to a distant relative, and that was all. You said you were going to think about that ridiculous proposition I made to you about going steady and give me an answer on your return. That was your condition, not mine. But of course, you never mentioned it again. And not only did I hardly see you when you came home, but you couldn't even find the time to call me."

"But, Cynthia . . ."

"No 'but Cynthia,' if you please. And it was you who said we mustn't let the path through the hedge grow over. Well, have you seen it? It would take a bush hog to clear it out again!"

"What do you know about bush hogs?" A stupid question, but out it came.

"There are lots of things I know that you'll never know I know, because you'll never ask."

"I just asked."

She looked at him, biting her lip. "I'm either going to punch you in the nose or bawl my brains out," she said.

"I deserve the former, but I'll leave the decision to you."

Great tears loomed in her eyes, and he rose to his knees on the bare floor and took her in his arms.

It was wonderful to sit close to her on the minuscule love seat, to smell the scent of wisteria, to have his arm around her and hear the silken voice he'd longed to hear again. Violet had sprawled across both their laps, purring like the engine of a compact car.

"I've missed you," he said. "I've missed you terribly. It's been like a death, having the little house empty, and no lights on, and not knowing . . ."

"I haven't exactly moved," she said, her eyes red from the storm of

weeping. "It's just that I had such a terrific deadline on the new illustrations that my editor said why not take his apartment while he's in
Europe for six months, and so I thought, of course, how perfect, and I
won't have to bother with . . . with my wretched neighbor!"

He kissed her hair.

"So I moved in there until I'm finished. I had most of my books
sent up, and my favorite drawing board, and my bed, which I'm never
without—just a few things. Actually, I didn't know what I wanted to
do. I felt very foolish, throwing myself at you like that and you backing away from me at sixty miles an hour."

"Forty-five."

"I prayed for you when you called."

"I knew you would." He kissed her temple.

"I thought it was very clever of you to ask me to do that."

"It was the Holy Spirit who had such a wild notion, not me."

She laid her head on his shoulder. What an extraordinary development. An hour ago he had been sitting at his desk in a hard-back
chair, laboring over his sermon with an aching heart, and now he was
holding someone soft and tender and fragrant and desirable, with a
vast furry creature in his lap. He might have sunk to the moss-covered
bottom of a clear pond where he was resting like a leaf.

But it was just such false content that had gotten him in trouble
before. "Where did you go to school?" he blurted, "and how is your
nephew?"

She raised her head and gave him an odd look. "Smith, and he's
fine."

"How is *The Mouse in the Manger* doing? Is it selling well? How did
I do as a wise man?"

"*Mouse* is selling very well, thank you, and sometimes I think you
are not very wise at all."

He had broken the spell, but she mended it with a dazzling smile.

"What do you want in a companion?" he asked.

"Someone to talk with," she said, stroking his cheek. "My husband
was too preoccupied to talk. He was too busy making babies with
other women . . ."

"Is that why you ended up in the hospital?"

"Yes. I tried to kill myself."

The pain of her confession pierced his heart.

"My parents were well-meaning, but they were always too involved socially to talk. And so, you see, what I want is very simple really."

"What do you want to talk about?"

"Everything and nothing. What you did today, what I did today, what we'll do tomorrow. About God and how He's working in our lives. About my work, about your work, about life, about love, about what's for dinner and how the roses are doing—do they have black spot or beetles . . ."

He kissed the bridge of her nose, smiling.

"Life is short," she said.

"Yes. Yes, it is."

He kissed her mouth, and it was as if he'd been doing it all his life; it was the most natural thing in the world. He felt he was taking a kind of nourishment that would make him strong and fearless.

She wasn't going back until Sunday afternoon. He would wine her and dine her, he would wrap her Waterford goblet in gold paper, he would fulfill that silly and heedless wish of hers, he would buy a dozen roses from Jena, he would buy a new jacket at the Collar Button sale, he would make her a peanut-butter-and-banana sandwich, he would buy a tango album—or was it the rhumba she liked? He would bathe Barnabas, he would give Violet a can of white albacore tuna in spring water, he would ask Dooley to put on his football uniform for her, he would pray for rain and take her walking in it.

He collapsed in bed. It went without saying, he supposed, that the love business could be exhausting.

CHAPTER FOUR

Banana Sandwiches

"I'll come home at Christmas," she said.

They might have been sitting together in just this way, slouching into the disheveled slipcover of his study sofa, since time began.

"I'll string the lights on your bushes to welcome you home."

"What a lovely thing to even *think!* Oh, Timothy, how could you not have loved someone all these years? Loving absolutely seeps from you, like a spring that bubbles up in a meadow."

"Maybe you can convince me of that, but I doubt it. I find myself niggardly and self-seeking, hard as stone somewhere inside. Look how I've treated you."

"Yes, but you could never deceive me into thinking you were hard as stone. You've always betrayed your tenderness to me, something in your face, your eyes, your voice . . ."

"Then I have no cover with you?"

"Very little."

" 'Violet only wanted a friend,' " he quoted, " 'but every time she tried to have one, she did something that chased them away.' "

She looked at him with a kind of joy. "You've read a Violet book!"

"Yes, and learned something about myself, disproving entirely that Violet books are only for ages five through ten. I really try to express my feelings for you, but I always chase you away. It makes me want to give up."

"Please! I can't bear it when someone says that. Remember what Mr. Churchill told a class that was graduating from his old school?"

"I confess I don't remember."

"When Mr. Churchill was a student, the headmaster had told him how hopelessly dumb and trifling he was, and then, years later, when he was prime minister and had written the history of the English-speaking people, for heaven's sake, they invited him back to address a graduating class. They anticipated one of his brilliant and lengthy speeches, and here's the entire text of what he told them:

" 'Young men,' he said, 'nevah, nevah, nevah give up!' And he sat down."

He laughed.

"Nevah," she said soberly.

"I regard that as wise counsel."

"It has counseled me for years."

"Will you have dinner with me on Friday evening?"

She looked into his eyes and smiled. "I would love to have dinner with you on Friday evening."

"How do you like your peanut-butter-and-banana sandwiches?"

"With the bananas cut in thick slices and smashed into the peanut butter."

"Smooth or crunchy?"

"Crunchy."

"White or dark?"

"White."

"With or without crusts?"

"With!"

With such knowledge now his forever, he felt invincible.

"Yellow or red?" asked Jena Ivey at Mitford Blossoms.

"Red," he said.

"Loose or arranged?"

"Loose."

"In a vase or a box?"

"A box."

He needed an assistant, a curate, a gofer, anybody, somebody. Puny had helped him put the tablecloth on and had polished the glasses until the lead crystal sparkled like gems. She had vacuumed the entire house, then cleaned out the rabbit cage in case Cynthia, who loved rabbits, wanted to hold Jack on her lap. She had washed the dining room windows, refilled the bird feeder outside the windows, changed the threadbare mat at the front door, waxed the entrance hall, and done the grocery shopping.

But that only made a dent in what had to be done. At last, and the thought made his heart hammer, he would have to take Walter's advice and let the Holy Spirit come up with Sunday's sermon, because there would be no time for carefully structured notes.

"What can I wrap this goblet in?" he asked Puny. He realized he had been walking around the house in a daze, carrying it in his hand.

"If you aren't the beat," she said, putting her hands on her hips. "I'm wore out jist watchin' you moon around."

"I am not mooning around. I am looking for wrapping paper."

"In th' buffet, don't you remember? That's where you told me you always keep wrappin' paper."

How could he have forgotten? He felt his face grow red. "Did you get the white albacore tuna?"

"I did."

"In spring water?"

"I don't know what it's in."

"I wanted it in spring water. I specifically wrote that on the list."

"Is that what you were talkin' about? I thought you wanted spring water, so I got two gallons."

Why wasn't this more fun? "The Collar Button is having a sale," he said, trying to sound casual. "I thought I might pick up a jacket. What color do you think?"

"What color does she like?"

He should have known there was no hiding from Puny Bradshaw. "Blue. I think she likes blue."

"Perfect! I'm sick of all that brown in your closet. It looks like a pile of dead leaves in there. Besides, it will bring out the color of your eyes."

"Dark or medium?"

"Dark. Get a blazer."

"Thank you," he said, sincerely relieved.

Now if he could get Barnabas bathed and find a rhumba album—
or was it the tango?—he would nearly be caught up.

"Here," she said, snatching the goblet from his hand, "let me do
that. White tissue paper or red?"

"White," he muttered, feebly.

"Of course!" she said, clearly disgusted.

That he had to drive to the far side of Wesley to find a music store
was no surprise. The surprise came when he discovered they had no
record albums.

"No record albums?" He was stunned.

"Just compact discs," said the sales clerk, eyeing him as if he'd
come from another planet.

No albums! What was the world coming to? Seriously? What did
one do, just throw out a perfectly good record player, which was
probably not even recyclable? What kind of sense did that make?

He didn't really want to know but thought he should ask. "How do
you use a compact disc?"

When he came out of the music store, he went straight to his car
and put the box in the trunk. He must not allow Puny Bradshaw to
lay her eyes on what he had just purchased. Never. He put the music-
store bag containing the rhumba and the tango discs inside the trunk
and closed it.

A little excitement was beginning to build, he admitted, but it had
not yet risen above the apprehension of where this whole thing might
be going and the deep, instinctive fear that he could not, in any case,
stop its progress.

"You are far too handsome in blue," she said.

The extraordinary thing about his neighbor is that he knew she
really meant this foolish remark. He could see it in her eyes.

"Impossible! I've been plain as a fence post as long as I can
remember."

"Well, now that you've started being far too handsome, there's
nothing you can do to reverse it." She smiled. "That's the way it works,
you see."

He was standing at her back door, having popped through the

hedge to fetch her to the rectory. Not knowing what else to say or do, he handed her the can of tuna. "For Violet."

"How lovely! And in oil, just what she likes best. Thank you!"

The stock market might have taken a radical upturn for the relief he felt.

"And thank you for the roses. Do come and see them!"

He smelled them as he came along the hall. They were in a vase in front of the bay window of her living room, illuminated by the last rays of light through the curtains. "Here," she said, removing a long stem from the vase. "This is for you."

She had taken his breath away when she appeared at the door. Her freshness, her inner vitality were dazzling. Everything about her stood out in the sharpest focus, as if he'd just gotten new glasses. "I . . . ," he said, taking the rose from her hand. He was sinking into her, somehow, and didn't know if he could swim.

He had waited until Dooley went to his room last night before attempting to hook the thing up and put on a disc. He was astonished when music came pouring out, nor had he ever heard anything like it; it was so clear, so lucid, so like the living sound. He confessed he would not miss the riot of static produced by ancient scratches or the scraping of a worn needle.

"It's been years since I danced the tango," he said, holding her close.

She laughed. "The rhumba!"

"Ah, well, I've always been a fox-trot man, to tell the truth."

"Fox-trot men usually have a streak of rhumba in them somewhere. It simply takes some doing to pull it out."

"Could you pull a bit harder then?"

When the dance ended, he stood with her in front of the fire, in front of the table so carefully set with his grandmother's old Haviland and the single rose in a vase.

"Look me in the eye," he said, taking her face in both his hands.

"I'm looking."

"I want to ask you a question."

"I love questions!"

He remembered asking her once, "Is there anything you don't

love?" "Yes," she had said, "garden slugs, stale crackers, and people who're never on time."

"Well, then . . . would you kindly consider the possibility . . . that is to say, the inevitability . . . of going steady?"

She burst into tears.

"Cynthia!"

"I always cry when I'm happy," she wailed.

"Well, answer me, then," he said, giving her the handkerchief from his pocket.

"Yes. I'll consider it!"

"Wait a minute. Will I never get this right? I asked you to consider it, but what I really meant was, will you do it? Starting now?"

"Yes. I'll do it."

He was going to kiss her, but his legs began to buckle under him.

"Timothy!" she said, holding him up. "Sit down before you fall down!"

He sank onto the sofa, laughing. "Hopeless," he said, feeling the trembling in his knees and the pounding of his heart. "Utterly hopeless."

She fairly hooted with laughter. "You'll get over it!" she promised, giving him a hug.

They were still in a frenzy of laughter, tears streaming down their cheeks, when Dooley walked in and looked around. "Mush!" he said, backing out the door.

She would be home for Christmas, which was only two months away, spend a week or ten days, and return to New York until March, when she would come home to the little yellow house for good.

Perfect, he thought, making the sandwiches on Saturday night. Couldn't be better! He would have plenty of time to adjust to what he'd just done, get through the inestimable pressures of the holy days, and be waiting for his bulbs to come up as she flew in.

Dooley had had a big football game this afternoon, which he'd attended while Cynthia packed, and was now spending the night with his friend Tommy. In view of that, he turned on the disc player and listened to the tango music again—or was it the rhumba?

Standing at the kitchen counter, shuffling his feet to the music, he caught himself smiling from ear to ear. For more than sixty years, he had been slogging along in wet concrete; now he felt as if he were swimming in a Caribbean pool.

"What is asked of us," Raymond John Baughan had said, "is that we break open our blocked caves and find each other. Nothing less will heal the anguished spirit or release the heart to act in love."

Break open our blocked caves!

What a lot of battering it had taken to break open his own cave, he thought. Among the many other things she deserved, Cynthia Coppersmith deserved a medal.

With that in mind, he made her peanut-butter-and-banana sandwich extra thick and wrapped it with a note.

"I can't help loving you," she read aloud from his note. "May God bless you and keep you and bring you back safely. Yours, Timothy."

They were sitting in the parking lot of the small commuter airport in Holding, eating their late Sunday lunch out of a paper bag and drinking root beer.

She smiled at him, her eyes the color of blue columbine. "Well, you see, we're just alike, then. I can't help loving you, either. Do you think I would have chased you like I've done if I could help it? Certainly not!" She took a bite of her sandwich. "Yum, yum, and a thousand yums."

"Are the bananas mashed in right?"

"Perfect!"

"I wanted this to be your main course last night, but I hadn't the nerve. I also prayed for rain, but that prayer went unanswered."

"You prayed for rain?"

"So I could take you walking in it. The news release at the library said you like to walk in the rain."

She laughed. He loved the sound of any laughter, but hers was a laughter that ignited something in his spirit.

"Oh, Timothy, there are so many lovely things to do, aren't there? I pray that we have hundreds of rains to walk in. I pray that I find out all your secrets and can do magical things for you, as you have done for me."

"One of my deepest secrets is that I like tapioca," he said, grinning.

"Tapioca? Gross! But I shall set my personal loathing aside, and you'll have all you can eat for Christmas dinner."

"Will you write?"

"Of course, I'll write. And when you write me, will it be one of those notes you'd send to a distant relative, or will it be deeply personal and sexy and delicious?"

"I'll see what I can do," he said, holding her hand.

"I hate to go."

"I hate to see you go."

"I loved your sermon."

"Is there anything you don't love?"

"Crow's feet, age spots, and good-byes."

"Kiss me, then," he said.

He stood on the tarmac and watched her little plane until it became a speck in the sky. He prayed for her safety, her peace, her ability to complete her work, and her joy. "Give her joy," he said aloud, turning back to the terminal.

In the car, he wondered if he should try to find Pauline, Dooley's mother. She had lived in Holding for years, but when Dooley had run away to her last Christmas, and the police had searched for her and him, it had been in vain. She couldn't be found, and not a word from her since. It was just as well; surely it was just as well. What could word from his broken, alcoholic mother do but tear Dooley apart all over again, after he had begun to reconstruct himself?

He wanted to help Pauline, but the way to do that, the only way he had available, was to help Dooley. Had he helped him? Perhaps. Certainly, he had grown to love him, to find even his aggravating ways familiar and comforting. Mush, indeed! His heart had clearly made its own mush for Dooley Barlowe.

An invitation from Edith Mallory arrived the following Wednesday. *Come for Thanksgiving dinner at Clear Day,* she wrote. *I hope I'm asking well in advance of any other demands on your schedule, and rest assured we shall have all your favorites.*

What did she know about his favorites? He would have Emma

reply that he and Dooley would attend the annual All-Church Thanksgiving, which the Presbyterians were hosting this year. Her monogrammed stationery reeked of some musky scent that fairly clung to his fingers after he read it. Why couldn't she leave him in peace?

When he laid the note aside, Emma grabbed it and tossed it in the wastebasket. "Whang-do!" she snorted.

At a quarter 'til twelve, Puny rang. "Are you comin' home for lunch?"

"I thought I'd have a bowl of soup with Percy."

"If I was you, I'd come home," she said mysteriously.

The dozen roses in a box took his breath away. Clearly, they were the finest specimens the zealous Jena Ivey could muster.

Cynthia had handwritten the card before she left: *With love from your neighbor, who misses you dreadfully.*

Dooley helped himself to reading the card that evening. "Double mush," he pronounced.

Two consecutive freezes downed the geraniums but enlivened the pansies in every border. Though mid-November had arrived, the curry-colored leaves of the oak refused to fall, providing a rich background for the remaining gold of the maples.

"A Flemish tapestry!" exclaimed Andrew Gregory, stirring a cup of hot apple cider with a cinnamon stick.

Percy Mosely sat on a stool at the Main Street Grill and declared he was glad to be rid of the tourists, so the locals could have a little peace and quiet. "Gawk an' squawk. That's what they do from May 'til th' leaves drop. Feller in here last week squawked to me about th' coffee, said it was s' weak he had t' help it out of the pot. That," he concluded, darkly, "was a Yankee lie."

"Winter!" grumbled J.C. Hogan, having sausage and eggs in the back booth. "I hate the dadgum thought of it."

"What you need," said police chief Rodney Underwood, "is a good woman to keep you warm."

"I doubt he could find one who'd want th' job," said Mule Skinner. "He was such an ugly young 'un his mama had to tie a pork chop around his neck to get the dogs to play with him."

At the first frost, Miss Rose and Uncle Billy Watson were rumored to have set their brand-new thermostat on seventy-five, and let the chips fall where they may.

Grocery man Avis Packard announced his excitement over the quality of collard greens and turnips he was getting from the valley.

Dooley moved Jack's cage from the unheated garage to his room.

The Chamber of Commerce, who had conducted a woolly worm festival on the school lawn, predicted a bitter winter, while Dora Pugh at the hardware designed a window display with snow shovels and had a plan-ahead sale on kerosene lamps and thermal underwear.

The vase of roses at the old rectory managed to last a very long time, as if defying what was to come. Before their petals fell on the polished walnut of the dining table, Puny decided to tie their stems with a string and hang them upside down to dry, figuring that, one day, they'd make a nice memory for somebody.

"Uncle Billy! How are you?"

"No rest f'r th' wicked, and th' righteous don't need none!" he said, cackling. "Jis' thought I'd call up to chew th' fat, and tell you things is goin' good up here at th' mansion."

"I'm always glad to hear that," said the rector, tucking the receiver under his chin and signing the letter he'd just typed.

"I don't know what you think about preacher jokes . . ."

"What have you got? I could use a good laugh."

"Well, sir, this preacher didn't want to tell 'is wife he was speakin' to th' Rotary on th' evils of adultery. She was mighty prim, don't you know, so he told her he was goin' to talk about boating.

"Well sir, a little later, 'is wife run into a Rotarian who said her husband had give a mighty fine speech.

" 'That's amazin',' she said, 'since he only done it twice. Th' first time he th'owed up and th' second time 'is hat blowed off.' "

He laughed uproariously. "That's a good one, Uncle Billy."

"I can tell that th' livelong winter. It'll do me 'til spring. You're th' first to hear it, next to Rose."

"Where'd you find it?"

"I like to get my jokes off strangers, don't you know, so they're fresh to th' town. Come off a feller down at th' dump, passin' through from Arkansas. He th'ow'd out a whole set of Encyclopaedia Britannica, good as new. We got 'em in th' kitchen. It's a sight f'r sore eyes what they do with drawin's of birds an' all."

"Cynthia tells me she's pushing her publisher to do something with those ink drawings of yours."

"Well, sir, that'd be good. I got more than a thousand dollars in m' mattress off that bunch of pencil drawin's we sold at th' art show. I hated t' take it, since some of my beagles looked like coons."

"What in the world will you do with a bankroll like that?"

"Set Rose up for Christmas, for one thing. It's th' most money I ever put my hands on. She thinks I'm rich. You ought t' see th' way she shines up to me since I got a little somethin' put away. A feller can't make that kind of money canin' chairs and buildin' birdhouses."

"That's a fact."

"We're goin' to have us a Christmas tree, don't you know, for th' first time in more'n thirty years. An' I'm goin' to be Santy and give 'er a dress or two an' some shoes I seen in a catalog—what they call sling-back pumps."

"How about a suit for yourself, my friend?" Uncle Billy had turned himself out in his wife's dead brother's clothes for as long as he had known him.

"Well, sir, I don't know about that."

"You're a good fellow, Uncle Billy."

"I don't think so, m'self, but I thank you, Preacher. Th' same to you."

When they hung up, he found he had a new zeal for his letter-writing. Uncle Billy Watson doeth good like a medicine, he thought, paraphrasing the Scriptures.

The door opened, but even before he saw who was coming in from the street, he felt a nameless dread.

"Hello-o-o," said Edith Mallory, closing the door behind her.

She marched straight to Emma's chair and sat down, as if it were her own. "I'm ravished!" she announced.

Not around here, you won't be, he thought.

"I haven't had a bite all day, except for the teensiest piece of toast for breakfast. Since you can't come for Thanksgiving dinner, there's the cutest new restaurant in Wesley, and I just know you'd love it. I've reserved a table for lunch, on the teensiest chance you can come. They have green tablecloths and green walls—I know how passionately you love green—and can you imagine, their dinner menu features elk and bison!" She peered at him with dauntless expectancy.

He did not love green, and anyone who would stalk and slaughter an elk or bison was a raving lunatic.

"Well? What do you think?" She opened her handbag and removed a compact. Looking into it intently, she twisted her mouth in a manner he found gruesome, then slathered it with a vivid orange lipstick. "Ummm," she said, poking out her tongue and licking her lips. When she crossed her legs, he saw for the first time that her skirt was ridiculously short.

He rose from his chair so suddenly that the silver bud vase on the windowsill above him went flying across the room and skidded to the door.

"Blast!" he said. "I was just leaving. Dooley is feverish, a wound to the knee. Football, you know."

He was stunned at the lie that came rolling out like so many coins from a slot machine. He fled to the peg and grabbed his jacket and was putting it on when she got up and came toward him. In one smooth, swift, gliding motion, she threw her arms around him and pressed her body against his.

"Timothy . . . ," she said, breathing onto his cheek.

He moved away from her, trying to wrench her arms from his neck. "Edith . . ."

"Timothy, I know how you feel about me, how you've always felt. I can see it . . ."

He flung the door open and ran into the street without looking behind him, without observing the careful, lifelong practice of locking up church property, without taking his briefacse, without considering that he might have handled the whole thing far better by meeting her head-on and coming, once and for all, to manly terms with an ungodly circumstance.

He struck the pillow on the study sofa with such force that a welt gaped open, releasing a pouf of white feathers.

The vestry. They could help him. Or should he call Stuart? What could the vestry do, after all? What did you do to provoke it, someone might ask, and well they might. The answer was simple: Nothing! He had done nothing, never, not the slightest thing. He had been kind to her over the years, he had gritted his teeth and been kind, that was all, nothing more than he had been to anyone else in the parish, including her beleaguered dead husband.

Had he passed Ed Coffey when he hurried out of the office and down the sidewalk? Had Ed sat watching him from behind the wheel of the Lincoln, as he fled like a hare before a hound? It was humiliating to think that Ed might even now be shaking his head with pity over the priest who could not hold his own with his employer. Would Ed have to watch him skulk about eternally, fleeing from church offices, trapped in rainstorms, until either he or Edith gave up and gave in?

Certainly, he would never give in.

But he felt a chilling dread that Edith Mallory would not give in, either. There was something indomitable about her; she had had her way with Pat Mallory for more than three decades. She was not used to giving in.

He was not pleased that he felt oddly fearful, like a child in a tale of a wicked stepmother. And why did it suddenly occur to him that her direct approaches were preliminary to something more subtle, something he might not be able to recognize and avoid?

Percy looked at him meaningfully. "That feller you got doin' up your nursin' home . . . ?"

"What about him?"

"He ain't my chew of tobacco."

"Is that right?"

"Started comin' in here two mornin's ago orderin' me around like some ninnyhammer, I like to shoved 'is head in 'is grits."

"Aha."

"Too bad you missed th' last two mornin's, he comes th' same time as your crowd, sits by hisself in th' front booth. Do this, do that, run here, run there. Makes Parrish Guthrie look like a church saint."

"They say he's the best in the business."

"I'll show 'im some business," said Percy.

After he left the Grill, he stopped in front of Happy Endings bookstore. He was looking over new titles in the window when Fancy Skinner got out of her car at the curb. He saw that Fancy had dyed a streak in her blond hair to match her 1982 pink Cadillac, and was wearing an angora sweater of the same hue.

"How you doin'?" she called, waving to him.

"Terrific. How's your new shop?"

"Couldn't be better. My Mister Coffee busted this mornin' and I'm goin' in th' Grill for a coffee to go. By th' way, that bozo of yours up at your nursin' home. . . ."

"Ah, which one is that?"

"Buck Leeper. Came in for a haircut, ordered me around like a slave. When he told me to give 'im his change, I told 'im to bend over. You oughtn't to let him run loose."

"Well." What else could he say?

"You ought let me take a little off your sides. That's kind of a chipmunk look you got there."

"Right."

So now Buck Leeper was *his* bozo, doing up *his* nursing home, and *he* was the one responsible for letting him run loose.

Dearest Cynthia,

Sometimes, if only for a moment, I forget you're away, and am startled to find your bedroom lamp isn't burning, and all the windows are dark. I must always remind myself that you're coming home soon.

I hope your work is going well and that you're able to do it with a light heart. I've never been to New York, and I'm convinced that my opinion of it is a foolish and rustic one. Surely much humor and warmth exist there, and I'll restrain myself from reminding you to hold on to your purse, be careful where you walk, and pray before you get into a taxicab.

I've mulched your perennial beds, and done some pruning in the hedge. I think we'll both find it easier to pop through.

To the news at hand:

On Saturday, Miss Pattie packed a train case with Snickers bars and a jar of Pond's cold cream and ran away from home. She got as far as the town monument before Rodney found her and brought her home in a police car. It appears that riding in a police car was the greatest event of her recent life, and Rodney has promised to come and take her again. Good fellow, Rodney.

I have at last heard Dooley sing in the school chorus, and must tell you he is absolutely splendid. Cold chills ran down my right leg, which is the surest way I have of knowing when something is dead right. Our youth choir, by the way, will have a stunning program ready for your return at Christmas.

Barnabas pulled the leash from my hand yesterday afternoon, and raced into your yard. He sniffed about eternally, before going up your steps and lying down on the stoop. I can only surmise that he misses you greatly, as does yours truly,

Timothy . . .

The Sunday of the Village Advent Walk was bright with sun, yet bitterly cold. He was glad to put on the camel topcoat Puny had brushed and hung on the closet door. He had let it hang there for more than two weeks, eagerly waiting for the weather to turn cold. Winters had become so mild, he had scarcely had it on his back in recent years. Let the hard winter come! he thought, whistling the morning anthem.

At four o'clock, the villagers poured into Lord's Chapel, teeth chattering, to stand expectantly in the pews as the choir processed along the aisle. "O Zion, that bringest good tidings, get thee up to the heights and sing!" Rays of afternoon light poured through the stained glass windows, drenching the sanctuary with splashes of color. It was enough, he thought, if no word were spoken or hymn sung.

After the service, he and Dooley followed the singing procession to the Methodist chapel, where the children's choir met them on the steps. "Hark, the Herald Angels Sing," they warbled, sending puffs of warm breath into the freezing air. People filled the nave and were standing in the churchyard as the ancient story of Christmas was read from Luke, and candles were lighted in every window.

Afterward, they trooped down the alleyway and across Main Street, singing to the tops of their voices in wildly random keys. They were led, at this point, by J.C. Hogan, who was walking backwards at a heedless trot while snapping pictures of the oncoming throng.

The Presbyterians joined them on the corner of Main Street and Lilac Road with ten pieces of brass, and led the frozen, exhilarated regiment across the street to First Baptist, where the the lower grades sang "O Little Town of Bethlehem," accompanied by their preacher on the guitar. They also saw a re-enactment of the manger scene, for which the preacher's wife had made all the costumes.

Then, everyone clattered to the fellowship hall, where the brass band was rattling the cupboards with "Joy to the World!" The women of the church had set out an awesome array of sandwiches, cookies, cake, homemade candy, hot chocolate, and steaming apple cider.

"I think we're about to get our second wind," said the rector to his Presbyterian colleague.

"One more denomination in this town and some of us couldn't make it around. We've just clocked a mile and a quarter."

"I don't think there is another denomination, is there?" asked Miss Pruitt, the Sunday School supervisor.

"Well, let's see. There's the Lutherans!"

Edith Mallory made her way through the crowd, carrying a sloshing cup of cider. There was a certain look in her eye, as if he might be a nail and she a hammer, determined to pound him squarely on the head.

"Lovely service at Lord's Chapel," she said, coolly.

"Yes, I thought so, and how did you like the walk?"

"Walk? I never walk on the Advent Walk, I always ride."

"I see."

He turned away so hastily that he knocked the cider out of Mayor Cunningham's hand, and took refuge in helping someone clean it up. When he got to his feet again in the milling crowd, Edith had disappeared.

Keeping his head down, he found Dooley and left for home, to steam himself like a clam in the shower, and reread the letter that waited by his bed.

Dearest Timothy,

No, scratch that. My dearest neighbor,
I have been riding in taxicabs the livelong day, and have taken your advice. I pray while hailing, as it were, and God has been very gracious to send affable, entertaining, and kindly drivers. One even chased me down the sidewalk to return a scarf I left on the seat. Can you imagine? I look upon this as a true miracle.

O! the shops are brimming with beauteous treasures. I would so

*love to have you here! I would hold on to your arm for dear life as we
looked in the windows and stopped for a warm tea in some lovely hotel with leather banquettes and stuffy waiters. You would overtip to
impress me, and I would give you great hugs of gratitude for your
coming.*

*My work is awfully labored just now. Sometimes it has the most
wondrous life of its own, it fairly pulls me along—rather like wind
surfing! At other times, it drags and mopes, so that I despair of ever
writing another word or drawing another picture. I've found that
if one keeps pushing along during the mopes, out will flash the most
exhilarating thought or idea—a way of doing something that I
had never seen before—and then, one is off again, and hold on to
your hat!*

*I am doing the oddest things these days. I brought home a sack of
groceries from the deli the other evening and, while thinking of our
kisses at the airport, put the carton of ice cream on my bed, and my
hat in the freezer.*

*Worse yet, I'm talking to myself on the street, and that won't do at
all! Actually, I'm talking to you, but no one would believe that.
"Timothy," I said just the other day when looking in the window at
Tiffany's, "I do wish you'd unbutton your caution a bit, and get on
an airplane this minute!" How did I know a woman was standing
next to me? She looked at me coldly before stomping away. I think it
was the part about unbuttoning your caution that did it.*

*I am thrilled to hear of Dooley's singing, and especially that it
ran a fine chill up your leg. As for myself, I know something is right
when the top of my head tingles. In any case, I am proud with you,
and can barely wait to hear him in chorus when I come home on
the 23rd.*

*A box has been sent to all of you, including my good friend,
Barnabas, with a delicious tidbit for Jack, as well. If I were to send
you everything that reminds me of you, you should straightaway receive a navy cashmere topcoat, a dove-colored Borsolino hat, a peppered ham and a brace of smoked pheasants, a library table with a
hidden drawer, a looking glass with an ivory handle, a 17th-century
oil of the 12-year-old Jesus teaching in the temple, a Persian hall
runner, a lighted world globe, and a blue bathrobe with your initials
on the pocket. There!*

Oh, and I haven't forgotten Puny. The truffles are for her, and do keep your mitts off them. They are capable of creating any number of diabetic comas.

Would you please have Mr. Hogan send my Muse *subscription to this address? I suppose I could call him up again, but each time I've tried, there's no answer at his newspaper office. I can't imagine how his news tips come in; he must get them all at the Main Street Grill.*

I will close and go searching for my slippers, which have been missing since yesterday morning. Perhaps I should look in the freezer.

With fondest love to you, and warm hellos to Dooley, Barnabas and Jack . . .

He didn't know how he felt about the Borsolino hat, and he already had a topcoat, but the peppered ham sounded terrific.

Humming "Hark, the Herald Angels Sing," he went downstairs, the folded letter crackling in his robe pocket. After supper with Dooley, he would sit in the study and read it again.

It was only the end of November, and a bit early, in his opinion, for stringing lights.

Mitford, however, had no such qualms—winking lights were strung from one end of Main Street to the other; fresh, beribboned greenery was hung on the light poles; and the merchants had stuffed their windows with everything from a Santa Claus with a moving head to a box of free puppies wearing red collars and mistletoe.

A Christmas tree lot was set up on the edge of Little Mitford Creek, across from Winnie Ivey's cottage, and fairly bristled with Fraser firs from the next county. In fact, everywhere he looked, he saw a tree lashed to the top of a car or truck, and an expectant driver headed home to an evening's festivity.

Carols poured from the music system at Happy Endings, enlivening that end of the street, and the town monument was respectfully draped with garlands of boxwood and holly.

Avis Packard filled the wooden bins in front of The Local with green boughs and mountain apples and ran a special on cider in the jug.

Sitting in the rear booth one morning at breakfast, he watched Percy Mosely lift the door of the hatch behind the grill and carry a box of fruitcakes down the stairs. They would be his holiday dessert special, served with Cool Whip and a cherry. Percy hand-lettered the counter sign, himself: You'll Be Nuts About Our Fruitcake.

The Lord's Chapel service of Lessons and Carols was coming straight ahead, and then, all the services and celebrations would be unleashed full force.

Suddenly, there was the quandry of what to give Cynthia, and what he might give Dooley, and yes, this year, he wanted to take gifts to Fernbank. The thought of it all made his head feel light and oddly empty, so that he had to go searching for sensible thoughts, as one might seek after pillowcases blown from a clothesline by high winds.

Several times, he found himself pacing the study in a circle, like a train on a track. The train! It would need to be brought down from the attic, which was a job for Dooley Barlowe. Delegate! That's what he needed to do. And why agonize over what people might want or like? Why not just ask them? He had never done such a thing, but he'd read an article recently that suggested this strategy was loaded with success.

"A jam box," said Dooley.

"A what?"

"A jam box—to listen to music."

What kind of music, he wanted to ask, but didn't—and how loud?

When he talked to Cynthia that evening, she said, "A neckrub! I've bent over these illustrations for such long hours that my neck is positively stiff as a board. A neckrub would be the loveliest gift imaginable."

A neckrub. He had never given such a thing in his life. How far did one have to unbutton one's caution to give a neckrub?

He heard the strain in her voice. "I'm working very hard to get finished, and with my editor in Europe, I feel all at sixes and sevens when it comes to knowing whether it's really working. There's such comfort in having someone say, Yes, that's lovely, or good heavens, Cynthia, what could you be thinking?

"But that's enough about me. What do you want for Christmas, Timothy?"

"I can't say that I haven't thought about it. I want you and Dooley and Barnabas, and a fire in the study, and a splendid dinner, and peace. The peace of having you home again, of seeing the boy finding his own peace, and feeling your contentment in having a rough task behind you. That, and nothing more."

"How dear you are to me."

"Am I? I wish I could imagine why."

"Perhaps if you could imagine why, it would spoil everything."

That, he admitted, was a thought.

"Isn't there any family left for you, except Walter and Katherine? Are we both so nearly alone in the world?"

"My mother had three sisters, but only one had children."

"Then you have other cousins!" She seemed hopeful for him.

"One of Aunt Lily's kids vanished after a divorce, another died in a train accident. At forty-five, Aunt Martha married a man thirty years her senior, and Aunt Peg was what we used to call a spinster. Immediately after college, she had her linens monogrammed with her own initials, declaring she would never marry."

Cynthia laughed. "What became of her?"

"She grew prize asters and headed up the local D.A.R."

"My!" said Cynthia, not knowing what else to say.

"So there you have it. No kin to speak of, except for that rowdy bunch in Ireland, of course. As I recall, Walter and I were related in some way to almost everyone at the tea party."

"I love the Irish!"

"The Irish would love you," he said.

A neckrub and a jam box made a wildly intriguing start to his gift list, he thought as he dialed Miss Sadie.

"What do I want? Oh, dear, I suppose I should spend more time thinking of my wants instead of my needs. I'd be more interesting, wouldn't I, Father?"

"It would be impossible for you to be more interesting."

"Oh, pshaw! Well, let's see." There was a pause. "I haven't the faintest idea! Let me ask Louella. Louella, what do I want for Christmas?"

"New stockin's, new rouge, and a new slip," came Louella's quick response from the background.

Miss Sadie put her hand over the receiver, but he heard the muffled conversation.

"I can't ask my priest for stockings and a slip!"

"Well, then, ask 'im for rouge, you lookin' white as a sheet."

"Louella says ask for rouge, Father. Not too red and not too pink. Oh, dear, this is embarrassing, maybe just some candy from the drugstore, we like nougats."

He sat back on the sofa, laughing. It had never happened in just this way before, but he was definitely getting the Christmas spirit.

He called Dora Pugh at the hardware and asked her to order a sack of special rabbit food; then he called Avis at The Local, and ordered five pounds of Belgian chocolates—four for the nurses at the hospital, and one for Louella. He asked Avis to put together enough food items to fill a dozen baskets, and to reserve his choice beef bones, starting now.

He had no intention of asking Walter what he might like. No, indeed. Walter would want a cashmere sweater, a blazer from Brooks Brothers, or a Montblanc pen. He might very well ask for a lighted world globe on an antique stand, or a leatherbound atlas, or both.

He ordered a desk calendar for Walter's law office, and a leather frame for Katherine, to hold the photo of the three of them in front of the family castle. They had given a pound note to a passing Irish lad, who used Walter's Nikon with the most amazing results. In the color print, in which they had all appeared to be years younger, one could see the crumbling remains of the castle in the background. Even now, he suspected with wry affection, this priceless photograph was swimming about in one of Katherine's jumbled drawers, getting dog-eared.

He went to the bank and retrieved five crisp one-hundred-dollar bills, and stopped by the drugstore for a compact of rouge,

There. He was nearly done, he thought. He whistled all the way to the Grill.

Grinning, Emma stood in front of his desk, and rattled a bag from Wesley's department store.

"It's your Christmas present," she said. "Guess what it is!" She rattled it some more.

Every year, as much as six weeks before Christmas, she couldn't stand it any longer and gave him his gift. Worse still, she never had gifts of her own to open on Christmas Day, as she always tore into a present the minute she received it.

"I can't guess," he said, dolefully. "A tie?"

"Wrong."

"Shaving lotion!"

"You're not trying."

"A solar calculator."

"Ha! Wrong again." She opened the bag and dumped something on his desk. Her presentation skills had never been noteworthy. "A restaurant guide to New York City!"

He looked at it without speaking.

"I know you've never been there before, so when you go visit your neighbor, you'll know how to do." She was as pleased as if she'd given him a Rolex watch.

"Who says I'm going to New York?"

"You mean you're not?"

"I most certainly am not."

"Not even for a *weekend?*"

"You said it."

"You mean you're going to let her stay in that godforsaken place all by herself, with no relief from home? Have you seen the kind of men they have in the publishing business up there? Handsome! Intelligent! *Tall!*"

She used this last jab for all it was worth.

"And what, may I ask, do you know about the publishing business?"

"I do watch TV, you know, which is more than I can say for some people."

"Aha. So men in the publishing business are often on TV?"

"All the time! Very good-looking and smart as whips."

"From what I've seen in the bookstores lately, they're on TV because they have nothing better to occupy their time. As for myself, Emma, I am presently occupied with five holiday services, a music festival, a youth choir concert, a baptism, a party at the hospital, a discussion topic for the men's prayer breakfast, and an overnight visit from the bishop. Thank you for your gift, and please—I beg you— take the morning off."

He had stumbled around in her basement under a 25-watt bulb, plowing through marked boxes. Though some attempt had been made to stack them in alphabetical order, Christmas Lights were nonetheless on top of Mud Room Odds and Ends.

If there was ever a task that wanted teamwork, it was stringing tree lights. When he got the box upstairs to her living room, he saw that she had put them away like so much cooked vermicelli.

It was a full three hours before the bushes on either side of her front stoop were glowing warmly. Life in the little house, at last! He stood back and blew on his frozen hands. Not a car had been up the street; there was not a soul to see the handiwork that cheered the whole neighborhood and proclaimed something wonderful. If it weren't so late, he'd drag Dooley over to look.

He went inside to her living room, switched off the lights on the bushes, and locked the front door. The house was hollow as a gourd without her, yet everywhere he looked, she had made it her own; it couldn't have belonged to anyone but Cynthia. He moved to the mantle and peered at a picture he hadn't seen before. She must have been sixteen or seventeen, and looked out at him with a poignancy that gripped his heart. Her blond hair was long and free, and her eyes full of hope.

"Cynthia," he said aloud, touching the frame.

There were other pictures on the mantle, one of her nephew, most likely, and one of her parents, her mother wearing a flamboyant shawl with fringe, holding on to the arm of a man who looked like Douglas Fairbanks, Jr., in a double-breasted suit. He saw that they were looking away from each other, and the small girl standing beside them seemed forlorn.

He turned the lights off in the living room and walked down the hall to her studio. It was bare of her drawing board and chair and many of her books, yet a light fragrance of wisteria greeted him.

"Cynthia!" he said, feeling a lump in his throat.

Why shouldn't he go to New York for a day or two, after all? It was not inconceivable. He had been far too hard on Emma, in the tone of his voice, chiding her for a foolish idea. But was it foolish?

He might take Cynthia to dinner at some legendary restaurant like Sardi's or the Stork Club. Was the Stork Club still in existence? If not, they could go to the Plaza, which he knew for a fact was still there; he had read about it in a magazine. Perhaps snow would fall, and they would ride in a carriage in Central Park, bundled under a lap robe. Perhaps they would look in the windows at Tiffany's, and perhaps, who knows, they would go inside and he would buy her something wonderful, something that would make the top of her head tingle.

He didn't want to think of the "men in publishing" who might, in actual fact, be seeking her company for dinner or a play or a concert. But why shouldn't she have the company of suave, dynamic movers and shakers, rather than languish in a strange apartment every evening, struggling to earn her very bread?

He stood by the phone in her studio and inhaled the scent that had become as much a part of her as breathing. He removed a card from his billfold, dialed the number written on the back of it, and charged the call to the rectory.

A man answered. It was such a shock to hear the deep, baritone voice, that he nearly hung up.

"I'd . . . like to speak with Cynthia Coppersmith, please."

"Cynthia? Oh, Cynthia's dressing just now, may I have her ring you tomorrow?"

Tomorrow? The word struck him with an odd force.

"Thank you, no," he said, slowly. "She needn't ring me."

CHAPTER FIVE

The Blizzard

He watched a sheep trot briskly toward the nave, trailed by two spotted cows, a donkey, and a camel. He noticed that the camel's hump had slipped and was bumping along the floor, but it was too late to do anything about it.

The wise men were already processing down the aisle to the altar, where the angel Gabriel and a heavenly host stood precariously on stepladders, gazing at the manger scene.

In the quarter-hour it would take for the children to deliver the pageant, he would just pop back to the parish hall for a drink of water and collect his sermon notes.

How extraordinary, he thought, entering the darkened room. It appears there's an angel in my chair.

Four-year-old Amy Larkin was curled up on the cushion of his favorite armchair, the pale organza wings trembling with her sobs.

"Amy," he said, going down on his knees. "What is it?"

She looked at him with streaming eyes and nose. "Them big angels hurted me! They pushed me and runned in front of me and wouldn't let me in my place! I was in the hall and they runned in front of me and . . . and . . ."

"And?"

"I gotted lost!" she wailed.

He lifted her from the chair and consoled her. He was struck by the happiness that flooded him at merely holding a child.

At the end of the pageant, he walked down the aisle at the rear of the procession, carrying Amy in his arms. As the acolytes settled into their places, he turned to the congregation.

"This small angel got separated from the heavenly host. Margaret Ann? . . ." He searched the pews for her mother.

Amy tightened an arm around his neck and announced in a loud voice, "I was with them big angels, and they runned in front of me and left me and I gotted lost!"

"It occurs to me," he said, "that many of us may be leaving small angels behind. As mature Christians, are we neglecting to help those who would benefit from our love and witness?"

He set Amy down as her mother came quickly along the aisle from a rear pew.

"Just a thought," he said, smiling at his flock.

He couldn't help but notice that Olivia was wearing one of her great-grandmother's hats this morning. On her, it was not merely an antique curiosity but lent a definite mystery to her violet eyes and striking beauty.

He saw from the pulpit that Olivia was holding Miss Sadie's hand, while Hoppy took Olivia's and Miss Sadie held tight to Louella's. A fine kettle of fish, he thought.

Though the facts of their kinship would almost certainly remain a family secret, Miss Sadie had told him her plans. "When Olivia gets married, I want to open the ballroom and give them a grand reception! It will be the first time it's been open in more than twenty years, and it will surely be the last. Do pray, Father, for it will demand a great deal of energy from these old bones. I wish I'd known about my great-niece before I got so decrepit. I could have done so much more!"

After the coffee hour, he was rinsing his cup at the sink when Edith carried in a tray of coffee cups. Though several people still mingled in the parish hall, they were alone in the kitchen.

She talked to him as she put the cups in the dishwasher, but she did not look at him. Her voice was cold and quiet. "Timothy, I know you are a man of passion. I've always seen this in you."

She spoke as if she might be reading aloud from a legal document. A fine chill raced through him.

"You know that I want you, Timothy, and I have every reason to believe you want me. I'm expecting you to get over this silly little game of cat and mouse and show me how you really feel."

"Edith . . ."

"You are behaving as if Pat were still alive. Pat is not alive. He is quite dead."

As he stood there, loathing the way the skin stretched over her face, he felt a sudden, warming sense of power, the conviction that he could face and handle anything. There was even a peculiar sense of being taller.

"Edith, there's something you need to know." He heard the ice in his own voice.

"Whatever it is," she said, continuing to load the dishwasher, "don't bore me with your priestly airs. I can't abide any more of your priestly airs."

"Oh, Father!" Ron Malcolm came into the kitchen, putting on his topcoat. "Before I leave, I need to talk to you about a little problem on the hill. Could we step up the hall a minute?"

He could have hugged his pink-cheeked building chairman on the spot. There was, however, a drawback to this providential escape, which he realized as he walked up the hall.

Standing at the sink, he had felt a surge of complete control; he had total confidence that, once and for all, he could tell Edith Mallory what was on his mind and in no uncertain terms.

He chose to believe he had not missed the moment.

The contents of Cynthia's gift box vanished rapidly. Puny shared the truffles with Joe Joe, Barnabas wolfed down the contents of the deli package inscribed with his name, and Dooley disappeared up the stairs with more than a fair share of cookies, candy, nuts, and chips.

His own portion was put in the cupboard, except for the elaborately boxed cookies that he stashed in his nightstand. Though they were utterly sugarless, he found them addictively delicious. He began to look forward to having one with a cup of tea before bed, while dreading the time they would all be eaten.

Don't think of it that way, he told himself. Think of it this way:

When the box is empty, she'll be home.

Stuart Cullen would arrive on Thursday for an overnight at the rectory on his way to a meeting down the mountain.

"Th' pope's comin'," he heard Puny announce to her sister on the phone.

"Stuart's not a pope," he told her, "he's a bishop. It's the Catholics that have a pope."

"My grandpa said he never met a Catholic that knew pea turkey about th' Bible . . ."

"Well, then," he said, heading off a diatribe, "let's do something with the guest room. It's been awhile since we had a guest."

"Never had one, period, since I been here. Needs airin' out, turnin' th' mattress, needs flowers—where'll they come from in th' dead of winter? Holly! We could use holly and save you th' florist bill."

"You're a good one! Let's do it. And let's put a copy of the *Muse* by the bed. Stuart likes a good laugh."

Puny would spend Thursday baking bread and a cake, and he would roast a tenderloin and do the potatoes. When he went by the Local, Avis gave him a bottle of Bordeaux, on the house.

"Seein' as it's th' pope," he said.

Dearest Timothy,

We've had snow flurries all morning and everyone on the street below is bundled in furs and hats and mufflers, looking like a scene from It's a Wonderful Life.

But, oh, it is not a wonderful life to be in this vast city alone!

Sometimes I think I'd like to fling it all away and go somewhere warm and tropical and wear a sarong! I would like to live in my body for awhile instead of in my head!

I've been working far too hard and find it impossible to turn off my thoughts at night. I lie here for hours thinking of you and Mitford and Main Street and the peace of my dear house—and then, the little army of creatures in the new book starts marching in, single file.

I review the tail of the donkey I did this morning, the snout of the pig I'm doing tomorrow, the heavy-lidded eyes of the chicken, wondering—should a chicken look this sexy??!

This can go on for hours, until I've exhausted all the creatures and go back and start at the beginning with the tail of the donkey that I'm afraid looks too much like the tail of a collie. That's when I get up and go to my reference books and find I'm wrong—it looks exactly like the tail of a jersey cow!

This is the price I pay for calling a halt to the Violet books. Yet, I should jump out the window if I had to do another Violet book! She, by the way, lies curled beside me as I write, dreaming of a harrowing escape from the great, black dog who lives next door in her hometown.

I'm thrilled at the thought of coming home and spending my second Christmas in Mitford. It is the truest home I've ever known.

I've looked and looked for a letter from you, and if I don't have one soon, I shall ring you up at the Grill and tell you I'm absolutely mad for you, which will make you blush like crazy while all your cronies look on with amusement.

There! That should compel you to write. I'm sure I'll hear by return mail!

With love, Cynthia

He hadn't wanted not to write, but where was the chance to sit down and begin? It was the busiest time of the year for clergy, not to mention the rest of the human horde. Besides, what was he going to do about the question that kept forcing itself in his mind—namely, Who was the man who answered your phone?

If a man answers, hang up! He never dreamed he would be the butt of such a classic, almost vaudevillian joke. The man had spoken her name with a certain familiarity. "Cynthia," he had said, "is getting dressed."

Getting dressed?

He hated this. It made his stomach churn. Number one, he clearly did not know how to have a romantic relationship; he had no idea what the rules were. And number two, he especially did not relish playing games, second-guessing someone, and generally suffering a gut-wrenching anxiety over what he would absolutely not allow to become jealousy.

He supposed the thing to do was write her at once and just say it:

Dear Cynthia,

Who was the man who answered the phone when I called you on Sunday evening?

Maybe that was the way to handle it. He hadn't the time, however, to figure it out. He would simply dash off a note that made no reference to the incident and forget the whole thing. If Cynthia Coppersmith were nothing else, she was guileless. She was not the sort to say one thing and do another; that was only one of the reasons he loved her.

But, then—did he really love her? Had he merely been swept along by the force of her own impulsive feelings?

Blast!

He slung the notebook against the study wall at the moment Dooley walked in.

"Hey," said Dooley, looking at the notebook.

His face burned. "Hey, yourself."

"When're we gittin' a Christmas tree?"

"Right now," he said. "Put on your jacket, and bring your gloves. I'll get the axe."

The snow began on Thursday afternoon.

He and Dooley had trimmed the tree the night before and he had gone home for lunch, simply to look at it again. Yes! The magic had invaded the rectory. He could smell it as he walked in the door, the permeating fragrance of fir and forest and freedom, which refused to be lost among the smells of baking bread. He felt fairly lifted off the floor.

Barnabas dashed from the rug in front of the study sofa and gave him a resounding wallop on the chest with his paws, followed by a proper licking. What more could he have asked of his life? A job to do, a warm home filled with intoxicating smells, a dog of his own, a growing boy, and all of it covered by the astonishing facts of the nativity.

"Come and see the guest room!" Puny called from the top of the stairs.

The room that was so often shut away and cold, with closed heating vents and a frozen toilet seat, was now warm and inviting. Puny had found extra pillows in the closet and covered them with starched shams. She had stolen a braided rug from the foot of his own bed and a rocking chair from the garage. Bottled water sat on the nightstand with a copy of the *Muse*, a worn copy of *Country Life* magazine, and a chocolate truffle from her own gift box from Cynthia.

She had placed a branch of holly atop the picture frame over the bed.

"You don't reckon it could fall on 'im in the night, do you?" She was clearly concerned.

"It'll be fine."

"Don't be mad about me takin' your rug. He's a bishop, you know, and you're just . . ."

"A lowly preacher."

"No offense."

"None taken!"

He reached in his pocket and handed her an envelope. "Merry Christmas! While I'm but a lowly preacher, you, on the other hand, are an angel. And that's a fact."

Her chin quivered as she opened the envelope and removed the hundred-dollar bill. "I jis' knew it!" she wailed, throwing her arms around his neck. "You'll never know how I needed this. My sister got laid off, and her least one is sick and needs shots, and this is jis' th' best thing in th' world!"

"Well, then, quit crying, if you don't mind."

"I cain't he'p it!" she insisted, wiping her eyes with her sleeve. He handed her his handkerchief.

"I jis' ironed that thing. I'll use toilet paper!" she said, fleeing to the bathroom.

The snow, which had begun as a light sprinkle of small flakes, was falling harder as he headed back to the office. "I'd stay home if I was you," Puny advised. "You know they're callin' for a bad storm."

One of his great failings was paying too little attention to the daily news. And since he had once again missed breakfast at the Grill, it was no wonder he knew nothing of immediate importance.

"I'm leavin' early in case th' roads get slick," she said, handing him his hat and gloves. "Be sure'n take that hall rug out of th' dryer. It's th' last thing I'm washin'."

"Consider it done."

"I'd stay in," she said again.

He opened the door and squinted at the sky. "It probably won't amount to much."

"I'd change my shoes, if I was you."

"Ah, well, Puny, you're not me and be glad of it. Otherwise you wouldn't be marrying Joe Joe come June."

He was surprised to see that everything was already well-covered, including the bushes at Cynthia's front door. Putting his hat on, he set off briskly.

Lay the train tracks after Stuart leaves tomorrow morning. Deliver the baskets. Get enough ribbon to wrap the jam box and tie a bow. Take the car to Lew Boyd. Carry the chocolates to the hospital. Remember to thaw two pounds of Russell's livermush to include in his basket.

Should he decorate Cynthia's mantel, put some greenery on her banisters, a wreath on her door? Surely, it would be no fun coming home to a house barren of Christmas greenery.

Passing Evie Adams's house, he saw Miss Pattie at the window, waving; a mere glance told him that Miss Pattie was excited about Christmas. He grinned, waving back. She would be even more excited if she knew her basket included a dozen Snickers bars.

The snow churned icily into his face as he walked. Beautiful though it was, it was not soft and friendly like some mountain snows; it was the sort one endured until it spent itself.

As he turned the corner toward the office, he saw that Mitford was fast becoming one of those miniature villages in a glass globe, which, when shaken and set on its base, literally teemed with falling flakes.

The mail had come late today. He had seen Harold Newland on Main Street, bowed under the weight of his mailbag and bundled above the ears against the cold.

"I won' send you a Christmas card," Emma had said by way of warning. "I've decided to quit sending Christmas cards, period. It's less for Harold to fool with."

"A noble gesture."

"Every little bit helps," she said, pleased.

He was thrilled to find the cream-colored envelope near the bottom of the pile of greeting cards.

Dear Timothy,

Thank you for the note that might have been written to a great-aunt who once invited you to a tea of toast and kippers.

Yours sincerely,
Cynthia

When he tromped home at three o'clock, barely able to see the green awnings of Main Street, he shucked off his coat and hat and sodden loafers and went at once to the phone, his feet frozen, and dialed her number. Busy.

Stuart Cullen appeared at his door with a hat brim full of snow and a black topcoat frosted across the shoulders like so much Christmas *stöllen.*

"Rough going," he said, stomping snow onto the hall rug and removing his gloves and muffler. "I thought I wasn't going to make it. Windshield started icing up. Cars off the road. Miserable! What smells so good? I'm starved! No time for lunch and running late for dinner! I could eat a table leg."

"Chippendale or federal?"

"A little of both, if it's no trouble."

He had never seen his old friend eat so hungrily, even as a penniless seminarian. "It's great to be at your table, Timothy. Some priests I visit can barely boil water."

They were having dinner in front of the fire, careful to watch the TV screen for a weather report.

"I've got to make it down the mountain in the morning, no fail. I'm praying this thing won't last."

"So far, no good," said the rector, nodding toward the window. The outside lights illuminated the steadily falling snow. "But—the town crew is good about keeping the roads clear, and the county will be working the mountain tonight. I think you can relax."

"Relax! That may as well be a word from a foreign language. What does it mean, anyway?"

"I don't suppose you'd like the lecture you gave me several months ago about kicking back, taking it easy, slowing down, letting up?"

"I most certainly would not. I was very tough on you, but it worked. In fact, you look the best I've seen you look in years." Stuart took a sip of the Bordeaux. "By the way, you'll never guess who I saw only a week ago."

"Bill Mutton!"

"No, thanks be to God. Peggy Cramer. I must say she's still very beautiful, but . . ." Stuart stroked his chin and looked vague.

But what? Cancer? Some crippling disease? "But what, for Pete's sake?"

"But boring."

"It could be worse."

"Perhaps. In any case, if you'd seen her, I think you'd be able to thank me for the advice I gave you years ago."

"But I do thank you, you know that. It was completely right. I've never once regretted my decision."

"I must say, Martha never bores me—in fact, it's quite the reverse. She studied my schedule and booked us into a villa in Aruba for a week. Aruba! What an astonishing choice. England, I would have thought, or France—but Aruba? I don't even know where it is. She says I need sun and a place where people aren't so serious about themselves. She says I must stop being a bishop for an entire week."

"Tough call."

"Perhaps the chartreuse swim trunks she bought me will help."

Laughing, they raised their glasses.

"To you, Stuart, your good health."

"And you, Timothy, your long life."

It was all in the past; it seemed as if he had never been in love with the petulant creature who had nearly caused the loss of his senses. Yet, he was tempted to ask more about Peggy Cramer. Was she married? Any children? But no, he wouldn't ask.

"She's married to a brain surgeon. Two kids, five grandchildren. She showed me their pictures. Anything else you'd like to know?" Stuart grinned.

Stuart had always had that odd sixth sense.

"You should know that she asked about you. When I told her you never married, she had that oh-poor-baby look on her face, so I preached her a sermon about your dedication, your devotion, your popularity with your parish, ad infinitum. Thank God, it was all true. She was impressed."

The bishop leaned down to scratch Barnabas behind the ears. "So, what's up? Where's the boy?"

"Reading a veterinary journal in his room. He'll be down to greet you in a bit. Doing pretty well, all things considered. Singing. Playing football. A fine and interesting lad. I believe in him."

"What else?"

"Not much. Terribly pushed right now, but who isn't?"

"Are you going to force me to pry?"

"Into what?"

"Into the women in your life."

"If you must know . . . do you remember Edith Mallory?"

"Yes. She gave a dinner party when Martha and I were here a few years ago. Married to a fellow in plaid pants, as I recall."

"Now dead."

"And something tells me she's after you."

"It's as if you're crossing the street, minding your own business, when suddenly you look up and there's an eighteen-wheeler about to nail you."

"It's serious, then."

"And frightening, somehow. She doesn't take no for an answer. What would you do?"

"Nail her first. Tell her hands off."

"She doesn't hear that. She has the deranged notion I'm lusting for her."

"Classic. You should know that. Clergy attract them like flies."

"That's the prognosis, but what's the cure? Frankly, she calls out something violent in me. I think I understand how a woman feels when a man won't back off."

"You'll have to confront her. I've had to do it in my time and not very long ago, either. Sometimes the problem disappears, like so much summer fog. You say she's a new widow. Maybe time will take care of it."

"I don't think so."

"Well, I trust your instincts. Do it soon, and get it behind you. I can tell it's eating at you."

"A bit, yes. Feels good to talk about it. You know how that is . . ."

"Absolutely."

They looked into the fire. A consoling thing, a fire. But clearly, the wind was getting up. The snow churned and swirled against the windows.

"Wonderful sight," said Stuart, turning his attention to the snow.

"I wish I could relax and enjoy it. But I cannot miss that meeting—it could be worth a million to the diocese. Literally."

"We'll get you out of here. You've got a good vehicle. How about a glass of port? Not as old as your host, but getting on in years, nonetheless."

"Splendid! And then to bed."

He delighted to see Stuart Cullen sitting in front of his fire, scratching his dog's head, drinking his port.

"I'm waiting," the bishop said, his eyes gleaming with mischief.

"For what?"

"Blast it, Timothy, a fellow has to beg on bended knee to get a word out of you."

"But I've talked your arm off, as they say."

"You sly rube. Cynthia! Remember her? Tell me everything, and for heaven's sake, don't tell me there's nothing to tell."

"Well. Where to begin?"

"You're going steady?"

"Yes. I asked her, and she said yes."

"And? So?"

Stuart was leagues ahead of Walter and Katherine when it came to sheer nosiness. But what were bishops and friends for? Why was he holding back at this perfect opportunity to spill it all and perhaps get some decent advice? "So, when I called her apartment in New York, a man answered."

He saw that Stuart nearly burst into laughter but controlled himself. "What did he say?"

"He said, 'Cynthia is getting dressed.' " He felt his face burn and the churning in his stomach. Galling. "He said, 'I'll have her ring you tomorrow.' "

"Did you say who was calling?"

"No."

Stuart drummed the table with his fingers, a habit he had always despised. "Ask her about it," he said at last, stopping the drumming.

"I considered that."

"How long have you considered it?"

"Several days."

"Too long! Call and ask her about it right now, why don't you? Then you can put it out of your mind. We can't be accumulating baggage, you and I, especially this time of year."

"Well, then . . ."

"I'll wait right here. I haven't sat in front of a fire, alone, in a hundred years."

When he went upstairs, he looked into Dooley's room and saw that he'd fallen asleep over his veterinary journal.

The phone rang three times before she answered. "Hello?"

His heart hammered. "Cynthia?"

"Timothy?"

"How are you?" That wouldn't do. She didn't care for casual conversation. She'd want something more direct, more specific, like "I miss you dreadfully." "I miss you dreadfully!" he said, meaning it.

"You do?"

He had no intention of saying what followed, not now, anyway. But out it rolled, like so much change from a vending machine: "Who was the man who answered your phone when I called Sunday before last?"

There was a long silence. It might have been the silence of a tomb. Then the phone went dead. Zero.

He jiggled the buttons on the phone cradle. "Cynthia? Cynthia!" She hadn't hung up; he was sure of it. It was definitely the phone. The wind howled and screeched around the corner of his bedroom. That was the culprit! How many times had he lost his phone service in these mountains, from weather of every known kind?

He slouched into the study, stricken.

"She gave you back your frat pin?"

"I asked her the question, and the phone went dead. The wind probably blew a line down somewhere."

"I prayed for you both as you went up the stairs."

"It's hard, being in love."

"No question. Then again, it's hard not being in love. You know how I feel about that, about finding Martha and what it's meant to me. It's meant everything, literally."

"I envy you. It seemed so easy for the two of you. For me—I don't know, I don't seem to . . . understand the process. From here, it looks like other people do it naturally, with ease and grace, while I fall in a ditch every two or three paces. So, in the end, it all seems a great bother. Too much aggravation."

"I have the sense that you haven't really given yourself up."

"Given myself up?"

"You're holding on to something, guarding yourself—just in case. I call to mind what George Herbert said—you know, the English cleric—'Love bade me welcome, yet my soul drew back.' Am I right?"

He thought about it. This was no time for self-delusion. "You may be right. I haven't . . . surrendered anything."

"So, there's a sense in which you're playing with her feelings?"

"Perhaps."

"I can tell you that a woman will find that out, and she will not like it."

"After the man answered, I felt . . . foolish, somehow. I had pitied her up there alone, never going out in the evenings, without friends. It took days to find the heart to write her. It was only a note, the best I could summon. Here was her answer."

He recited the indignant missive about the kippers and toast.

Stuart roared. "I like this woman! I like her better every time you talk about her. She doesn't beat around the bush, and she doesn't let you get away with anything. My friend, a woman like that is one in a thousand, one in a million. You'd better hunker down and be willing to give yourself, Timothy, or you could lose her."

"I think about the thing with Peggy . . . that was a stunning blow, all of it."

"Right, it was. But it was also more than thirty years ago. Why are you still sporting the bruise from that encounter? Good Lord, man, we've all been knocked around. Wasn't Susan Hathaway my Peggy Cramer?"

"Possibly."

"No possibly about it. I could have taken a dive along with you. Right into the pool, with no water. I can still break a sweat just think-ing about it. But I don't hold it against myself, and the Lord has thrown the whole matter as far as the east is from the west."

"Bottom line, Stuart . . ."

"Bottom line? . . ."

"Marriage. That's what it all comes to. At my age, it's all or nothing at all. There's no in-between."

"Quite. But look here, in-between is precisely where you seem to have stationed yourself. Going steady, but no real commitment. Lov-ing, but afraid of the future."

Barnabas yawned and rolled over on his side before the fire.

"Don't kid yourself," Stuart said. "It's not easy for other people, either. Martha and I had our own struggles. I was forty-nine, she was forty-seven, and neither of us had ever been married. But we knew, Timothy. I knew I wanted the shelter of this woman, and God only knows what she wanted in me, but apparently she's found it.

"What do you want, in the long run? To end up tottering around on a walker, muttering to yourself, having missed the bliss and the hell of love?"

"The bliss and the hell. I'm afraid of both those things. I never thought of that before. I've never admitted such a thing in all my life." He felt astonished to discover something so new, and raw, in himself.

"Good! We're getting somewhere. This woman wants a fun-loving, unpredictable relationship, and who does she pick? A serious-minded, rather predictable fellow who, just underneath the zipper, is every-thing she's looking for."

"But is it all worth . . . unzipping for, if you'll pardon the expression?"

Stuart smiled. "I've found it to be so," he said.

At six o'clock in the morning, the Bronco was fairly buried. Though the streets had been cleared, the plow had knocked an even greater pile of snow onto the vehicle.

The phones were working again. He called Rodney at the police station.

"Any passage down the mountain?"

"If you're goin', better hop to it. Th' roads are pretty clear, but more snow's comin'. They're closin' th' mountain at eight o'clock. I just got a call."

He and Dooley worked with the bishop under the light of a street lamp for a full hour, shoveling the car out. Bundled to the eyes, Stuart got in the Bronco. "Pray for me!" he called before closing the door. Then he turned his car around in the frozen street and disappeared in a cloud of vapor from the exhaust.

White on white, as far as the eye could see. But a million bucks was a million bucks.

They stomped back into the house as a gray dawn broke.

Around noon, the snow started falling again.

Barnabas bounded to the hedge, making a path wide enough for a small sleigh, did his business, and returned at once. White on black, racing through the house, shaking snow from backdoor to front. "Good fellow!"

"Good ol' pooper," said Dooley.

Lord, he prayed, don't let us lose power. There was enough wood in the garage to last two days, maybe less, and no one would be hauling logs in weather like this.

He set the Christmas baskets on the counter, finished filling them, and tied the bows, then looked for the fur-lined boots that laced to his knees. He mustn't sit around mooning, as Puny called it. He needed to move along smartly. No argument could convince Dooley to accompany him.

"Listen, buster," he snapped, "you want Santa Claus, you'll help me take it to others." He was inevitably cross in foul weather. It worked, however. They each carried two baskets, leaving the fifth behind until the weather cleared. There would be no walking along the creekbank to visit Homeless Hobbes today, nor would his Buick get farther than the sidewalk, if he bothered to back it out of the garage.

At Evie Adams's house, he warned Dooley. "We mustn't get Miss Pattie started or we'll be here all day."

Dooley looked daggers at him as Evie opened the door.

"Oh, Father!" she said, bursting into tears. "I'm so glad to see you! And Dooley! How you're growing! Come in, come in. Oh, do come in!" He felt rather like the pope.

There was only one thing to make of her tears. "What's Miss Pattie done now?" he asked. They were standing in a puddle.

"Crawled under the bed and won't come out!"

That ought to be a godsend, he thought.

"Under there, singing to beat the band, and won't come out unless I buy her a baby doll with long, blond hair and a blue pinafore. Where am I going to get a baby doll in weather like this—much less in a blue pinafore?"

"Would you like me to talk to her?"

If looks could kill, Dooley Barlowe would have dropped him right there, dead as a doornail.

At the sagging Porter mansion, he had a word of caution. "Don't eat anything here."

"I'm about t' starve t' death," Dooley said, glaring at the rector.

"You'll live. After all, you're full of baloney."

"Real funny."

"I thought so."

Uncle Billy opened the door. "I'll be et f'r a tater if it ain't th' preacher! Rose, come an' look! It's th' preacher an' th' boy!"

He heard some rustling sounds, and Miss Rose appeared, looking fierce. "The preacher? What's he want?"

"Wants t' give us Santy Claus, looks like."

"Tell him to come in, then."

They dripped a large puddle in the foyer, where a hand-carved banister railing lay on the floor exactly where it had fallen years ago. He looked up at the portrait of the handsome, intense Willard, who was almost certainly turning over in his grave.

Dooley handed them a basket stuffed with fruit, nuts, candy, a tinned ham, and a pecan pie. "Merry Christmas!" he said.

"Looky here, Rose," said the old man, obviously elated. "Ain't this th' beat? Well, come on back to th' warm place. We'll all be froze t' popsicles standin' here. Rose baked a cobbler that'll melt in y'r mouth. You'll have t' set an' have a piece."

"Oh, no, no, Uncle Billy. Can't stay, have to run. They're calling for eight inches tonight and high winds. Have to get along."

"I'm sure this boy would like a piece," said Miss Rose, looking fiercer. "Preachers don't eat like the rest of us. All they like is fried chicken."

"I b'lieve it's th' Methodists as like chicken," said Uncle Billy.

Miss Rose grabbed Dooley by the sleeve. "Come along! Let these men stand an' jaw 'til th' cows come home. We'll have us a bite to eat. I like boys!" She grinned, revealing a frightening display of dental conditions.

Dooley looked back in desperation as she hauled him through the tunnel of newspapers that packed the dining room toward the heated apartment at the rear.

Ah, well, no rest for the wicked and the righteous don't need any, the rector thought, following meekly.

They stomped up the hill to Fernbank, against an increasingly bitter wind, and down the winding driveway that was thigh-deep in snow.

Miss Sadie gave Dooley a set of shoelaces, wrapped in aluminum foil and tied with a ribbon, as they stood in another puddle in another foyer.

"Father, I'm so upset. I ordered you the nicest can of mixed nuts, but if this weather keeps up, UPS will never get through."

"Don't even think about it," he said.

"Louella, why couldn't we just give him a check for the value of the nuts?"

"You askin' th' elf, Miss Sadie. You th' Santy!"

"You wait right here," she said, leaving the room and returning with a check. In her spidery handwriting, she had made out a check for five dollars and thirty-two cents. "Merry Christmas!" she said brightly. "Just in case the nuts don't get through! I didn't include shipping and handling, but I did add state tax."

He literally dragged himself to the door of Betty Craig's snow-bound blue house. It was exhausting to walk through heavy drifts, up-hill and down, hither and yon, and keep a smiling face while crawling under beds and eating cobbler you didn't want.

He had never been so glad to see the rectory, which looked like a cottage on a Christmas card, set as it was into a deep bank of snow with a drift of wind-tossed smoke rising from the chimney.

"I'm give out," Dooley announced at supper, over a fried bologna sandwich. "You can git yourself somebody else next year. That's church stuff. You need to git you some church people t' carry that stuff around."

"My friend, you are church people."

"I wouldn't be if you didn't make me."

"I make you?"

"I reckon you think I'd go if you didn't make me."

"Well, then, I'll quit making you. Why don't you just stop going?"

"I might."

"Nobody should have to go to church against their will." Sometimes he had to, but that was beside the point.

At a quarter to seven, Dooley came into the study. "I'm outta here," he said vaguely, putting on his down jacket.

"Out of here to where, may I ask?"

"Church. Choir practice."

"You don't have to go, you know."

"Yeah. Well, bye."

"Bye, yourself."

He went at once to the phone and dialed her number. He was too tired to speak, but it had to be done. No answer.

Nobody but Dooley and Jena Ivey had shown up at the Youth Choir rehearsal.

At eight, Martha Cullen called, distraught. Stuart had not arrived at the meeting, nor had he called home.

"I bought him a car phone, but he said it was too elitist, and it's still in the box. Timothy, I'm beside myself. He always calls."

"He's fine, I'm sure of it. Chances are he's stranded on the side of the mountain. Perhaps there's been an accident. It can back cars up for miles."

"I've protected him so, that I sometimes think of him as a child. I confess this to you, Timothy. I'm not proud of it, but I sometimes treat him like a mindless boy, God forgive me."

"Whatever you're doing, it must be right. You should be a fly on the wall and hear him sing your praises. Don't worry. Please! Call me when you hear."

He got a call from the adult-choir director, who was stranded at the foot of the mountain. Would he contact everyone and cancel the rehearsal?

The head of the Altar Guild phoned to say that forty-four memorial poinsettias had been left by the florist on the church stoop and had frozen solid.

The winds increased. Walter rang.

"We hear you're under three feet of snow, for Pete's sake."

"Nearly. It's losing power that concerns me—there're so many old people in this community . . ."

"Including yourself, of course."

"Ha. There goes your cashmere jacket for Christmas."

"Have you gone through any of the family papers yet?"

"What do you think?"

"You've been too busy, you haven't gotten to it, you apologize for the long delay, but you'll get right on it after the first of the year."

"I couldn't have put it better myself."

"We're off to a party. Keep in touch. Stay warm. Best to Dooley."

"Did the package arrive?"

"Under the tree."

"Great. I love you, you big lout."

"Same here, Cousin. Katherine sends her love. Let's have another trip together in the new year. By the way . . ."

He could hear it coming. To avoid an interrogation about his love life, he put his hand over the phone and yelled, "Be right there!"

"Have to go, Walter. So long. Merry Christmas! God bless you!"

The wind roared around the house, moving the curtains and rattling pictures on the wall.

The evening news reported that major airports across the state were closed, the interstate highways were closing, and the word for the storm was officially "blizzard."

"One of nature's most life-threatening storms is the winter blizzard," said a newscaster, standing hatless in the TV station parking lot, looking bewildered.

The houses of Mitford were frozen like so many ice cubes in a tray. Lights shone from windows onto the drifting snow, as leaden skies made even the daylight seem one long dusk. Everywhere, spirals of chimney smoke were violently snatched by the wind and blown through the streets, so that the stinging drafts of arctic air contained a reassuring myrrh of wood smoke.

The high winds did not cease. In some places, snowdrifts covered doors and windows so completely that people had to be dug out by more fortunate neighbors. Cars that had been abandoned on the street appeared to be the humps of a vast white caterpillar, inching up the hill toward Fernbank.

Percy Mosely lived too far from town to make it to the Grill and open up, but Mule Skinner, who lived only a block away, managed to open the doors at seven on Tuesday morning, brew the coffee extra-strong, and fry every piece of bacon on hand. J.C. Hogan, who was waiting out the storm in his upstairs newspaper office, came down at once. The weary town crew, unable to start the frozen diesel engines of their snowplows, were the only other customers.

Unlike most snows, this one did not bring the children to Baxter Park. The sleds stayed in garages, the biscuit pans shut away in cupboards. This was a different snow, an ominous snow.

Martha called. Stuart was safely ensconced in a motel outside Holding, after being stuck on the mountain behind a brutal wreck for five hours and stranded in a drift on the side of the road for three.

He learned that long-distance calls could not be received because of overloaded circuits, and there was still no answer at Cynthia's apartment.

The winds howled and moaned without letup. He could see the drapes move in the living room but couldn't see across the street for the brilliance of the whirling snow.

He checked the kitchen drawer for candles and matches, the flashlight for batteries, and the lantern for kerosene. He refused to look at the woodpile.

In just two days, she would be home. Surely, the weather would change, she would get through, and she would rush toward him from the little commuter plane, laughing, her eyes blue as cornflowers.

The very last thing to think about was who had answered when he called.

At four o'clock, he discovered the telephone lines were again dead.

Two hours later, he put the kettle on to boil. At the moment he turned the stove dial, the lights went out. It was as if he, himself, had pulled a switch that brought the whole thing down into darkness.

CHAPTER SIX

Water Like a Stone

On Sunday, the alarm rang at five o'clock.

He lay there, frozen as a mullet, listening to the ceaseless roar of the wind. There would be no heat in the church, nor any sensible way for the congregation to get there. He had never before missed a Sunday service because of weather.

In his mind, he counted the logs in the garage. He thought he could count six or seven and not a stick more.

"I'm freezin' m' tail," said Dooley, who appeared in sweatpants and a ski jacket and crawled under the covers. Barnabas yawned and pushed in between them.

"I ain't goin' t' no church," said Dooley. His teeth were chattering.

"Me either."

"What're we goin' t' do?"

If there was anything he didn't like about having a boy in the house, it was feeling he should have all the answers. "Blast if I know," he said, huddling against Barnabas. "What do you think we should do?"

"You could get up an' fry some bacon and baloney."

"How? By rubbing two sticks together?"

"Poop, I done forgot." He soon heard Dooley's whiffling snore.

Hello, Cynthia? Timothy. How's the weather up there? His mind turned once again to what he might say, if only he could reach her.

"Don't start that nonsense," he said aloud. Think, instead, of how Miss Sadie and Louella and Uncle Billy and Miss Rose will be faring on this miserable and wretched morning, and pray, for God's sake, for their welfare.

He crossed himself and prayed silently. Assist us mercifully, O Lord, that among the changes and chances of this violent storm, your people may ever be defended by your gracious and ready help . . . Hello, Cynthia? Timothy. We were cut off the other day, and when I tried to reach you again, there was no answer. Then the lines went down for three days, and so, how are you? . . . O Lord, create in me a clean heart, and renew a right spirit . . . Hello, Cynthia, Timothy. How are you?

There was only one way to knock such idiocy in the head. He got out of bed and fell to his knees on a floor that felt like an ice rink.

The fire was fairly crackling, and he closed his mind to the fact that its cheer would be short-lived.

"This is neat."

"Bologna to die for," he said, picking two thick, browned slices out of the skillet with a fork and putting them on Dooley's toast. "Eat up, my friend, and don't hold back on the mustard." As for himself, he hadn't tasted such bacon since he was a Scout. He looked at their camp mess spread around the hearth. Not a bad way to live, after all.

The wind had cast torrents of snow against the study windows, where it froze solid, shutting out the light. They might have been swaddled in a cocoon, filled with an eerie glow.

He took a swallow of the coffee that he'd brewed over the fire in a saucepan. "Whose name did you draw at school? I've been meaning to ask."

"I drawed ol' Buster's name, but I didn't git 'im nothin'."

"Why not?"

"I traded for somebody else's name."

"Really?"

"Yeah. Jenny's."

"Aha."

"Had t' give ol' Peehead Wilson a dollar and a half to swap."

"Not a bad deal, considering."

"I got 'er a book."

"A book! Terrific. Best gift out there, if you ask me."

"About horses."

"She likes horses?"

"She hates horses."

"I see."

"So I got 'er this book so she can git t' know 'em and like 'em."

"Good thinking, pal."

They drew closer to the brightness of the fire.

"You like ol' Cynthia?"

"Yes. Very much."

"You love 'er?"

"I . . . don't know. I think so."

"How come you don't know?"

He really did dislike feeling that he had to have all the answers. "I don't know why I don't know! Do you love Jenny?"

Dooley looked forlorn. "I don't know."

"One thing's for sure," said the rector, "this is the dumbest conversation I've heard since the vestry made its new ruling on toilet paper."

In some places, the drifts were twenty feet high, and everywhere ice gleamed upon the snow like glaze on a sheet cake.

It was impossible to walk in this glittering ice kingdom, nor was there any standing up on the slick crust that lay over the ground.

Twice, he put on multiple layers of clothing and his warmest boots, determined to check on Miss Rose and Uncle Billy and fight his way up the hill to Fernbank, but the ice turned him back before he was scarcely clear of the garage. Attempting to leave by the front door, he made it down the porch steps but slipped and careened down the bank, slamming into the telephone pole at the sidewalk.

They stuffed towels along the sills of the aged windows and at the base of every door. They kept the faucets open, to delay, at least, the freezing of the pipes. In the garage, they found a ladder-back chair intended for the rummage sale and a set of decrepit pine folding tables.

"We'll use the chair tonight and save the tables for tomorrow," he said, unconsciously looking around his own study for firewood.

He was finding that Dooley Barlowe could go the mile. He might be a complainer when life was soft, but he knew how to be tough when the chips were down.

"You're OK, buddy."

"When's ol' Cynthia comin' home?"

"Day after tomorrow."

"I bet she ain't."

And what gift would he give her if she did come home? As was often the case, he'd left a crucial decision until the last minute, hoping the solution would fall out of the sky.

He thought of his mother as they dozed on the sofa under piles of blankets and the radiant heat of one large dog. She had loved Christmas like a child.

When he went home from seminary, most of the room he slept in would be filled with boxes, wrapping paper, and endless yards of her signature white satin ribbon.

The armoire would be stuffed with gifts she'd been making and buying all year, and the house would smell the way she loved it best— of cinnamon and cloves, oranges and onions, coffee with chickory, and baking bread.

She would expect him to bring his friends and make the house merry, and when they begged her to sit down at the table and stop serving, she would always say, "But it's my joy!"—and really mean it.

Peggy Cramer had been with them for his mother's last Christmas, and Tommy Noles and his fiancée, and Stuart Cullen had called long-distance. He remembered the call because Stuart had spent nearly an hour talking to his mother and making her laugh as she sat by the wall phone in the kitchen.

He automatically loved anyone who made his mother laugh.

He had given her the brooch that year, a lovely thing, costing far more than he could afford, but when he saw it in the jeweler's window, he knew this was the gift that must try to convey his gratitude for the years of encouragement, for the fact that she had believed in him from the beginning, no matter what his father said to the contrary.

One small amethyst brooch with pearls had been required to speak volumes. Above all, he wanted it to say, Thanks for your support when you, more than anyone, wanted me to become a Baptist minister and I did the unthinkable and became an Episcopal priest.

That had been the coldest of affronts to her family and even to her own heart. But she loved him and stood with him, as stalwart as an armed regiment.

"Mother," he had said, "there's no way I can tell you . . ."

"You needn't try," she told him. "I can see it all in your eyes."

He looked at Dooley, asleep under the mountain of covers. It was almost this time last year that he had run away, racing down the mountain in a freezing wind on his Christmas bicycle, desperate to see the face of his own mother.

He prayed for Pauline Barlowe and the children scattered like so many kittens from a box.

"In the bleak midwinter, frosty wind made moan . . ."

He heard the faintest singing somewhere and sat up and listened. Barnabas growled.

"Earth stood hard as iron, water like a stone . . .

"Snow had fallen, snow on snow, snow on snow . . .

"In the bleak midwinter, long ago . . ."

Someone was singing his nearly favorite Christmas hymn, but who? And where was it coming from?

Barnabas bounded off the sofa, barking. "Angels in the garage!" he shouted, slipped his feet into frozen shoes.

A soprano and a baritone from the choir had pulled a sled to his house, wearing hobnail boots that bit into the ice. Lashed to the sled was a load of seasoned oak, and while it was no half-cord, it would give them respite.

They might as well have parked a Mercedes in the garage and presented him with the key. Gleeful, he and Dooley picked a log and split it into kindling.

Next, they chose a second log, as fuel for their supper.

Then they broke the chair into pieces, agreeing to save the folding tables for a Christmas Day blaze.

Things were definitely looking up, though there was no news from the outside world to prove it. The last report, the baritone said, was of helicopters dropping food into the coves and a forecast of freezing rain for tomorrow and the next day.

There was enough oak left to heat the study tomorrow, giving them a chance to write and read, instead of sitting in a frozen stupor, watching their breath vaporize on the air. He could not remember when his heart had felt so full of ease. A load of wood had been delivered and, with it, the spirit of Christmas.

"You know this one," he said to Dooley, who was laying kindling over the crumpled newspaper. "Sing with me! 'What can I give him, poor as I am? If I were a shepherd, I would bring a lamb . . . if I were a wise man, I would do my part . . .' " Hesitantly, Dooley joined in. " 'Yet what can I give him . . . give my heart.' "

He held out hope until the morning she was to arrive. It had rained the day before, and now, at dawn, he heard the relentless freezing rain still rapping sharply against the windows. Flights would be canceled, airports shut down.

He prayed they would be able to go forward with the hanging of the greens and with the afternoon and midnight services on Christmas Eve. After the death of winter had lain upon them like a pall, they needed the breathing life of the Child; they were starving for it.

He continued to pray for Miss Rose and Uncle Billy, Miss Sadie and Louella, and for all who were elderly, sick, or without food or heat. He was bold to ask that angels be sent, and step on it.

He was going to the kitchen door to let Barnabas out when he did an odd thing. Without thinking, and out of sheer habit, he turned on the dial of the burner under the kettle.

The television blared in the study. The light came on in the hall. The kitchen radio announced a Toyota sale.

He shouted, "Hallelujah!" Dooley hollered, "Hot dog!" Barnabas barked wildly. And the washing machine went into a spin cycle in the garage.

He would never bet on it happening again, but he felt he had somehow managed to shut down, and then restore, power to an entire county.

When the phone rang, he jumped as if shot at.

"Father! I just had to talk to somebody . . ."

"Margaret Ann . . . what is it?"

"The most awful thing has happened. I hid all of Amy's Santa Claus at Lisbeth's house, and I was going to pick it up on Christmas Eve. Well, Father, you know that awful hole my sister lives in down by the town cemetery, and now she's frozen in like . . . like . . ."

"A stick in a popsicle."

"Yes! And there's no way I can get my car out of the yard, Father, much less make it to Lisbeth's. What can I do? It's the prettiest little doll you ever saw, it wets like crazy, it cost somethin' awful, and no check from her daddy since Easter. Oh, and there's a little pink wagon with lights on it, and a nurse set, and a blue dress, and socks with lace. Oh, Father!" She was crying. "Amy is *counting* on Santa Claus!"

"I'll see what I can do. Give me a half hour."

Ron Malcolm's son was out, helping the town crew spread salt and slag. Lew Boyd's Esso was closed tight as a clam. The young man who once raked his leaves could not be found.

He called the baritone. "Is there any way I could borrow your hobnail boots for a couple of hours? Terrific. Just leave them inside your porch door." He called the soprano. "What size are your hobnails? Perfect. We won't come in, just set them on the stoop."

"Dooley," he shouted over a TV ball game, "can you come here a minute?"

"I ain't doin' this n' more," said Dooley, whose face was red as a lobster. He stomped along, carrying a doll and a wagon in a sack on his back. The rector's sack contained a dress, socks, and nurse's set, plus the doll carriage Margaret Ann had forgotten to mention.

"You fall and bust your butt," said Dooley, "and you cain't preach. I bust mine, I cain't play football."

"Good thinking." He had to stomp hard on the crust of ice with each step in order to keep from falling. He would pay for this by morning in every aching muscle. "We've only got three more blocks to go. Just keep in mind those steaks sizzling in the skillet . . . those oven-roasted potatoes with all the sour cream you can eat . . . and that triple-chocolate cake, sent by some well-meaning parishioner before the storm, which is currently hidden in the freezer. You can devour the whole thing!"

Dooley grunted.

The Main Street Grill was dead as a doornail, which was a sorry sight to behold.

"Yo, Santy Claus!" called one of the town crew, who was sliding along Main Street, trying to dump salt.

"Bring me a dolly!" hollered another. "Blond hair, blue eyes—and a red pickup with a CD player!"

"Merry Christmas, Father! Merry Christmas, Dooley!" The crew boss grinned and waved. "A package of fifties will suit me just fine, thanks."

"We'll get right on it, boys. Clean your chimneys."

All the reports were in.

Miss Sadie's bedroom had stayed warm as toast with a kerosene stove. Louella slept on the sofa at the foot of Miss Sadie's bed, and they had lived off Nabs, Cheerwine, white bread, Vienna sausages, and cereal. Keeping the gallon of milk cold had been easy—Louella merely raised the window and set it outside on the roof. For recreation, they had looked through Miss Sadie's picture albums and scrapbooks, read the Bible aloud, and sung Christmas carols, seeing who could remember the most words.

"The only thing missing was a hot bath!" said Miss Sadie, "but we're making up for it."

Miss Rose and Uncle Billy had spent a good deal of time in bed. "Th' only trouble, don't you know, is Rose sometimes pees in th' bed, it bein' too cold t' git up an' all. I wouldn't want you to tell that, Preacher."

"Absolutely not."

"We had a big fight about a box of crackers. Rose wanted th' whole thing. Boys howdy, that was a predicament. But I'd saved back a can of sardines, don't you know, and pretty soon we got t' talkin' about it and turned out we split what we each had right down th' middle, so I cain't complain. You don't want t' git low on food with Rose around, no sir."

"I hear you."

"Boys, that basket you delivered over here saved th' day. There it was, a-blowin' like jack outside, and us settin' in bed eatin' honey-baked ham and soppin' th' sauce with yeast rolls. But I'm glad it's over."

"Amen. Stay warm, and don't go out. It's still slick as hog grease on the streets."

"An' bring th' boy back, anytime. Rose likes 'im, wants t' bake 'im a pan of cinnamon stickies."

Since Homeless Hobbes had no phone, he couldn't inquire. But then, he supposed he didn't need to. The richest man in town was probably faring better than anybody, with a wood stove that kept the place like the inside of a toaster and cooking skills that could turn a creekbed rock and a cup of snow into a banquet.

And how had Evie Adams pushed along with Miss Pattie, and Betty Craig with Russell Jacks?

According to Evie, the snow had done wonders for her mother, who bundled up in a rummage-sale ski suit and sat by the window for days counting snowflakes. "One hundred thousand and forty-three!" she announced proudly, showing Evie the totals in her dead husband's sales ledger. "It was like a vacation," said Evie. "I kept a fire going and got to read a detective story all the way through!"

The report on Russell Jacks was not so good. Just when he was considering whether Russell should return in the spring to his house in the junkyard, the sexton had gone out in the snow against Betty Craig's wishes and fallen down while fetching in wood.

"He must have laid out there close to twenty minutes before I missed him!" said his distressed nurse. "I could just kill the old so-and-so!"

He felt immeasurably relieved. Keeping Russell at Betty's was costing Ron Malcolm and himself four hundred dollars a month, but every time he thought of the old man going back to that ramshackle house on the edge of town, he knew Dooley would have to go with him. That would not be good, for more reasons than he cared to consider.

He prayed for Russell's recovery and Betty's sanity.

"The storm of the century," as the media called it, had traveled along the East Coast to New York, where snow accumulation was up to five feet and still piling on. All circuits, he discovered again, were busy.

"Merry Christmas, Timothy!"

Could it be? It was Edith Mallory, sounding different somehow. "I'm sending Ed down with a little something for you and the boy tonight after the five o'clock. Two services on Christmas Eve can be exhausting, and you surely won't want to cook."

"Oh, no, please, we . . ."

"Do let me have this little Christmas joy," she said pleasantly. "I'll be sending baskets around to others down your way, as well."

"It's too good of you, Edith. Why don't you let someone else have ours, someone . . ."

"Less fortunate? Well, perhaps next year! Actually, I'd like to talk with you about the less fortunate. I think I'm ready, Timothy, to do what you recommended!"

"And what's that?"

"I want to help the Children's Hospital in Wesley. I know it's your pride and joy. But we'll talk about it soon. Since the storm, I've been just deluded with calls, people wishing me happy holidays . . ."

"Yes, and let me be one of them. Happy holidays, Edith!"

He felt queasy when he hung up. Was she undergoing some odd conversion? Did he sense she may be willing to back off and leave him in peace?

He had never minded a few empty pews if the people were filled with the Spirit. The faithful remnant that attended on the eve of the Christ child's birth celebrated with joy.

The great joy commingled freely with the smaller joys. A warming trend is predicted! The sun will come back! The roof didn't leak, the pipes didn't burst, we made it through!

He had seldom seen such hugging and kissing, and over it all, the green wreaths adorned with white gypsophila and the candles flickering on the windowsills lent rapt hosannas of their own.

"Joy to the world, the Lord is come . . ."

He prayed that the earth might truly receive her King.

Ed Coffey passed them on their way home from the five o'clock and insisted they get in. With the tire chains lashing the street, Ed drove to the rectory, then walked them to the door, carrying the basket.

As he and Dooley unpacked it on the kitchen counter, he felt compelled to say something positive. Here was a woman, after all, who had sent food still warm from the oven to feed two hungry men on a cold night.

"Mrs. Mallory is . . . very thoughtful to do this," he said, unwrapping a steaming plum pudding.

Dooley looked at him as if he'd lost his mind. "She's a dern witch."

"Is that so?"

"I hate 'er ol' butt."

"Please rephrase that," he said, meaning it.

"I don't like 'er. She seems two-faced t' me, sayin' one thing, doin' another."

"Really?" Roast beef, done to perfection.

"Said she'd give th' Sunday school a barbecue—ain't done it. Said she'd send us t' Grandfather Mountain—ain't done it."

"Hasn't done it."

"Somebody said she was after you. Said she'd like t' git you in th' bed."

"Who said that?"

"I don't know. Somebody. Is 'at right?"

"Let's just say that I have no intention of going to bed—or anywhere else—with Mrs. Mallory."

"Gittin' ahold of her'd be like gittin' ahold of a spider."

"Please. Forget what you heard. And no matter what you think, be respectful when you see her, regardless. Understand?"

He must have understood, for he said something the rector rarely heard: "Yes, sir."

"If this is what it's like to go steady," he muttered, "no wonder I waited so long to do it."

He dialed her number again. The circuits were still busy, as the storm raged through New York state and headed out to the Atlantic.

People thronged to the midnight service, as if the manager were the last way station on earth. Though patches of ice still gleamed lethally throughout the village, Ron Malcolm's son had doused the church walks with salt and sand, giving many the first sure footing they'd had in days.

Deprived of their pre-Christmas concert, the Youth Choir sang with such gleeful energy it fairly rocked the nave.

" 'Go tell it on the mountain, over the hills and everywhere. Go tell it on the mountain, that Jesus Christ is born . . .' "

"Go tell it on *this* mountain—every day, in every way," he said at the close of the service, "and go in peace, to love and serve the Lord."

"Amen!" said the congregation, revived and wide-awake, though it was hours past their bedtime.

Several parishioners had pressed envelopes into his hand. Others had brought cookies, cranberry bread, and a can of his known favorite, mixed nuts, so that he walked home carrying a full paper sack. Not a few had said what his parish was never too shy to say, "We love you!"

In other years, he had often felt a great fatigue after the midnight service. Tonight, he could have shouted through the streets, blown a trumpet, waved a banner. His Christmas adrenaline was up and pumping, and so was Dooley's.

"Well done, old fellow!" he said as they headed toward the rectory. "I heard you hang those high notes in 'Once in Royal David's City.' " He put his arm around the boy's shoulders. Here was another miracle, walking right beside him. "Why don't we open just one present tonight?"

"You ain't goin' t' like what I'm givin' you."

"That's what you said last year, and haven't I carried that glasses case with me everywhere, even to Ireland and back?" When would this boy stop shooting himself in the foot? "I'll tell you one thing—you'll jolly well like what I'm giving you."

Dooley looked up and grinned.

Sitting on the floor in the study, the winking tree lights reflected in every window, he unwrapped the book on veterinary medicine. It was true. He didn't like what Dooley gave him.

"Now you can doctor Barnabas if he gits sick."

"Aha."

"You can doctor ol' Vi'let if she's tryin' t' puke up a mouse."

"I'll let you handle that."

"Looky here. It tells how you can fix up Jack if he gits worms or mange."

"You're the doctor in the house, not me."

"Yeah, but I might not always be here."

"Not always be here? And where might you be?"

"When Grandpa gits well, I guess we'll be goin' back t' 'at ol' house, if it ain't fell in."

He could tell this had been on Dooley's mind for some time, but he hadn't been wise enough to sense it. "We're going to do something about that, but I don't know what exactly. I want you to stay here, for things to stay the way they are."

"Good," said Dooley. "Where's my present?"

He was sitting on the side of the bed, taking his shoes off, when the phone rang. It would be Walter, who often phoned after the late service. "Merry Christmas, potato head."

"Timothy?"

"Cynthia!"

There was an awkward pause.

"Are you all right?" she said. Her voice sounded new to him somehow.

"Yes! Yes, we're fine. A rough go in some places, but fine. I turned your faucets on to drip and put the thermostat at sixty-two . . . shouldn't be any problem. I think the worst is behind us."

"Thank you. I appreciate it."

"I thought you were Walter. That was . . . ah, what I used to call him." He could tell the conversation was having trouble pushing off, like a sled poised at the top of a hill but snared on a rock.

"I hope you're not disappointed that it isn't Walter."

"Why, no. Certainly not! And you—are you all right?"

"I haven't had any spills on icy sidewalks, or power outages, or empty cupboards, if that's what you mean. But my heart is not all right—not in the least," she said coolly.

He felt his own heart pound as the sled pushed off. He sensed that this would be Olympic tobogganing, as opposed to a playful dash down Old Church Lane on a biscuit pan.

"Why don't we start where we ended, all those days ago?" she said. "You were asking me a question."

That question, once so alive in his thoughts, was now a fossil. He was embarrassed even to think how peevish it would sound.

"Yes, well. It's really not worth asking again."

"It must have been worth something—it cost days of trying to figure out the answer.

"The answer, Timothy, is that the man you spoke with on the phone was my editor and friend, James McNeely. He came back from

Europe on business in New York, where he rang the bell of his own apartment, only to find me in a bathrobe, with my face set like papier-mâché in a green mud pack. He needed something in his desk and said that if I'd consider washing my face, he'd take me to dinner.

"It was terribly late, but I was wild to be out of here and have the lovely privilege of talking about my work to somebody who not only understands it but is vastly interested."

"Of course," he said, barely able to speak.

"I didn't even hear the phone ring while I was getting dressed. I had my head stuck so far in the sink trying to dissolve that mask! Days later, I called him in France, wondering if he'd answered my phone, and he said he'd asked whoever it was to leave a message." There was a pause. "So, why didn't you leave a message?"

"I don't know."

He felt as if he had committed a schoolboy crime, like smoking on the bus or putting a frog in the girls' toilet. He fairly squirmed with the agony of having made so much ado about nothing.

He knew he would have to hold on tight and steer. "If I had it to do over, of course, I would insist on speaking with you. 'Haul that woman out of the shower or wherever she is, and put her on the line—at once! This is her neighbor calling!' "

She laughed the breathless, throaty laugh he loved.

"Your laughter is the Christmas music I've been longing to hear. I'm sorry, terribly sorry to have been so petty. Please forgive me."

"Oh, Timothy! How awful it's been, not being able to get home, not hearing from you, getting that dreadful little frozen note that I stuffed in the incinerator, and wondering what was wrong. And all the circuits busy for days, and no way to talk . . . to make contact. And your Christmas present sitting here on the sofa . . . I've felt so alone, so isolated from you . . ."

"I miss you," he said. Without meaning to, he said, "I need you . . ."

"Can you imagine how I love hearing you say that? That is the Christmas music I've longed to hear."

"I have no photograph of you. Sometimes I can't remember what you look like—do you mind my saying it? I want so much to see your face."

"I'll pop into one of those little booths and make dozens of funny faces and send them out as soon as the snow melts."

"Wonderful! And when will you come home? Soon?"

"Not until March. If I could get home now, I wouldn't have but three days. And the ice and rain have begun here, and the work is pressing me so . . ." She sounded anguished.

"What can I do for you. How can I help?"

"Love me! Long for me! Yearn for me! Oh, Timothy, you were jealous, weren't you?"

"Yes. Terribly. It was churning around in me for days, and when you answered the phone, it just popped out. I didn't mean for it to come out that way at all."

"How lovely that you can still surprise yourself. I couldn't love you if you were completely buttoned up. It's that little place you can never quite manage to get closed that makes me love you."

"But it's such a small place. Wouldn't you rather it was a bigger place?"

"Infinitely rather, my dearest."

He felt a kind of thaw, a snow melt. Something was being released and healed, and he sank back on the pillows.

"I love you, Timothy."

"I love you, Cynthia. Truly I do. You are a godsend."

"Do you think God would have me batter through your locked doors?"

"I think that you and only you could do it. I read something the other day—'What is asked of us in our time,' the writer said, 'is that we break open our blocked caves and find each other. Nothing less will heal the anguished spirit, nor release the heart to act in love.' Locked doors, blocked caves, it's all the same. It is so hard to . . ."

"To be real."

"Yes. Terribly hard. Frightening. But there's no other way."

"Ah, you talk tough now, you big galoot, but wait 'til I come home and fling myself into your arms . . . will you run?"

"The very thought takes my breath away," he said, meaning it. "And I don't know if I'll run. I don't want to. But . . ."

"But it could happen?"

"The odd thing is, I don't trust myself with you—yet I trust you. I trust you to be real with me, but I'm afraid that I can't give that back . . ."

"You're giving it back right now."

"Yes. But it's . . . frightening."

"Hold me, Timothy. Just be still with me. Where are you, dearest?"

"Lying on my bed. Can you hear Barnabas snoring?"

"No, but I should like to. I should like to be there with you, only holding you and you holding me."

All the tension of the past weeks, the angry weather, the increased duties of church, the luncheon speeches and invocations, the conflicts of his heart—all had concentrated to feel, somehow, like an inpouring of cement. Now, at last, came the outpouring.

"I need you," he said again, warmed and happy.

"Let's burn 'em ol' tables!" Dooley shouted over the music on his jam box.

"Let's burn 'at ol' jam box!" he shouted back.

Actually, the folding tables made one of the finest fires they'd had all winter.

With the Christmas Day service behind him, he did something he'd nearly forgotten how to do. He undressed and put on his pajamas and robe and made a pot of Darjeeling. He at last sent Dooley to his room, where all he could hear of the music was boom, boom, boom.

There was only one thing for it.

He put the disc on his player in the cabinet and, smiling, fell sound asleep listening to the rhumba—or was it the tango?

Jena Ivey of Mitford Blossoms didn't have the faintest idea which florists in New York would be certain to send roses that didn't drop their heads, but he remembered a magazine article he'd read in the dentist's office that said the Ritz-Carleton was known for its stunning flower arrangements. So he called the hotel manager in New York, was given the name of a florist, and proceeded to order a dozen red roses and a bouquet of fresh lavender, at a price he at first thought was a joke, to be delivered in a box tied with a satin ribbon—and step on it.

CHAPTER SEVEN

More Than Music

My Dearest,

You can't know how the living freshness of roses and lavender has rejoiced my heart. The whole apartment is alive with the sweet familiarity of their company, and I'm not so loath now to come home from the deli, or the newsstand, or the café.

Thus, I'm not thanking you for the roses precisely, which are glorious to look at, nor the fast bundle of lavender that appears to have come from the field only moments ago. I thank you instead for their gracious spirit, which soothes and calms and befriends me.

I tried to call your office after the flowers arrived, but the line was busy again and again. And so, I take this other route, this path made familiar by pen and paper, reflection and time.

What a lovely thing it is to begin to love. I shall not dwell on the fear, which seems always to come with it. I shall write only of victory, for that is what is on my heart tonight.

When I met you, Timothy, I had no thought of loving anyone again. Not for anything would I pay the price of loving! I had shut the door, but God had not.

I remember the evening I came to borrow sugar. Though I did nothing more than gobble up your leftover supper, I felt I'd come home. Imagine my bewilderment, sitting there at your kitchen counter, finding myself smitten.

Over your home was a stillness and peace that spoke to me, and in your eyes was something I hadn't seen before in a man. I supposed it to be kindness—and it was. I later believed it to be compassion, and it was that, also.

Yet, I sensed that God had put these qualities there for your flock and your community, to help you do your job for Him. For a long time, I didn't know whether He might have put something there just for me.

Years ago, I went to Guatemala with Elliott. While he was in meetings, I was on the road with a driver and a sketchbook, slamming along over huge potholes, our teeth rattling. We drove in the jungle for miles, seeing nothing but thick, unremitting forest. The light in that part of the world was strange and unfamiliar to me, and I felt a bit frightened, almost panicked.

Suddenly, we drove into a clearing. Before us lay a vast, volcanic lake that literally took my breath away. The surface was calm and blue and serene, and the light that drenched the clearing seemed to pour directly from heaven.

I shall never forget the suddenness and surprise of finding that hidden and remote lake.

I feel that I have come upon a hidden place in you that is vast and deep and has scarcely been visited by anyone before. It is nearly unbearable to consider the joy this hidden place could hold for us, and yet, tonight, I do.

"Love is like measles," Josh Billings said, ". . . the later in life it occurs, the tougher it gets."

May God have mercy on us, my dearest Timothy!

I close with laughter and tears, the very stuff of life, and race to the drawing board with every hope that I can, at last, make the zebra stop looking like a large dog in striped pajamas!

I kiss you.

Love,
Cynthia

Dearest Cynthia,

At the library today, Hessie Mayhew announced that Latin American dance classes will be held at the Community Club, some-

time in February. I told her I have my own private Latin dance in-structor, which she found to be astonishing.

Then I popped into the children's section and talked to Avette about reading Miss Coppersmith.

*"*Violet Goes to School *and* Violet Plays the Piano *are my two personal favorites," she said, "although* Violet Goes to France *is hilariously funny. What will it be?"*

"The complete works!" I said.

I must tell you that Hessie Mayhew is no dummy. When she saw my selection, she approved. "The Proust of juvenile authors!" were her exact words.

Now I have innumerable photographs of you, though they are all on the backs of book jackets. I am currently displaying the backside of Violet Goes to the Country *on my desk in the study, where I meet your winsome gaze as I sit and write this letter. I'm afraid the author herself looks exceedingly juvenile, and if that's what writing children's books can do, then I'm willing to have a go at it.*

I shall begin this evening at the top of the pile and plunge straight through to the bottom. Never think that I dismiss lightly the hard work and devotion that go into each small volume. I feel privileged to see behind the scenes, if only a little.

Uncle Billy asks about you and says they'd like to have us over when you come home. You and Dooley can go along for the home-made banana pudding he mentioned as a refreshment, and I'll meet you there later.

He was telling me about the money he keeps hidden between his mattress and box spring. He says Miss Rose usually asks him for ten or fifteen dollars on Monday. On Wednesday, she wants twenty, and every Friday she asks for twenty-five.

When I asked him what she does with all that money, he says he doesn't know; he never gives her any.

I believe that's his newest joke, though he didn't say so.

Your letter spoke of victory, and I hesitate to end on a note that is less than uplifting. Yet I can't ignore your allusion to the hidden lake.

Your analogy was extraordinary to me and made me feel at once that I should surely disappoint you. The lake you discovered in Guatemala was tropical and warm. The lake you say you have found in me suffers a climate entirely of my own making—and there is the rub.

Please pray for me in this, my dearest Cynthia. I am well along in years to have such a terrific case of measles. In truth, I am broken out all over and no help for it.

You are ever in my prayers.

Dooley asks after you, as do Emma and Puny. A candle flame has gone out in this winter village, and we count the days until you are safely home.

Love,
Timothy

Dearest Timothy,

It was lovely that you called tonight after reading Violet Goes to the Country. *That is my personal favorite, and I'm so happy it made you smile.*

I'm happy, too, that you read it to Barnabas and that he approved. For one as steeped in Wordsworth as he, I'm not surprised that he could appreciate the pastoral setting, though I'm sorry he was upset when you showed him the picture of Violet chasing the sheepdog.

Violet receives a great swarm of attention wherever we go. I put her in the little carrying case with the top undone, and there she rides, licking her paws. The ladies behind the cosmetic counter at Bergdorf's come crowding into the aisles to give her lots of free samples—both salts for her toilette and mascara for her lashes. They like to spray her with French perfume so that I can hardly bear to be in the taxi with her on the way home!

When James was here, he asked me to do Violet Goes to New York.

He took me to such a vastly expensive restaurant and gave such a persuasive argument that I was fairly undone. I did not tell him I would do it, though I did say I'd think about it. The advance would be the largest amount I've ever received. I will appreciate it if you'd pray for me in this. It's confounding to be asked to do something I said I'd never do again!

Thank you for liking my work and finding the fun in it. I look forward to having the letter you wrote tonight before you called— altogether an embarrassment of riches!

Here are those ridiculous pictures taken in a booth on the street.

In the spring, you could tack them on a post in your garden to keep the crows away!

I've taken stems of lavender from the vase, dried them a wee bit in the toaster oven, and put them under my pillow. Lavender is said to give one sweet dreams, which is what I wish for you tonight.

You are always in my prayers.
With fondest love from—
Your neighbor

Dearest Cynthia,

It is Friday evening, and I've just come from a late meeting. This is only to say hello and that I've switched on the lights in your bushes.

The fog is as thick as lentil soup, and they give a cheering glow. As they were not turned on during the holy days, I hope you won't mind a few hours now, as a send-up of my thoughts of you on this wretched but beautiful winter evening.

God bless you and give you wings for your work. Nay, use them to fly to me here in Mitford. I shall watch for you to glide over the rooftop of your little house and eagerly open my window to let you in.

With loving thoughts,
Timothy

Timothy, dearest,

Violet has been invited out to dinner this evening by Miss Addison, who lives down the hall.

The invitation was delivered by the lady's footman or something—this is a very swanky place—and was for six o'clock, which is when her elderly cat, Palestrina, likes to dine.

Can you imagine?

I have met Miss Addison several times in the hallway or in the foyer, and she is rather old and quite adorable, wrapped from head to toe in furs.

The footman, or whoever he is, came for Violet on the stroke of six, after I'd brushed her until she shone.

But oh, she is wicked! What did she do five minutes before the bell sounded? I was bringing a flowerpot inside when she dashed to the terrace that is forty stories above the street, leapt onto the railing, and stood looking with absorption at the lights of the Chrysler Building.

She will stay until eight, because they are all watching a video after dinner (surely not 101 Dalmatians*?).*

I went to dinner the other evening, quite alone, and confess it was a bit pricey. The waiter finally came over and asked, "And how did you find your steak, Madame?"

"Purely by accident," I said. "I moved the potatoes and the peas, and there it was!"

Oh, Timothy, I'm trying so hard to bloom where God planted me. But I am very homesick. I look forward to our talk on Sunday.

Much love to you and to Barnabas. Do tell Dooley hey for me. I should like to see his frank expression and hear his wonderful way of speaking. When I come home, let's all do something together—like— well, you think of something!

I pray for you.

Warmest regards to Emma and my love to Miss Sadie and Louella.

Sunday eve
Dearest Cynthia,

We've just hung up and it seemed so many things went unsaid. Now that I'm sitting down to write, however, I have no idea at all what they were.

I'm delighted that Violet has made a friend, even though her fancy dinner sent her to the litter box throughout the night. Sautéed quail livers with Madeira sauce are notorious in this regard.

As for us, we had our usual Sunday evening banquet. Fried bologna for Dooley with double mustard, and no sermons about a balanced diet, please. This case is beyond me. Unless I'm mistaken, he has not eaten a vegetable in four or five months, and I'm dashed if I know what to do about it. Any ideas?

I forgot to mention that we had a mild, almost balmy day on Saturday. Miss Rose pulled on galoshes and spent the noon hour directing traffic. After a long confinement, it put the bloom back in her cheeks, Uncle Billy says.

Fancy Skinner has nailed me again about my hair and insists I let her give me a haircut. I hesitate to do this to Joe, who, I'm told, may go with his sister to Tennessee for a week. Possibly I could use his extended absence as an excuse. What do you think?

I've seen Andrew Gregory, who looked smart as all get-out in a cashmere topcoat, and he asked about you. He seems to think that because you're my neighbor, I know all there is to know about you. Yet it occurs to me that I don't even know where you were born.

Well, there you have it. All the urgent things I left unsaid.

Clearly, there's nothing of importance to tell a famous author and illustrator living in New York, whose cat has a more interesting life than most people.

Cynthia, Cynthia—my face grows red when I think of what you said. I hope you will seriously reconsider that outrageous idea, lest I take you up on it.

With something like amazed laughter, and, of course, love,

Timothy

Sunday evening
Timothy!

You rake in a collar! I positively blush like a sophomore when I think of what you said!

You may want to reconsider that outlandish proposal. What if I should take you up on it?

Or was it my idea?

Oh, well, when two hearts beat as one, who knows? And who cares?

I do love you to pieces. You are so funny and wonderful. I knew it the minute I saw that barbecue sauce on your chin, when I came to borrow sugar after just moving in.

Violet has gone down the hall to play with an electronic mouse while Palestrina, who is too old for such nonsense, looks on.

I shall be happy to be home again with people who are ordinary.

Well almost ordinary.

Much love,
Cynthia

My dear neighbor, it was your outlandish idea, not mine, and please do not forget it! I certainly haven't forgotten it. Good grief, I can barely keep my thoughts on my duties. And there's the rub.

I struggle with what old men with measles fear most: not being able to think straight, forgetting their Christian names, wandering in a daze on the street, being late for meetings and early for luncheons, dwelling everlastingly on some woman who only professes to have measles but in truth possesses a case so mild that she can go about her duties as cool and elegant as you please, while the other chap stumbles around trying to locate his shoes or even the very house where he lives.

Cynthia, Cynthia. Be kind.

yrs,
Timothy

Dearest Funny Person,

Your wake-up call this morning—how wonderful it was! It was coffee with brandy, it was eggs Benedict, it was a hot shower and a walk in the park! Words fail me, but not entirely!

So glad you liked the pictures, though I'm sure you were being kind. I can be terribly grave in front of a camera, and that fur-lined hood made me look exactly like an Eskimo woman who has spent the morning chewing a piece of reindeer hide.

Dearest, I really and truly can't come home. I must work some part of each day in order to reach the deadline. If I were to pull up stakes at this point and move home, I should do nothing more than lose time and gain confusion.

Thus far, I've been given God's speed. Now, if I keep going and nevah, nevah give up, I shall come to the finish line on schedule.

And so, I have a question that will make your heart fairly leap into your throat—

Why don't you come to New York?

You could stay here, and while I'm working, you could read or visit the bookshops or pop over to my little café where they've not only adopted me but would take the fondest care of you.

You would have lots of privacy, for this is a very large apartment— and I promise I will not seduce you. Since we've never discussed it, I want to say that I really do believe in doing things the old-fashioned way when it comes to love. I do love you very dearly and want every- thing to be right and simple and good, and yes, pleasing to God. This is why I'm willing to wait for the kind of intimacy that most people favor having as soon as they've shaken hands.

But enough of what I shall not do, and on to what I shall!

I shall buy fresh bread and fresh fish and vegetables and all the things you love and cook for you right here, and you will save hundreds of dollars on pricey restaurants, which you can give to the children's hospital!

I shall take you to a play with the tickets from my publisher and to the shop with the lighted antique globe, not to mention the Metropolitan Museum and the New York Public Library.

Last but not least, I shall give you as much love and affection and happiness as I am capable of giving. Which, I believe, dearest Timothy, is quite a lot.

There. How can you resist?

Your loving Cynthia

from the office
dearest cynthia,

but i am a rustic, a country bumpkin, a bucolic rube of the worst sort—in a word, a hick.

I can see why you didn't mention this on sunday when we talked—you wanted me to have time to think it over. That indeed is one of the grandest benefits of a letter. it gives one time to reflect, so that one doesn't shout some impulsive, spur-of-the-moment nonsense like yes i'll come to new york and fly in a plane and be stranded in an airport and get lost or maimed, or even killed, not to mention buffeted by throngs on every corner.

Nope. i can't do it. you think i'm kidding, but i am dead serious. I am infamous for my fear of flying—which is chiefly why I hemmed and hawed for twenty years over the trip to Ireland. Large cities are another of my rustic phobias—they literally make me sick—which is the sole reason Kthrn and Wltr and I lodged in the countryside when we went to sligo.

I am willing to take any flailing you dish out—but i cannot come to new york. you're right, the very thought makes my heart leap into my throat. blast, i am sorry,

with love,
Timothy

Dearest Cynthia,

It is Monday evening, and I have read your letter again, feeling like a heel.

Your bright spirit is the light of my life. When I read the gracious things you would do to make me happy, my foolish limitations and fogyisms are humiliating to me.

I can only hope you'll forgive me and know that somehow, in some other way, I shall be forthcoming and good for you.

I, too, hate it that you must be there alone. Emma assures me that men in the publishing field are good-looking, enormously successful, and invariably tall, some of them verging perhaps on nine feet or more.

She went on to suggest that if I don't mind my p's and q's, I will surely lose whatever ground I have gained with you, and you'll be swept away. I would not be surprised if this were true, but I pray it will not be so.

It was consoling to read your brave announcement of what you would not do. No, we have never discussed this, but the time, clearly, was right for you to say it. It is amazing to me that you and I share the same ideal for sexual intimacy, which, needless to say, the world finds exceedingly outdated.

Another consolation is that the world has nothing to do with us in this.

Your openness has widened the door of my own heart, somehow, and I feel a tenderness for you that is nearly overwhelming. I can't think how I could be worth the care you take with me, the effort you expend, and the ceaseless patience you bring to our friendship.

For this alone, I must love you.

My dearest,

You would be amused if you knew how long I have sat and looked at the two words just above, words that I have never written to anyone in my life. Can it have taken more than six decades for these words to form in my spirit, and then, without warning, to appear on the paper before me, with such naturalness and ease?

Even for this alone, I must love you.

I've come across a letter from Robert Browning to EBB, in which he says:

"I would not exchange the sadness of being away from you for any imaginable delight in which you had no part."

To this sentiment, I say Selah.

I also say goodnight, my dearest love. You are ever in my prayers.

Timothy

Timothy,

I understand. I really do. I could feel the intensity behind your typed note. At one moment, your horror of this place makes me laugh. At another, I wonder what on earth I'm doing here myself!

I feel we should go on as we're going and try to enjoy, somehow, this process of working and waiting. I know there is wisdom in that! But it keeps escaping me, like the flea I picked off Violet this morning.

Can you imagine? Forty stories up, in the dead of winter—and a flea? Certainly, she did not get it at Bergdorf's. Which leaves only one consideration.

Palestrina!

I shudder to think what I should do when her next social invitation arrives in the letter box!

I must get something ready for the pickup service that comes at five, so I'll dash,

with love and understanding,
Cynthia

Dearest Timothy,

When I reached into the letter box yesterday morning, I somehow missed your wonderful letter written on Monday evening. How very odd that I didn't feel it in there yesterday, but odder still that I would have looked in there again this morning, knowing that today's mail had not yet arrived.

I so needed your letter with Mr. Browning's words to Elizabeth and the tender things you spoke to me from your heart. Because, though I honestly do understand your refusal to come, it made me sad that you will not.

I had hoped we could be together here, as free as children from everything familiar. Most of all, I wanted to share what I know of this strangely compelling city and take you 'round and show you off!

But you have called me your dearest. And that is worth any window-shopping at Tiffany's or tea we might have sipped at the Plaza.

More than that—it fills me with happiness that you were able, for your own sake, to speak to me so.

It wasn't easy for me to tell you what I shall not do—it was very hard to know when to say it! So, perhaps you can imagine how comforting it was to learn that we agree in this sacred thing—and to find that you are just as silly and old-fashioned as your neighbor.

When Elliott and I were divorced eleven years ago, the first thing my friends did was "fix me up."

Oh, how I hated being "fixed up!"

Practically the first man I went out with said, "Hello, blah, blah, blah, cute nose, I'm wild about your legs, let's check into a hotel."

I wish I could tell you that I poured scalding coffee in his lap! But all I really did was curl up inside in a tinier knot than I'd curled up in before! I refused to go out with anyone again for nearly three years.

The secret truth, dearest, is that I cannot bear dating. I find it absolutely ghastly. I am so glad we have never ever dated and never ever will! You are just the boy next door, which I find to be the most divine providence since France was handed over to Henry the Fifth.

But please don't think our friend Andrew Gregory was anything less than lovely. He is a prince! Yet, among a variety of other sweet incompatibilities, he is too tall. Yes! When he kissed me on the cheek, he had to practically squat down to do it, which made me laugh out loud every time! Poor Andrew. He deserves far better.

You and I, on the other hand, are the perfect size for each other. As we're very nearly the same height, we're just like a pair of bookends.

I close with sleepy wishes for a riveting sermon at Lord's Chapel on Sunday. Please make a photocopy at Happy Endings and send it to me. I shall be sitting on the gospel side at the little church around the corner.

Love and prayers, Cynthia

P.S. My work is simply pouring through. I am thankful beyond telling. James writes from France that my zebras fairly leap with life.

There's not a pair of pajamas in the lot. Pray for me, dearest, I shall be home sooner than we think. Love to Dooley. Here's a bit of a drawing I did of him from memory.

from the office
dear bookend,

i'll have you know i stand 5 feet 9 in my loafers, while you are a mere 5 feet 2. that leaves 7 whole inches waving around in the breeze above your head, and i'll thank you not to forget it.

Dooley laughed at your drawing and must have liked it for he took it to school today. That someone would make a drawing of him was a marvel he did not take lightly. Puny thought it pure genius, and i promised to make her a photocopy when i copy the sermon, which, by the way, was less than riveting, though Miss Rose, to my great surprise, pronounced it stirring.

she refused to wear the sling-back pumps that Uncle billy ordered out of the almanac. She put them on the mantel in the dining room, instead, as a kind of display. She was arrayed in her Christmas finery. Uncle Billy was wearing a new shirt and held himself so stiff and erect i suspect he had left the cardboard in.

Things are back on schedule on the hill and i could hear the hum and buzz of the equipment as i walked in this morning. emma wanted the week off, so i am quite alone here, half-freezing one minute and roasting the next, as the heater has developed a tic and goes on and off at odd moments.

You sounded strong yesterday, so glad Miss Addison invited you for that swell Sunday tea and that you brought home no fleas.

Again, i enjoyed your books more than i can say. i seemed to find all sorts of meaning between the lines.

Love, Timothy

p.s. Dooley says hey
thnx for telling me when you were born, though I forgot, as usual, to ask where. So there'll be no forgetting, i have written your birth date on the wall beside my desk, my first graffiti—except of course for the legend, TOMMY NOLES LOVES PATTY FRANKLIN, that i once chalked on the cafeteria door and which

nearly cost my life at the hands of the principal, not to mention Patty Frnkln.

Perhaps you entered the world in maine? or was it massachusetts? You are definitely a Yankee, no doubt about it

Here comes harold

Dearest Timothy,

I've been very sleepless recently. I wish I could call you now, but a ringing phone at such an hour stops the very heart. It would also set Barnabas "to barking" and Dooley "to fussing." So I shall have to be consoled with talking to you in this way.

I've read something wonderful. "Deep in their roots," Roethke said, "all flowers keep the light."

My mind went at once to my tulips, frozen into the black soil of the bed you helped me dig. My imagination burrowed in like a mole and saw, in the center of a frozen bulb, a green place—quick and alive and radiant and indefatigable, the force that survives every winter blast and flies up, in spite of itself, to greet spring.

I am keeping the light, dearest. But sometimes it grows so faint; I'm frightened that I shall lose it entirely.

Why am I not doing the things I should be doing? Going to the library and the bookshops, seeing plays, hearing concerts, looking at great art?

The answer is, there's scarcely anything left of me after bending over the drawing board for hours, and so I send out for Chinese or make the quick walk to the café and am in bed before the late news, only to find I cannot sleep!

I am, however, going faithfully to confirmation class at the little church around the corner, every Thursday evening—and liking it very much.

I pray for us to have long walks together, to dash out into the rain and jump into puddles! Would you jump into puddles with me? I think not, but it's a hope I shall cherish, for it makes me smile to think of it.

Now that I've gotten out of bed, and located the stationery, and rounded up the pen and filled it with ink, and fluffed up the pillows, and adjusted the lamp, and told you I can't sleep, I'm nodding off!

Life is so odd. I can't make heads or tails of it. I'm glad you're a parson and can.

Lovingly yours, C

My dearest C,

Have been pondering our dinner here before you vanished into the sky in that minuscule plane. I can't seem to remember what I fed you, when or how I prepared it, nor even discussing the order with Avis. Though I was sober as a judge, I think I was in a kind of daze—the most I can recall is that we danced, I asked you the question that was so infernally difficult, and you were tender and patient and full of laughter.

This recollection should be more than enough, yet I'm astounded at such a lapse. Something was clearly going on that had little to do with either dinner or dancing and causes me to consider the wisdom of Aiken's poem:

"Music I heard with you was more than music,

"And bread I broke with you was more than bread . . ."

So glad you called last night. It was no disturbance at all, quite the contrary. I hope it's some comfort, however small, that you can call me anytime.

Do you hear? Anytime. Please take this to heart.

I've been in parishes where the phone might ring at any hour, from midnight to morning. Mitford, however, is a reserved parish, and I think the last late-hour call was from Hoppy's wife who was in the agony of dying and wanted prayer—not for herself, but for him.

It occurs to me that I'm not only your neighbor and friend, C, but your parson, as well. All of which seems to make a tight case for your freedom to call me as your heart requires it.

With fondest love to you tonight and prayers for sleeping like an infant,

Timothy

My dear Bookend,

I've had a load of wood carted in and a more splendid fire you've never seen. All this seems to occasion a letter, though I just sent one to you yesterday morning.

A meeting was canceled, thanks be to God. Dooley is spending the night with Tommy, and Barnabas is amused with scratching himself. Wish you were here. It is another night of jollity in our frozen village.

I've just heard from Fr Roland in New Orleans, who complains that my letters to him have dried up like a pond in a drought. Can't imagine why.

Am cooking a pork roast and a pot of navy beans, one more reason I wish you were here. I told Puny I needed to put my hand in again, so she did the shopping with Avis, and I'm handling the rest.

The house is fairly perfumed with a glorious smell, which causes me to remember Mother's kitchen. She always added orange rind to a pork roast and a bit of brandy. Her strong favorite with any roast was angel biscuits, so named for their habit of floating off the plate and hovering above the platter.

I can't help but think how my father never came to the table when called. He would sometimes wait until we were finished or the food had grown cold before sitting down without a word. I remember my mother's disappointment and my own white fury, which often spoiled the meal she had laid.

Later, I could see it was his way of controlling the household, of being the emperor, far above the base need for eating, for loving, for feeling. I remember his refusal of anesthesia when he had an operation on his leg and again a serious abscess on his jaw.

If my mother had not been fashioned of something akin to marzipan, my father's composition of steel would have been my very death.

But why do I waste ink telling you this? It came into the room with the fragrance from the pots and would not let me be.

Sometimes I consider not mailing a letter I've written to you, but you insisted that nothing should be struck through or torn up or unmailed, so there you have it.

Someone has said again that I should work on the book of essays I've long considered. Perhaps when I retire, if I ever do such a thing.

Stuart says I should be making plans for retirement—but his advice mad me want to say, oh, stop being a bishop and let me stumble around and fall in a blasted ditch if that's what it takes.

I am homesick for your spirit.

With love,
Timothy

Darling Timothy,

I've dried the lavender and tied it into small bundles that are tucked everywhere. Here are a few sprigs for your pillow. If that seems too twee, as the English say, perhaps you'll find a place for them in your sock drawer.

I've plucked every petal from every faded rose and have two bowls filled with their lingering fragrance. I cannot let them go! I'm enclosing a handful of petals for you to scatter over the last of the snow.

James says the new book must be a different format than the Violet *books and even larger than* Mouse in the Manger. *"These creatures must have room to breathe!" he says, and I do agree. I'm going to the publishing house tomorrow afternoon and work with the designer. I shall be thrilled to have someone to talk with, though the lovely people who run the café do make the days go faster. I wish you could meet them.*

The weather is still terrible here. A water main froze and broke in the neighborhood, and the streets have been flooded for two days. I've bought fleece-lined boots after weeks of tripping around in the footwear of a Southern schoolgirl!

I got your letter mailed Saturday a.m. You must have given it wings! Thank you for writing about your father. One day, I shall tell you about mine. Alas, there was no steel in him at all. He was constructed entirely of charm, French cigarettes, and storytelling. He was often sad, utterly defenseless, and I loved him madly. He was thrilled that I was a girl, once saying that he didn't know what he would have done with a little person who wanted to kick around a football or go fly-fishing.

Oh, Timothy! I feel wretched. I cannot look at another zebra, another wildebeest, and certainly no more armadillos! I am so very tired.

I want more than anything to scratch through that last remark or start over, for that is what my mother always said. She always said she was tired, and I vowed never to say it, especially to you. But I am tired, and there you have it. I am exhausted in every bone.

I should love to kiss you over and over. Like at the airport. Our kisses made me feel I was flying, long before I got on the little plane. I am weary of having my feet on the ground, dearest. I should like to poke my head in the clouds!

With inexpressible longings,
Your loving bookend

Dearest Bookend,

    Hang in there. i have just this moment heard a male cardinal singing. He is sitting on the branch of an icebound bush outside the office window. It is so reviving to hear his song i had to tell you at once. It has gone on and on, as if he can't bear to end it. His mate swoops and dives about the bush, expressing her own glad joy for the sunshine that is with us at last. Let this be a comfort, somehow, and a hope for us. Am off to Wesley with Dooley to buy a parka, as his was ripped on a fence when we delivered Christmas baskets. Know this comes with tenderest love and fervent prayer, and yes, my own longings.

yrs, timothy

CHAPTER EIGHT

Keeping the Light

He awoke with a start, crying out, and saw Barnabas looking at him with alarm.

In the dream, he'd been standing on the site of Hope House, where Buck Leeper had been seriously hurt. The wound above Buck's knee lay open to the bone; blood soaked his pants and was spreading upward to his shirt.

He rubbed his eyes, trying to wipe away the image of the nearly mortally wounded man whose face he had not seen but whose suffering had been palpable.

He had never been one to try and sort out the meaning of dreams, as a dog might worry a bone. He wanted to put it out of his mind, at once.

It was a half hour before the alarm would go off, but he got out of bed and took a hot shower, scrubbing his head more vigorously than usual, as if to drive out the image of the worst dream he'd had in a very long time.

"I ain't seen you in a month of Sundays," said Percy, who looked up from the grill.

"I'm having breakfast with Dooley these days."

"Th' boy gets you for breakfast, your house help gets you for lunch, an' I ain't open for supper, so there's that." Percy was hurt.

He grinned sheepishly. If ever you got on the good side of Percy Mosely, he would make you feel wanted and needed, no matter how big a scoundrel you turned out to be. Why, indeed, had he stayed away so long when the Grill was his favorite medicine?

"Where's Velma?"

"Waitin' on your buddies over there."

He turned and saw Ron Malcolm and Buck Leeper at the table by the window. The dark pall of the dream settled over him again. He noticed Velma was standing by the table like a stone, her order pad poised.

"Howdy," said J.C., as he slid into the back booth.

"How's it going?"

"You ought to get you some of this gravy," said the *Muse* editor, who had ordered biscuits and gravy, sausage patties, two fried eggs, and grits.

"And have a stroke before I hit the sidewalk? No thanks, pal."

Mule came up to the booth and slapped him on the shoulder. "Where in th' heck you been? Slide over. I been lookin' through th' obituaries to see if I could trace you."

"A lot going on. Glad to see you. How's business?"

"Slow as molasses. How's yours?"

"Steady."

It was a comfort to be back.

He could cook rings around Percy's eggs, but Percy's grits were another matter. While his own grits could be a dash watery, Percy's had a good, firm texture and were yellow with butter. He hadn't recently tasted anything so satisfying. And no wonder. For two mornings in a row, he'd weakened and had fried bologna with Dooley.

"Hope you haven't been eatin' your own cookin' all this time," said Mule, who tucked into an omelet with a side of livermush.

"Bologna two mornings in a row. The obituaries missed me by a hair. What's new?"

"The Presbyterians are raffling off th' Cadillac this month, but they're doin' it at the Legion Hall, to keep it ecumenical," said J.C.

"Aha."

"The school got a new flag, one that flew at the White House, and the Mixed Chorus is going to sing on Thursday while they raise it."

"I heard about that. Dooley's singing."

"Rodney Underwood caught somebody climbin' out th' back window of th' Collar Button. The burglar ran off, but they nabbed two suits of clothes, a sack of underwear, a dress shirt, and a fancy umbrella."

"Keep this up, I won't have to buy a paper on Monday."

"This," said J.C., "is old news. Already run in the paper last week. I figured you hadn't read it. If you're lookin' for new news, buy Monday's *Muse*."

"A poet and don't know it," said Mule. "Did you hear about ol' Miz Cranford goin' off to visit her daughter and asked Coot Hendrick to watch her house?"

"Didn't hear about that."

"Came back and Coot and his biggest boy had washed it. Top to bottom. Borrowed every ladder they could get hold of."

J.C. was not a pretty sight when he laughed with his mouth full.

"I don't get it," said Father Tim.

"Coot thought she said wash 'er house, not watch it."

"Um," murmured the rector.

"You had to be there," said Mule. "You know Joe Ivey's down sick with th' flu . . ."

"Uh oh. I needed to walk up there this morning and get a haircut."

"You're lookin' a little shaggy, all right. It's hangin' over your collar."

"That bad, is it?"

Mule peered at him over his glasses. "A good time to step over and see Fancy."

The rector ducked his head and buttered his toast.

"She cut J.C. last week."

The rector inspected J.C., who turned red.

"He looks the same to me."

"Well, that's the beauty of it," said Mule. "You go to just any jackleg, and you come out lookin' like a total stranger. Go to a professional and you come out lookin' like yourself."

The rector grinned. "So, you're going the unisex route, J.C.?"

"I hope to God you won't spread it around that I went to a beauty shop. Dadgummit, Mule, I asked you to keep that to yourself."

"All I've told is the preacher, here, hope t' die," said Mule.

Father Tim roared with laughter.

J.C. sopped his plate with the last crust of toast. "I ought t' stop comin' in this place . . ."

"Twenty percent off for clergy," Mule assured him. "That's five more'n what you get in Wesley, plus you burn gas runnin' over there, not to mention th' potholes from all th' bad weather that'll take your hubcaps off, plus your exhaust pipe. About a two hundred dollar run is what you'd have, not includin' th' tip."

"How long can the flu last? I can get by another day or two."

"Yeah, but Joe just took sick. He'll probably be down for a couple of weeks. You know Joe. He won't barber with the flu."

Puny Bradshaw sprang instantly to mind. She was the one for the job. She could trim him up in no time.

"I'll think about it," he lied. Actually, J.C. did look different, after all. He appeared as if he might be wearing bangs.

"Slide in," J.C. said to Ron Malcolm, who walked up to the booth. "I'm leavin'. Some people in this town have to work."

"I'm bustin' out of here, too," said Mule, who stood up and took his meal check. "Listin' a new house. Speakin' of which," he said to the rector, "how's that good-lookin' woman I slipped in next door to you? Haven't seen her around."

"Living in New York for a while."

"I got him a neighbor and a half," Mule told Ron. "Nicest pair of legs you'd ever want t' see."

Mule Skinner had no qualms about taking full credit for an act of providence, thought the rector. All he'd done was handle some paper-work on the little yellow house, which was deeded to Cynthia by her uncle's estate.

Velma came around with the coffeepot. "It's me again," said Ron, looking sheepishly at Percy's wife. "I'll take a fresh cup, if you don't mind."

Velma grunted and stomped away.

"She's sour as milk about Leeper. Any friend of his is an enemy of hers."

"What now?"

"Same old, same old. He's short with her, demanding, kind of high and mighty. She'd like to stab him with a fork."

"I had a horrifying dream about him last night. An accident on the job. Terrible, haunting."

"Worst that ever happened to him is he lost two fingers. One off each hand, a matched set, he says. You ever notice?"

"Our social exchanges have been pretty hasty. No, I didn't notice. What about his family? A wife? Kids?"

"No kids. Three wives. I won't go into what happened with the last one. I promise you don't want to know, and it sure didn't sweeten his temper any."

"Where does he live? What does he find to do around here?"

Velma set Ron's coffee on the table, with two packages of Sweet 'N Low. "There you go," she said tersely.

"Rents the old Tanner cottage, remember it? Go to the end of Church Hill, take the right that goes off in the woods. The cottage sits down in there. Pretty secluded. Beats me what he does. Not much, probably, after the kind of days he puts in. Somebody told me he used to do models, maybe of airplanes, I don't know."

"You said he hits the drinking pretty hard."

"Bottom line, it's not known to interfere with his work. Same way with his daddy for a lot of years, then it got him."

"What's his poison, anyway?"

"Vodka. Straight up."

The rector whistled.

"I have to tell you," said Ron, "there's something about him I like. Nope, I'm not condoning his social behavior, but there's something in the man . . . kind of like that little piece of nut you can't quite get out of the shell, even with a pick. Just that little piece stuck in there, somehow, that's all right."

"How's the job coming?"

"The weather poked a hole in us, but Buck's got it back on line. I tell you, he's the best in the business. If his ol' daddy hadn't kicked his butt so hard when he was a kid . . ."

"There's the rub. How's Wilma?"

"Cuter than a speckled pup." Ron's eyes sparkled with merriment at the mention of his wife of forty years. If there was a man to be turned to and counted on, it was Ron Malcolm, who, in his opinion, occupied the pedestal with Hal Owen. With these men flanking him on either side, he was a rector on whom providence clearly smiled.

"I feel like somethin' th' cat dragged in," said Emma. Her face was blotchy, her hair looked unkempt, and her eyes were swollen.

"What do you think it is?" he asked, truly concerned.

"I ate a whole cheesecake last night."

"You what?"

"Th' whole thing."

"Good Lord!"

"Direct from the freezer," she said, barely moving her lips and appearing to have gone numb in the face.

"How? . . ." He was at a loss.

"Dumped it out of the aluminum pan right on the countertop and busted it into five chunks with a knife handle."

"Good heavens! Where was Harold?"

"Gone. Went off to talk to somebody about plantin' Christmas trees on that four acres behind th' barn. He never leaves me at night. It was th' first time we've been separated in th' evenin' since we got married. Soon as he walked out th' door, somethin' came over me—that cheesecake popped in my mind like it was up on a drive-in theater screen."

"I know the feeling."

"He wasn't hardly out of the driveway 'til I jerked open th' freezer and hauled that cake out of there.

"At least I could have waited for it to thaw, but no sirree, whop, chop, down th' hatch." She sighed deeply, looking mournful. "I could have called in sick, but I knew you needed this report for the buildin' committee."

This was the first time he'd ever seen her too ill to be ill-tempered. She was meek as a lamb, which, regardless of the price she was paying, was not an unwelcome turn of events.

She had a strained look as she peered at him over her glasses. "Knowin' how cheese clogs me up, the worst is not over."

"Well," he said feebly, trying to be helpful, "try not to do it again."

He went up the hill at Miss Sadie's request, for an impromptu lunch of collards, navy beans, hot rolls, and fried chicken.

"Miss Sadie," Louella had said over their early breakfast, "we've crackered and san'wiched that poor preacher half to death. Let's give 'im somethin' can stick to 'is ribs."

Miss Sadie sniffed. "Fried chicken in the daytime is too heavy if you've got work to do. Why not chicken salad?"

"Too much trouble—skinnin', stewin', cuttin' off th' bone. Besides, I feel a cookin' spell comin' on."

"Oh, dear." Miss Sadie drew a deep breath. If Louella was too long discouraged from what she called "real" cooking, she would suddenly take a fit of meal preparation that cost a fortune, the results of which they couldn't possibly eat at one or two sittings. This meant all the leftovers had to be frozen in a veritable stack of containers. She knew for a fact that loading up the freezer made the refrigerator motor work harder, which reflected on the electric bill.

She tried, however, to be reasonable. She didn't mind losing a battle or two if, in the larger issues, she might win the war.

Miss Sadie's eyes were sparkling. "You know why I asked you up for lunch?"

He hardly ever knew why Miss Sadie asked him up for lunch. One thing he did know, however—it would be a surprise; it always was.

"They're going to get married!" she announced.

"Well, now, that's wonderful. Marvelous!" He leaned to her at the dining table and kissed her cheek. "Congratulations! The best news!" He couldn't deny that he felt a dash overlooked that no one had called him.

"Olivia wanted me to be the first to know, and Hoppy was going to tell you second, but he got that awful case of that whole family with food poisoning, and Olivia said I could tell you." He had never seen her look so radiant, as if she, herself, might be a bride. Here was one of the benefits, the bonuses, the perks of being a parson.

He sat back happily in the Queen Anne chair. "I don't know when I've had better news. When will it be?"

"June! Olivia said, 'Aunt Sadie'—oh, if you could know how I love hearing her call me that!—she said, 'Aunt Sadie, we were thinking of May or June. What do you think?' I said, 'Why, June, of course! It's traditional!' And she said, 'But aren't we a bit long in the tooth for that sort of tradition? Isn't that for young brides?' And I said, 'But my dear, you *are* a young bride. Your heart is only a few months old!' And so— June it is. The seventeenth! Oh, Father, I'm beside myself! It's the first family wedding I've ever known.

"How I wish everyone could know that Olivia is my blood kin." As she said that, her eyes lost their dancing light.

"Miss Sadie, you've bossed me around for years, and I've loved every minute of it. Now, I'm going to boss you on something. Forget your disappointment that no one can know. Don't let that rob you of even a moment's joy. You and Olivia have found each other. What a miracle! What grace! And all this joy depending upon a little coat that was spared down the years, so you could at last open this gift of the heart. I'm scolding you, Miss Sadie. Cheer up!"

She smiled and patted his arm. "You're right as rain, Father. You keep after me, you hear? You know I'll keep after you."

"Oh, and it's a privilege to have someone keep after me. I need it."

"Father, I've heard . . . rumors. You know how things get around. There are some who say you might have . . . well, that you might have a special fondness for your neighbor and she for you." Miss Sadie colored slightly. It had taken some courage to ask.

"You've heard right."

"Then, one day, there could be someone besides me to keep after you?"

"There . . . could be." He paused. "Perhaps."

"Father, don't be too cautious. I would never tell anyone to throw caution to the winds, for caution is a good thing." She looked at her hands in her lap for a moment and then looked at him. "But caution can be carried too far."

He shook his head, silent. He had learned to be as comfortable and trusting as a child in Sadie Baxter's company.

"Now," she said. "I have a surprise."

Ah, well, what else was new? Where else did one get genuine surprises these days, if not from Sadie Baxter? Of course, Cynthia Coppersmith was no slacker when it came to surprises . . .

"You're beaming!"

"Weddings," he said. "I like weddings. Baptisms. Confirmations. Even funerals, in a sense. Life events are wondrous."

"I'm going to be cremated, you know."

"Yes, I know."

"I certainly don't want to be laid out in a coffin for everyone to gawk at. Besides, it costs a fortune. Thousands and thousands of dollars, and now they're selling you a liner into the bargain. A liner! That's to go around the casket! As if the casket itself weren't up to the job!"

"Watch your blood pressure," he said, laughing.

"Make sure you put my urn in the rose garden. Don't stick me in that rhododendron grove. It's too shady. Where is Parrish Guthrie, anyway? Is he planted out there? If so, move me across the churchyard!"

"Gosh, I should have brought my notebook to take down all these directions."

She laughed with him. "Isn't it wonderful that we can have such a lively time talking about dying?" She pulled at his arm. "Come, Father, I'm going to show you the ballroom. And I hope you know how privileged you are, for Louella and I are the only ones who have seen it in twenty-four years. Oh, wait. I did let Luther in one day to trap a squirrel."

He walked with her slowly, offering his arm for security. "I'm going to give Olivia and Hoppy the grandest ball you could ever imagine," she said. "I want to give her something she'll remember for the rest of her life."

The ballroom doors were located in the foyer at the foot of the impressive staircase.

"Papa designed the ballroom to go here, so our guests could come sweeping down the stairs in their fine clothes and go right into the festivities. We had friends from all over, 'til Papa's health suffered."

"I've heard," he said gently. "I believe the president visited here."

"President Wilson! I remember he gave me a piece of toffee wrapped in silver paper. I kept it for years. Then, one day I just unwrapped it and ate it! It was still good."

She took the large key out of her pocket and turned it in the lock. "Louella keeps the lock oiled. We use WD-40. What do you use for locks?"

"The very same," he said, feeling excited.

The doors swung open and Miss Sadie stepped over the threshold.

"There, now. What do you think?" She looked at him for signs of the admiration this room had always inspired.

"Ah," he said, stricken, needing a place to sit.

"Leaves you speechless, doesn't it, Father?"

"Yes, indeed!" Tattered sheets and blankets were nailed over the windows, furniture of every sort sat moldering along the walls, covered with dust and cobwebs. Great pale splotches appeared on the once-shining parquet floor where water had leaked in and stood in puddles. Some of the parquet tiles had come off their moorings and were scattered about, and the rococo mirrors on every wall needed resilvering, a process of staggering cost, he once learned.

He could have been standing in almost any room of the old Porter place, he thought. How could all this be turned around before June?

"You haven't looked up even once!" Miss Sadie sounded a trifle disgusted.

He looked up, and the sight took his breath away.

"You see! People keep their nose to the ground when they ought to be looking up!"

"A good sermon," he gulped. "Well taken."

Cherubim and seraphim frolicked along the borders of the ceiling and darted among blush-colored clouds. Angels swarmed toward the center of the ceiling in gold-bordered robes of blue and scarlet and purple, their iridescent wings brushed with silver. They bore garlands of roses in their arms, with loose blossoms tumbling down over the borders, so seemingly real that one might rush to catch them as they fell.

"Bravo!" he said quietly, still looking up.

"Papa called it the Heaven Room, after something he'd seen in England in the house of a duke or an earl—I can't remember which."

"It's heavenly, all right." Fortunately, there appeared to be water damage in one area only, which might easily pass for a dark cloud among the shining cumulus variety.

"One day I'll tell you about the time it was painted and who painted it," she said. "Oh, Father, you'll grow weary of my stories."

"Never!" he said, meaning it.

He had laughed today; he had been happy. He didn't know why he had not counted more sunny hours in his life, but he hadn't. God had clearly asked him to, but he was intent on having his own nature, and his own nature could be inward, even melancholy. He didn't like it, but there it was.

At the end of this day, what he wanted more than anything else was the solace of her letters.

A new one had come this morning, and he carried it to his desk, unopened. He put the letter in the drawer, looking forward to sitting down with it after Dooley was upstairs and the little clamor of their supper together was over.

He reminded himself that he needed to have a key made for the desk drawer where he kept her letters. The worn lock was there, but he hadn't inherited the key. Even more than not wanting anyone to discover them, he wanted to protect them for their rarity, for their . . . he couldn't find another word . . . fragility.

As he turned toward the kitchen, the longing he'd felt all day welled up in him again and he went back to the desk. He would read only one line, just the opening, something to sustain him.

My Bookend,

The winter here continues bitter and dark, the work on the book goes poorly, and my heart aches for the consolation of your company. Even so, I am keeping the light . . .

"There's nothing better for the inside of a boy than the outside of a horse," said Hal Owen when he called in the evening. "Let him come for the weekend."

Ah, he'd grown selfish with Dooley. He liked the sound of his tennis shoes on the stairs, the look of astonishment on his face when he ate fried bologna with him for two mornings in a row. He was attached to the bright questions in his eyes, to the occasional breakthrough of a smile or one of those wacky laughs he'd developed with Tommy. He had even made a certain peace with the sound of that blasted jam box thumping above his study.

"He can bring Barnabas," said Hal, sensing the hesitation.

"A boy shouldn't be hanging around the house with a doddering old parson," said the rector.

"Hanging around the house with a parson has saved the day, if you ask me. I'll pick him up after school and you'll get him back after church on Sunday. How's that? I expect you'd like some time to yourself . . ."

No, he thought, he would not like some time to himself. He'd had time to himself for more than sixty years, which was enough for any man. He felt shocked at this odd revelation.

"Timothy? Are you all right?"

"Absolutely. Just a bit jealous of the chicken pie I hear Marge is baking this weekend."

"You know you're invited. It's a standing invitation, has been for twelve years."

"Thirteen, my friend. And thank you. But another time. The boy's backsliding, you know, in the 'ain't' department. I was after him with a stick for a while but slacked off. Marge will send him home talking like a Rhodes scholar."

"I don't suppose there's anything from his mother?"

"Nothing. And Russell is just recovering from the relapse after his fall in the snow."

"What are you going to do about all that?"

"I don't know. I can't seem to come up with a plan that works for anybody, much less everybody. If Russell goes home, Dooley would have to go with him."

"Have to?"

"Hoppy says Russell would need someone to monitor him. If Betty hadn't been around, he could have lain in the snow 'til the buzzards started circling."

"Could you hire somebody to do the monitoring?"

"Who would live in that unheated shack in the middle of a junkyard?"

"True."

"Another thing. If Russell goes out, Miss Pattie goes in. Betty Craig would be done for. She's begged me to protect her from Miss Pattie."

"What about the gardens? Anybody to pitch in there?"

"Not a soul that I can think of. Fortunately, Russell's done such a grand job over the years they won't be that difficult to maintain. But they must be maintained." He heard himself sigh.

"I expect it's costing somebody to keep him at Betty's."

"About four hundred a month, in addition to his social security."

In his opinion, the four hundred covered a lot more than health care for Russell Jacks. Indeed, it was a small price to pay for Betty Craig's sanity, his own peace of mind, and, last but not least, the boy's freedom to keep his mind on his education.

"Considering the circumstances," said the senior warden, who usually got the gist of things, "it sounds like a bargain to me."

The thought came to him as he stopped by the rectory to change jackets for the flag-raising program.

Fun—that thing he was always thinking of having, or feebly attempting to have, or trying awkwardly to figure out how to have—

well, that's what he would have this weekend. He would lighten up and have some fun—he would do something different, something new.

He ran over the list of possibilities. He would, of course, call Cynthia, and he would call whenever the notion struck, whether the rates were down or not. He would go see Homeless who, for all he knew, still hadn't thawed out from the blizzard. He would . . .

He gazed unseeing into the mirror over his chest of drawers, straightening his tie.

"Call Cynthia and visit Homeless" was absolutely as far as he could get with this list. Wasn't there something else he could do, something more innovative, like other people? Didn't people always look forward to the weekend, to eating out or watching a ball game? Well, and there was no place to eat out other than the Grill, except for Mack Stroupe's hot-dog stand next to the Esso station. He was sure it was his imagination, but Mack's hot dogs always tasted like motor oil.

As for watching a ball game, he had never, not even once, been able to follow a game to the end. His mind would wander, he would fall asleep, or he would get up and leave the room, forgetting to come back until after the game was over.

The truth was, he didn't know a blasted thing about having fun. Cynthia, on the other hand, not only seemed to have it, she was very good at making it. In actual fact, they hadn't done much that one could describe as fun, yet they always seemed to have it. With Cynthia, it just naturally happened.

He pulled on his jacket, smiling. Friday afternoon and all day Saturday. That would be his allotment for fun. He would see if he could pull it off. He would call Cynthia tonight and ask her to suggest something.

Not a word had Dooley let slip, not even a hint. And though he'd seen Miss Pearson in front of the bakery the other afternoon, she, too, had kept the secret that Dooley Barlowe was going to sing a solo with the full force of the Mitford School Mixed Chorus behind him.

No wonder the boy had been jumpy as a cat, he realized later. When he wasn't wandering in a daze, he was cussing Barnabas under his breath.

"I heard that," the rector said at breakfast the morning of the flag-raising.

"Heard 'at ol' dog fart is all I heard."

"Dooley . . ."

"All I said was . . ."

"Dooley . . ."

The boy looked at him defiantly. "What are you goin' t' do about it?"

"Same as last time."

Washing someone's mouth out with soap was not a remedy he liked, but it had worked for him when he was a kid. He was sure there were newer techniques, all much smarter and written up in books with deep psychological insights. As for him, he had not asked for this job and was not interested in learning what today's cutting-edge punishment for cussing, if any, might be.

He would, however, make one modern concession.

He let Dooley wash his mouth out himself, as he stood at the bathroom door, recalling the penalty his mother extracted for his own abominable language.

"That ain't so bad," Dooley said, wiping his mouth and looking him squarely in the eye. "It's a whole lot better'n 'at ol' soap in th' kitchen."

Good fellow, he wanted to say, but didn't.

It was what came out of the boy's mouth as the flag was being raised that caused him to catch his breath with unbidden joy. Dooley was doing this? His own Dooley? Why hadn't he thought to invite Puny and Miss Sadie, Percy and Velma, Hal and Marge and Rebecca Jane, Emma—the whole lot? But, of course, he hadn't known about the solo.

He was dashed if he could swallow without choking.

Miss Pearson would need someone to hold her feet on the ground, he could see, or she would float up and over the schoolhouse in a kind of rapture.

They met on the sidewalk after the program, as he and Dooley were leaving for home.

"Good heavens, Miss Pearson!" was all he could find to say.

"Father!" she exclaimed, which was all she could find to say.

There were tears in their eyes as he shook her hand again and again, unable, somehow, to let go.

Jenny passed, carrying her book bag. "You were really great," she murmured softly.

"Mush," said Dooley, bouncing his basketball.

"I can't tell you how terrific that was. It was a glorious thing, hearing God's gift pour out of you like that. And the way your chorus backed you up—strong stuff! I'm proud of you."

"It ain't nothin'."

"No, my friend, it's quite something. I wish Cynthia could have heard you. And your grandfather. And Miss Sadie. Everybody!"

Dooley shrugged. "Jis' ol' school stuff."

"Blast it, Dooley, how did it make you feel to stand up in front of all those people and belt out 'God Bless America'?"

He saw that Dooley couldn't stop the grin that suddenly began spreading across his face. It happened without warning and clearly could not be controlled. "Neat," he said.

"It was, I suppose, the soap that helped do this marvelous thing . . ."

Dooley glared at him. "Yeah, I cain't sing f'r poop usin' 'at ol' stuff in th' kitchen."

Before he turned the corner at Mule's house, he looked up and down the street. If he saw anybody coming, he would stop and examine his fingernails or look more closely at the bark on the tree that had grown through the sidewalk.

He had never been into a beauty shop in his life, nor had a woman other than his mother ever cut his hair. There was absolutely nothing wrong with beauty shops, nor with a woman cutting a man's hair. It's just that it was too strong a dose for him at one sitting after thirteen years with Joe Ivey who, in spite of the brandy he kept sitting in plain view with the hairspray, gel, and setting mousse, knew what the rector liked and how to deliver it.

Another thing—how much would it cost, even with a 20 percent discount? Twice as much as Joe, most likely, to pay for the new sinks she had put in and the carpet, not to mention those color prints of poodles that Mule said cost two hundred dollars to have framed, even without mats.

Double. That's what he should be ready to cough up. If Joe was six bucks, Fancy Skinner would be twelve. He had heard that a tip of ten percent was an insult these days. It was a full twenty or don't bother. That pushed it up to fourteen dollars and forty cents, which he might as well make fifteen, to round it off.

Misery! He would never do this again if his hair grew as long as John the Baptist's. Puny had absolutely refused to do this thing. She claimed it would look butchered, and she wanted no part in giving him an appearance that was beneath his station. He threatened to do it himself, which had not softened her heart.

Thanks be to God, he didn't see a soul when he pushed open the door. But the sight of pink carpet and pink walls gave him a distinct sinking feeling. He would turn around and go home and drive to Wesley as hard as he could go. Losing a hubcap or two was no big deal.

He was starting up the driveway when Fancy yelled from an upstairs window, "Are you my three o'clock? Oh, hey, Father, I thought you were my perm. I'll be right down, don't go away, make yourself at home. You want a glass of tea? It's unsweetened, or I can give you sugar, whichever—you tell me. Maybe you'd like a Coke. I have Classic or Diet, what do you think—you tell me."

If Cynthia Coppersmith had not suggested he go through with this, he would have run and not looked back.

"I like to color-coordinate with my shop," said Fancy, who was wearing pink tights, a pink cashmere tunic, and pink high-heel shoes with ankle straps.

"I'm glad you're here. Cuttin' your hair will put me over th' top this week." She swiveled the chair around, so that he stared at himself in a mirror. At Joe Ivey's, he was able to look out the window at the tops of trees.

"I set a goal every week. Last week I came a bitty bit under. Th' week before that, a bitty bit over. You never know which way it'll go. Now that you walked in, I'll top last week by a hundred dollars!"

His heart sank. Fifteen dollars was clearly a low estimate. Well, let this be a lesson. Let this be a lesson! He felt a wrench in his stomach as she slipped some kind of scarf over his head and around his shoulders. It was such an intense shade of pink it reflected on his face.

"I'll bet you don't put this thing on Buck Leeper."

"Honey, if Buck Leeper ever shows his butt in here again, excuse me, I will personally chase him out with a butcher knife."

"That bad, huh?"

"Have some gum. It's right there on th' magazine. Mule said, 'Fancy, you don't have to cut his hair and take his insults. I'll give you double whatever he spends.' Was that sweet of Mule or what? So, next time Mister High an' Mighty walks through that door, I'm runnin' his tail out of here. *If* he walks through th' door, that is. I iced him so bad when he bossed me, he might never be back. He might cross th' street when he sees me comin'.

"Man, have you got a tight scalp. That's tension. You prob'ly use your brain all th' time. That's what does it. Some people, their scalp just rolls around on their head like baggy pantyhose. You want a little massage? See, that feels better already, right? Oops, these nails. Lord, I nearly poked a hole in you. They're acrylic. Mine won't grow for shoot. I wouldn't drink milk when I was a baby. That's what did it."

"Who's your three o'clock?" he asked darkly. Who in God's name was going to come in here and see him helplessly decked out in this shawl thing?

"Nobody you know, honey. Somebody new from Baltimore. Oh, look at this neck. What a mess. Who does you? Joe Ivey, of course. Joe Ivey has never been to New York City to learn the latest things."

"You go to New York, then?"

"No, but I read the magazines. Th' way he cuts you makes your face look too wide. I'm goin' to just trim it right through here. It's like some kind of *bush*."

He felt panicked. Why hadn't he brought a hat? He could have brought that old twill garden hat that folded up flat. He could have slipped out of here and been wearing it when he rounded the corner.

"Please," he said, sensing that he was about to croak, "don't do anything different. Like I said, I just want the same thing. Please. Just a trim. Nothing serious." It was as near to pleading as he'd come in years.

"Oh, phoo, that's what they all say. You should've seen J.C. hunker down in this chair like I was goin' to snatch his eyeballs out. You trust me on this, OK?"

She scissored something from above his left ear that fell with a positive thump on his shoulder. He was afraid to speak, and why bother? It was too late.

Not bad, he thought, looking at himself in the mirror at home. He had been too shy to examine himself at the beauty shop. Not bad at all. Yes, his face looked thinner; his jaws looked perfectly hollow. And he could hardly believe she charged only six dollars. He was so grateful he had given her ten. Amazing, he thought, peering intently at his head—he even seemed to have more hair on top. Probably the massage.

He heard the bells toll at Lord's Chapel as he stuffed a canvas bag with a few items from the refrigerator and took a can of water chestnuts from the cabinet.

He missed his dog and his boy. But he was not going to dwell on it. He was going to have supper with Homeless Hobbes. Finally, he was going to have some fun.

CHAPTER NINE

Going On

Winter had been hard; its ravages were revealed in everything from loose roof tiles to crumbling stone walls. With the late-February sunshine predicted to last three days, the town was busy piling up limbs brought down by ice storms, and stomping around on roofs, looking for snow damage.

The sound of hammering drifted down from Fernbank.

According to rumor, this wasn't the much-needed new roof the village had hoped for; this was patching.

When one of the Fernbank roofers named what it would cost to replace "the whole shebang," a hushed reverence moved upon the crowd at the Grill.

They wondered why anyone of Miss Sadie's age and financial security would live in a place that was falling down around her head. It was a comfort to discuss this familiar topic, which had been a town favorite for years. To a man, they were dumbfounded and amazed that she had gone on so long.

"She ain't goin' t' quit, neither," said the roofer, as if he had some confidential information from Miss Sadie herself.

The sound of hammers on the hill and the sight of limbs piled along the curbs seemed to awaken new hope in Mitford. Several people reported hearing a robin sing, and Jena Ivey declared that three purple crocuses had bloomed in her backyard.

"Git over it," said Coot Hendrick. "Winter ain't done yet, and you can take that t' th' bank."

Dearest Timothy,

Miss Addison had a cocktail party, as she calls it, for four cats in the building. Thank goodness, Violet was not able to go, as she has just had a shot and was not feeling sociable. According to the superintendent, who came to fix my faucet, Miss Addison's butler or footman or whatever he is put little heaps of catnip on a silver tray and set the tray on the drawing room floor.

All the cats, it's reported, went absolutely berserk.

They climbed Miss Addison's silk shantung draperies and gave her Louis XIV sofa a good drubbing with their claws. Then they leapt onto the kitchen counter and gobbled up the smoked salmon intended for the horrified people who owned the cats.

It's enough to make one wish for a dog.

Miss Addison said she was told that catnip is a spring tonic and ordered this stuff all the way from a farm in upstate New York. I had entertained the thought of buying some for Violet but have squelched this notion permanently.

Our streets are full of a general sloshiness that lingers and won't go away, as if a glacier is deicing to the north. I forgot to ask on Sunday if anything has poked its head up in my perennial bed. Would you look? I am so homesick I can hardly bear it. I've worked on this stupid book until my eyes are crossing. You won't recognize me. At the airport, you will peer at me and say, "Cynthia?" Then you'll mutter, "No, no, can't be," and walk on.

But oh, this book will be good, I think. I really do believe so. Everyone here seems excited about it, and I pray fervently it will be loved by its readers. Do you know that one of my favorite things is seeing a child reading one of my books? They don't even have to like it. It is merely the sight of a small head bowed over the pages that gives me indescribable joy.

Do you feel the same when your sermons pierce our hearts and

*convict us of something that must be carried forth or changed in
ourselves?*

*Thank you for sending your typed sermon. I needed to hear all of
it. Yes! Intimacy is always about openness, about transparency. Until
the Holy Spirit led me into intimacy with Christ, I was as transparent as your iron skillet. It is terribly scary to go around with your
very spleen on display, yet, how can He shine through anything that
is not made transparent? Well, of course, He could—but well, you
understand.*

*I loved your note confessing that your feelings for me have made
you more transparent. Sometimes—well, only once, actually—I've felt
a little guilty for falling in love with you. Guilty that I have taken
something from you, something very private. I try not to dwell on this.*

*With much love from
Your bookend*

*the office
thursday, fog on the heels of sunshine, 56 deg., barnabas snoring,
emma making deposit*

*dear Lord! taken something from me? words cannot express what
you have given, do give. that you would love me at all continues to per-
plex me, i am sorry to say. as we go into Lent ii ponder again and
again how the apostles must have felt at losing him, at losing the love
that had captured and ennobled and given them something higher
than they could have ever known without him. there must have been
the deepest despair and disbelief, greater than the ordinary loss of a
loved one, until the Holy Spirit arrived on the scene and filled in the
blanks. ii have known something of loss, also, in these weeks, these
months you have been away, months in which winter has breathed its
frost upon our spirits continually. yet i think it is good somehow that
we discovered, confessed our feelings for one another and were forced
apart to think it through. that at least is true for me, and i am being
philosophical about it at the moment. at other moments i could not ask
for anything more than to have you here and cook your supper. Afterward, we might sit by the fire and look at the new garden catalogs.
there, now, I've run you away with the prospect of such dull evenings,
while you might be at the club playing cards or doing the tango.*

*please do not ever think that you have taken anything from me,
but know that you have given me something too precious and amazing to contemplate. and never worry that i won't recognize you. ii
would know those blue eyes anywhere, crossed or no.*

*i kiss you. God bless you and keep you. marge and hal pray for
you, as does dooley on occasion.*

harold cometh

love, timothy

p.s. nothing poking up, will advise

"He's workin' on his sermon right now, Esther. Can he call you
back? He said he has something goin', for a change. He'll call you, or I
will. I know it's important. Thirty minutes. Bye."

He could hear her drumming the desktop with her fingers, waiting
for him to put the cover on the typewriter.

He swiveled around in his chair. "Well?" he said, pleased with what
he had accomplished in less than a half hour. "What did Esther
want?"

"You know that big Presbyterian car thing at the Legion Hall on
Friday night?"

"Vaguely."

"They asked Esther to do the cakes."

"That was smart," he said, calling up the memory of the cake that
had nearly taken him home to glory. Her splendid orange marmalade
cake was famed among all the local churches.

"Well, she wants to do something' in the triple chocolate category,
for a change, something' called Better Than Sex Cake. But she's nervous as a cat about makin' a change . . . torn, she says."

"Aha."

"She wants to know should she come out with a new cake and
throw over the old one that's made her famous? She was wantin' to get
your answer by eleven, when she has to start bakin'."

"I have an answer, all right."

"What is it?"

"If it ain't broke, don't fix it."

"Amen!"

"Tell Esther I vote for the orange marmalade, hands down."

"That's what I say! Besides," she said, peering over her glasses, "what could be better than sex?"

He thought he was the last person on earth who should be asked such a question. Nonetheless, he had an opinion. "Certainly not a cake."

"I'll call her back," she said.

He was putting on his jacket to leave when the phone rang.

"Timothy?"

Her voice gave him a fine chill, something like that produced by chalk scraping over a blackboard.

"I'm so glad you're still there," said Edith Mallory.

"What can I do for you, Edith?"

"I think it's what I can do for the Children's Hospital," she said mysteriously.

"And what is that?"

"Remember how you urged me to get involved? Well, you were right, of course. Absolutely right, as always."

"Aha."

"Guess what?"

"I can't."

"Oh, Timothy, do loosen up a weensy bit. I'm calling with good news!"

He couldn't help but notice that when the phone rang, the sun had disappeared behind a cloud. "Fire away."

"I'm going to give ten thousand dollars to the Children's Hospital!"

He wished his heart might have leapt at the thought. Ten thousand would help enormously, but words seemed to fail him.

"Oh, all right!" she said, peeved at his silence. "Fifteen!"

He had never before raised five thousand dollars by keeping his mouth shut. "Wonderful, Edith. You'll never know how desperately it's needed and how thoughtfully it will be used."

"I'd like you to take me there to find out, firsthand."

"You mean, you'd like to look around?"

"Of course, meet the director, talk to the doctors. I'd like some personal contact, after all." She sounded petulant.

"What's your schedule?"

"Could we do it right away? Monday, perhaps? Or Tuesday? Which shall it be? Ed can drive us over. Perhaps we'll have lunch."

The very thought gave him a knot in his stomach. "Monday, I speak at the ECW luncheon about Hope House. There's a long meeting on Tuesday with the building committee. How about Wednesday or even Thursday?"

"Impossible."

"Well, then."

There was a frozen silence. She was waiting, he knew, to be courted and cajoled. Perhaps he should break over a little for the Children's Hospital. Maybe Ron Malcolm could fill in with the ECW.

"Oh, Timothy," she crooned, suddenly thawing. "Why argue over a day or two when children's lives might be in danger? I know how busy, busy, busy you are—of course we can make it Wednesday."

"Thanks for being flexible."

"Flexible? Me? How sweet of you to say that." He heard her take a deep drag on her cigarette.

"Well, then, Wednesday. What time?"

"Ten would be good."

"Let me call the hospital, and I'll get back to you."

"Perfect!" she said.

It wasn't a word he would have chosen.

Ever since Christmas, the thought of the amethyst brooch seemed to hover in his thoughts. Where was it, anyway? He felt a mild distress that he might have lost it. He hadn't seen it in—how long? Had he seen it since he moved here? Yes, he remembered thinking it should be taken to a jeweler and cleaned.

He closed his eyes, trying to visualize where he had put it. Why hadn't he come across it from time to time, if it weren't altogether lost?

He dug through the top left-hand drawer of his chest, where he kept things he didn't need but didn't want to toss out, either. Not there.

He opened his closet door and peered at the top shelves. Maybe. He took the chair that stood by the blanket chest in the hall and set it inside the closet. He took down several of the smaller boxes and put them on the floor by the bed.

Little puffs of dust rose up as he opened them, one by one. Christmas decorations from his last parish. He had searched high and low for these. What were they doing up there?

Buttons. An entire box of buttons. All emptied out of his mother's sewing-machine drawer. He would set them aside for Puny.

Then, the box of his mother's monogrammed handkerchiefs, her silver vanity mirror, a beaded evening bag, a lace collar, a hat pin with filigree work. There, too, was her gold wedding band, with a ribbon slipped through it and tied firmly. She had tied the ribbon herself, he suspected, when she had to remove her ring toward the end.

With the scent of age and mustiness, he also smelled her special smell; perhaps it had been gardenias. So faint, so elusive, it was scarcely there.

"Mother . . ." he said aloud, feeling an odd comfort in the word, the old familiarity of it.

He thought of Miss Sadie coming across the little socks and the certificate. Her departed loved ones seemed bent on speaking to her down the years.

Nearly six decades ago, Willard Porter had carved a message on a crossbeam of the home he hoped to give Sadie Baxter as his bride. Last summer, Miss Sadie had asked her rector to go look at the beam and tell her what was carved there. The legend he found was full of Willard's passionate belief that they would marry and that peace would reign in their lives at last.

Now, Miss Sadie's mother had spoken, helping her find Olivia. In his opinion, Rachel Baxter meant for her daughter to discover the certificate soon after her death. Why would it have been placed so casually in a dressing table, where a daughter would surely look when going through her mother's effects? Clearly, Rachel Baxter had tried to say, Run and find your sister!

What would his own mother say if she could speak to him now? He looked at the lace collar that she had prized, that had been so beautiful on her.

He realized his leg had gone numb, that he'd been sitting among the boxes for a long time. Yet, he hadn't found the brooch. He slid the boxes under the bed and got up, feeling as if his mind had gone away on a short trip and returned to find the surroundings oddly unfamiliar.

He got out of bed on Wednesday morning, feeling the same dread he might feel over an impending root canal. Two root canals.

At the Grill, he was inspired to order a treat that might help him go on with this aggravation.

"Two eggs, scrambled—with bacon and a side of hash browns."

Percy inspected him as if he were a sack of onions. "You sure about this?"

"Dead sure. I'm fed up with eating right."

Percy frowned. "Well, but just this once."

It was a terrible thing when you couldn't watch your own diet without the whole town jumping in to watch it too.

What he'd really like to have was a half-dozen of Winnie's fresh doughnuts, three chocolate-dipped and three glazed, which would leave just enough room to squeak in a napoleon.

"What're you dreamin' about?" Mule slid into the booth, looking dapper in a salmon-colored sport coat, which he had found last summer at Evie Adams's yard sale. Knowing that her dead husband was his exact size, he had appeared at Evie's door at six a.m., well before the crowd, and bought everything Barney had owned, with the exception of his shoes that were triple A's.

"You got your money's worth on that jacket," said the rector.

"Three bucks. You hear about the town museum gettin' started?"

"Esther told me about it yesterday. They're going ahead with fixing up the outside. Hope to have the whole thing operating full-scale in about two years. She said ask around what to put in it, starting with something historic."

"Put Percy's grill in there. That's historic," said J.C., who dropped his loaded briefcase on the seat and slid in. "Or how about his fry grease. That's even more historic."

Percy shook his spatula at the back booth. "Keep talkin' like that, buddyroe, and you'll be history your own self."

"Well," said the rector, "the mayor told me to make a list. What do you think, Mule?"

"Don't ask him," said J.C. "He's so slow it takes him an hour an' a half to watch *60 Minutes*."

"I got one," Percy called from the grill. "That bench in front of

Lew Boyd's. Been there long as I can remember. A lot of lies been told on that bench."

"Miss Sadie's car," said Mule. "That's about as old a car as you'll find on th' open road. Write that down."

J.C. poured sugar in his coffee and stirred. "Winnie Ivey's oil tank. Nothin' but pure rust, sitting' right on the street in plain view of God an' everybody."

"Somehow, I don't think this is going anywhere," sighed the rector.

"Yeah, well, leave it to Esther. She'll come up with somethin'."

He didn't mention it, but he thought the entire collection of his neighbor's books would be a splendid addition, in case they wanted anything current.

"Oooh," said Edith Mallory.

They arrived at the Wesley Children's Hospital, on a bitterly cold Wednesday, as the sun broke through leaden clouds and shone on the facade of the building. "It's a sign," said Edith, "I just feel it."

All he could feel was a vague gnawing in his stomach, which he reckoned was the beginning of an ulcer.

The meeting in John Brewster's office was worse than he could have imagined. After handing over the check, Edith told the director what color to have his office walls repainted and suggested he get rid of his furniture and start over. "Just because you're a charity," she said, sniffing, "doesn't mean you have to look like one."

John Brewster, whose cheerful personality appeared undaunted, took them to the cafeteria for an early lunch, where Edith cast a withering look at her vegetable plate, telling them how much she hated hospital food.

He was vastly relieved when John winked at him. *I can handle this,* the wink implied, *so relax and eat your tuna sandwich.*

There, thought the rector, *is a personality trait I desperately need to cultivate. Laissez faire! Easy come, easy go!*

The trip through the halls to visit the children, however, could not be taken so lightly. He loathed the way she poked her head in the rooms, looking at the children as if they were so many stuffed sausages. His own heart was breaking.

"Father!" Nine-year-old Gillian Murphy called him from her bed and stretched out her arms.

He stooped and received her hug as if it were a benediction. He was thankful that Edith and John continued down the hall, for tears sprang to his eyes and coursed down his cheeks.

"Blast!" he said, fumbling for the handkerchief he hadn't brought. "See what you've gone and made me do?"

Gillian looked at him almost maternally. "You're sad."

"No," he said, grinning, "I'm happy. You made me happy because you gave me a hug."

"You make me happy," said Gillian, whom he'd visited in this room since he started driving again.

"You look like an angel with that blue ribbon in your hair."

"Nurse Moody put it in. I wanted pink, but she didn't have pink."

"I'll send you a pink ribbon," he promised, having no idea where he'd find one.

Walking up the hill behind Edith in her expensive suit, it occurred to him that, in the language of Coot Hendrick, he'd like to knock the woman upside the head with a two-by-four.

He sat as far away from her in the car as he could. He would have stood on the running board, if cars still had such things. The sliding panel that separated them from Ed Coffey was firmly closed.

Edith studied her fingernails, which he did not take for a good sign. "I certainly don't think your Mr. Brewster was very appreciative."

"I . . ."

"It isn't every day, from the look of things, that someone gives them fifteen thousand dollars."

"You . . ."

"From the look of things, I doubt they know how to use it properly. Perhaps I was too hasty."

Rector Murders Woman in Car, Flees to New Jersey.

He would hide out at Walter's. They'd never find him in that basement room where his cousin kept the paint cans.

"Perhaps so, Edith."

"You know, of course, that I did it for you." She turned and looked at him. "That's what really counts. I did it to give you joy." She smiled then and opened her lizard-skin bag.

Here it comes, he thought.

She took a cigarette from a monogrammed case and held it between her teeth, grinning. Still looking at him, she flicked her lighter and inhaled deeply.

"Ahhh," she said, leaning back. Their compartment filled with blue smoke.

"Thank you, dear, dear Timothy, for the opportunity to do something for . . . for our God."

He could not speak.

"Oh, my," she said, seeing that her skirt had risen well above her knees. "How naughty!" She looked up at him, grinning again. "Do you think I'm naughty, Timothy?"

He would croak if he opened his mouth, so he kept it shut.

She moved closer to him and put her hand on his leg.

"Oh, my dear Timothy, if only you would let me . . . touch you. You would never ever again have even the weensiest doubt about your adoring Edith."

"Edith . . ." he said.

"Timothy."

Her hand moved again as she came closer, and he felt her breath on his cheek.

"Stop!" he cried, lurching forward and banging on the panel. "Pull over at once!"

Ed wheeled into the parking lot of the Shoe Barn, and he leaped from the car while it was still moving.

"I seen you pass th' school in 'at ol' car this mornin'."

"Yes. Well." The walk from the Shoe Barn had been wretched. Twice during the five miles he walked, Ed Coffey pulled the car alongside and called, "Father, Miz Mallory says you shouldn't be walkin' in this cold."

He never once looked around. If he spoke, he would vent the most wicked and abusive language he had ever imagined, much less expressed. No indeed, he would press on in the biting wind and no looking back.

"I thought you said you wouldn't go nowhere with 'at ol' witch."

"I did say that. But circumstances alter cases." He was struggling with an anger so black it made him tremble as he diced the eggs for potato salad. John Brewster would have to take it from here. He was through trying to be accommodating.

"It's m' birthday," said Dooley, looking him in the eye.

"Blast. I forgot. I didn't mean to, I promise."

"I was waitin' t' see if you'd say somethin', but you ain't said nothin', so I'm tellin' you."

"I feel like a heel."

"That's OK. I prob'ly ain't goin' t' remember your birthday, either."

"Please. Don't say ain't. Anything but ain't."

"You know what I want for m' birthday?"

"Let me guess."

"Twenty dollars."

"Really?"

"Jis' one big ol' fat twenty. No fives, no tens, no ones."

"And clearly no small change."

"Nope."

"Where do you expect it to come from?"

"I don't know. It's jis' what I want, that's all. I was jis' tellin' you, like you tol' me you wanted 'at world globe. I ain't—I'm not goin' to get you one, but I reckon it helped you t' tell me you wanted it."

"If you had a twenty, what would you do with it?"

"Carry it in m' pocket, wrap it around them two ones you tell me t' tote. I'd jis' pull it out and ol' Buster, 'is eyes'd pop like a frog's." Dooley made a face so grotesque that the rector nearly fell on the floor laughing.

"So. You want twenty bucks, but just to carry around?"

"That'd be cool."

"In the meantime, what do you want for your birthday dinner? I'll step over to The Local and pick it up. You name it."

"Steak."

"What else?"

"Ice cream."

"Steak and ice cream. No bologna?"

"I'm half-sick of baloney."

"Hallelujah."

"I wouldn't mind t' have some ol' cake or somethin.' If it was chocolate."

"I wouldn't mind to bake you one after we eat."

"Cool," said Dooley. "Can Tommy come for dinner?"

When Tommy left, they walked upstairs.

"Well, buddy, I'd like to congratulate you on becoming thirteen. Shake."

He had folded the twenty three times. Dooley felt it against his palm.

"Man!" he said, unfolding the new bill. "Neat!"

He had become an out-and-out sucker for seeing a smile on that boy's face.

The thought seemed to swim up from some dark grotto in himself, floating to the surface as he picked up the newspaper from the study floor.

His mother's brooch was in the lockbox at the bank.

As he carried it home in his pocket, in the blue velvet pouch, he knew at last why he'd been searching for it, why the thought of it had hovered around him for weeks. The truth was, he wanted Cynthia to have it.

Site of the Mitford
Town Museum

"What do you think?" asked Esther Cunningham.

They were standing in front of the freshly painted sign in Miss Rose's front yard. They might have been looking at Monet's water lilies.

"Beautiful!" said the rector, meaning it.

"Have you ever in your life? Why, they don't even have a town museum in Wesley! You mark my words, this'll bring their TV station runnin'!"

"As well it might. When do we see the statue?"

"Oh, law, that statue! It looks to me like his head's too big. I hope it's just me. But all in all, pretty nice-lookin' and costin' a fortune. Now, listen, Father, I know how you hate to raise money . . ."

"Esther . . ."

"Just this once, you could do somethin'. And I'm not talkin' about bakin' pies. I'm talkin' big money."

"Big money, is it? Why pick on me? What about the Baptists?

What about the Presbyterians? They could auction off another Cadillac."

"Shoot, they didn't raise the price of a used Subaru. All those people just swarmed in there to eat Esther Bolick's cake."

"Aha. Well, about raising money, here's my answer . . ."

Her eyes gleamed.

"I'm not going to do it," he said, standing his ground for dear life.

Esther laughed uproariously. "For a minute there, I thought I had you."

"Your eternal optimism is part of your charm. You persist in thinking you're going to nail me to the wall."

"Oh, and I will," she said, grinning. "One of these days, I will."

Lent would soon be over and the fresh hope of Easter upon them. Cynthia would be home, and the forsythia in Baxter Park would be blooming. He heard the Lord's Chapel bells toll ten o'clock when the phone rang.

"Hello?"

He couldn't precisely identify the sound at the other end.

"Hello?"

There was a long silence, then a sort of squeak. "Tim . . ." It was Cynthia, and she was crying.

"It's OK," he said. "Take your time. I'm right here."

He could hear her muffled sobbing, as if she were holding her hand over the phone.

"I'm right here," he said again, his heart hammering. Was she ill or in some kind of peril? Please, God.

"I . . . ," she said, then another pause. "I can't stop," she said. "I'm OK, it's just that I . . . can't stop." She didn't hold her hand over the phone now but wept unabashedly, as if the weeping were a language of its own and he would understand it.

"I'm so glad . . . you're there," she said. "I just can't do this anymore. It's too hard . . ."

"I understand. I do."

"I think I can't bear it any longer that you're there and I'm here, and all there is, is work, work, work and this . . . this horrid longing. And I know it's going to be over soon, but right now, it seems it will never end. And James absolutely hated the last pages of the book. I'm so angry with him. Why was he so busy careening around Europe if he's so vastly picky about it? Why isn't he here, giving me the kind of direction he's so good at dishing out at the final hour? And I know its wrong to say it, Timothy, but oh, I want to say it, I must say it, Timothy—I'm so very, very angry with you!"

He heard the fresh storm of weeping and knew it was coming from a place he had never touched or known in her. There was an intimacy in the way she bared herself to him, something so oddly intimate that he felt his face grow warm.

"Cynthia . . ."

"Don't . . . don't even speak. I knew I shouldn't have called. I knew I would be hysterical when I heard your voice. I know this is going to take until the end of April now. I won't be able to come home in March.

"Oh, Timothy, why aren't you here? Why aren't you here for even one weekend? Why must you be so tight and controlled and peevish about riding in a taxi or getting mugged or something? I think it is horrid of you, just horrid, horrid, horrid!"

"How long have you worked today?" he asked.

"Twelve or fourteen hours—I don't know."

"Have you eaten?"

"I ate some cottage cheese," she said. He thought she sounded exactly like Gillian Murphy, the day she clung to him and cried because her mother had missed the Sunday visit.

He felt utterly helpless. What could he say, Go wash your face, get some rest, and you'll be fine? He felt the agony of the distance between them in a way he hadn't felt it before. He knew he had denied it. He had never once really faced her absence. He had numbed himself to it. When he missed her, he had simply made himself busy.

"Blast," he said softly.

"What did you say?"

"I said that I love you, though I know you don't believe it."

"No, I don't! I don't believe it at all. I think you like the idea of being in love as long as I'm far away and can't be any trouble to your feelings."

"Cynthia . . ."

"There. I've hurt you. I knew I would somehow hurt you if I made this call."

"I don't know what to say. I . . . am the one who's hurting you, and I regret it."

"Oh, poop! Stop regretting! Don't fall into that bottomless mire of regretting. Just get up and do something, Timothy—I don't know what!" She sounded exhausted.

He didn't know what either.

He put the blue pouch in his breast pocket, though it made a slight lump.

The book Emma gave him for Christmas went in his briefcase, along with a change of socks and underwear and a fresh shirt, nothing more. If he looked like a hick, well then, so be it.

He told Emma he would be away for two days and turned his back on her before the grin even started spreading across her face.

"I'm going to see Walter," he announced to the bookcase, which was true. He would pop into Walter's Manhattan office for precisely five minutes, just to see the look on his cousin's face. He would be only too happy to dial 911 when Walter slumped over in shock, unable to speak.

Of course, he was insane to make the trip. There was absolutely no question at all in his mind, especially with Easter only ten days away and the preparations that had to be made. But how often did he do something insane, after all? The last time was so far in the past that it was no longer considered insane—now, half the population was doing it.

The thought of arriving at the New York airport alone, with only her address on a slip of paper, gave him palpitations. But he must swallow it down like a dose of bitters and get on with it.

"My, my," said Emma, her eyes glittering. She wasn't sure she could put her finger on it exactly, but she felt suddenly proud of her rector. He looked handsome, even taller, and—she had never thought this particular thing before—very distinguished.

He stood at the sink, washing the supper dishes, consumed with plans for her happiness.

He would take her to one of those restaurants in the book, one with four stars, certainly. Yet, if there was anything he couldn't abide, it was a snooty maitre d'—weren't you supposed to give them twenty dollars just for letting you in the door, or was it fifty? The very thought made his knees weak.

He wanted it all to go smoothly, right down to hailing a taxi. When it came to that, he could whistle as well as the next one. Hadn't he and Tommy Noles been world-class whistlers in Holly Springs, able to wake the dead a half-mile away?

He washed the hamburger platter and whistled as loudly as he could, just for practice.

He heard Barnabas hit the study floor running, scattering a braided rug to kingdom come. He skidded to the sink and stood on his hind legs, thrilled to be summoned.

"Here," said the rector, proffering a tea towel, "I'll wash and you dry."

Perhaps he should have let her know; he should have called to say he was coming, but somehow, he couldn't do it. He kept seeing her as she opened the apartment door and the blue surprise in her eyes, and he knew he wanted it this way.

That he made it to her apartment building intact gave him a great sense of triumph. He was trembling inside like a schoolboy as he took the scrap of paper out for the last time and looked at her apartment number, which, though he knew it by heart, he kept forgetting.

"May I help you, Father?"

It was the doorman, he supposed, all gotten up in braid and gold buttons. "I'm seeing someone on your tenth floor. I should have brought flowers . . ." He looked up and down the street, as if flowers might appear at the curb.

"May I ask who you're seeing on our tenth floor?"

"Miss Coppersmith. Miss Cynthia Coppersmith. I'm her . . . priest."

"Very well. I'll buzz you up."

They went into the lobby, where the doorman, inordinately well-dressed to be pushing buzzers, gave 10C a sharp blast.

They waited.

"Must be in the shower," the rector said, helpfully.

"I'm thinking I saw Miss Coppersmith leave early this morning, as I was coming on. I can't be sure."

The doorman pushed again and waited.

"Has the volume up on Mozart, very likely. Do keep ringing."

The doorman gave another long alarm. "I don't believe she's in, sir."

He had what his mother always called "a sinking feeling," as if some vital force went out of him, and he needed to sit down.

"Just once more, if you'd be so kind." He hadn't meant to sound plaintive, but there it was.

The doorman rang again. "Not in, I think. Perhaps having a bit of shopping."

He felt for the brooch, as a child might feel for a blanket. Then, he looked up and saw an elderly woman in a dark fur coat leaving the elevator.

She walked with a cane and was accompanied by a man in a uniform, who carried an aging, long-haired cat of considerable size.

He waited until she nearly passed him.

"Miss . . . Addison?"

She turned and peered at him, squinting. As rustic as he may be, he could tell that Miss Addison had enjoyed a number of face-lifts and was wearing contacts. Close up, she seemed at once forty-five and eighty-three.

"Yes, and who are you?"

"I'm a friend of Cynthia Coppersmith—my neighbor. Ah, your neighbor, to be exact."

"Lovely Southern accent. You're that father she's told me about, I presume."

He felt suddenly daring, expansive. "And what, exactly, did she tell you?"

"Oh, just that you're wonderful, among other things." She smiled a very sophisticated sort of smile, he thought. "I do hope that being wonderful hasn't gone to your head, however."

"Miss Addison, let that be the least of your concerns!" He had to restrain himself from giving her a hug.

"You've come a long way, I should think."

"Yes, very. Up before dawn!"

"Well," she said, leaning on her cane, "I dislike exceedingly having to tell you where she is."

His heart hammered. "Please," he said.

"She's gone home to Mitford."

CHAPTER TEN

Cousins

"Was he expecting you, Father?"

"Not in the least."

"May I give him your name?"

"Just say it's one of his Irish cousins. It's a surprise."

She smiled. "He hates surprises."

"I know."

"But I'll do it for the clergy."

"Thank you."

Walter opened his office door and peered out. "Good God!" he said, freezing in his tracks.

"Ah, and He is good, cousin."

"I can't believe it!"

"I can't believe it myself."

"In New York? Here? A country bumpkin, a bucolic rube . . . ?"

"A hick," he said, grinning.

They embraced heartily, Walter kissing him on both cheeks, which he'd once learned in France and thought a splendid idea. "There was a lot of backslapping and general punching about, like two boys," his secretary later told a friend.

❋

"This, Timothy, is New York!" Walter yelled above the clamor of the restaurant. He held up an enormous deli sandwich as evidence and bit into it with conviction.

"Powerful attorneys eat like this? What happened to nouvelle cuisine?"

"Completely out of fashion! Now, tell me everything. Why are you here? How long are you staying? I'll ring Katherine to take the Christmas ornaments off the guest room bed!"

He didn't have the heart to tell the truth—that he'd flown all the way to a place he never intended to visit, only to discover that the one he'd come to see had passed him in the air, hurtling in the opposite direction.

"It's like this . . ." He couldn't think of a lie if his life had depended on it. "I came to see Cynthia."

"That's the spirit!"

"And she wasn't home."

Walter suspended his garlic pickle in the air. "She let you come all the way to New York—and she wasn't even home?"

"She didn't know I was coming," he said, feeling miserable. "It was supposed to be a surprise."

"And you got the surprise."

Thank heavens, Walter wasn't laughing like a hyena. In fact, his cousin considered this piece of information very soberly.

"She flew to Mitford this morning."

"Rotten luck, old fellow. But Katherine will be thrilled to see you. You're staying the weekend, of course!"

"I'm on my way to the airport, actually."

Walter looked at him and shook his head. "I've known you for fifty-six years, and you never cease to amaze me."

"What's so amazing?"

"That you mustered the courage to come here in the first place— we know how disconcerting this sort of thing is for you. And that you came without telling Cynthia! Quite a romantic piece of business for a country parson."

"Foolish would be the word."

"Actually, I like my word, and I'm sticking with it. You've always been a slow starter, Cousin, but once you get going, stand back."

"There's a rye seed between your front teeth."

"You love her then?"

"What do you think?"

"Just answer my question."

"Yes. She's . . . good for me."

"In what way?"

"Oh, gets me out of myself."

"There's an accomplishment."

"Makes me laugh."

"Go on."

"I trust her. She's real."

"Like Katherine."

"Well . . ."

They both laughed then, with affection for the outspoken, salty-tongued Katherine.

"Not like Katherine, exactly," said the rector, "but in that league."

"The big leagues, then." After nearly thirty years, Walter still thought his wife the most compelling woman he'd ever known. "What are you going to do about all this?"

"I've never understood why people think I should do something about it. Isn't loving her enough?"

"Nope. That's the way it is with feelings like this. You've got to take them somewhere. They can't be allowed to merely dangle around in space. Ask her to marry you."

He felt his heart hammer.

"Either you're blushing or your blood pressure is going out the roof," Walter said.

"Sometimes I'm afraid to move forward, but I'm terrified to turn back."

"There comes a time when there is no turning back. You'll know it when you get there."

"Thanks for your understanding. Sometimes you can be rather . . ."

"A cad," said Walter, finishing his sentence.

"I love you, pal."

"And we love you, Timothy, and want the best for you. You know we pray for that."

"And please don't stop. I've got to get out of here. Which side of the street should I stand on to hail a taxi for the airport?"

"I'll walk you to the best place. Katherine will never believe you've been here. She'll think I'm hallucinating on the antibiotics I'm taking for a sinus infection."

"Is there a store of any kind nearby? A shop?"

"What are you looking for?"

"A pink ribbon," he said, feeling brighter.

When he turned the corner at Wisteria, he saw lights in Dooley's room but could see no lights in the little house next door. He had stood by for more than four hours, which he'd spent dozing in an airport chair, refusing to think of the precious time being wasted.

He felt utterly exhausted. "Lord," he said aloud, which was both an appeal and a thanksgiving.

It started to rain as he pulled the car into the garage. He could hear Barnabas barking wildly in the kitchen.

After receiving a good lathering about the chin, he went with Barnabas to Dooley's room and found him sleeping, the jam box going full blast. He turned it off, covered the boy with the blanket, and went wearily across the hall.

He felt the little bump in his breast pocket and removed the blue pouch and put it on the dresser. Then he unpacked his briefcase.

Why were there no lights next door? Was she sleeping? Was she, in fact, safely home?

He went to the window and looked out at her house. He saw a light come on in her bedroom, just before the Lord's Chapel bells tolled eleven.

He hurriedly splashed water on his face, washed his hands, brushed his teeth, and combed his hair, regretting every moment it took to do it.

The rain had become a downpour as he ran through the hedge and up her back steps, huddling close to the door as he knocked. At last, he opened her never-locked door and shouted, "Cynthia! Are you there?"

"Cynthia!" he called again, going through the kitchen to the stairs.

She appeared on the landing in her bathrobe, her hair bristling with the pink curlers he knew so well.

"Hello," he said, dripping on the carpet. There was a long silence. "You'll never guess where I've been."

"I can't imagine." Her voice was as frozen as the dark side of the moon.

"New York. I've been to New York. I went looking for you."

"You . . . were in New York?" Even in the dim light, he could see the utter astonishment in her eyes.

"It was supposed to be a surprise."

"I don't believe it!"

"Miss Addison invited me to lunch, but I went to a deli with Walter instead."

He saw a thousand fleeting emotions in her face, then she flew down the narrow staircase and into his arms, weeping.

In all his life, he had never had such a hug. It was as if his neighbor poured every power she possessed into it. He became warm all over and full inside. "Cynthia," he murmured, wanting to weep himself, but only for joy.

"I'm so happy to see you!" she said, sobbing. "I can't believe you went to New York, that you really did such a wonderful thing, and then . . ."

"And then you weren't there. I was . . ."

"Devastated! Exactly the way I felt when I came home and you weren't here. Dooley said you had gone away for two days to see your cousin. I had so wanted it to be a surprise! I was going to knock on your door, and you would come padding out from your study, and Barnabas would jump up and lick my face, and you would kiss me, and . . ."

"And I was going to knock on your door, and you would open it and be astounded, and you would know that I really do . . ."

"Do what?"

". . . love you. You would know it, then. I would have somehow . . . proved it. And you could be at peace about it."

She took his face in her hands and looked into his eyes. He thought her curlers had never been more beautiful.

"I'll never forget that you did this thing."

He kissed her. It was a long, slow kiss that penetrated some ancient armor. He felt the top of his head tingle, as if Joe Ivey had applied a lavish dose of Sea Breeze.

They sat on the bottom step, holding each other.

"I think the top of my head just tingled," he said hoarsely.

"I thought you were supposed to get cold chills on your right leg. It's me whose head is supposed to tingle!"

"You mean, it didn't?"

"I cannot tell a lie. It didn't."

He looked so crestfallen that she laughed deliriously. "Goofy!" she said, kissing his cheek. "My goofy, goofy guy!"

He called the office and told Emma he would be late. "Late? I thought you were in New York City!"

"I was in New York, but now I'm in Mitford."

"Well, that explains it," she said airily.

At nine-thirty, Cynthia popped through the hedge to the rectory.

He had laid the table for breakfast in the dining room, something he had done only a few times in thirteen years. On the other side of the window, the birds were at the feeder, and the sun shone warmly on every wet branch from the night's rain.

"Timothy!" she said, with something like wonder. "You've outdone yourself!"

And he had, rather. Grilled sausages from the valley, grits, an omelet with mushrooms and Monterey Jack, Avis Packard's home-made salsa, English muffins with a coarsely-cut orange marmalade, and coffee that was still in the bean only moments ago.

"I love salsa!" she said, helping herself after the blessing. "I love grits!"

His heart swelled at the very look of her; he was thrilled to see her eating like a stevedore.

She dipped into the salsa. "I've decided I'm not going to do *Violet Goes to New York*. James thinks I'm some kind of milk cow, I suppose, made to bring forth whatever strikes his fancy.

"Besides, I'm not going to work myself to death doing a book I don't even want to do. If anything, I'll do *Violet Goes to Mitford!* How's that?"

"Terrific! That's the spirit!"

"*Violet Visits the Parson! Violet Takes a Much-Needed Holiday in the South of France! Violet Gets Sick and Tired of Being a Cat and Becomes a Dog!*"

"You're on a roll," he said, buttering her muffin. "Best-sellers, every one!"

"Oh," she giggled, leaning back in her chair. "I'm so glad to be home."

"Let's go for a walk after breakfast."

"And see Miss Rose and Uncle Billy?"

"Do we have to? She was threatening cinnamon stickies the last time they invited us, or was it banana pudding? Well, at least we can see the new sign the mayor put up in their yard."

"Let's go shopping at The Local, too, and I'll make dinner for you and Dooley tonight."

"Excellent! I accept. And we can stop off and see the new kneelers at Lord's Chapel. But of course, you'll see them on Sunday."

The light faded from her eyes. "I have to go back tomorrow afternoon."

"No . . ."

"It's the revisions, you see. There's no help for it. This . . . my dearest, is stolen time."

Stolen time.

He took her hand and turned it over to see the small, uplifted palm. He kissed its softness and placed her palm against his cheek.

Stolen time.

He would willingly be the blackest of thieves.

He remembered a speaker at a seminar who had put five large stones in a glass. Those were the important things in life, the speaker said and went on to demonstrate how the small stones, or less important things, could easily be put in and shaken down among the cracks.

However, if the small stones were put in first, it was impossible to add the large stones.

He called Emma. "I won't be in at all, actually."

The last time he hadn't come in at all, she remembered, he'd been deathly sick. He certainly didn't sound sick this time. He sounded like he had never felt better in his life.

They were going out the back door when the phone rang.

"Father?"

"Yes, Evie?"

"Forgive me for calling you at home, Father, but I just had to ask . . . Can you, would you please come by for a few minutes?"

He could hear Evie trying to suppress the tears that always threatened when she talked with her priest.

"It's nothing really bad this time, it's just . . ." She hesitated for a moment, then wailed, ". . . it's just *general!*"

"I'm on my way," he said.

"What did you get in your stocking?" Miss Pattie wanted to know.

"My stocking?" asked Cynthia, who inspected her legs at once.

"She thinks it's Christmas," said Evie, helping her mother to the sofa, where she sat down, plump and serene as a cherub.

"We baked it all morning!" Miss Pattie exclaimed.

Cynthia joined the old woman on the sofa. "Really?"

"I baked, Evie basted. But we do our cornbread dressing separate. We don't like stuffing." Miss Pattie wrinkled her nose.

"Now, she thinks it's Thanksgiving," said Evie, looking desperate. "She likes holidays."

"Have a drumstick!" Miss Pattie passed a green ashtray to Cynthia, who stared at it, then selected something imaginary from it and took a large bite. The rector noted that she also pretended to chew.

"Delicious!" she said bravely, wiping the corners of her mouth with her fingers. "Just the way I like it! Juicy on the inside, crisp on the outside!"

"Not too dry, is it?" Miss Pattie leaned forward with interest.

"Not one bit!"

"I like the part that goes over the fence last, myself."

"Mama, for Pete's sake!" said Evie.

Miss Pattie turned to the rector. "Have some cranberry sauce, and pass it to your wife." She gave him a copy of *Southern Living* from the lamp table. "It's homemade, you know."

"Thank you," he said, handing the magazine to Cynthia as if it were a hot potato.

"Oh, mercy, I forgot." Miss Pattie lifted the hem of her dress and tucked it into her collar. "Father, would you say the blessing?"

"You're wonderful," he said. They had detoured to a bench in the bookstore garden.

"I am?"

"To eat the drumstick."

She leaned her head to one side and smiled.

"I thought," he said, feeling oddly moved, "that was the most generous thing I've ever seen anyone do."

"Wouldn't you have done the same?" He saw the laughter in her eyes.

"You know I wouldn't, and I'm less the man for it. But for you, it was . . . natural."

"Yes, well, you see, I prefer dark meat."

They laughed so hard that someone passing on Main Street looked suspiciously into the tiny garden.

"To tell the truth, I was frightened to death," she said at last.

"Whatever for?"

"Because I didn't want to embarrass you, or hurt Evie's feelings, or disappoint Miss Pattie. But I couldn't just sit there staring at that ashtray in the shape of a frog. So I ate the drumstick."

"Well done," he said, squeezing her hand.

"It's the first time I've been part of your . . . work. It was an honor, Timothy."

As they walked to The Local, he thought of the relief they'd seen on Evie's face and Miss Pattie sitting upright on the sofa, snoring peacefully. Yet, the visit had been nothing more than a Band-Aid on a gaping wound. He had always wrestled with the frustrating smallness of the things he was able to do. "Let God take care of the big stuff," a seminary friend once said. "It's our job to fill in the cracks. Kind of like caulking."

As they shopped for vegetables at The Local, Miss Pattie's singsong voice came to him: ". . . and pass it to your wife."

When Cynthia glanced up from the artichokes, his face grew suddenly warm, and he could scarcely look her in the eye.

She had made a superb dinner in his own kitchen. Dooley had eaten like a horse and, after washing the dishes at lightning speed, had gone to spend the night with Tommy.

Now they sat together on the sofa, holding hands and listening to one of her Mozart CDs on his player. Tonight was certainly not a night for the tango. Or was it the rhumba?

The smallest of fires crackled on the grate, and he thought how this very thing was what he had wanted all his life. In some unspoken place in himself, in a place he had never regarded or chosen to recognize, had been the longing to sit with someone in this inexplicable peace. He felt oddly complete, as if the final piece of a jigsaw puzzle had been slipped into place.

"How was it for you in New York?" she asked, putting her head on his shoulder. "Were you frightened?"

"Frightened? I was frightened of going, but once I got there, I was . . . almost happy, I think. Flying seems to be the worst of it, the taking off and the landing. But in the end, old fears passed away, and there was the good fellow in the taxi and Miss Addison and Walter. Miss Addison felt woefully sorry for me. She said that very thing had happened to her in Vienna."

"Really? Tell me."

"She went there as a surprise to meet her husband while he was on a business trip, and all the while he was flying to her in Paris."

"Paris to Vienna, New York to Mitford, it's all the same," she murmured against his cheek. "You're my hero."

He had been a lot of things but never ever a hero. He cleared his throat. "I don't think I'd like to do it again." He thought he should say that, just for the record.

"Did you see Palestrina?"

"The Barnabas of the cat kingdom! Large! She had it in for me. I could tell by the look in her eyes. I would not want to be in a closed room with that cat."

"Oh, Palestrina is all bark and no bite."

They laughed uproariously.

Ah, but it felt good to laugh! Why didn't he laugh more often? He had asked himself that very thing a hundred times. Well, and who would he laugh with? Not Emma! And getting a grin out of Dooley Barlowe was like looking for a needle in a haystack.

He drew her close and said, "I have something for you."

"A new joke from Uncle Billy!"

"I haven't had a joke from Uncle Billy in months."

"Well, then, I can't guess."

"I'll be right back," he said, noting that Barnabas helped himself to the warm place he left on the sofa.

When he came down again to the study, she had curled up with his dog, who was fresh from an afternoon bath. "If Violet Coppersmith could see you now . . ." he said.

"Cardiac arrest!"

He passed on to the kitchen, where he took a dog biscuit from the cabinet. "All right, old fellow, off with you!" Barnabas leapt from the sofa and dashed after the biscuit that had skidded under a wing chair.

Why did he have to feel winded from the stairs as he handed her the blue velvet pouch? Why did his knees creak like a garden gate when he sat down beside her? In any case, he thought her face lighted up like the bush he strung outside her door at Christmas.

"May I take my time looking inside?" She drew her bare feet under her and leaned against the cushions.

"There's no hurry."

She held the pouch in both hands, happily feeling the contours of what it contained. "It's the moon, I think!"

"Yes! You've hit it on the head. And the stars are in there somewhere, too—I collected them last night after the rain."

Sudden tears sprang to her eyes.

"Cynthia! Blast!"

"I'm sorry!" she said, laughing and crying at once. "I don't mean to do it. It's just that I love your . . . heart, Timothy."

She reached at last into the pouch and felt the brooch and drew it out.

"It was my mother's," he said. He had intended to say more, had in fact rehearsed a small speech, but it left him.

She held it in her palm and gazed at it, as if stricken, tears streaming down her cheeks. Good grief, he thought, would this never end? She was worse than the man in the attic, who had bawled his head off every time something touched him. Worse than that, weeping was nearly as catching from his neighbor as was laughter—he felt himself choking up.

"Cynthia, stop it this minute!" he said in a voice from the pulpit.

She looked at him then and laughed and touched his face with her hand and leaned to him, kissing his forehead. "Thank you," she said.

Later, he remembered that his mother had done that very thing—kissed his forehead and thanked him and wept.

They walked to her house, passing single file through the gap in the hedge.

"I'll see you tomorrow, then," he said on the porch stoop. "What time shall we leave for the airport?"

"No later than noon."

"Consider it done," he said, tracing her cheek with his finger.

"Bookends," she whispered, putting her arms around his neck. "You are the most beautiful thing I've ever seen in my life."

She gazed at him, the joy beating in her. "I'm not going to ask you to marry me."

It took a moment for what she said to sink in. He stood very still, as if moving or breathing would expose him, like a rabbit before a hound in the field.

In the glow of the porch light, he saw her eyes turn that mesmerizing shade of periwinkle. She smiled and said, "You'll have to do the thing yourself, my dearest."

"Aha." He thought she looked exactly as Violet might look when sitting at the edge of a fish pond.

Safely through the hedge, he discovered his circulation seemed to have shut down; he felt he had turned to stone. Marriage!

He carried the brooch upstairs, his mind crowded with thoughts. Why was fear always so close upon the heels of his joy, overtaking it every time?

He laid the brooch on the dresser, thinking of her reluctance to leave it with him to be cleaned and the catch repaired. She had at last relented, saying she would wear it always and especially for her confirmation at Lord's Chapel. He went to bed with the image of Stuart Cullen placing his hands on her head at the altar rail.

Lying there, he prayed for deliverance from his fear and confusion, ashamed that he could not do what others appeared able to do every day—take a stand and stick by it.

At midnight, he remembered that he still didn't have a title for his Easter sermon.

He had planned to preach "The Glad Surprise," for that, after all, is what the resurrection had been, coming as it did after the horror of the execution, a hasty funeral, and the loss of hope among the disciples.

On the other hand, "All for Love" contained the entire message of Christ's birth, death, and resurrection in a mere three words. That was the gist of it, the condensed version, the bottom line.

The issue of love, he thought, was surrounding him on all sides.

". . . and pass it to your wife," he heard Miss Pattie say in his dreams. ". . . and pass it to your wife."

After the mournful watch of Maundy Thursday, Mitford awoke to falling snow on Good Friday.

"What'd I tell you?" grinned Coot Hendrick, who was doing his part to steam up the windows of the Main Street Grill.

"Man," groaned J.C. Hogan, who despised snow and especially didn't relish a fulfillment of prophecy by someone with stubs for teeth.

Miss Sadie's extensive roof patching was finished, and the work in the ballroom went at a pace.

"Father," she said, ringing up soon after the ground had turned white, "what do you think of this snow?"

"I'm trying not to think of it at all!" he said with feeling.

"Louella bought a straw hat for Easter, but she declares you can't wear straw in the snow."

"Easter is not about weather. Tell Louella to wear her new straw. We'll be looking for it."

Miss Sadie turned from the phone and warbled into the distance, "He says wear it anyway, he'll be looking for it!"

"How's it coming in the ballroom?"

"Oh, Father! You won't believe how much it's costing. I nearly fainted when I heard what it takes just to scrape the window casings. I had to sit down—the room was spinning every which way. But I'm going through with it! Do you think the Lord will look on this as wrong stewardship, spending so much money on a room we probably won't step foot in again?"

"Miss Sadie, when you consider all those harpists crowding around in heaven, and the mansions and streets of gold, well then—I believe the Lord knows something about big doings, Himself."

"She's my only family, Father."

"Absolutely. I agree one hundred percent. Make that a hundred and twenty."

"I've never had anyone to do for 'til now."

"You can't take it with you, Miss Sadie, and I don't believe Lord's Chapel could bear the blessing of . . . your further generosity."

"Guess who I'm thinking of inviting?"

"I can't guess."

"Absalom!"

"Excellent."

"But his sister won't come. I'm sure of it. Wouldn't you think, Father, that a person who calls themselves a Christian would have forgiven and forgotten after all these years?"

"What makes you think she hasn't?"

"I asked Absalom when he was preaching at Lord's Chapel and you were in Ireland. I said, 'Absalom, has Lottie forgiven me for not marrying you?' I was very direct!"

"The only way to be."

"Absalom just shook his head, and said, 'No, Sadie, I'm afraid not.' I could see it troubled him. And I blurted out something I've been wanting to say for more than sixty years. I said, 'It seems to me she'd be grateful I didn't marry you, so she could keep you for herself!' "

"Strong words," he said, smiling.

"Absalom laughed, but deep in my heart, Father, I felt mean as a snake for saying it."

"Christians hardly ever live up to our expectations, Miss Sadie."

"I think you should know, Father, that I've forgiven her for not forgiving me."

"That's the spirit!"

She sighed, and he heard the rare weariness in it.

"It seems to me you could use a hug."

"A hug?"

"Have you had one since Sunday?"

"Not that I can think of, but the man doing the plasterwork shook my hand."

"I'll be right up," he said.

Miss Sadie leaned on her cane in the rubble of the ballroom and peered at him. "What about Dooley?"

"What about him?"

"Haven't you done your part yet?" she asked tartly. "You're supposed to do your part and be looking into schools."

"Yes, well, how right you are. And I haven't done my part because, to tell the truth, I hate the thought of sending the boy away. Now, don't flog me, Miss Sadie. I'm just telling you the way it is."

"I hope you don't mind my saying so, Father, but that is very selfish thinking."

There was a meaningful silence. "I'll do it," he said at last, feeling as if he had choked down a dose of paregoric.

" 'Love is an actual need, an urgent requirement of the heart,' " he read aloud from an old essay on marriage that he found in his files.

" 'Every properly constituted human being who entertains an appreciation of loneliness . . . and looks forward to happiness and content feels the necessity of loving. Without it, life is unfinished . . .' "

Barnabas dropped his head on his front paws.

Was it true that without love, life is unfinished? Without Christ's love, yes, no doubt, definitely. But the love of another earthly being? He had never thought his bachelor life without love was unfinished, but then, he'd had plenty of love coming from other quarters.

" 'The bosom that does not feel love is cold, the mind that does not conceive it is dull . . .' " His voice trailed off. Still snowing. Dooley studying. Barnabas snoring. The house chilling.

" 'What is to be sought is a companion, a congenial spirit . . . who, under any given combination of circumstances, would be affected, feel, and act as we ourselves would . . .

" 'This is a companion who is already united to us by the ties of spiritual harmony, which union it is the object of courtship to discover.' "

Already united to us by the ties of spiritual harmony . . .

What a man wanted at a time like this was a good pipe, but he didn't smoke. What a man might crave at such an hour was a dram of old whiskey, but he didn't drink. Then, the thing he yearned for most became plain as the nose on his face:

He needed someone to talk to.

Who would it be? Not Walter. Walter had already put in his two cents' worth. Not Katherine, who would give him a proper upbraiding for not having done the thing already.

He thought of Marge Owen, the first friend he had made when he came to Mitford. They had shared many confidences over the years, but he hadn't seen much of her since Rebecca Jane came to Meadowgate and Dooley arrived at the rectory. Besides, he knew precisely what she would say:

"Follow your heart, Timothy."

Blast it, that was the problem. One moment, his heart was filled with longing for Cynthia, and the next moment, the mention of marriage could turn it to stone. His heart was jerking him this way and that, precisely as Barnabas had done when being leash-trained.

What did he want to talk about, anyway? What was his question?

He sat at the desk in the study, staring into the hedge at the rear of Baxter Park, unseeing.

Could he love her fully, freely, without betraying his love for God? Wasn't their love, after all, *from* God? He believed this.

Well, then, how would marriage affect his ministry? What might be lost? No, he thought. That's not the question. Try this: What might be gained?

But he was avoiding the real issue, and he knew it. The issue was not love, nor betrayal, nor even whether his labors might gain or lose meaning.

The real issue was fear.

He tried to name the fear and felt the discomfort of naming it. It was the fear of giving in, of going under, of losing control.

He had made a full surrender once, thinking it the end of surrender. And now, this came, and he had to face it and be just with her and with himself. But was it too late for justice?

If they were to marry, what about his infernal diabetes and his set-in-his-ways sort of life? Could he even share a bed with someone after years of sleeping alone?

Another thing. It was no small matter that she confessed to sleeping with her cat. And did he not sleep with a dog the size of a sofa? And weren't cats and dogs natural enemies from the beginning of time? He could see them now, the whole lot of them, piled on the bed like so many coats at a party. One wrong move . . .

It was one thing to consider the broad view of marriage, as the idealistic essayist had done. It was another to think of the sore details, the nitty-gritty, the way things really were, day to day.

Yet, he knew that he wanted her urgently—her encouraging companionship, her bright candor, her grand good humor. He knew, too, that kissing her and holding her were often excruciating and made all the worse by his holding back and holding in and laboring to keep a wall of defense around himself, so there would be no spilling over like a bursting dam.

Yesterday, he and Dooley had bumped elbows in the kitchen, splashing soda from their glasses onto the floor. As they squatted down to wipe it up, the dark liquid of Dooley's Coke ran into the colorless liquid of his Diet Sprite. You couldn't tell where one began and the other left off. Was he willing to blend into the life of another human being for the rest of his days, and have her blend into his?

That, of course, was the Bible's bottom line on marriage: one flesh. Not separate entities, not two autonomous beings merely coming together at dinnertime or brushing past one another in the hallway, holding on to their singleness, guarding against invasion. One flesh!

If he could do the thing at all, could he stick it through? Would he be of one mind at the church altar and of another mind later? Could he trust himself?

The essay had called the power to love truly and devotedly "a sacred fire, not to be burned before idols."

A sacred fire. And if sacred, then durable? The word held a mild comfort. A durable fire.

Lord, take this fear and dash it. Rebuke the enemy who is the creator of all fear, and give me grace to be the man you've called me to be, no matter what lies in store. If I'm to spend the rest of my life with her, with this lovely . . . this gracious spirit, then open the door wide. Swing it open, I pray! And if this is not pleasing to you, well, then . . .

He could not imagine the other, could not imagine going on without her. Even in prayer, his heart was fickle and deceitful, turning this way and that.

With a bare two hours of daylight left, he fixed Dooley's supper, put it in the oven, snapped the red leash on Barnabas, and headed out to see Homeless Hobbes.

He hadn't talked with Homeless about much of anything, really, but he came away refreshed.

It meant something for a parson to have a place to go where no one judged him or asked anything of him or expected him to be anything special. They had sat together before the wood stove, contented with one another's company, each doing the other some profound good without even trying.

He was headed up to bed when he heard the antiquated blast of the front doorbell.

Barnabas dashed down the stairs and crouched by the mail slot, growling.

He had no earthly idea who the tall, bony, red-haired woman was who stood on the porch stoop, flanked by suitcases, squinting at him through heavy bifocals.

"H'lo, Cousin Timothy," she said in a throaty voice. "It's Cousin Meg from Sligo."

CHAPTER ELEVEN

Meg

Behind the bifocals, her eyes looked like the magnified eyes of a housefly that he'd seen on the cover of Dooley's natural-science book.

"Cousin . . . Meg?" He held Barnabas, who was still growling, by the collar.

"You know," she said, pushing her hair behind her ears, "Cousin Erin's tea party. You invited me for a visit when I came to America."

"Aha," he said, standing awkwardly in the doorway.

"We had a gab by the china dresser. You were drinking sherry."

He remembered Erin Donovan's notable family china dresser, but as for gabbing with anyone by it . . .

"Didn't you get my post a couple of months ago?" She seemed to loom over him.

"A letter?" A letter! On mauve writing paper. "Of course! Please . . . come in . . ."

"Could I borrow a twenty for the driver? Had to be fetched up in a taxi. I'll repay."

"Certainly," he said, digging into his pocket and handing over a twenty.

As she went off to the driver who was parked at the curb, he reached in the foyer closet and brought out the extra leash. He snapped Barnabas to one end and tied the other around the banister.

He picked up the suitcases, which nearly took his arms from their sockets, and set them in the foyer, then watched her walk back to the porch stoop in the glow of the street lamp.

A loping gait, he thought, with something tired in the way she hunched forward. He was reminded of a leggy cosmos.

"Cousin Meg," he said, stepping aside to let her enter, "welcome to Mitford."

She brushed past him in a trench coat that smelled of damp newspapers and peanut butter. "Good heavens, what a dog!" she exclaimed.

He closed the door and turned the lock, completely flabbergasted.

He had lugged the bags to the guest room and set them inside the door, then went downstairs to fix his guest something to eat.

"I'm starved," she said intensely, pushing her hair behind her ears. She sat at the small table under the kitchen window and peered into the empty plate. It might have been a crystal ball forecasting Russian caviar for the hopeful look in her eyes.

"Perhaps it will do 'til morning," he said, serving her a meatloaf sandwich that he'd made extra thick. She peeled back the bread and looked. "I prefer not to eat flesh foods, except on Sunday."

"Aha. Well, I'm dashed if I know what to give you, then. There's soup in the cabinet . . ."

"In a tin?"

"I'm afraid so."

"This will suffice," she said, taking a bite so vast that he turned his back to give her privacy for chewing.

"I'm trying to remember our gab," he said. "Let's see. I suppose we talked about Cousin Erin's china dresser that made its way to America, then miraculously found its way home again."

Clearly, he couldn't stop there, as he heard her still chewing. He stood at the sink and pretended to dry a dish that wasn't wet. "Perhaps you can give me some help on the family tree. We collected a lot of notes and papers in Ireland and stuffed them in a bag, and I'm supposed to make some sense out of it all. Frankly, I haven't opened the bag once and dread it like the toothache."

What else could he say? She wouldn't be interested in the Porter place museum, he didn't think, or the fund-raiser to buy special hymnals for the Youth Choir. He plunged ahead. "We'll have lots to discuss about Sligo, I'm sure. But only when you've rested, of course—I know how jet lag can fog the mind."

He turned around to find her wiping her mouth on her sleeve and having a draught of tea.

"Ah . . . how about another sandwich?"

"Right-o. Splendid. I'm famished."

He gave her the sandwich and hauled himself up to sit on the counter by the sink. "So, tell me, Cousin, how are we related?"

"Your great-grandfather and my great-grandfather were half-brothers, of course."

Clearly, she didn't mind being stared at while she talked with her mouth full.

"And Great-aunt Fiona," he said, "was in there somewhere . . . my grandfather's sister, I believe."

"*My* grandfather's sister," said Meg, gulping down a half glass of tea.

He hated losing Great-aunt Fiona to the other side, straight off.

"Your great-grandfather, Michael, married Glynis Flanagan, and they had Lorna, Fergus, Sybil, Tyrone, Cormac, and Lisbeth. Fergus emigrated to America when he was fourteen and later married Letty Noonan. They had Matthew and Stephen and, of course, Little Betty, who died at birth from the fever."

"Good heavens! How can you contain all that?" Perhaps if she stayed a day or two, she could make short work of the bag that sat on his closet floor.

"Your uncle Stephen married Katie Crain of Pennsylvania, who, they say, was a great beauty. Walter was their issue. Two years earlier, your father had, of course, married Madelaine Howard of Mississippi, whose great-grandfather served in the senate with Mister Jefferson. Matthew and Madelaine had you, and neither you nor Walter ever chose to carry on the family line."

Perhaps he only imagined that she said this coolly.

"My great-grandfather," she said, taking a large bite, "married Gillian Elmurry, who had Reagan, Fiona, Brian, Kevin, Eric, and Inis. Reagan married Deirdre Connors, and they had Allie, Meg, Nolle, Anthony, Stephen, Mary, and . . ." He thought she said Joseph. Clearly, it was a challenge to talk with your mouth full while reciting one's family tree.

"Nolle, as you may recall, flew with Lindbergh on several occasions, before he had Arthur, Allen, Asey, and Abigail.

"Anthony, of course, married Daphne, who had me. I was the only child. In an Irish Catholic family, a laughingstock . . ."

"So we are? . . ."

"Third cousins."

"I see," he said, although he didn't.

Perhaps it was because he had been up since five o'clock and it was now eleven, but he felt as if someone had just read him the entire first Book of Chronicles.

He cautioned Dooley when he came downstairs on Saturday morning. "There's someone sleeping in the guest room."

"I never heard s' much bangin' an' scufflin' around in th' middle of th' night . . . sounded like a dern gang of convicts was let loose in there." His grandfather made over, thought the rector. Dooley Barlowe often woke up as an old man, though he generally went to bed as a boy.

"Who's in there, anyway?"

"A cousin. From Ireland."

"Ireland. 'At's over there in Scotland."

"Try again."

"Somewhere in England, maybe."

"Check it out."

Dooley looked at the world globe on the rector's desk. "I was pretty dern close."

He walked to the office, oddly in step with the throbbing sound of machinery on the hill, and went through his Easter sermon twice. Orating to the rear windows, which showcased the branches of trees in expectant bud, he felt convinced that "All for Love" had been the right theme—he felt the burning fact of its rightness.

He called home at one o'clock and talked to Puny, who had come in to bake an Easter ham. She was shocked to hear there was anyone else in the house.

"She's in the guest room," he said. "Jet lag, more than likely. She'll come down before long, I'm sure."

"You want me to fix 'er somethin' to eat if she does?"

"She ate two meatloaf sandwiches last night and drank a half pitcher of tea, but I'm sure she'll want something before dinner. Oh, yes—she doesn't eat flesh foods except on Sunday."

All he got from the other end was a stunned silence.

At three o'clock, Puny called the office. "You better come home. Your cousin's still up there, and th' floorboards ain't even creaked. I knocked on th' door at two o'clock—that's long enough for anybody to be layin' in bed, if you ask me—but not a peep out of 'er. She must've found that key hangin' on th' wall and locked herself in, 'cause I tried th' knob, thinkin' she might be, you know . . ."

"*Mort?*"

"Whatever. So maybe you should come home."

Puny was waiting for him at the back door. "She came down right after we talked."

"Oh?"

"Wanted somethin' to eat. I fixed 'er salad and a roll, put it on a tray. She high-tailed it back upstairs, said not to look for 'er at th' dinner table."

"She's pretty trouble-free, I'd say."

Puny appeared thoughtful, or was it his imagination?

At six o'clock, he knocked lightly on her door.

"Cousin Meg?"

Silence.

Must have eaten and gone straight off to sleep. Jet lag could do that, and didn't he know? Arriving home from Ireland, his head had felt stuffed with sheep's wool. For another two days, he hadn't been able to think straight, and finally, it all ended with the odd perception that everything—and everyone—was more poignantly real than he'd ever known, as if a veil had been lifted from his senses.

After midnight, he awoke to a sound he couldn't identify. Barnabas pricked up his ears and growled.

He got up and went to the bedroom door, then stepped into the hall and listened. He would know that sound anywhere. It was coming from the guest room. It was a typewriter, thumping along loudly at sixty miles an hour, as if every key were a mallet pounding the floor.

A Royal manual, he concluded, or he'd eat his hat.

He went back to his room and closed the door. If Dooley could sleep through it, so could he.

All over town, green shoots poked from earth still damp from melting snow, and nearly everyone felt a shiver of delight at a certain fragrance in the air.

Easter morning had "turned off fair," as one villager said, and the various Mitford congregations poured out of church with new hearts.

On the lawn of the Presbyterians stood a wooden cross, massed with blooming vines, fern, galax, and woods moss. Dozens of potted white lilies lined the front walk of Lord's Chapel, and the Baptists draped their wayside pulpit with a banner proclaiming *Hallelujah!* The Methodists had chosen to peal their agreeable chimes at sunrise.

Uncle Billy Watson, according to the rector, had put the whole spirit of the morning in a nutshell. "I'm about t' lift off," the old man announced as he left the churchyard with a sprig of forsythia in his lapel.

Father Tim walked home with Dooley after the eleven o'clock, expecting to see their guest up and about. To that end, he had set the dining room table before the early service, using his grandmother's Haviland.

He found the ham sitting on the counter, loosely covered with foil, minus a vast chunk from one side. He looked under the lid of the green-bean casserole and saw that a full third of it was missing. A pop top from a Coke can lay in the sink.

He went up and knocked on her door. "Cousin Meg?"

No answer.

He knocked more loudly.

"Right-o." He heard the bed creak.

"Happy Easter! Wouldn't you like to have lunch with us?"

"I've had it, if you don't mind."

He stood for a moment, rubbing his chin. Then he went downstairs, wrapped the ham, put it in the refrigerator, and said to Dooley, "Don't take your church clothes off. We're going to Mayor Cunningham's family Easter dinner, then we'll visit your grandpa."

Dooley looked at him approvingly. "It's about time we went somewhere. We never go anywhere."

"There's a first time for everything," he said, admiring the way Dooley had turned himself out this morning.

"Good heavens, Timothy, who answered the phone while you were out? Tallulah Bankhead?"

"My cousin Meg. From Ireland."

"She doesn't sound terribly Irish to me," Cynthia declared.

"Schooled in America."

"Um. There for a visit?"

"Yes. She's a writer."

"Oh, dear!"

"Doing a book on descendants of the Potato Famine emigrants."

"Are you one?"

"No, but she says these mountains are full of them."

"How long will your cousin be with you?"

"I don't know."

"You don't know?"

"No."

"Oh."

"And how is the city?" he asked, changing the subject.

"Grimy. Intoxicating. Tedious. How's Mitford?"

"Quiet. Clean. Comforting. And a dash boring, to tell the blessed truth."

"Boring?"

"Because my neighbor isn't here. I haven't had a good laugh since she left."

She proceeded to tell him a joke so corny that Uncle Billy would have flatly refused it for his own collection.

He laughed, lying back against the sofa cushions, able at last to let go of the week and the intensity of the services and the glory of Easter, which always knocked him winding, somehow.

"There!" she said. "Is that better?"

"Infinitely." He felt the foolish grin on his face.

"At the end of April, I'm moving out, James is moving in, the book will be ready to go to press, and I'm coming home. For good."

"Are you sure?"

"Positive! You won't be able to run me off with a stick. Now— guess who's visiting *me*."

"Palestrina!"

"David. He's helping pack a few things, and I'm taking him to a play this evening. He's so handsome and successful and such a comfort to have with me. I look forward to the day when you meet."

"I look forward to it, also. Have a wonderful evening, and give him my regards."

"I will. And Timothy?"

"Yes?" His heart was full, yet oddly frozen.

"Philippians four-thirteen, for Pete's sake."

"H'lo."

She was standing at the kitchen sink in a faded chenille robe and scuffs, making up a dinner tray. Her mane of red hair was tied back with what appeared to be the sash of her robe. It would be a terrific stretch, but he supposed she could be oddly attractive if she would dress herself and quit hunching over in that defeated way.

"Ah, Cousin. How's it going?" He took his shoes off at the door, so he wouldn't track mud, noting that his radio had been tuned to a country-music station.

"Booming along," she said in her throaty voice. "You've popped home early." There was a Coke can on her tray, but whatever was on her plate couldn't be identified.

"And what did Puny leave us for supper?"

"Stewed chicken and rice."

"And you're having? . . ."

"Rice with raspberry preserve and cottage cheese."

"Aha."

"You may recall that I eat flesh foods only on Sunday."

He thought she looked like a stalk of Evie Adams's Asiatic lilies, which needed staking every summer.

"You'll join us for supper, of course."

She left the kitchen and started down the hallway. "Sorry, but I have momentum on the book."

"I thought you were going 'round and talk with people. Do research, you might say."

She turned and stared at him with her magnified green eyes. "That comes later, of course."

How much later, he couldn't help but wonder, eyeing the pop top she had left in the sink.

"Are you sleeping through it?"

"Sleepin' through what?" Dooley wanted to know.

"All that rumble in the guest room."

"What rumble?"

He supposed that answered his question.

"I hear you've got company," said Emma.

"A cousin. From Ireland."

"Umm. Nobody's seen 'er, includin' your house help. You'd think your house help would see 'er."

"Doesn't get out much, but she's going to. She'll be talking to descendants of Potato Famine emigrants."

Emma peered at him over her half-glasses. "Descendants of *what?*"

"How's Harold?"

"Grouchy."

"Whatever for? His wife is a fine cook with an income-producing job and the housekeeping skills of a barracks sergeant."

"I'm tryin' to make him sleep in pajamas."

"That explains it."

"Says he never will. Baptists are hardheaded, you know. Episcopalians sleep in pajamas, and so do Lutherans. I'm not sure about Methodists."

"You can never tell about Methodists."

"He says he's wearin' his birthday suit, an' that's enough for him."

"Maybe you should concentrate on more important things. What if you won this battle, only to lose the war?"

"Sometimes I don't have a clue what you're talkin' about—win a battle, lose a war . . ."

"Are you putting in a garden this year?"

"Harold is. I told him no more pole beans or I was leavin'. That garden nearly worked me to death last year. Came back from the honeymoon, had to jump in and go to pickin' beans and tomatoes and cucumbers and squash, then put it all up in jars. Harold won't eat anything put up in freezer bags." She sighed deeply.

"That Harold!" he said, in an attempt to be consoling.

At 11:15, the Grill was still quiet. Having had a meeting in lieu of breakfast, he was famished and feeling in the mood to sit at the counter.

"We got two choices on today's lunch menu," Percy told him.

"What is it?"

"Take it . . . or leave it."

"I'll take it."

"Better watch what you're sayin'. It might be liver."

"So give me a tomato sandwich on whole wheat, not much mayonnaise."

"Tomatoes ain't any good yet. Too early. I'd take th' grilled cheese."

"Too much fat. Let me have an omelet with mushrooms."

"All I got today is canned, no fresh."

"Plain omelet, then."

"I'm out of those brown eggs you like. White's all I got. Wait a minute. I might have some brown down th' hatch."

"No, that's OK. Too much trouble."

"Hold your horses. Won't take a minute."

Percy disappeared behind the grill, opened the hatch in the floor, and went down the steps where he stored certain food items. He came back up quickly and lowered the hatch door.

"Nope."

The rector scratched his head. "I'm worn out trying to get a bite to eat around here. How about a hot dog, all the way?" Live a little, he thought.

"My buns ain't come in yet. Be here any minute."

"Plain omelet with white eggs, and make it snappy," he said, feeling his blood sugar plummet.

"I'd sure like to hear a dose of scandal this mornin'," said Percy, taking two eggs out of the refrigerator. "Preachers hear scandal all th' time. What's th' latest?"

"Uncle Billy got a new jacket for Easter. First clothing purchase in thirty years."

"That news is too mild t' mess with. Keep goin'."

"Omer Cunningham's come back to town."

"Shoot, I heard that more'n a week ago. You're about as up t' date as th' *Muse*."

"Here's a good one. Homeless Hobbes has a dog."

Percy rolled his eyes. He could get better gossip out of a brick wall.

"It's a nice little brown and white spotted dog, but it can't bark. He named it Barkless. Homeless and Barkless, how do you like that?"

Percy thought his customer seemed thrilled with his dog story. "I had somethin' more in'erestin' in mind. Like, I hear you were out strollin' with your nice-lookin' neighbor before Easter. Velma told me this mornin' to find out what's goin' on or she'd bust."

The rector stared at the splatter board behind the grill.

"I figured you'd clam up. Here's your omelet. What d'you think?"

"Looks a little dry."

"Have some salsa," said Percy, shoving two jars across the counter. "From Los Angeles to New York City, salsa's th' latest thing."

"Which flavor?"

"Try th' hot. It'll roll your collar back."

He recklessly spooned the stuff onto his plate.

"Lookit this," said Percy, who took a napkin from under the counter and showed it to him. "Don't that beat all?"

He instantly recognized one of Buck Leeper's intricate doodles.

"Buck Leeper done that this mornin'. Looks like it was engraved or somethin'. 'Course, I couldn't tell you what it is if you held a gun t' my head."

"A chambered nautilus."

"Well, anyway," said Percy, "what am I supposed to tell Velma?"

He should have gone home, as originally planned, where the menu was more varied and nobody asked hard questions.

"What about you and your nice neighbor?" inquired Puny when he walked home from the Grill to pick up his checkbook."

"What do you mean?"

"I'm hearin' stuff."

"Stuff?"

"You know."

Barnabas sat down at his feet and peered up at him. Odd, but he thought he saw a questioning look in his eye.

"No, I don't know. Do I pry into your affairs with Joe Joe?"

"It seems to me you'd be proud to talk about it."

"Talk about what?"

"Bein' in love."

"Am I in love?"

"If you ain't, I'll eat your refrigerator."

"That would be a pretty sight," he said, tersely.

"I'm your house help. I ought to be one of th' first to know, don't you think?"

She looked so pretty in her green and white striped apron that he found it hard to refuse her anything. If he ever lost Puny Bradshaw, and the bright light that switched on every time she entered his house, he would be up the creek.

"Ah, Puny." He sat down on the stool at the counter, feeling suddenly deflated.

"I know how you're feelin'," she said.

"You do?"

"Pretty much."

"Well, it's good that somebody does. I hardly know, myself."

"I thought so."

"You did?"

"I'd give you a big hug if you wouldn't take it wrong."

"I wouldn't."

She came and put her arms around him and squeezed. He squeezed back. "You're the best of the best," he said, trying not to croak.

"Same back and ditto. Now, get your chin up off th' floor."

He laughed. "Consider it done."

Walking to the office, he felt that the eighteen-wheeler that had been parked on his shoulders for days had miraculously moved to another parking lot.

He couldn't figure what to do about Meg Patrick.

But why do anything, he wondered, as long as she wasn't a bother? He seldom saw her, and he closed his door at night to the thumping that sounded like a barn dance for field rabbits. Obviously, she was cleaning her own room, for she was no trouble to Puny. She was even doing her own laundry, he supposed.

It was a peculiar circumstance, but why worry about something that clearly wasn't worth it?

Emma answered the phone, then held her hand over the mouthpiece. "Whang-do," she said, looking sour.

"I'm not in," he snapped.

He got up and briefly stepped outside to avoid telling an outright lie.

Edith Mallory came in waves, like the ocean. Roar in, roar out seemed to be her style. If jumping from her moving car had not been a sufficiently eloquent expression of his feelings, what would be?

"She wanted prayer," said Emma, setting her lips like the seal on a Ziploc sandwich bag.

The last person on earth he wanted to pray for . . .

"Said she's got a lump." Emma drummed the desktop with her fingers. "I hope I don't get struck by lightnin' for sayin' this, but I'd like to give 'er a lump."

It was useful that Emma Newland sometimes expressed his true feelings, and he didn't have to take the licking for it.

"Yes. Well. I will pray." And he would. Right after he prayed to be forgiven for the smoldering anger that didn't want to go away.

"I heard you was gittin' married." Grinning, Coot Hendrick stood at the door of Lew Boyd's Esso, which, after all these years, hardly anybody called Exxon.

"Where did you hear that?" he asked, feeling the color drain from his face.

"At th' Grill." Coot was prepared to block the door until he got a satisfactory answer.

"Yes, well, I suppose they also told you that intelligent life has been found on Mars? Not to mention gas is dropping to fifteen cents a gallon."

"No kiddin'," said Coot, wide-eyed.

"I guess you also heard that Elvis Presley was seen shopping at The Local."

"Well, I'll be dadgum."

Coot stood aside, scratching his head, as the rector of Lord's Chapel strode through the door.

He checked Cynthia's perennial beds for signs of life, even though he knew it was too soon. Early April was still a frozen time in Mitford, and spring a full six weeks away.

No local ever put a seed or a plant in the ground before May 15. That date might as well have been engraved in stone, because every time he planted earlier, he paid the price.

Row upon row of impatiens, planted on May 14 three years ago, had ended up as watery mush at the border of his front lawn. A year or two earlier, he had tried to sneak by with planting fifteen cosmos seedlings on May 12, only to find them keeled over the next morning from the hardest freeze they'd had all winter. No, indeed, you did not mess with that date in these mountains.

dear cynthia,

nothing up in your beds, whats up with you? saw miss rose in a t-shirt from presbyterian rummage sale, proclaiming SuPPort WildlifE, Throw a Party. she wore it well. will be glad to see yr new book esp the zebras. all quiet here. dooley warbling like a bird in yth choir, though his voice is beginning to crack a bit and we are definitely in for a change. have started jogging again, as hoppy has come down on me without mercy, feeling stronger for it. are you doing the neck exercises we talked abt, pls do this / everyone asks for you, i pray for you faithfully.

Yrs, timothy

Dear Timothy,

I have received yet another letter addressed to me but clearly written to a distant relative. You are afraid, I can just feel it. You are afraid of your feelings, and if you think you are the only one who is afraid, you are wrong. I am terrified.

Why? Because I love you, and you are not up to it, after all, which makes my heart sink within me and leads me to believe that I have done it all wrong again.

I am closing my eyes and mailing this letter but forcing my heart to remain open.

Yrs
Cynthia

He sat at the desk in the study and put his head in his hands. Why had she insisted on bringing up the subject of marriage? Wasn't the experience of going steady still fresh enough to last for a while, to count for something?

She was a complicated woman, after all, with deep feelings and a sensitive spirit. And, for the moment, he greatly resented that.

Father Roland, the hopeless romantic, wrote to say he was leaving his large New Orleans parish and going off to Canada: . . . *to the wilds, Timothy! Yes, indeed, a parish of a mere one hundred souls, many of them lodging in cabins. Rather the sort of place I imagine Mitford to be. No more stress, Timothy, no more burn-out . . . just the call of wolves in the frozen night, and fresh trout, and time to seek refreshment of the spirit.*

The people are grand in every way. In fact, it is to their credit that I'm willing to take a compensation package that would make you roar with laughter, and which, I can assure you, will keep me humble. Thanks be to God!

A parish in the wilds of Canada. Now, there was an idea, if he ever heard one. And to think he was perfectly free to consider the very same thing.

But, no. Come what may, he was stuck to Mitford like moss on a tree.

"Doing her own laundry, I take it?" He was going through the mail that came to the house, looking for his *Anglican Digest*.

"Must be. Leaves th' washroom jis' like I leave it, clean as a pin. But it's creepy she's been here a whole week an' I ain't laid eyes on 'er. Only way I know she's up there, I hear th' toilet flush."

"That's one way," he said. "Next time you're upstairs, maybe you could bring down the *Country Life* magazine I stuck in the guest room for Stuart during the blizzard. There's an article I'd like to review for a sermon—about basket weavers. There's an intriguing dash of theology in basket weaving."

"I still cain't get in. Her door's locked tight as a drum."

"Aha."

"I hate locked doors. They git my dander up."

"Ummm."

"How's your neighbor? When's she comin' home?"

"End of April," he said, feeling a constriction in his chest.

"I'm prayin' for you," announced Puny, heading toward the dining room with a bottle of lemon oil and a dust rag.

The phone woke him from a light doze on the study sofa.

"Timothy?"

"The very same. How are you, Cousin?"

"Only just recovered from seeing you in New York, to tell the truth. Katherine says you must never do that again—I could have a stroke."

"Tell her not to worry."

"Once was enough, was it?"

"You might say so."

"And how are things with your neighbor? Rotten shame about your planes crossing routes in the air."

"Walter, do you remember meeting Meg Patrick at Erin Donovan's tea? One of the cousins."

"Meg Patrick. Meg Patrick . . ."

"Tall. A Niagara of red hair. Wears bifocals."

"Well, of course, *you* would remember all that, since you were only having sherry. Everyone else was drinking Irish whiskey out of teacups."

"You don't remember, then?"

"How many cousins were there—twenty-four? Thirty-two? No, I draw a blank. Why?"

"She's turned up on my doorstep, out of the blue."

"No warning?"

"Well, there was a letter some weeks ago, thanking me for inviting her. Blast if I can remember doing it. But . . . no matter. How's Katherine?"

"Volunteering four days a week. Singing to the elderly and can't carry a tune in a bucket—they love her. Doing art classes with handicapped kids and can't draw a straight line—they adore her."

He laughed. "Put her on. Then, I'd like to discuss a legal matter."

"Teds!" How many times over the years her voice had cheered him. "How are things with your neighbor . . . with Cynthia? We let you get safely through Easter without calling to find out, but now the jig is up."

"Katherine . . ."

"And don't play your cat-and-mouse game with me! Inquiring minds want to know, Timothy! You would not fly to New York if it weren't terribly serious—either a death in the family . . . or love!"

"Katherine, you're a nuisance."

"I know it, old darling. Now tell me everything."

"I think I hear the phone ringing . . ."

"Timothy, you are *on* the phone."

"Rats," he muttered darkly.

"From the beginning," she said. Hundreds of miles away, in a suburb of New Jersey, he could hear her settling back in the plaid club chair, putting her feet on the ottoman, and clinking the ice in her eternal glass of ginger ale.

He was in for it.

The statue of Willard, which he saw at the sculptor's studio in Wesley, was precisely as the mayor had said—the head was too big. He would never have spoken up if it hadn't been for the fact that Miss Sadie would pass the statue every time she went to shop at The Local.

"The head . . . is too large," he said in what came out as his pulpit voice. He didn't like to pass judgment on a work of art, which was clearly a subjective matter.

The sculptor walked slowly around the clay model as the rector stared at the floor.

"You're right, of course," said the sculptor.

There! What if he hadn't spoken? The size of Willard's head would have rivaled that of a Canadian bull moose. Miss Sadie would have been so disgusted with the whole thing that she would have done her food shopping on the highway, where making a left turn into Cloer's Market would be plain suicide—if she didn't die from eating their produce.

Uncle Billy had gone with him to Wesley but didn't say a word in the artist's studio. On the sidewalk, he took the rector's hand and shook it soberly.

"Rose'll be proud that you're lookin' after things, Preacher. I'll be et f'r a tater if that statue didn't look like a feller with a washtub settin' on his shoulders."

"What did you think," he asked Emma, "of the wedding on Sunday?" As for himself, he thought it fine and beautiful, and it had been grand to see his old parishioners and their daughter, who, though now living in Virginia, still considered Lord's Chapel their home church.

"Did you see that lizard pocketbook sittin' on that little shelf to the left of the altar?"

"Lizard pocketbook?"

"Stuck up there next to th' holy family like a sore thumb. Must've been left there by somebody doin' the flowers. I could not believe my eyes."

"But there was so much else for the believing eye. Sixteen in the wedding party—beautiful young women, handsome young men— and all glowing like so many candles."

"Just stickin' up there like a crow on a limb . . ."

"The trumpet voluntary was outstanding, every bit as good as some recordings I've heard. And the flowers—absolutely the most glorious flowers ever to grace Lord's Chapel, don't you agree?"

"It seems to me the flower people would have stepped back and taken a good look at the whole caboodle before they went rushin' out the door. If they'd done their job, they would have seen a lizard pocketbook sittin' on the shelf."

"The retable never looked more magnificent . . ."

"It's not even the *season* for lizard!"

"Emma, Emma, Emma." What else could he say?

He'd forgotten to take the brooch to the jeweler when he went to Wesley yesterday. He would take it today and pay a visit to the Children's Hospital while he was there.

Remembering that he'd seen a pink ribbon among his mother's things, he got on his knees and fished the box from under the bed. He rolled the ribbon up and put it in his jacket pocket and went to his chest of drawers to collect the brooch.

But it wasn't there.

"It was up there when I dusted," said Puny. "In that little velvet bag."

"Maybe I put it in my coat pocket when I went to Wesley to see the sculptor. What jacket did I wear?"

"Beats me. Try th' blue."

"That's the trouble with having too many clothes," he said sharply. He could remember a year or so ago when he had only two jackets. Now he had five.

Would he have put it in his pants pocket? But those pants went to the cleaners this very morning. Every other Wednesday, Puny Bradshaw bundled up the clothes he had been wearing and, whether they needed it or not, sent them to be cleaned. He argued that the English almost never have their clothing dry-cleaned, and she argued that not only was he not English, but sometimes he sweated, so that was the end of it.

He called the cleaners and begged them to go through his pants pockets the moment the truck drove in. To take his mind off a creeping anxiety, he went through all his suits and jackets, including those he wasn't currently wearing.

If Cynthia had once put her hat in the freezer and a quart of ice cream on the bed, who knows what he might have done while his mind was elsewhere—which it usually was these days.

When Evie Adams called the office at ten, he found himself wishing for a curate, a deacon, anybody. He had two meetings today, recklessly scheduled so as to disallow lunch, a hurried trip to Wesley that included buying two shirts and some poster paper for Dooley, and a visit to the Hope House site to see the progress they'd made in only a few days of good weather. Needless to say, there was plenty of work that needed doing on his sermon.

Evie wanted to know if he could come by as soon as possible, and this time he didn't ask what Miss Pattie had done now. He only wished again for help and then suddenly realized he was wishing for Cynthia. Cynthia would know what to do; she would take care of it and leave Evie with new hope in her heart.

Cynthia could fix things without even trying.

Cynthia could eat the drumstick, and he could not. No matter how hard he tried, he would never be able to eat the drumstick.

CHAPTER TWELVE

Faith Not Feeling

His feeling of panic had passed once before; it would pass again, he told himself. He must go forward on faith, not feeling.

He remembered, too, what Emily Dickinson had said: "The truth must dazzle gradually, or evermore be blind." After the trauma of being asked to go steady, hadn't he settled down and gotten used to the idea? Hadn't he been dazzled, after all, and hadn't it been gradual?

Well, then. He would put his mind to other issues, one of which was sobering in its own right.

No, he could not send Dooley away to school, because, Walter said, he was not Dooley's legal guardian. His heart had leapt up when he heard that.

"However," his cousin advised, "his grandfather can do it. Even though Russell isn't the boy's legal guardian, he is closest of kin, and it can be done on the basis of his verbal consent. It wouldn't hurt to have it in writing, of course."

Getting Russell to go along with such an idea would be one thing. Explaining it to Dooley would be another. And how would the boy fare among affluent kids who had probably never heard the word "ain't" in their lives and who thought "poop" was the latest news in the school paper?

Could he handle the English compositions, the algebra, the science? He felt sure of the algebra, with a little coaching, but the rest of it . . .

On the other hand, he could easily see Dooley scrubbed up and wearing a navy blazer—yes, indeed. And singing in some school chorale and surprising himself on the ball field.

"Be good for him," he said, pumping up for the task.

He called Meadowgate Farm and asked Marge to pray for this crucial thing.

"Ah, Tim. Isn't plain love more valuable than fancy education? But of course, we must let him go, mustn't we?"

"I think so, yes. Such opportunities are once in a lifetime. We're talking twenty thousand a year, here. Certainly nothing I could easily fork over, and clearly, no one else will offer to do it. Sadie Baxter is an angel with wings, a harp, a halo . . ."

"The works!"

He called Cynthia to discuss the school issue. He saw no reason to mention her last note, which boldly stated that he was not up to loving. Perhaps she was right, but he would forge ahead. Faith, not feeling!

"What are you up to today?"

"Taking Miss Addison to lunch at my café. She's never been to a café! She says she wants to drink strong coffee out of a mug and eat something hearty like a plowman's lunch. Why, she's never drunk out of anything less than Baccarat and Sevres in her life!"

"There you are, being a grand influence on yet another neighbor."

"Have I . . . been a grand influence, Timothy?"

"More than I can say." He felt a lump in his throat, for no earthly reason. "I needed your help yesterday."

"You did?" She sounded as if he'd told her some wonderful news.

"Evie Adams called and I went over, but my heart wasn't in it. I thought how you would have made things seem all right."

"But of course, they aren't all right."

"No. And won't be until Hope House is built."

"Do you think it's important to make things seem all right when they aren't?"

"Not always. But in this case, yes, very important."

She was silent for a moment.

He decided not to mention the brooch. It would turn up. Even if the cleaners couldn't find it, it would turn up.

He left the office much later than usual—it was nearly dusk—and saw Buck Leeper walking on the other side of the street, leaning into the strong wind that had been blowing all day. He thought the man looked utterly desolate; perhaps it was something in the slope of his shoulders, but he really couldn't say.

"What will we do? Carry him off kicking and screaming?"

"He wouldn't be the first boy carried to school that way."

"Not meaning any disrespect, Miss Sadie, but what do you know about boys being carried off to school?"

"Father, you do not have to be a villain to act one in a play, nor do you have to be a boy to know that kicking and screaming about private school is more rule than exception."

He pondered this.

She leaned on her cane and gazed at him steadily. "It was Mr. Oliver Wendell Holmes who said that a mind stretched to a new idea never returns to its original shape. That boy needs his mind stretched."

"Why are you so interested in Dooley's development?" He'd been wanting to ask that. At twenty thousand a year, he was curious.

"He's a diamond in the rough, clear as day. My father was, and so was Willard Porter. They both made something of themselves, with no help from anybody. I'd like to see what happens when help comes to a boy who's rough as a cob yet loaded with possibilities."

"Miss Sadie, isn't this like what Uncle Haywood did to you? He convinced your parents to send you to a fancy school in a foreign country, and you hated every minute of it. A fancy school, no matter where it is, will be like a foreign country to Dooley Barlow. Actually, he'll go there speaking a foreign language, if you know what I mean."

"Uncle Haywood thought a fancy school was the right credential for catching a husband," she said crisply. "It had nothing to do with stretching my mind with new ideas!"

More than seventy years later, the very mention of Uncle Haywood was still distasteful to Miss Sadie. She made a face like she'd just eaten a persimmon.

Dooley looked up from his homework at the desk in the study. "I seen that woman today. I come up th' steps and she was in th' hall closet, gittin' an armload of toilet paper."

"Aha."

"Seen me, went back to her room, locked th' door."

"Ummm."

"Got some eyes, ain't she?"

"Green, I think. We need to have a talk."

"When?"

"Oh, soon, I guess." Not now. Not tomorrow. Not necessarily next week or the week after that. But . . . soon.

"What about?" Dooley stared at him, expressionless.

"Oh, this and that."

"I ain't done nothin'."

He sat on the edge of the desk. "Haven't done anything."

"That's what I said."

"Well, then, there's nothing to worry about. Not a thing. Just a talk, that's all."

"Anyway, I ain't smoked but two. Buster Austin sucked down a whole pack."

Rats! He didn't want to know that. "Really?"

"He's th' one stole 'em, not me. Me an' Tommy stood across th' street while he done it."

No, he didn't want to know any of this. But here it was, and he'd have to deal with it, which would result in another kind of talk, entirely.

Dooley dived into the pause to change the subject. "You git me them shirts?"

"I did. No plaid. Just blue."

"Where're they at?"

"Your prepositions dangle terribly," he said, quoting Cynthia Coppersmith.

Those boys in their navy blazers would make chopped liver out of this kid; if he made it through alive, it would be a blasted miracle.

He thought his words had sunk in during their talk at breakfast, but he couldn't be sure.

Hadn't he smoked a few cigarettes in his time? He and Tommy Noles had nearly burned the Noles's barn down, but, thanks be to God, they'd put the fire out by flinging themselves onto the smoldering hay and rolling in it.

They had shoved the blackened hay under the pile in the rear loft, and he'd gone around with singed hair for weeks, his father peering at him in his strangely abstracted way.

Stealing, however, was another thing. Hanging out with a boy who was not only smoking but stealing into the bargain—this was serious business. He hoped he had made his point and that it had been well-taken. Sometimes, talking to Dooley Barlowe was like talking to a fence post.

He was glad it was Emma's day off when Mitford Blossoms made a delivery. Jena Ivey knocked on his office door and stepped inside, carrying a long box.

"Good morning, Father!" He could see the mischief in her eyes as she held it out to him. "Your birthday isn't 'til June, so it must be something really special."

"Aha." He looked at the box as if it contained a set of barbecue tongs.

"They're my best, Father. I know how picky you are about roses."

He should have felt delighted, he thought. Instead, he felt interrupted. "Thanks, Jena. Well, then, see you later. I know how it is when there's no one to mind the store." He held the door open for her.

"Don't you want to peep in before I go?" Jena liked a chance to see the look on people's faces when they received flowers from her shop. " 'Course, you don't have to read the card 'til I leave."

Obliging, he lifted the lid and stared with spontaneous admiration at the dozen roses. They appeared to have come from a country garden only minutes ago—in fact, morning dew still clung to their petals.

"Sprayed with mineral water," Jena said proudly, reading his mind. "What do you think?"

"I think you're the best florist in these mountains—no contest."

She looked disappointed. "Somebody once said the East Coast."

"The East Coast, then! I'm sure of it." He gave her a hug, knowing that his Sunday-school supervisor thrived on hugs.

"Well, enjoy the roses, Father. We're sure loving Dooley's contribution to the choir! Having him, I think we can build something wonderful over the next couple of years."

The next couple of years? He nodded bleakly.

She stepped out to the sidewalk. "Do you need a vase? I can run across the street and bring you one."

"No, thanks. I have just the thing." He called after her as she hurried away, "God bless you! Thank you!"

The roses had already begun to change the very air in the room with their subtle freshness.

He set the box on his desk. All his life, he had been a fool for roses, and she knew it. Perhaps she had been thinking of him as he had been thinking of her, both of them frightened in their own ways, for their own reasons.

He remembered the plaintive way she had said, "Have I been a good influence?"

Well, of course, she had. She deserved a medal for even recognizing his existence. What was he, after all, when you came down to it, but a country parson? Not tall and trim and debonair like Andrew Gregory, who owned a closetful of cashmere jackets, could speak Italian, French, and a bit of Russian, and drove a Mercedes the size of a German tank.

That she would wear a path through their hedge was wonder enough. But to love him into the bargain? That was supernatural.

He put the roses in the vase, stem by stem, and set it on top of the file cabinet, where the morning sun rimmed their petals with a bright glow.

It was as if a light had come on in the room.

He stopped by the rectory after a noon meeting and found a note from Meg Patrick on the kitchen counter: *C Cpersmth rang.*

He put Barnabas on the red leash and hurried to the office, thinking how he didn't deserve the roses, not at all. He didn't deserve anything from her, not even the consolation of her voice.

What was wrong with him, anyway, to have thought he loved her, to have felt the certainty of loving her—only to have this frozen impotence grip him?

He had the image of one of Hal's Guernsey cows going up against the new electrical fencing and stumbling back, dazed. The mention of marriage was for him an electrical fence; it was a barrier with its own raw shock through which he could not force himself to go.

Why was he, after all, fearful of marriage? He trusted her completely not to make a fool of him, or wound his pride, or do some sort of damage that he couldn't foreknow.

The trouble was, he kept making a fool of himself, wounding his own pride, and doing his own damage—which always included disappointing her.

When he talked with Katherine on the phone, he had fought to keep his concerns to himself. But, little by little, like grinding a kernel of corn to a fine powder, she had got it out of him.

"Teds, fear is not of the Lord. You know that."

"I know that."

"So who do you think it's of?"

"The Enemy, of course."

"Bingo! If this weren't right in God's opinion, he would put sensible caution in your heart, not paralyzing fear. But until you have peace about it, it can't be right—no matter how right it all looks on the surface. And believe me, it looks very right . . . at least for you. I don't know about her, of course, but she could probably do a great deal better."

"I don't deserve her honesty," he said.

"Well, of course you don't. You hardly deserve the time of day from her the way you keep yanking her feelings around. But it seems to me this relationship is grace, if it's anything at all, so what's to deserve? The good Lord plunked her down practically on your doorstep, while the single people I've talked with at church go scrambling over hill and dale just to find a dinner companion!"

Katherine could give you an earful, all right.

"I definitely think you should stop moaning about how you don't deserve this or that. Men who're scared silly always say that, thinking they sound gallant or modest. Well, they don't. They sound pompous and artificial."

"Katherine, is this friendly counseling or a bloodletting?"

"You wanted the truth. And the other thing I think is, you need to get out of this retreat mode. Tell her you needed time with the idea of going steady, and you need time with this. Why back off when she's not pushing you? She didn't even ask you to marry her!"

"Yes, well." It was true. Cynthia hadn't asked him, but the implications were . . . numbing.

"Maybe I should go into the city and take her to lunch."

Good grief! "Please," he implored, "don't even think such a thing." If he thought he was in trouble now . . .

Hoping to improve his heart rate before he made the call, he ran in place in front of his desk, causing the old building to rumble on its moorings. He thought it sounded like Meg Patrick composing an index to her book.

Stop saying I don't deserve . . .

Ask for time . . .

But first, thank her for the roses . . .

He had broken a light sweat when he sat down and dialed her number.

"Hello?"

"Cynthia?"

"Timothy?"

"Yes."

"What's . . . up?" she asked.

"Oh, lots of things. A few green leaves on your double hollyhocks . . ."

"I spoke to your cousin earlier."

"Aha."

"She sounds quite . . . settled in."

"Yes."

There was a pause that he wanted to dive into but couldn't.

"You're out of breath," she said.

"I've . . . been running."

"Oh."

". . . to thank you for the roses. They're even lovelier than the ones you sent before. I . . . can't tell you how . . . I hardly know what to say . . ." He desperately wanted to say he didn't deserve them, for that was the complete and utter truth.

"Cynthia, you are . . . so gracious and thoughtful, always . . ." He could hardly bear to go on. Why had he forgotten to pray before he called? He was positively babbling. ". . . and so, I thank you again and again. They have transformed this room . . ."

There was an empty silence on the other end.

"Cynthia? Are you there?"

"Timothy," she said in a voice he hardly recognized. "I didn't send you roses."

"You . . . ?"

"The thought wouldn't have occurred to me," she said in that unfamiliar voice.

He was aware only that his chest hurt.

"Nor will it ever occur to me, Timothy."

After the click and the dial tone, he sat at his desk in an agony he could hardly endure.

The Lord's Chapel bells chimed two o'clock. He had never heard them sound so mournful, as if they were ringing for the dead.

Dazed, he reached into his pocket and removed the small florist's envelope that he'd wanted to save until evening. He drew out the card and read:

> *Lump benign.*
> *Your prayers worked, as always.*
> *Love, Edith*

Dooley had wolfed down his dinner and run upstairs to his homework, leaving the rector to eat alone at the kitchen counter. He hadn't knocked on the guest room door and offered a bite of dinner—frankly, he'd forgotten that anyone else was in the house.

He went to the study and crashed on the sofa, the pain still gripping his chest, when he heard the toilet flush. Immediately afterward, he heard the typewriter.

Thumpetythumpetythumpthumpthump . . .

She was starting early tonight, about five hours early, by his calculations. Perhaps she was coming out of whatever jet lag she had suffered and returning to a normal schedule. Why jet lag would persist for more than two weeks, he didn't have a clue. Perhaps there was a complication because of some medication she was taking.

Thumpetythumpthumpthumpthumpety . . .

Where was the blasted thing sitting, anyway? On the little desk he had inherited with the rectory? Or on the floor? It sounded like she was typing on the floor, which was enough right there to injure someone's back and keep them bedridden for days.

At seven-thirty, Dooley apparently finished his homework and turned on the jam box.

Boomboomboometyboomboomboomthumpetythumpthumpetythump . . .

Barnabas stood at the foot of the stairs, howling, while the rector sat on the sofa, frozen.

His sandwich had turned to a rock in his digestive system.

He stared at the wooden tray in his lap and the stationery on which he'd written two words.

Dear Cynthia . . .

"Cousin Meg!" At nine o'clock, he banged on the door like a federal agent, striving to be heard over the din.

"What is it?" she finally answered.

"Come to the door, please. I'd like to have a word with you."

There was a long pause. "Right-o."

After what seemed an eternity, she opened the door a full two inches and pressed her face to the opening. "What is it?" she said in the voice that slightly resembled the lower octaves of a French horn.

"I must tell you that your typewriter sounds like a construction crew working up here. Could you move it onto another surface, please?"

"Right-o," she said, shutting the door.

"Whoa! Wait up. Open the door!"

She turned the knob and peered through the crack.

"Look here. I think you need to be getting around, getting some fresh air. I've had an idea. I'll wake you at six in the morning and we'll have breakfast at our Grill on Main Street. You'll meet a lot of interesting people, very likely some Potato Famine descendants. No need to dress. It's casual."

He turned on his heel toward the stairs.

"I can't possibly. I have a schedule I must keep to," she called after him.

He didn't turn around. "Haven't we all? I expect you to be dressed and ready at seven—I'll knock at six."

When he knocked, she didn't answer.

"Cousin Meg!" He could wake the dead when he put his mind to it.

He heard the bedsprings creak. "It's six o'clock!" he shouted. "I'll fetch you at seven!"

Silence.

He'd just looked in the refrigerator and found the squash casserole that Puny had made for the weekend. It appeared that a family of raccoons had gotten hold of it. Worse than that, her fresh lemon curd had been reduced to leftovers.

At seven o'clock, he was knocking again.

No answer.

"Cousin Meg! Either you come out or I'm coming in!" Blast if the words didn't roll out of their own accord, and he meant every one of them.

He heard her stomp across the floor as if she were wearing combat boots.

She opened the door and slipped through sideways, then closed it, locked it, and dropped the key in her pocket.

"Good morning, Cousin," she said, pushing her hair behind her ears.

On the sidewalk at the Grill, they met Buck Leeper. "Mr. Leeper, my cousin, Meg Patrick."

"Pleased," she said, thrusting her hands into the pockets of her trench coat.

The Hope House superintendent nodded and flipped his cigarette over the curb. "Miss Patrick."

"Things are looking good on the hill," said the rector.

"Not good enough."

Leeper sauntered through the door ahead of them and went to his table at the window.

The rector greeted the Collar Button and Irish Woolen crowd who were sitting at the counter. He felt every head in the place turn as they walked to the rear booth.

After Velma poured their coffee, Percy came around, wide-eyed with curiosity. "Percy, meet my cousin, Meg Patrick. From Ireland."

"Ireland, is it?" Percy peered into the booth as if into a cage containing a rare panda. "Mule Skinner claims t' be Irish."

"We're distantly related to Skinners," she said, adjusting her bifocals. "Very distantly."

"This one ain't so distant. Here he comes now. How d'you like your eggs?"

"Fried," she said, "and a broiled tomato."

"A what?"

"A broiled tomato." Saying "tomahto" did not cut it with Percy Mosely.

"Grits or hash browns is all we got." Percy appeared to say this through his teeth.

"Are your hash browns freshly peeled and cut, or are they ... packaged?"

Father Tim stirred his coffee, though there was nothing in it to stir.

"Packaged, like every other hash brown from here t' California."

"Is your cooking oil saturated?"

"You better believe it."

"Just eggs, thank you, and whole-wheat toast. Unbuttered."

"Better have you some of Percy's good sausage t' go with that," said Mule, slipping into the booth.

Please don't say it, thought the rector. But, of course, she did.

"I eat flesh foods only on Sunday."

Percy Mosely would not let him forget this anytime soon.

Puny stopped by the office the next morning to pick up her check. "Here," he said, handing her the vase full of roses, "take these home."

"Law, they're beautiful! Who give you these?"

"Whang-do."

"Whang-*who?*"

He didn't answer.

"Sometimes, I don't know what you're talkin' about."

"You aren't the only one," he said.

She thought she'd never seen such a strange look on his face.

Where was the brooch? The cleaners hadn't turned it up. He had searched the entire room, including the closet, on his hands and knees, not to mention every pocket and drawer.

It was maddening. After all, if something so important could slip away so easily, what else might disappear or run to neglect because of his carelessness? There was the rub.

He was finding scant peace in his own home these days.

Puny was cleaning every blind, curtain, cornice, and shade on the premises, so the rectory could hardly be visited for lunch.

Half the seventh grade was ringing his phone in the evenings to get Dooley's help with their math homework.

And last, but certainly not least, his cousin had turned his home into a hotel, with food vanishing as if into a bottomless pit.

He could remember the time when there was no one here but himself, when the very ticking of the clock could be heard.

Who could hear a clock tick above the din of a Royal manual, a jam box with twin speakers, a vacuum cleaner, a washing machine, a ringing phone, and a toilet that flushed over his head every time he tried catching a nap on the sofa?

It occurred to him that all the people coming and going under his roof, other than himself, were redheads. He wondered if that could have anything to do with it.

"We are not necessarily doubting," said C. S. Lewis, "that God will do the best for us; we are wondering how painful the best will turn out to be."

He had spent an hour on his knees, asking for the best, believing in the best, thanking God in advance for the best. No, he didn't doubt that God would do the best for her and for him. But yes, he was wondering how painful the best might be.

At the office, he typed a note to go out with the morning mail.

Dear cynthia

flowers were thankoffering from parishioner who tho't she might have cancer, asked for prayer, and discovered all is well. sorry for mix-up.

i know this is a distant relative note but am meeting with adult sunday school teachers in five mins. Will write long letter soon.

He stared at what he had written and then typed:

I think of you.

Not knowing what else to say, he took the note from his typewriter and signed it by hand.

With love,
Timothy

He didn't add that no one had ever hung up on him before.

"Knock, knock!" said Puny, pushing the door open. "I had to go to Th' Local to git cornmeal. I'm bakin' you a cake of cornbread tonight."

"Hallelujah!" Puny allowed him this sterling indulgence once a month. Golden brown, steaming on the inside and crying out for butter, Puny Bradshaw's cornbread could win a blue ribbon at the state fair.

"I want to ask you somethin'." She sat on the visitors' bench, holding the grocery bag in her lap.

"Shoot."

"You know I said th' washroom always looks jis' like I leave it? That's 'cause it *is* like I leave it. Your cousin ain't usin' it." She raised her eyebrows and looked at him.

"Ummm."

"The question is, three weeks on th' same sheets? An' how many changes of underwear do you reckon she *has* in there, anyway?" From the look on her face, the thought was appalling.

"Well . . ."

"An' when does she bring 'er dishes down, for another thing?"

"The middle of the night?"

"I suppose you know she shoves 'em in the dishwasher whether th' stuff in there is clean or dirty. I found a clean load settin' in there with a dirty plate an' glass an' silverware."

"Ah," he sighed.

"For another thing, where does she empty 'er wastebasket?"

"Good question. I don't know."

"Not in th' bag under the sink, I can tell you that. An' not in th' garbage cans in th' garage."

She let him ponder that.

"I'm makin' you a nice, lean roast tonight, an' I intend to stay there 'til you git home, or there might not be a bite left, if you git my meanin'."

He hated to say it. "Don't worry. She eats flesh foods only on Sunday."

Puny shook her head, disgusted.

He might have walked into a graveyard for the odd silence that hung over the Grill on Wednesday morning.

Over the years, he'd gotten used to the noise in the place, hardly noticing it. Now, he noticed the lack of it.

He was ready for Percy to give him plenty of heat about his cousin, but Percy looked up from taking an order and didn't even acknowledge that he'd come in.

He sat in the rear booth, strangely anxious. Yesterday morning, he had breakfast with Dooley, skipping the Grill. What had he missed? Was something going on that he hadn't heard about?

He turned around and looked at the door. Where was Mule? Where was J.C.? He heard only forks against plates and shoe leather against bare floors, as if the Grill were observing a wake.

Velma poured his coffee, wordless.

"Has somebody . . . died?"

"I wish," she said curtly, taking the pot to a nearby table.

He might have been a tourist for all they cared.

J.C. slammed into the booth, throwing his briefcase in the corner. He thought how the editor's red face was not a good sign along with sixty pounds of extra weight. "I hope you been on your knees," he growled.

"About what?"

J.C. stared at him, wide-eyed. "You don't know what's goin' on?"

"I don't have a clue."

"Edith Mallory has stuck it to Percy with a hoe handle." He wiped his perspiring face with a much-used handkerchief. "That's who owns this place, in case you didn't know. Kicked up his rent . . ."

"How much?"

"Double, can you believe it? Nobody in this town goes up double."

"What does double mean?"

"Double means highway robbery—better'n two thousand bucks a pop. The only way Percy can swing a rent like that is to raise prices on the menu. You wanna pay four bucks for a poached banty egg on toast? This crowd'll never go for it. Mack Stroupe is circling like a vulture, even as we speak. If Percy moves off Main Street, Mack is fixing to add on to his hot-dog stand and serve breakfast. He'll have grits tastin' like they were cooked in a crankcase."

"Edith Mallory . . ."

"Look," said J.C., "I respect that you're not big on foul language, but I gotta say it. You know what the woman is."

In case he didn't, J.C. told him.

"So if he doesn't come up with the rent, he's out?"

"Big time."

"And if he does, he jacks up his prices and stands to lose his trade . . ."

"You got it."

"I thought somebody had died."

"Yeah, well, somebody could, and it might be Percy. This could kill him. This place is his life. And lest you forget, buddyroe, th' *Muse* is right up those back steps there. Who knows when I'll get *my* little notice in th' mail?"

"Where's Mule?"

"Out lookin' for a place Percy can move into."

The Main Street Grill not on Main Street? It was unthinkable.

"Pat Mallory wouldn't have done a thing like this in a hundred years," said J.C. "He ate his breakfast at the Grill every morning of his life, desperate to get away from that barracuda. He would have paid Percy to keep it open."

Velma stopped to pour J.C.'s coffee.

"Don't worry," the *Muse* editor told Percy's wife. "There's still such a thing as th' power of th' press . . ."

"Whatever that means," said Velma.

Mule slid into the booth. "Let me tell you, it ain't out there."

"No luck?" J.C. said.

"One little old bitty place stuck off behind the Shoe Barn, and she owns that, too."

"Does she really think Percy can cough up the new rent, or is she trying to run him out?" asked the rector.

"Tryin' to run him out is the deal. Has some fancy dress shop from

Florida she wants to bring in, th' kind that would draw customers from Wesley and Holding, all around."

He didn't think he could eat a bite for the churning in his stomach. "How much time do we have?"

"This is the twelfth of April, right? We got to the middle of May and not a day longer. Percy begged for time, but did she give him any? No way."

"There's got to be something we can do." One look at the anguish on Percy's face as he worked the grill was about all he could take.

"There might be somethin' . . ." said Mule. The rector wondered why the realtor was staring a hole through him.

"I could dig up some dirt," said J.C., "and spread it across the front page. First thing you know, she'd come runnin' in here to hand over the deed, forget droppin' the rent . . ."

"Stop talkin' junk and talk sense," snapped Mule.

"See there?" said J.C. "Everybody's got their back up. It's enough to make you sick to your stomach."

Velma appeared and slid J.C.'s order to the end of the table and set down the rector's poached eggs. "You done eat?" she asked Mule.

"Cornflakes at six a.m.," he said. "I could gnaw th' legs offa this booth, but Fancy's got me on a low-fat diet."

"Fancy barks, he jumps," grunted J.C., busting open his egg yolk with his fork.

Mule looked at the rector. "I hear you know Edith Mallory pretty well . . ."

"She's a member of Lord's Chapel."

"You've been carted around in that Lincoln of hers a few times, not to mention you've been seen over in Wesley ridin' around . . ."

"Purely business." His toast suddenly tasted like so much Styrofoam.

"You know what people say . . ."

"No," he said coldly, "I don't know what people say, and further-more . . ."

"They say she's got you marked off with a red flag . . ."

"I suppose you believe everything you hear?"

"Well, knowin' you as I do, and knowin' her as I wish I didn't, I don't put any stock in what I hear. But what I'm gettin' at is this . . ."

"What you're gettin' at is him suckin' up to a snake," said J.C. "If you ever opened the cover on your Bible, you'd see how that don't work."

Mule put his hand on the rector's shoulder, looking earnest. "One word from you and this whole thing could be turned around. No skin off your nose whatsoever. 'Scuse th' language, but if she's got th' hots for you like people say, you could talk sense to 'er and she'd listen."

"I appreciate that Percy's been driven to the wall, but I won't be thrown on the sacrificial fire. The answer is no."

This was not the usual morning banter. It was serious business; he felt the life-or-death of it. Even so, he despised being made the goat on the altar. He had no intention of humbly submitting to this tactic.

"Nobody's sayin' do anything you'd be *ashamed* of," said Mule, as if the rector's speech had gone in one ear and out the other. "Just take her to a nice dinner over in Wesley. Tell her how th' Grill is one of the oldest businesses in town. Percy's daddy opened it fifty-two years ago. It's a dadgum *historic* landmark . . ."

"Listen. I don't have a lobby with Edith Mallory—I don't give a blast what people say. If she wants two thousand dollars a month, and she can get it, what could I say that would change her mind? You think she's going to turn down twenty-four thousand a year because she thinks I'm . . . I'm . . ."

"Yeah," said J.C.

"Besides," said Mule, "aren't you in that business?"

"What business?"

"Persuadin' people."

"How's it going?" said Ron Malcolm, sliding in beside the *Muse* editor.

"Rotten," growled J.C., which seemed to express the feelings of the entire booth.

Ron took his cap off and looked at the rector. "Father, I've been thinking . . . you know Edith Mallory pretty well. I was wondering if there's anything you could do, anything you might say. I get the feeling she'd listen to you."

If J.C. Hogan had the guts to grin at him, or if Mule Skinner laid on that insipid wink he was famous for, he would puke, plain and simple.

CHAPTER THIRTEEN

A Rock and a Hard Place

They had swarmed over him like so many fire ants.

Then, Percy had joined them when the breakfast crowd thinned out, his eyes filled with some mute pleading that was clearly aimed straight at him.

It was a conspiracy.

Given the ten and a half she was now collecting, what could possibly make Edith Mallory give up an easy twenty-four thousand a year? Nothing that he would be party to.

So what was the use?

On the other hand, what if he got tough and came up with something that would, perhaps, result in only a token rent hike?

Maybe a room in her name at the town museum . . .

Under the circumstances, he thought he could talk Esther Cunningham into it. Sliding it by the town council, however, was another matter.

What about a garden planted in her honor? He and the rest of the Grill regulars would gladly grub the stumps out of the town lot with their own hands.

But he could forget that—the town lot was hidden behind the post office. Edith would want something people could see from Main

Street, with a plaque they could read a block away—lighted at night on both sides, possibly by an eternal flame.

How did he get in a fix like this?

And, come to think of it, how *did* Cousin Meg dispose of her trash?

When the old man called the office, he felt instantly encouraged.

"Uncle Billy, how are you?"

"Pretty Good, considerin' I done fell off a twelve-foot ladder."

"Good Lord! Is anything broken? Why, it's a miracle you survived!"

"Well, sir, t' tell th' truth, I only fell off th' bottom rung."

"Aha."

Uncle Billy sounded disappointed. "That's m' new joke, don't you know."

"I was supposed to laugh?"

"That's th' general thinkin' behind a joke."

"Better get a new joke, Uncle Billy. You scared me with that one."

"You ought t' know I don't git on no ladders, no sir. Th' last 'un I got on, I left it leanin' against th' house to rot down. I don't mess with ladders no more."

"A good idea, all around. How's Miss Rose?"

"Sly as a fox."

"How do you mean?"

"Every day she gets in my money and moves a little bit around to her side of th' mattress."

"What are you doing about it?"

"Why, I'm comin' along behind her when she ain't lookin' and movin' a little bit back where it come from."

"Makes sense."

"How's your boy? I seen 'im in church. He's gittin' gangly."

"That's right, he is. He's prospering, I'd say."

"We want you'uns to come up and have cobbler with us this summer when th' berries are on. And bring that nice blond-headed woman what crawled in Rose's playhole and found my ink drawin's."

He remembered Cynthia crawling behind Miss Rose into the dark space under the eaves that had been Miss Rose's childhood playhouse.

"We'll come," he said, meaning it.

"Have you discussed it with him yet?" asked Miss Sadie.

"No, ma'am," he said, feeling despondent.

"Have you come up with anything yet?" Mule wanted to know.

"No, blast it," he said, feeling pressured.

"Have you done anything with those family papers yet?" Walter inquired.

"What do you think?"

"Ah, Timothy. And with an Irishwoman living right under your roof . . ."

"So, sue me," he said.

He had come home early and found her rifling through the shelves in his study. "How's the book coming?" he asked.

"Straight on," she said, burying her nose in a volume of Irish poetry. He thought she looked precisely like a barn owl in a bathrobe.

"I've been wondering . . . how are you disposing of your trash? We did give you a wastebasket, I hope?"

"I'm recycling," she said.

"Aha."

"Paper products in one bag, aluminum cans in another."

"That's terrific. We can take the bags to Wesley next trip, get them out of your way."

"Right-o," she said. "No hurry."

"I'd like you to go with me to the Grill in the morning."

"Ah, no. Too much staring at me just now."

A cattle prod, that would be the thing. But he must be kind. After all, blood was blood. "I'll knock at six, as before. And Cousin . . ."

She pretended not to hear but licked her forefinger and turned the page.

"I'll look for you at the dinner table this evening. Six-thirty."

"I don't think so . . ."

"Sharp," he said, meaning it.

His cousin sat at the kitchen table, glowering.

Where was the Irish wit, he wondered, the droll humor, the unend-

ing stories their ancestors were famous for? What was she, anyway—
Scottish?

He put Puny's low-fat meatloaf on the table, still sizzling from the
oven, and went to the stove to dish up the green beans.

"Man!" said Dooley.

He turned around to see that his cousin had helped herself to a
vast portion and was going at it, full bore, with her fork and knife. "I
ate only grapefruit on Sunday, so this will be my substitute day for
flesh . . ."

"We'll wait for the blessing," he said evenly.

Holding her fork in one hand and her knife in the other, she sat
hunched forward in her chair. What in heaven's name could he do that
might bring a smile to those startled eyes?

At the blessing, he reached for Dooley's hand, but hers was gripping the fork.

How could she eat so heartily and never put an ounce on her bony
frame? Metabolism, he supposed. Where in the dickens had he been
when the hyperactive metabolisms were passed out?

"How many times have you been to the States? I can't seem to recall if you told me."

"Several times, on and off."

"Staying with cousins, were you?"

"On occasion."

"And where was that?"

"Once in Oregon."

"And where else?"

"Massachusetts."

"Who were you seeing in Massachusetts?"

"No one you know," she said.

"Try me."

"Cousin Riley."

"Umm. That wouldn't be Riley Kavanagh, would it?"

She glared at him. "No, it wouldn't."

He took a deep breath, only to have it end in a sigh. "Dooley,
what's going on at school?"

"Nothin'," said Dooley.

Conversing with this crowd was about as reviving as lugging a rock
straight uphill. "Well, then, tell us about your book. How does it . . .
begin?"

She deftly piled green beans on the back of her fork. "It begins as the horror itself began."

"Aha."

"One morning in 1845, an Irish farmer discovered that something was dreadfully amiss. The book opens with what he had to say, and I quote:

"'It was a warm day when I saw a thick white fog gradually creeping up the sides of the hills. When I entered it, I was pained with the cold. I at once feared some great disaster. The next morning when I traveled about . . . I found the whole potato crop everywhere blighted. The leaves were blackened and hanging loosely on their stems, and a disagreeable odor filled the air.'"

"Gross," said Dooley.

"Moving," said the rector, knowing how that tragic event had scattered, and nearly destroyed, a nation. Oddly, the longest speech he had heard her make was someone else's.

"When do you expect the book to be finished?"

"It will be done when it is done."

"I see. And how long do you think you . . . might be with us?" Among the Irish, cousins from across the pond were treated with great favor, but he didn't know how much more favor he could fork over.

She pushed her hair behind her ears and gazed at him soberly. "As long as you'll have me, Cousin."

Dear Timothy,

> *Hanging up on you was a silly and immature thing to do, but I couldn't help it. It just happened. Something came over me.*
>
> *Your note arrived, telling me about the mix-up, and I've tried to feel remorseful for what I did. Actually, I don't feel one bit remorseful, but I do feel forgiving.*
>
> *As I thought how you flew to New York to surprise and comfort me, the ice around my heart began to melt and I could not help but love you.*
>
> *Hasn't our timing, and especially mine, been atrocious? If only I had been here when you arrived, do you think things might have been different? Do you think the ice around your own heart might have melted for eternity?*

I've decided I will come home to Mitford at the end of the month and live there always, no matter what the future holds. Nothing can run me away again, not even a neighbor who is kind and loving one moment and distant and indifferent the next.

Somehow, the mention of marriage has strained even the sweet pleasure we found in going steady. It is grieving to think we might throw it all away because we've come to a hard place in the road and cannot cross over it. One would think that two people with brains in their heads could stand in the road and ponder the obstacle and come up with some ingenious way of getting over or round it! I mean, look what Mr. Edison, quite alone, managed to do with the light bulb!

Perhaps we could be friends, Timothy. But it's time for me to quit suggesting what we might do or be together and let it rest in God's hands.

If you think that sounds spiritually noble, it is not. I simply don't know what else to do.

Cynthia

He went to his desk and numbly opened the lower drawer where he kept her letters and laid the envelope on top. He stared into the drawer for a moment, trying to focus his thoughts.

He could have sworn the pile of letters had been deeper, that there had been many more. But then, everything now seemed less than it had been.

Dooley, how would you like to go away to school next fall?
(Suspiciously) Where at?
Virginia, perhaps. Just one state away. You could come home on holidays, and I could come up for special occasions and bring Barnabas.
(Long silence) I wouldn't like it.
You would be given every privilege, not to mention friends for a lifetime—and a chorus to sing with that's twice the size of your group at Mitford School.
(Firmly) I ain't goin'.

That was precisely how the conversation would proceed. It might as well be scripted on a piece of paper.

He was suddenly faced with persuading two people to do

something they had absolutely no intention of doing. Why was a preacher expected to be so all-fired able to accomplish the impossible when that, clearly, was God's job?

The Lord had never spoken to him in an audible voice, not once. But there were times He had spoken to his heart and in no uncertain terms.

As he labored in prayer on Friday morning, he received a strong but simple message:

Go to Buck Leeper and talk.

This message, which he felt no keen delight to receive, was persistent. Not only did it come when he was on his knees, but again as he washed his hands at the office sink and, later, as he jogged to the hospital.

He knew the consequences of delay when it came to obeying what he'd been asked to do. Oswald Chambers had found this topic of special interest. "It is one thing to choose the disagreeable and another thing to go into the disagreeable by God's engineering. If God puts you there, He is amply sufficient.

". . . There must be no debate," Chambers had gone on to say. "The moment you obey the light, the Son of God presses through you in that particular. . . ."

If a parson could not reach out to the desperate, then who could— or who would?

On the way to the site of Hope House, he made a decision to speak simply. No games, no hidden agendas, no beating around the bush. And let the chips fall where they may.

Buck Leeper was alone in the trailer. He swiveled around in the creaking desk chair and looked up.

"I'd like to talk," said the rector.

"What about?"

"I don't know, to tell the truth. Just talk. Get to know you better."

The superintendent took a long drag off his cigarette and inhaled deeply. "Sit down," he said.

Leeper swung his feet onto the desktop and crossed his legs. In your face, his muddy boots seemed to say, but the rector sat across the desk from them, unflinching.

"You probably need to know I don't like preachers."

"You wouldn't be the first."

"This hill is not a missionary field."

"I'm off-duty." That was a lie, but he told it, anyway.

"My granddaddy was a preacher," Buck said, narrowing his eyes.

"So was mine. Baptist."

"Ditto."

"Did you know your grandfather?"

"Never knew him. Heard about him all my life. Nothin' good." He stubbed his cigarette in the ashtray.

"Your dad's father?"

Leeper toyed with a silver lighter, and the rector saw where his fingers were missing. "Yeah. He turned my old man into the meanest preacher's kid in Mississippi."

"You're from Mississippi?"

"Born and bred."

"Same here."

Leeper barked an expletive. "Small world."

"What part?"

"Northeast. Booneville."

"Holly Springs," said the rector. "Forty miles from Booneville, as the crow flies."

Another expletive and an odd laugh. "Son of a gun."

Leeper glanced at his watch.

"Maybe you'll join us at the rectory for dinner—one of these days."

The superintendent pulled a cigarette from an open pack in his shirt pocket. He lit it with the lighter and inhaled. "I don't think so."

"Drop by the office, then, for a cup of coffee . . . anytime."

Leeper suddenly got to his feet and walked to the door, where he took a jacket and hard hat off the hook. The rector followed him.

"That redheaded kid yours?"

"Dooley?"

"I don't know his name. Tell him if he comes messin' around on this job again, I'll kick his butt. That goes for his sidekick, too."

"They . . ."

"Tell him I mean business. You can get killed out there."

Leeper opened the door. The machinery vibrated the trailer as if it were a toy. "Got to get to th' hole," he said, putting on his hat. "Some people have to work in this town."

Springtime was on its way, no doubt about it.

Hessie Mayhew's gardening column made its annual appearance in the *Muse*, under a photograph of the author taken thirty years ago. The first column of the season always disclosed Lady Spring's current whereabouts.

It seemed she was tarrying on a bed of moss and violets down the mountain, where the temperature was a full ten degrees warmer.

Do not look for her, Hessie cautioned, *for she never arrives until we've given up hope. Once you've sunk into despair over yet another snowfall in April or a hard freeze after planting your beans, she will suddenly appear in a glorious display of Miss Baxter's apple blossoms—not to mention lilacs along south Main Street and wild hyacinths on the creek bank near Winnie Ivey's dear cottage.*

Lest anyone forget what a wild hyacinth looked like, Hessie had done a drawing from memory that J.C. reproduced with startling clarity.

The old sexton was sitting in a chintz-covered armchair, fixing Betty Craig's alarm clock. The contents of the clock were scattered over the top of a lamp table.

"You look comfortable," said his caller, sitting on the side of the bed.

"Dadgum clock's been stuck on high noon since I moved in here. How are you, Father?"

"Fine as frog hair."

Russell Jacks laughed and emitted a racking cough. "Lord have mercy," he said, his eyes watering.

"Might as well tell you straight out, Russell. We've found somebody to look after the gardens. He's not your caliber, not by a long shot. I don't think there are any true gardeners left out there for hire. But we had to have help, and it's going to take time for you to knit. When the doctor gives you a clean bill of health, we'll put you back. How's that?"

"Fair enough. I thought I could hold on t' my job, but I cain't. I'm tryin' to help Miss Betty all I can. How's our boy? Is he troublin' you?"

"No, sir. Not a bit." His heart sank. Here goes, he thought. "Russell, I was wondering if you'd agree to . . . if you'd let us send him off to a fine school next fall, where'd he learn more, think harder . . ."

"Send 'im off?"

"Maybe to Virginia. Close by. You and I could drive up once in a while to see him, and he'd come home for holidays."

Russell studied two small clock springs in the palm of his hand, silent. Finally, he said, "What do you want t' do, Father?"

"I don't want him to go. I'd like to keep him right here in Mitford, but we have an opportunity. Someone is offering to pay his tuition, give him a once-in-a-lifetime chance." He stared at the rug, feeling a chill in the room. "I think we should let him go."

"I want t' do what you want t' do," said Russell.

"I'll bring the papers when the time comes."

His heart felt heavy as a brick when he left Betty Craig's house, and he hadn't even gotten to the hard part yet.

He got no providential word on what to do about Edith Mallory. And he had exhausted every foolish possibility he could think of.

What was the worst scenario?

He could go and talk to her—plead for the continuity, the history, the tradition of the Grill and the place it occupied in the heart of the village. Then he thought of her hand on his leg or being trapped in that blasted car at a speed that did not warrant leaping to safety.

If Percy Mosely and Mule Skinner and J.C. Hogan and Ron Malcolm knew what they'd asked of him, they would never have asked it. After all, they were friends. A man wouldn't ask this of his worst enemy.

Of course, all they expected him to do was give it a shot, just one. Nobody said he should keep going back for punishment.

They tried to puff him up by saying how Edith would listen to anything he said, do anything he wanted. To hear them talk, he might have been the pope. But he saw through it; they didn't fool him. While they had aimed straight for his ego, he'd seen it coming—and ducked.

On Sunday, Ron dragged him to the country club after church, while Dooley begged to go home and make a sandwich and ride bikes with Tommy.

He saw Buck Leeper at a table in the corner, eating with a man in a business suit.

"The honcho," said Ron. "Came to check on the job. They're here as my guests. I figured you wouldn't care to join them."

"I went up to see Mr. Leeper the other day."

"No kidding."

"We were born forty miles apart—in Mississippi."

"I'll be darned. Amazing. What did he think of that?"

The rector repeated what the superintendent had said, expletive and all. "End of quote."

Ron laughed heartily. In fact, he hadn't gouged such a good laugh out of anybody since the opening remarks of a recent sermon on spiritual apathy.

"We'll drop by the table on the way out. You'll like Emil Kettner. Devout. Solid. He's protective of Buck, views him as a real cornerstone of the company."

"What does he think about his drinking . . . about the way he pushes himself?"

"He knows it. He keeps after him—makes it mandatory for him to get a physical every six months."

"The goose that laid the golden egg . . ."

"In a way. But it's more than that. I think Emil loves the son of a gun."

Andrew Gregory stopped to say hello, appearing, as far as the rector could determine, more charming than the last time he'd seen him. His mother's warm Italian blood had clearly fought it out with his father's English reserve and won.

"I have a book you might enjoy looking over. Very early. Splendid engravings, gorgeous binding. Drop by for coffee one morning. Ron, I hope you'll do the same. For you, a book on bridges. German. Eighteenth-century."

"Consider it done," said the rector.

"I'll look forward to it," said the retired building contractor. "Who knows what you might learn from an old book?"

"Our priest and our building-committee chairman!" exclaimed

Edith Mallory. He thought she swooped down at their table like a crow into a cornfield.

"Hello, hello!" she said.

Both men stood. "Edith . . ."

"Timothy, I thought your sermon was excellent. Believe me, I needed to hear all you had to say about fear. I was absolutely eaten up with it for days when I was waiting for the tests to come back. I loved what you said about—what did you call it, the prayer of re . . . re . . ."

"Relinquishment."

"Yes! Just turn it all over. Give it to God."

"How are you feeling!"

"Great! Never better. Can't you tell?" She grasped his hand, and he saw that her blouse was cut considerably lower than he'd noticed at the church door an hour ago.

Seeing Ron Malcolm gaping like a boy, she fingered a diamond pendant at her neck. "A little momentum Pat gave me," she crooned.

"Aha . . ."

"I can tell you're having boy talk, so I'll get back to my veal chop. I'll call you sometime tomorrow, Timothy—just a weensy thing I'd like to get settled before I go to Spain in May. *Hasta vista!*"

Ron shook his head as she walked away. "There for a minute, I thought she was going to have *you* for lunch—forget the veal."

He felt queasy. "That crowd at the Grill is sticking me between a rock and a hard place."

"Don't I know it?" his friend said, grinning.

Buck Leeper had disappeared toward the men's room as they got up to leave. Ron introduced the rector to Emil Kettner and was snared by the club treasurer for a five-minute meeting.

Kettner was a big man, cordial, with steel-gray hair, steel-rimmed glasses, and penetrating blue eyes.

The two men sat over a cup of coffee.

"Well, Father, I hope Buck isn't more than you bargained for."

"He is, actually."

They laughed.

"I like your candor. Of course he is. I don't know how we get away with sending him to certain jobs. But then, we couldn't get away with not sending him. This is a big project, Hope House."

"Agreed."

"I'm here to look it over, check it out. It's a courtesy to your building committee. The job is humming like a top." He paused. "Buck has it in for clergy, you may have noticed."

"I think I noticed, yes."

"His grandfather was a preacher who was brutal to his son. It passed right on down the line. The sins of the fathers are visited upon the children . . ."

". . . unto the third and fourth generation," said the rector, completing the scripture from the Book of Numbers.

"Buck's work is the one place he doesn't fail or mess up. There's not a better man in the business."

"I believe you."

"I make no excuses for him. But something happened to him a long time ago, while he was still in Mississippi. Nobody back here ever got the gist of it, exactly. Some loss, something tragic. He felt responsible. That's all I know."

"Thanks for your candor."

"Thanks for your understanding. I'm going to walk over the job again, then bust out of here to Memphis." He took a business card from his jacket pocket. "I'm at your disposal if you need me."

The superintendent came back to the table, grabbed his jacket off the back of the chair, and nodded curtly to Father Tim.

"Let's hump it," he said to Emil Kettner.

"I've got it," J.C. announced on Monday morning. "I was up 'til two a.m. trying to knock this thing in the head. This is it. This'll work."

Mule caught Percy's attention. "Can you step here a minute, buddyroe? J.C. says he's got it knocked."

Percy came over from the grill. "Make it snappy. I got enough bacon goin' to feed a camp meetin'."

J.C. took out a handkerchief and wiped his face. "Didn't ol' Pat Mallory come draggin' in here every morning of his life after he retired? Didn't he think he'd died and gone to heaven every time he ate Percy's sausage with Velma's biscuits? Didn't he hole up in that first booth and read the paper 'til it fell apart? I was pacin' the floor last night when *boom*—it hit me."

J.C. paused and looked at his listeners. "We change the name to *Pat's* Grill. Anybody's widow would go for that one." He sat back as if he'd divested himself of the brightest idea since sliced bread. "What do you think?"

"Over my dead body," said Percy. He threw his hand towel over his shoulder and stalked back to the bacon.

"Oh, well," said Mule.

"Dadgummit," snorted the editor.

"Good try," said the rector. For a few blissful moments, their eyes had been on J.C. Hogan. Now, every head once again swiveled in his direction.

They waited for the crowd to thin out, so Percy could have a cup of coffee with the rear booth. "Kind of like sittin' up with the dead," said Mule.

"Do you think you'll get a rent hike for upstairs?" Father Tim asked J.C.

"I got the letter yesterday. No rent hike, but I can't run my presses 'til after seven o'clock at night. That burned me. I thought this was th' land of the *free* press."

"Shouldn't be any skin off your nose," said Mule. "You never ran your presses 'til after seven o'clock, anyway. Midnight's more like it."

"Whenever I bloomin' well please should be the big idea here," said J.C. "She also said the stairs to the Grill would be blocked off and I'd have to use the back entrance." He wiped his face with his handkerchief. "Witch on a dadgum broom . . ."

"Who'd want t' walk down th' steps into a shop full of women, anyway?" said Mule.

J.C. looked around the quiet room. "Where's Percy?"

"Down th' hatch," said the rector. "I saw him go down there a minute ago."

"What's this going to do to Velma? We know it'll kill Percy, so that's th' end of that deal," J.C. said.

Mule drained his coffee cup. "Velma said she'd have to go to work. They've got savings, but not much. You know how they've done with their kids, settin' 'em up in college, buyin' one that little house . . ."

"Here he comes," said the rector.

Percy slid in with a coffee mug, looking glum. "On top of everything else, my back's out. Not only that, they shipped me white grits instead of yellow—I can't sell white grits."

"Just want you to know I've been talking with someone who handles real estate," the rector told Percy. "I believe he's got the perfect place for the Grill, whether it's right here . . . or out there."

"Who is it?" Mule scowled.

The rector grinned. "God."

"Oh," said Mule.

"He's th' very one that put my daddy in this buildin' fifty-two years ago," Percy said, brightening. "They claimed my daddy was crazy to go to feedin' people with a war on. But he was a prayin' man, and when th' good Lord opened th' door of opportunity, my daddy walked through it and went to cookin'. Bread was fifteen cents a loaf, tomatoes was four cents a pound, and rent was ten dollars a month."

"Oleo margarine," said Mule, "was white, came in a plastic bag with a little colored capsule in there. You popped that capsule and out oozed this colored stuff and you mashed it all around in that bag 'til it colored your oleo and you thought you had butter."

"Don't think I haven't prayed a time or two myself," Percy said, "especially in '74. There was a whole week when th' single biggest ticket I wrote was for a fried-egg sandwich and a Baby Ruth candy bar."

The conversation slacked off, and they all looked at the rector.

"I've got to get out of here," he said, meaning it.

"When are you goin' to do it?" asked Mule.

"Today."

He planned everything he'd say when she called about the "weensy" matter she mentioned. He also worked out what he'd say when they drove to lunch . . . in *his* car.

He wrote it all down, working on it like a sermon. Then he paced the floor, speaking his lines.

He would plead for a dramatic reduction of the proposed rent hike, stating that the Grill had been a faithful, long-term lessor who had paid its rent on time and never asked for anything more than a little paint and a new toilet. What would a dress shop demand? Everything from wallpaper to carpet, not to mention the repair of the water stain on the ceiling that had been spreading like a storm cloud ever since the blizzard.

If she wouldn't budge on the rent hike, then he'd plead for more time, to the end of June, say, until Percy found another situation.

In case she called, he didn't go out for lunch but drank a Diet Sprite and ate a package of crackers. He dusted his bookshelves, tried writing a note to Cynthia but failed, and wrote notes instead to some of the kids at Children's Hospital. Since he refused to let Emma get call waiting, he made no calls in case Edith tried to get through and was brief with whoever phoned the office.

He wanted to be ready, and he was ready; he was champing at the bit. He even found two positive things he could say to Edith Mallory about herself and wrote them down in case he forgot what they were.

He would ask her to lunch in Wesley, tomorrow, at that place with the green tablecloths—and he'd give it everything he had, once and for all.

As for strategy, he would keep it simple. And—he would stay in control.

There was just one problem.

She never called.

CHAPTER FOURTEEN

Home Again

He waited two days.

When she didn't call, he called her. Magdolen said she'd gone to Florida unexpectedly, something about old business of Mr. Mallory's. No, she didn't know when Miss Edith was coming back, and yes, she was going to Spain in May, the minute that new shop moved into her building on Main Street.

He asked for her number in Florida and carried it around in his pocket like a hot potato.

He also dodged the Grill.

Thumpetythumpetythumpthumpthumpthumpety . . .

He pounded on her door. "Cousin Meg!"

Silence.

"Blast it, move your typewriter off the floor!"

He had turned away from the door when she opened it a crack and glared out at him. "If you don't *mind,*" she said, "I work better on the floor. I cannot *think* in a chair."

A chair isn't the only place you can't think, he said to himself. He turned and looked at her. "Off the floor."

It must be hard to slam a door when it had been opened less than three inches.

He was doing his homework.

He spent several hours on the phone, compiling a list of schools and contacts, including a priest who helped socially and economically disadvantaged boys get into major boarding and prep schools.

Dooley would need testing, along with English, science, and algebra placement. Clearly, he would need tutoring in English. And no, it wouldn't be the way he spoke that could make or break him but the way he pulled an English composition together.

Last but certainly not least, they would need the strong approval and support of two or three current teachers.

At three o'clock, he left the whole exhausting task and, for refreshment, went to make hospital calls.

If making hospital calls was his idea of refreshment, he later realized, he was in trouble.

Joe Ivey was out of town for the day, with a *Closed* sign on his door at the top of the stairs. Feeling like a sneak thief, he called Fancy Skinner who had a cancellation and could take him.

"Good grief! I can't believe what's goin' on with this stuff over your ears. It's that chipmunk look again. I thought I *cured* you of that.

"If I was a man and saw Joe Ivey comin' down th' street, I'd cross to th' other side. What did he use to cut your hair, anyway, a rusty saw blade?

"Do you know how much coffee I've had this mornin'? You won't believe it. A potful! I never drink a pot*ful* of coffee! I declare, it makes me talk a blue streak. Look how my hands are shakin'. I hope I don't cut your ear off or jab a hole in your head. Hold still, for gosh sake. See what I mean about those clumps over your ears? There you go! Look at that. A hundred times better—and I'm not even finished.

"I guess you know what's goin' on at the Grill. Mule is so depressed, you wouldn't believe it. You'd think he was losin' the roof over his head. He said you're goin' to work on changin' her mind. Bein' a preacher and all, you can probably talk her into whatever. I personally don't care if we get a dress shop. I order everything out of catalogs. That is the latest thing, orderin' out of catalogs, which is fine except for shoes. I wouldn't order shoes out of a catalog, would you?

"Oh, no, can you see that little bitty nerve jumpin' in my eye? That is so embarrassin'. I forget that happens if I drink a potful of coffee. Why I did it, I don't know. I don't have the slightest idea. Mule said, 'Don't drink this potful of coffee,' but then he went to the Grill and I drank it. Do you ever do somethin' somebody tells you plainly not to do, and you know they're right, but you can't help yourself?

"Your scalp is tense. You should try to relax. I bet bein' a preacher is hard. I mean, all those people lookin' to see if you're walkin' what you're talkin', right?

"I never did ask if you want a Diet Coke. Or would you like a Sprite? You tell me. I offer cold drinks as a courtesy. I would offer coffee, but it's a mess to clean up—like a fireplace. Mule said, 'Do you want to burn the fireplace this winter?' I said, 'No, it's a mess to clean up.' I bet you burn a fireplace, though. You look like you'd burn a fireplace.

"Oh, mercy, wasn't that some winter we had? Have you *ever?* I am not over that yet. A blizzard! Can you believe it? And snow in April. Or was it March? I don't know. Since I opened this shop, I can't keep up.

"I declare, look at you. You are handsome as all get-out. Do you have a girlfriend? Mule told me somethin' about your neighbor. What was it? Let's see. Oh, yeah. I shouldn't tell that, but what the heck— he said she has great legs. Do you really like her? You don't have to answer—I know that's a personal question. But I hope you do, be- cause people shouldn't live alone. It's not good for your health. Of course, you've got a dog. They say that helps.

"Well! What do you think? See how it slenderizes your face? You ought to let me give you a mask sometime. No, I mean it. Men in Los Angelees and New York do it all the time. It cleans out your pores. Oh, and Italians, they do masks. They even carry handbags, did you know that? Italian men are different. My girlfriend used to date an Italian. He was so macho, you wouldn't believe it. How can you be macho and carry a handbag, I wonder? I don't have the slightest idea.

"Oh, law, this coffee has got me flyin' to the moon. That'll be ten dollars. No, six! I forgot—you're clergy."

He closed the door to the study, then closed his eyes and prayed.

He might as well expect water to flow uphill as to expect this phone call to do any good—but where was his faith?

Ed Coffey answered the phone at Edith's condominium in Boca Raton.

"She's with someone on the patio, Father."

"I can call later."

"Oh, no, sir. I'm sure Miz Mallory would like to talk to you."

He waited an eternity.

"Hello," Edith said, exhaling smoke into the receiver.

"Edith, it's Tim."

"Yes, Timothy." He might have been someone from the IRS for all the enthusiasm he heard in her voice.

"How's the weather down there?"

"Fine."

He pushed on. "Same here. You mentioned you wanted to talk about something before you go off to Spain . . . ?"

"Nothing urgent."

Was she talking through clenched teeth? "Aha. When are you coming home, may I ask?"

"I don't know. But I do know why you're calling me."

"Yes, well, to find out what you wanted to talk about before Spain . . ."

"You're calling because your precious Grill is going to be yanked out from under you, and you think you can talk me out of it."

"Edith . . ."

"I don't know what you men find to love about that tacky hole in the wall. My husband went there every morning of his life. You would have thought they were paying him to open up the place. Magdolen and I begged him to eat something sensible in his own home, but no! He marched right down there and ate God knows what and came home reeking of grease—which, in my opinion, killed him."

"Grease?"

"Gorging himself on sausage and biscuits and grits and every other thing that wrecked havoc with his doctor's orders, and where is he now?"

At peace, he wanted to say. "A double rent hike is . . ."

". . . is the smart thing to do, Timothy. My accountant is here. That's exactly what we've been discussing. Put yourself in my shoes." He heard the familiar whine overtaking her indignation. "If I don't look after Edith, who *will?*"

Her mood was changing. She was batting her eyelashes, he could just feel it. "I'd like to talk with you when you come home," he said.

She breathed into the phone. "I won't let you get away with one single, weensy thing, though I do hope you'll try."

"I don't have a clue," said the mayor, sucking up the last of her Diet Coke through a straw. "If somebody wants to hike rent, they hike rent. It's still a free country, though God knows how long that'll last with th' rabble we've sent to Washington."

"Can't we declare it historic or something?"

"That won't change a thing. Come to think of it, why don't you talk to th' landlord about it? I hear she's taken a shine to you."

He blanched. "Mayor, if you can't help us fight progress around here, who can?"

"Truth is, I'm feelin' too old to fight progress. And if you let on I said that, I'll say you lied. I just want to get in th' Winnebago with Ray and go to Colorado for a little fishin'."

"Take me with you!" he implored.

They had concluded the antiphonal reading of the psalm when he looked up and saw an extraordinary sight.

Barnabas was trotting up the aisle, as a couple of astonished ushers stared after him.

He arrived at the front pew on the gospel side and halted, turning to stare into the face of an alarmed congregant.

Was this a dream? No, it was a nightmare, for Barnabas was now licking a perfect stranger—a visitor, no less—on the right ear.

" 'Let love be genuine,' " said the lay reader, carrying on with the Scripture reading, " 'hate what is evil, hold fast to what is good . . .' "

How had he forgotten to close the garage door? He had never forgotten to close the garage door. He could hear laughter breaking out like measles.

" '. . . *outdo* one another in showing honor. Do not lag in zeal, be *ardent* in spirit . . .' "

Barnabas looked toward the lectern, then gave a sigh and lay down, his head on the visitor's foot. The man wiped his glasses and his ear with a handkerchief and, smiling broadly, gave his rapt attention to the remainder of the reading from Romans.

" 'Do not repay anyone evil for evil, but take thought for what is noble in the sight of all. If it is possible, so far as it depends on you, live peaceably with all. Beloved, never avenge yourselves, but leave room for the wrath of God; for it is written, "Vengeance is mine, I will repay, says the Lord." ' "

That his dog stood for the Nicene Creed and again for the dismissal hymn was, he concluded, something to marvel at.

Dear Cynthia,

It won't be long until lights will burn again in the darkened windows of the little yellow house; bushes will bloom, trees will leaf out, the wrens will build a nest under your eave. So, hurry home, and help these good things to happen.

If you'll let me know when you're arriving, I'd like to fetch you from the airport.

All is well here, only one upset which I'll tell you about. Am investigating schools for Dooley. Thankfully, there are quite a few out there, but must get some tutoring into him before fall. Will likely go on a tour of schools as soon as his classes at Mitford School are over in June.

We will be glad to have you home.

He pondered how to sign it. He might even have agonized over it, but he refused. Did he love her? Of course. That had never been the question.

Love, Timothy

"Where are th' KitKats that was in the kitchen drawer?"

"Where are the KitKats that *were* in the kitchen drawer?"

"Yeah, where're they at?" asked Dooley.

"Where are they."

"I'm askin' you. They ain't in there."

"They aren't in there."

"That's what I said."

He was unable to keep from laughing. "Dooley Barlowe, I'd like to wring your neck."

"You'll have t' catch me," Dooley said, grinning.

"Ask the question in proper English, for Pete's sake. You talk like a Rhodes scholar for Marge Owen. Come on—give me a break."

"Where are the dern KitKats?"

"That's better. And the answer is, I don't know."

"That woman eat 'em is what I think."

"Did you eat them and forget you did it?"

"I don't forget stuff like that. I remember eatin' candy, 'specially since I was savin' those for me and Tommy."

"I'll look into it." he said. Which was worse—the nervous tic that had lately begun to jump in his right cheek or the wrenching in his stomach?

"Cats?" she said, staring at him blankly. "I despise cats."

"No. The candy. The candy that was in the drawer to the left of the sink. That is Dooley's candy drawer."

"I don't know anything about candy," she said with distaste, "as I never touch sweets."

What could he say?

The fog was dense, the afternoon was cold, and her plane was late.

He drank coffee in the terminal café that was the size of his bedroom closet and stared out the window, searching the skies. "Heavy weather in Charlotte," they told him at the flight counter. "It's going to be an hour, maybe two."

He read an abandoned newspaper, checked his urine, jotted sermon notes on the back of a napkin, paced the floor, and observed the reading material of a few desultory air travelers. Grisham, Clancy, and Steel seemed to win, hands down.

The fog had turned to rain when the Fokker commuter descended, two and a half hours behind its scheduled arrival.

He watched her come through the door and down the steps of the plane as an eager airline attendant thrust an umbrella over her head.

He felt that some connection had been broken, as if he might have to start all over again to know her, and that she was walking toward him as if from a very great distance.

Holding on to an airline umbrella with one hand, he helped Cynthia into the front seat, put Violet's crate on the back seat, and piled luggage into the trunk.

His feet were soaked. Who had known the skies were going to give way, when all had been sunshine and birdsong in Mitford at noon?

He returned the umbrella to the desk and dashed to the car.

"Blast," he said, sliding under the steering wheel. The faintest scent of wisteria greeted him.

"Thank you, Timothy."

"For what?"

"For waiting. For coming at all. For getting drenched into the bargain."

"My pleasure." he said, trying to mean it.

As they neared Mitford, she grew silent and rummaged in her purse.

"Oh, no!" she said.

"What is it?"

"My house key! It was on the key ring I left in the apartment. Oh, no."

"Don't worry. I have your key, remember? That's how I got in to find the lights at Christmas."

"Thank heaven!" She sank back against the seat and smiled at him.

He was struck by her warm presence and the way she looked in the purple wool suit the color of hyacinths.

Although their conversation hadn't flowed like wine, he felt better—consoled, somehow.

But he couldn't find her key.

She sat in the kitchen with Violet howling in the crate and Barnabas going berserk in the garage while he searched his bureau drawers. He had meant to put the key on his key ring but had never done it, and he kicked himself for the stupid way in which he managed to lose important things. He wouldn't even think about the brooch, not now, for it was all too much.

He went back to the kitchen. "You're not the only one who can't find your house key. I put it in the bureau drawer, and it's simply not there." He switched on the burner under the tea kettle and sat down across the table from her.

"Oh, dear," she said.

Violet howled. He heard Barnabas lunging against the door from the garage to the hallway.

"Perhaps one of your windows isn't burglar-proof?"

"I never lock the windows on the side toward your house, because I raise them so often in summer."

"Then I could use your stepladder—mine isn't high enough to reach—and we'll have you in your house in no time."

"Wonderful! I shall make all this up to you, somehow."

"Don't even think about it. Let's have a cup of tea first, shall we?"

"I'd love a cup of tea! And do you have a bit of milk for Violet?"

"If Dooley hasn't downed the whole gallon," he said, foraging through the refrigerator.

He left Cynthia with tea and a plate of shortbread, and Violet with a dish of milk, to fetch his slicker that was hanging in the garage.

As he stepped back into the hall, he heard voices in the kitchen.

"H'lo."

"Hello. I'm Cynthia from next door."

"Meg Patrick."

"Yes, well . . ."

He heard the refrigerator door open and shut. His cousin was probably dressed in that moth-eaten chenille robe and those scuffs that were out at the toe. He shuddered to think.

"Are you . . . enjoying your visit?" Cynthia asked.

"Right-o. Very pleasant, all the comforts. And such a thoughtful man, my cousin."

"Yes, he is that. Are you . . . close cousins?"

"Actually not. Third. Although in Ireland, third cousins often become very close, indeed—it's not unusual for them to marry."

"Really?"

"My own mother married her third cousin."

"I see."

"Well, cheerio."

"Cheerio."

He stepped into the kitchen as his cousin stomped up the stairs, and he saw that Cynthia's eyes were wide with a kind of wonder.

He was rummaging in the kitchen handy drawer for a chisel and hammer when the phone rang.

"Would you answer, please? Just tell them I'm busy and I'll call back."

He could hardly wait to lug that blasted stepladder out of her basement and drag it around her house in the pouring rain, looking for a burglar-friendly window.

"Hello?" said Cynthia.

"Hello-o-o, is the man of the house in?"

"He's busy now. May he call you back?"

"Just tell him Edith is home and dying to have the little chat we talked about the other evening. Perhaps over dinner. Why doesn't he ring me later? Tell him I can have my car sent down . . . anytime."

"Oh?"

"You must be the little house help I hear so much about."

Cynthia slammed the receiver on the hook.

"Good heavens," she whispered, turning a scorching shade of red. "I hung up on her. I don't know what came over me."

"Who was it . . . exactly?"

"I don't know what's gotten into me, I . . . I've never hung up on anyone in my life, and now I've done it twice in a row."

He slowly put the hammer in one pocket.

"It was Edith," she said. "That woman in the Lincoln."

He put the chisel in the other pocket.

"They're positively queuing up for you."

There was a very odd look on her face. Was she going to burst into tears or throw something at him? He stood unprotected in the middle of the floor. "Queuing . . . up? he croaked.

"First your so-called cousin who seems to have moved in permanently, and thanks for never telling me she's a raving beauty! And now this . . . this *Edith* who says she'll send her car down for you anytime, so you can have the little chat you're so looking forward to. I'm terribly sorry you had to fetch me from the airport, as it has clearly taken you away from a very demanding social schedule."

She grabbed Violet's crate and flew out the door and down the steps before he could gain any locomotion whatever.

"Cynthia! Where are you going?" he shouted from the back door. The rain was not only steady, it was pouring.

She turned around and glared at him, already drenched. "To a place where people are honest and decent and tell the plain truth instead of lies!"

"I hope this Valhalla isn't next door, because you can't get in."

She looked abashed for a moment. "Then I'll live in my car!" she yelled and dashed toward the hedge.

He had gotten as far as his back stoop when it hit him.

He couldn't use her stepladder to find a point of entry because her stepladder was in the basement and the only way to get to the basement was through a door in her hallway.

If he were a drinking man, he would have a double Scotch. On the rocks, and make it snappy. What was his brain made of these days? He couldn't seem to think straight for five minutes in a row.

The option was to break out a basement window. But could he then get through the door at the top of the basement stairs and into her hallway? If he remembered correctly, she liked to keep that door locked.

Could he even get that leviathan ladder of hers through a basement window, if he managed to crawl through, himself? Didn't he remember seeing the windows when he hauled Violet out of the coal chute, and weren't they unusually narrow?

A locksmith. That was the answer.

But when he called the only advertised locksmith in the area, there was a recording. He left a halfhearted message for the smith to call him back and hung up, feeling mold beginning to form under the slicker.

He splashed through the hedge toward the far side of the little yellow house, passing her garage on the way. He saw the dim outline of her head in the driver's seat of the gray Mazda.

Meg Patrick a raving beauty? The very thought boggled his mind. Had she worked so hard in New York that her eyesight was failing?

The basement windows were not only too narrow to push the ladder through, they were far too small for him to crawl through.

He went into the garage, dripping, and knocked on her car window. She rolled it down halfway.

"Hello, is this Miss Coppersmith's residence?"

"It is," she said, unsmiling.

"Ma'am, we have a problem. I am too large to crawl through your basement window and fetch out your ladder, which is too wide to be fetched out in the first place. So there you have it, and would you care to change your address temporarily and move to the rectory, where a fire and a bowl of soup wouldn't be a bad idea?"

"Don't you have a boy?"

"A boy?"

"Yes, a boy who is small enough to crawl in the basement window."

"We're awfully short on boys right now, ma'am. In any case, the basement door to your hallway may be locked, which means we couldn't gain access to your house even if I rounded up a dozen boys."

She stared straight ahead at a garden hoe hanging on the garage wall and sighed deeply.

"Do you know if the hall door to your basement is locked?"

"I always lock it when I go away, so nothing can . . . crawl up the stairs."

"Quite," he said, sighing also.

"I don't suppose you could crawl up the coal chute?" she said, still not looking at him. Violet howled from her crate in the passenger seat.

"No ma'am, we aren't trained to crawl up coal chutes. It's company policy. We tried it once, but our men kept slipping back and landing where they started."

"A definitive portrait of my relationship with my neighbor," she snapped.

"Why, yes, it is," he said, pleased with himself.

They sat at opposite ends of the study sofa with a box of Kleenex on the middle cushion.

Violet was curled on Cynthia's lap, sleeping, and Barnabas lay on the kitchen rug, leashed to the knob of the back door. The rector had decided he had only a couple of choices: Leave his dog in the garage, feeling punished through no fault of his own, or leash him to the knob where, should Violet get loose, a door torn from its hinges would be the worst that could happen.

The rain lashed the windows, the fire crackled, the clock ticked.

"I love the ticking of a clock," she said, sounding mournful.

He sneezed. "Does anyone else have a key?"

"Bless you. Not a soul, except David, who's traveling on business in the Far East."

He could break the glass pane in her storm door, but he didn't mention that."

She sneezed.

"Bless you," he said.

"You could stand on the back stoop and Dooley could kneel on your shoulders and lean over the railing and pry up the window in the downstairs bathroom," she said.

"That's a thought." He could see such a circus act crashing into the mud below, with only minor fractures as a result. He sneezed.

"Bless you. Maybe the locksmith will call you back."

"Maybe."

She hugged herself. "I'm freezing."

"Why don't you lie down, and I'll stir up the fire?"

"I've been up since four o'clock this morning," she said, looking miserable.

He brought a pillow from the armchair, and she lay down obediently. He covered her with the plaid afghan that was folded over the back of the sofa. "How's that?" he asked, looking at her huddled form.

He could barely hear what she whispered. "Heaven."

He put his hand on her forehead. "Warm," he pronounced, and sneezed.

She spent the night on the sofa, under a pile of quilts, refusing the offer of his bed.

He had brought her a pair of his socks and sat at the end of the sofa with her feet in his lap, sleeping in an upright position until two a.m.

He awoke when Cousin Meg flushed the toilet over his head,

and he added two logs to the fire. Then he crept up the stairs, feeling feverish.

After the locksmith arrived the next morning, he walked her through the hedge, lugging Violet's crate in one hand and her carry-on in the other. He went back to his car for the two suitcases, which were easily as heavy as Meg Patrick's, and popped those through the hedge and up the stairs to her bedroom.

She stood on the soft carpet in the room that he had never before seen and looked at him. He was somehow not surprised that he read his own thoughts and feelings in her eyes, though he had no idea what his thoughts and feelings were.

He took her in his arms and they stood for a moment, wordless.

Then he went down the stairs and home, where he searched for a handkerchief in his upper bureau drawer and found her house key.

He had breakfast with Dooley but stopped by the Grill for coffee.

"Edith Mallory is home," he announced. "I'll talk to her this week."

"Better get a move on," said J.C.

His muscles ached and his head felt the size of a Canadian moose. "For Pete's sake, don't expect miracles." He'd rather take a whipping than see Edith Mallory.

"Percy's decided it's not going to happen," said Mule. "He says somethin's goin' to come up that'll stop it."

J.C. wiped his face. "That's called denial, buddyroe."

"Let me ask you something. Do you think my cousin Meg is . . . good-looking?"

"With those glasses on," said Mule, "she's ugly as homemade sin."

"Without her glasses?"

"I've never seen her without glasses. Probably not bad. Tall, slim, nice legs, great hair. But too weird, you know what I mean?"

Percy came to the booth and sat down. "Yessir, I've lost my last night of sleep over this thing."

Then why, the rector wondered, did Percy's hands shake when he put cream in his coffee?

The crowd at the hospital called to ask if they might drop by before lunch.

He sneezed. Good! He could ride back with them and check into the emergency room.

At eleven, three nurses and Hoppy Harper in a Navy peacoat over a green scrub suit came through his office door with J.C. Hogan.

"Ta-daaa!" said Nurse Kennedy, handing him something.

Several bright flashes went off in rapid succession.

When he could see again, he read what was engraved in brass on the wooden plaque:

> *For Father Tim—*
> *Beloved friend*
> *and confidant—*
> *For thirteen years,*
> *you have doctored*
> *the gang at*
> *Mitford Hospital*
> *with the best*
> *medicine of all:*
> *love.*
> *We love you, too!*

"I wrote it," said Nurse Kennedy, grinning proudly.

"I told her what to say," announced his doctor.

"I corrected their terrible spelling," Nurse Phillips assured him.

Nurse Jennings threw her arms around his neck. "I didn't' do a blessed thing but come up with the whole idea!"

J.C. reloaded his camera as Emma took the plaque out of the rector's hands and looked for a place to hang it. "Sit down and have a cup of coffee. And no offense, but it's fourteen years he's been runnin' up th' hill to th' hospital," said his proud secretary.

"Father, I believe you know who this is."

And he did, more's the pity. It was Dooley's school principal, Myra Hayes.

"This is to inform you that Dooley Barlowe is being suspended for ten school days for the possession of tobacco products and for smoking on school grounds."

There was a deafening silence. The decision might have come

down from a Supreme Court judge, so awesome was Myra Hayes's indignation.

He sneezed and his eyes watered. "When shall I pick him up?"

"Immediately," she said.

And just when they needed the blessing of every teacher they could get their hands on . . .

"Go to your room until I can deal with this thing," he told Dooley. He was shaking with a chill, and all he wanted to do was to lie down.

He managed to get his clothes off and his pajamas on and haul the quilts from the sofa to his bed. Then, he put on the socks Cynthia had worn and crawled between the icy sheets.

He was asleep before he could turn the lamp off.

CHAPTER FIFTEEN

Lady Spring

He couldn't remember being so sick.

For three days, Dooley fetched and carried through the hedge, ran to the drugstore and The Local, heated soup and delivered it upstairs, and generally made himself useful.

Timing is everything, thought the rector, who was getting plenty of mileage out of Dooley Barlowe's recent indiscretion.

A new and virulent strain of flu, complicated by sinus infection, said Hoppy, who made a house call wearing a mask and gloves. His doctor looked down his throat, listened to his breathing through a stethoscope, thumped him like a melon, and darted through the hedge to do the same to his neighbor.

Apparently fearing contamination, his cousin came out only at night, like a cockroach. She was rustling so many books from his shelves that he once heard her make two successive trips downstairs. On the last trip, he groaned loudly, making sure he could be heard beyond his closed door.

Dooley came in the next morning, looking pale. "I heard you hollerin' in here last night like you was dyin'. Are you dyin'?"

"No such luck," he said, feeling his sinuses drain like pipes.

"Well, try t' hold it down in here if you don't mind—you like t' scared me t' death."

"Speaking of being scared to death, wait 'til I get well, buster. You haven't seen anything yet."

Dooley turned paler still. Good! He needed to be scared. Getting himself thrown out of school like so much wastepaper, breaking the blasted law, shooting himself in the foot . . .

"You want ginger ale or tea?"

"Tea, thank you, and ask my dog to come in here while you're at it," he said darkly. "I know he's sleeping on the foot of your bed."

"Cynthia was sick as all get-out when I seen her last night."

"Tell me about it."

"Ol' Vi'let eat a mouse that got in while she was in New York City. Dropped it right on Cynthia's bed. Gross."

"I thought she liked mice."

"Not half eat, she don't," said Dooley, who appeared to know.

"When you bring up the tea, I'd like you sit in the chair under the lamp and read to me."

"What d'you want me to read?"

He might as well reach for the moon. "Shakespeare."

Dooley pointed a finger down his throat. "Gag."

When the boy went downstairs, he dialed her number, but it was busy.

Dooley delivered the *Muse* to his chair in the study, along with a fried bologna sandwich. "You want mustard or catsup?"

"Mustard." This was living. Or it might have been, if he weren't still nearly dying.

There was that blasted photo on the front page, as if nothing else was going on in this town. Why did his nose look like the bulb of a tulip? And that smirk on his face—is that what he looked like when he was smiling? If he never saw another picture of himself, it would be too soon.

"Here," said Dooley, "it's time for your medicine. I hope it makes you better. I'm about give out."

"If you're going to be a vet, you'd better get used to caring for the sick."

"Can I go to Tommy's after school?"

"Are you out of your *mind?*"

Dooley rolled his eyes.

"In case it hasn't occurred to you, you're grounded. Big Time. We'll talk as soon as I can manage it. Now, onto other matters. That was a grand reading from *Hamlet*. We'll have Dickens tonight."

"Who's Dickens?"

"Only one of the finest storytellers in the English language, but long-winded, so eat your Wheaties."

"Man," said Dooley, wishing he were back in school.

"And I'd like to have a look at that English composition you're writing about my dog.

"He ain't . . . isn't . . . just your dog. I live here too, y'know."

"Yes, well, and who feeds and brushes and bathes him?"

"I could brush 'im. An' I could feed him sometime . . .'"

"There's a thought. Go to it." Why had he mistakenly assumed that a ten-day suspension was all bad?

He made his usual search for J.C.'s way with words but found only one gem:

Local Man Convicted of Wreckless Driving

He tore the story out to send to Walter.

On page three, Hessie Mayhew continued her annual saga.

Lady Spring has been sighted in our village at last, and skeptics are now convinced that she is here to charm us for the season.

Arriving less discreetly than in times past, she has already covered several banks with fuchsia phlox and tossed bouquets of violets hither as well as yon, showing special favor to the wooded pathways behind the post office.

One always looks for her touch, of course, at Lord's Chapel, where the gardens created by sexton Russell Jacks give pleasure year in and year out. Here, Lady Spring has entreated the redbuds to bloom a dash early, presenting themselves in glorious array behind the old tombstones. Do stroll down and have a look, as they make quite a show.

There's hardly any need to notify you of the great white cloud that is, as we write, settling over Fernbank. As all can see, Miss Baxter's apple trees are once again doing their best to make us the prettiest town in creation.

But take heed: don't plant yet. We've ten days to go, so do try and contain yourself.

Hessie ended with a quote from John Clare:

> *The snow has left the cottage top;*
> *The thatch-moss grows in brighter green;*
> *And eaves in quick succession drop,*
> *Where grinning icicles have been,*
> *Pit-patting with a pleasant noise*
> *In tubs set by the cottage door;*
> *While ducks and geese, with happy joys,*
> *Plunge in the yard-pond brimming o'er.*
> *The sun peeps through the window pane;*
> *Which children mark with laughing eye,*
> *And in the wet street steal again*
> *To tell each other spring is nigh.*

The timeline for planting, May 15, was also the Grill's timeline.

He let the newspaper drop to the floor. How had the days passed so quickly? For there was the shock of hearing the news, which took its own kind of time. Then, the brainstorming sessions and Edith's trip to Florida, and now he was sick.

Unless a miracle happened, they were looking at God knows what—a stroke for Percy, a strange job for Velma, and no way to get a decent cup of coffee, except by standing straight up at a shelf that ran along Winnie Ivey's bakery wall.

It was more than the probable loss of a landmark. It was, he concluded, a violation of ordinary lives made larger by continuity and connections.

He went to the sofa, uttered a brief but loaded petition, and dialed her number.

"Hello-o?"

"Edith?"

"Hello, Timothy. Magdolen has just gone out to The Local, so I'm my own social secretary."

"I'm sick . . ."

"Yes, I've heard. *So* sorry."

"That's why I haven't called sooner . . ."

"Not since your house help hung up in my face . . ."

"Something wrong with the phone lines, no doubt."

"What are you proposing, Timothy? And oh, you may as well know that I have no intention of seeing you while you're contagious, even if you are my priest."

"I should be completely over it in a couple of days. What about lunch in Wesley on Thursday?"

"We'll see," she told him, in a tone that said she had no intention of seeing.

His cousin still refused to accompany them to church. In reply to the note he left under her door, she left a note for him on the kitchen table:

I shan't come with you, though I do appreciate the invitation. Csn Meg

He couldn't help but notice she'd left the lid off the pickles.

"Hello."

"Hello, yourself," he said, noting that the receiver felt like a barbell. "Feeling better?"

"Better than what?"

"Better than if you'd been pushed from a tall building."

"Only slightly. And you?"

"Rotten, if the truth were known."

"The truth is seldom known, Timothy."

He moved quickly. "The truth is, Edith Mallory is involved in something I didn't have a chance to tell you about, which is why she called and invited me to dinner, and if Cousin Meg is a raving beauty, I am Michelangelo's David." There. He hadn't meant to sound so angry about it, but he was angry, he suddenly realized. Why was he having to report his personal life to Cynthia Coppersmith?

Clearly, she didn't want to talk about it. "Thanks for sending Dooley over. You've no idea how it's helped."

"Actually, I do have an idea. He's a boon to me, as well. Couldn't get out of bed the first two days. What did Hoppy say?"

"I have everything you have."

Bookends, he wanted to say, but didn't.

"Everything, that is, except a sinus infection, thanks be to God."

"There is a balm in Gilead."

"I'm making soup with the ounce of energy I got from eating a cracker," she said. "May I send some over?"

"Wonderful! I told Puny not to come in 'til the germs die down, so we're pushing along on our own over here. What time do you want Dooley to make a pickup?"

"Around five," she said, "and I'll leave out the carrots so he'll eat it. Now, with or without a cream base?"

"Without," he said.

"With or without a thin, golden-crusted little morsel of cornbread hot from the oven!"

"With!" he exclaimed, not feeling angry anymore.

Edith Mallory wanted him crawling on his hands and knees. All he was prepared to do, however, was call her again—just as soon as he went to the drugstore for Dooley's prescription.

Dooley had eaten a vast bowl of Cynthia's soup, cleaned up his share of the cornbread, crumbs and all, and fallen on the sofa, unable to move.

"You've done worked me to death," he said, his teeth chattering from the chill that raced through him.

"Tit for tat," replied the rector, covering him with the afghan.

"Timothy, I am not a charity organization." Edith's brown cigarette lay smoldering in the ashtray on the table."

"That's not what I'm saying, Edith."

"Priests are so idealistic—they're like children, really. They know nothing about business."

"I do realize your need to make investments lucrative, to be a wise steward of what you . . ."

"Then do stop nagging me to do what you're asking. A twenty-percent rent increase is not worth bothering about." She stirred sweetener into a glass of tea, while lunch progressed into his digestive system like so much gall.

"The mayor has done everything in her power to stop progress in this town, and while you may think those tacky shops on Main Street are charming, they're an economic liability of the worst sort. Look at that hideous awning on the Grill and that peeling paint."

"May I remind you that hideous awnings and peeling paint are a responsibility of the property owner and not the tenant?"

"Don't mince my words. A fine dress shop from Florida, where people know how to *do*, Timothy, will bring in more shops like it. It will raise rents all along the street. It will . . ."

"It will destroy the character it has taken more than half a century to create. It will erase something central to the core and spirit of the town and demolish a sense of connectedness that is disappearing throughout the country—something we're desperately longing to return to, though in most places it's far too late . . ."

"Oh, for heaven's sake," she said, "stop preaching to me. Save that for the pulpit! I always knew you were old-fashioned, but I never dreamed you were so set in your ways."

"That may be. I'm also saying that doubling the rent is unfair and is clearly a strategy to get the Grill off the street. Another thing. How carefully have you considered the cost of leasing this space to a fine dress shop and the amount of upfitting they'll require of the owner?"

"It has all been considered, and it is all decided. Unless your people can pay the rent I'm asking, which is perfectly legitimate for Main Street, the dress shop will occupy the property on May 16. And no, I can't wait until your people find a new location, if there is such a thing, because the shop owners must occupy on the sixteenth or go elsewhere. Believe me, I'm going to see they don't go elsewhere."

"Waiter," he said, "would you bring the check?"

She crushed out her cigarette. "And don't expect me to pay it, like so many clergy do."

There was one thing he could say for her, but only one:
She hadn't strung him along.
Percy had better be ready to pack up and not look back.
He couldn't separate the anger from the sorrow. "Vent your anger," the bishop had said a few times, "or it turns into depression—then you're down in the mire with half your parish."

He didn't feel up to racing his motor scooter out to Absalom Greer's country store, though the weather was certainly good for it. He was not yet well enough to jog, and smashing glasses into the fireplace was too theatrical.

Instead, he put on a pot of soup, gave Dooley his medicine, read to him from a veterinary book, and brushed Barnabas. Then, while the soup boiled over on the stove, he fell asleep on the sofa, exhausted.

"Are you well, Cousin?" she called through the three-inch opening.

He let out a racking cough and shoved his handkerchief to his face. Then he blew his nose as loudly as he could.

She shut the door.

There, he thought. That ought to hold her for another day or two.

"She's set on it, Percy. I did my best."

Percy looked thinner, and there were dark circles under his eyes. "Thank you, Father. I know you did. I ain't worried about it."

"Percy's cookin' is starting to reflect his mood," said J.C. "Lookit this sausage." To make his point he tried to puncture it with a knife, only to have it skid across his plate.

Mule scowled at Percy. "You got to keep up, buddyroe. You can't let down, especially not here at th' last."

"Depression," said J.C. "That's what it is. That and denial."

"Depression comes from anger," said the rector. "You need to let off steam."

"We could all go to Wesley and get drunk," said Mule.

"Fine," said J.C., "except nobody drinks—besides th' father, that is, who knocks back a little sherry now and then."

"I forgot," said Mule, "that J.C. goes to A.A., I don't drink anything stronger than well water, and Percy was raised Baptist and never touched a drop."

J.C. raked the last of the buttered grits onto his toast. "Bein' raised Baptist can drive you to drink, if you want my opinion."

"So how could Percy let off some steam?" asked the rector. "We need to brainstorm this."

"I'll tell you how,' said J.C. "Let Omer Cunningham fly you

around in that old airplane, upside down and backwards. That'll do it. You'll be so glad to get on th' ground, they could take this place and turn it into a hubcap museum, for all you care."

"Let Fancy give you a face mask," said Mule. "No charge. On the house."

"A what?" asked Percy, looking done in.

"A face mask. It cleans out your pores."

Percy got up and went to the men's room.

"We're makin' him sick," said J.C.

"We've only got eight days to the fifteenth." The rector took off his glasses and rubbed his eyes. "So, what's the answer?"

"There isn't one," said Mule, sounding oddly philosophical.

He had never seen Dooley Barlowe look so haggard and pale. He opened a can of ginger ale and went upstairs and sat on the side of his bed.

"I got you another week of KitKats," he said, holding up the bag. "Thanks for using them as we agreed."

"One every other day, and no cheating," said Dooley, looking feverish. "Leave 'em in here or that woman'll git 'em."

The rector pushed the bag under the bed. "There. Completely out of sight. So how are you feeling?"

"I'd as soon be dead."

"I know the feeling. We'll have a talk when you're better."

"Who's lookin' after ol' Cynthia?"

"I am. The torch has passed to me."

"How's she doin'?"

"Still a bit down."

"Are you goin' to marry her?"

"Well . . ." he said, as if the wind had been knocked out of him.

"Are you or ain't you? I would, if I was you."

"You're not me."

"I'm dern glad of that."

"Why are you glad of that?"

"You ain't no fun."

"Aren't no fun. Come to think of it, you're not exactly a million laughs, yourself. Why would you marry Cynthia if you were me?"

"Because she's neat. She's fun."

"What's so fun about her?"

"She picked 'at ol' mouse up by th' ear and th'ow'd it at me when I laughed at 'er."

"Throwing around a dead mouse is fun?"

"It is if you don't have nothin' else to do," said Dooley.

Dooley's flu hung on longer than his own had done, but then, he had pushed himself. Cynthia was still moping around in her bathrobe and curlers, with scarcely enough energy to bring in the mail.

"It's all right to take your time getting well," he said, having a cup of tea in her workroom. "You've worn yourself out on the book. Allow time to rest. Don't push yourself." He had never been able to take his own advice.

He picked flowers and left them on her kitchen cabinet and brought her a book of quotations from Happy Endings. He stopped by Winnie Ivey's for a napoleon, which he was tempted to step into the bushes and devour on the way home, but delivered it straight to her door.

He sat and read to her one evening while she put her feet on the ottoman and looked pale, and he also endured her infernal sighing.

He even opened some foul-smelling concoction and fed it to Violet, who scratched him on the ankle for his trouble.

If this was what marriage was like, he thought, he was getting a good dose. Cynthia Coppersmith was lapping up his doting attention like cream, without so much as bothering to take the curlers out of her hair.

"That woman left!" Dooley yelled from his bedroom.

He walked to the boy's doorway and looked in. "Left? When?"

"After you went to your office. I seen 'er creepin' down th' stairs."

He went to the guest room door and tried the knob. Locked.

"She'll be back," he told Dooley.

"Poop."

"Tomorrow night is when we'll talk. You'll be well enough and in the nick of time, too. You start back to school on Monday."

Dooley pulled the covers over his head.

"Well! I see you went out. That's good news."

"I went out for personal items," she said, ducking through the kitchen in her trench coat.

"I love you," he would say, meaning it.

"That's the first thing I want you to know."

Then, he would talk about school laws and how they're designed for the common good, not to mention individual good, which, in this case, had everything to do with health.

Then, he would deal with the issue of wrong friends and once again go over the ramifications of stealing as it affected personal character and spiritual freedom.

He would close with the warning Buck Leeper had commanded him to pass along. Here was yet another infraction of rules, another instance of disregard for set boundaries. He would not allow this sort of behavior to become a pattern, and neither did he want to make any threats he couldn't keep.

He pondered what Dooley liked best:

Playing with Tommy, singing in the chorus, listening to his jam box, eating hamburgers.

To underscore the ten-day suspension, he could remove everything but the chorus—but should he remove them all at once or in descending order? And for how long? He would call Marge Owen, who had raised two and was sufficiently skilled to be doing it all over again.

This was treacherous ground, and for Dooley's sake, he didn't want to step in a hole.

To accommodate two working mothers, the ECW changed their morning meeting to an evening meeting but failed to tell him. As he was the speaker, along with Mayor Cunningham and a Wesley town official, he had to change his own plans and be there.

"We'll talk when I come home," he told Dooley, who was well enough to watch TV.

But when he came home, the boy was in bed, snoring, his red hair lying wetly on his forehead.

He looked down at his freckled face and the arm thrown over the covers, grateful for all he had brought into the silent rectory, including the worry and aggravation.

Barnabas, who was sleeping at the foot of Dooley's bed, didn't raise his head but opened one eye.

Right there was some of the best medicine Dooley Barlowe had ever had. His dog could positively cure what ailed you—not to mention the fact that he was an upstanding churchgoer into the bargain.

He looked out his alcove window before getting undressed and gave his neighbor a quick call.

"Hey," he said when she answered the phone.

"Hey, yourself."

"What's going on next door? Do I see your Christmas lights burning?"

"I'm celebrating."

"Alone?"

"I wouldn't be, if you'd come over."

"Well . . . ," he said, uncertain.

"No strings attached."

That was fair enough. He went over.

She invited him to sit on the love seat in her workroom.

"What are you celebrating?" It must be fairly momentous, as she had taken the curlers out of her hair and looked terrific.

"Being alive."

"You were that sick?"

"It has nothing to do with being sick. We breathe, we run around in our underwear, we go to the store, we dig up the tulip bulbs or plan to, we make soup and pay the electric bill, and we never stop to think—we're alive! This is a gift!

"I wasn't even pondering this. I wasn't being poetic or introspective. It's just that I glanced at the floor—right there—this afternoon and saw how the light came through the window and fell on the wood.

"It bowled me over. It took my breath away. I could hardly bear it."

He was silent, looking at her.

"There was so much life in the light on the wood, the way it folded itself gently into the grain. That little spot on the floor radiated with tenderness. And then it was gone."

He couldn't stop looking at her and didn't try.

"Do you know?" she asked softly.

"I know," he said.

"Not everyone knows," she said.

"Yes."

They heard the ticking of her clock in the hallway outside her workroom.

She was perched on the stool at her drawing board. "Why don't you come and sit here?" he said.

She slid off the stool and came to him and sat down, and he took her hand. They were quiet for a time, in a soft pool of light from the lamp.

It occurred to him that he wanted to kiss her, to hold her close, but he didn't deserve it. He didn't deserve even to be sitting here, a man who couldn't make up his mind from one hour to the next.

She leaned her head to one side, in that way of hers. "What are you thinking?"

"That I want to kiss you," he said. "More than anything."

She smiled. "No strings attached?"

"Yes," he said. "No strings attached."

He couldn't help it that Dooley had a mild relapse on Saturday night and that he didn't feel so good himself. Nor did he intend to fall asleep on Sunday after church and nap until the afternoon, which is when Dooley fell asleep and was out like a light until dinnertime. He meant to discuss the whole thing with him that night, before the boy went back to school the following morning, but when he sat on the side of Dooley's bed, it was all he could do to say, "Listen, this can't happen again. Do you hear me?"

Dooley had seemed to hear him, but he couldn't quite forgive himself that he hadn't handled it right. No, he hadn't handled it right at all.

The lilacs bloomed so furiously that not a few of the villagers turned out to view the bushes.

"You've got to walk down behind Lord's Chapel," Hessie Mayhew told Winnie Ivey. "There's a white bush you won't believe! Take a camera!"

"Come and look!" Cynthia called through the hedge one morning. Barnabas nearly pulled him down racing to her yard where an ancient purple bush, half-hidden by the garage, was massed with fragrant blooms.

Andrew Gregory invited two friends from Baltimore to "come for the lilacs" and took them up and down Main Street to meet everybody from the postmaster to Dora Pugh, whose window display at the hardware store had changed to seed packets, bonemeal, garden spades, and wooden trellises.

On Sunday, the rector felt a lightness of spirit like he'd seldom known.

He walked toward home, as if on air, until he saw Percy and Velma driving down Main Street after the Presbyterians let out.

Percy didn't see him, but he saw Percy—and he was shocked at the grief so plainly revealed on his friend's unguarded face, as if it could no longer be hidden.

CHAPTER SIXTEEN

Down the Hatch

"And the name of the slough was despond," said J.C., who couldn't eat a bite.

"Th' last supper," said Mule. "With its own Judas."

They had all seen the sign on the door.

LAST DAY
After lunch,
the Main Street Grill
will be
officially closed.
New location
to be announced.
Thank you for
your business.

J.C. stared into his coffee cup. "I helped pack last night. It was awful."

"I'll help tomorrow," said Mule, "and Fancy's comin' to help Velma. Omer's loadin' this end. Lew Boyd's unloadin' the other end. We got four college kids from Wesley, and Coot and Ron are runnin' their trucks to the warehouse."

"Well done," said the rector. "I'll be here tomorrow at daylight."

J.C. rolled his eyes. "Good luck with what's down th' hatch."

"What's down there?"

"Fifty-two years of bein' in the food business. You got creamed corn in cans big as this booth, not to mention stewed tomatoes and sauerkraut out th' kazoo. You got busted display cases, old counter stools, rusted tin signs, milk crates, and a jukebox that'll take four men to lift it. Did you know this place had a jukebox in 1950? His daddy was trying to loosen up and go after a new demographic. Percy won't throw away a bloomin' thing, so eat your Wheaties."

"You're not packin' tomorrow?" Mule wanted to know.

"I've got a paper to get out."

"How are you going to treat the story?" asked the rector.

"I'm blaring it across the whole front page. Big photo of the sign on the door. Headline says, *Read It and Weep*. We'll run a black border around the front page—which hasn't been done on the *Muse* since World War Two. What do you think?"

"Check your spellin'," said Mule, looking distraught. "This is important. It needs to be respectful."

J.C. wiped his face with his handkerchief. "This is goin' to change my dadgum life. I don't take kindly to things that change my life."

"Get you a hot plate and start cookin'," said Mule. "You bachelors lead a sheltered existence."

"Rave on," said the rector.

J.C. leaned out of the booth and looked toward the front of the Grill. "There's Mack Stroupe with a toothpick stuck in his jaw. He's about to finish roofing that shed he built to snatch Percy's trade.

"There's your Collar Button man. He's shakin' Percy's hand like an undertaker. And there's Esther and Ray, both of 'em bawlin' like babies. Man, this is giving me an ulcerated stomach."

"In two days, they'll be nailin' boards over your stair steps," said Mule.

"I sent her a note, said she better fix th' back steps or I haul my presses out of here."

"I wouldn't get too high-hat with that witch on a broom," said Mule. "You'll be printin' your paper on th' creekbank."

J.C. squinted toward the front. "Velma's breakin' down."

"Let me out," said Father Tim.

He walked with Velma Mosely to the Sweet Stuff Bakery, where

Winnie set her in a chair in the back room and let Velma do something she said she'd been needing to do: cry her eyes out.

A letter from Father Roland in his "rude cabin in the wild":

He'd been taken in a canoe to a parishioner's house, where a meal for fourteen church members consisted of salmon steaks roasted over live coals. He declared he had never tasted anything so fine since his preseminary days in southern France. Clearly, his honeymoon with the rugged north woods of Canada remained in full swing, albeit the pay was minuscule.

A letter from the man in the attic, George Gaynor, who had discovered several prison inmates with whom he was praying and searching the Scriptures:

In this hard place, I have been greatly blessed to find hearts softened by the gospel of Jesus Christ. You're faithfully in my prayers.

A note from Cynthia, faintly reminiscent of wisteria:

Thank you for taking care of me while I was sick. I really was an old poop, but you didn't seem to notice, for which I'm truly thankful.

She had drawn a picture of herself in her bathrobe, looking frazzled, while he sat opposite her in a suit of shining armor, reading aloud from Wordsworth.

Ah, but he liked mail. Always had. One never knew what might turn up in the mail. It was like a lottery in which one could hit the jackpot at any moment.

The letter from Dooley's principal was not the jackpot.

Dear Father:

Dooley has told me that you did not rebuke him in any way for his flagrant conduct, and I am both shocked and disappointed to learn of this.

To cast the full burden for correction upon the school is a gross neglect of moral responsibility, though unfortunately it is a course of behavior almost always chosen by today's new breed of woefully indifferent parents.

You have only to look at the newspaper and watch your television to discover at once where such neglect inevitably leads.

I shall expect you to devise and deliver a proper punishment in the home and report it to me at once.

Myra Hayes

Dear Mrs. Hayes, he might reply, *I have kicked Dooley Barlowe's tail clean across Baxter Park for betraying my moral laxity to your office. For the crime of having smoked cigarettes on school property, I haven't yet come up with a suitable punishment, but when I do, rest assured it will be something that you'll most gleefully approve. Sincerely.*

He woke at five, as usual, and called the hospital to say he wouldn't be around to visit on the wards this morning, but he'd be there tomorrow, without fail.

He read morning prayer and lections and spent time on his knees for Percy and Velma. Then, he asked the Holy Spirit to open his heart for any special prayer for others. Buck Leeper was first in line.

At six, he pulled on an old pair of corduroy workpants and a denim shirt and woke Dooley and their houseguest. He didn't think he was up to looking at his cousin over breakfast, but he knocked anyway.

"Rise and shine!" he shouted, loud enough to be heard to the Presbyterian parking lot and beyond. Two of his dearest friends were being dumped on, and he was plenty mad about it. If his cousin was thinking of ignoring his knock, she had better think again.

When she showed up in the kitchen in her robe and slippers, scowling, he acquainted her with a few rules he should have laid down in the beginning—and in no uncertain terms.

Dooley stared at him with his mouth hanging open.

"And," he informed his charge, "if you think that's something, just wait 'til I get through with you. In other words, my friend, you ain't seen nothin' yet."

Dooley Barlowe didn't say one word during breakfast, nor did his cousin, nor did he.

"Where's Percy?"

Velma's eyes were red and swollen. "Down th' hatch," she said.

The place was a tomb. He could hear his footsteps on the hardwood floor, even though he was wearing tennis shoes.

"You'll open again," he said, meaning it.

Velma didn't reply. She was dumping flatware in a box with egg turners, colanders, and a metal grater. The sound seemed to echo off the walls, which was denuded of its usual array of outdated calendars, prints of covered bridges, and a collection of Cheerwine and Dr. Pepper signs.

The autographed photo of Percy and the former governor was gone, as was the photo of Percy's daddy wrestling an alligator in Florida. The photos of their grandchildren had been peeled off the back of the cash register, and they had stripped off the battered sign that read, *Good Taste, Ample Portions, Quick Service, Low Prices.*

He sighed, not knowing what else to do.

"Mule's runnin' late," said Velma. "Help yourself to coffee."

He poured a cup of coffee and descended broad wooden stairs to the basement.

He'd never been underneath the Grill before, in the room lined with shelves built over earthen walls and lighted by two bare, weak bulbs.

"Percy?"

"Over here," said Percy, appearing from behind the furnace. In the gloom, the pallor of his friend's face was startling.

He'd known priests who could make people laugh in the jaws of disaster, but he wasn't part of that breed. In all his years in the clergy, he'd never been able to think of witty remarks that, even for a moment, might obscure the pain of loss.

"How's it going?" he asked quietly.

Percy looked away from him. "I cain't hardly seem to go on from here."

"Why don't we take a load off our feet before we get started?"

"I thought I'd be able t' handle it," said Percy, sitting with the rector on the bottom step. "But I ain't able, it seems like."

"Thirty-four, thirty-five years. It's a long time."

"Longer'n that. I was ten years old when I stepped behind th' counter. My daddy had a bad toothache and put me in charge of the grill while he went to the dentist."

"How did you do?"

"I stood on a bread crate and fried bacon like a man. I'd never fried bacon in my life, nor anything else. My mama had to drive my daddy. He was in awful pain. She looked back at me as she was goin' out th' door, and said, 'Percy, you can do it.' I'll never forget that."

"She's right. You can do it."

"You mean . . . this?"

"Right. This."

"How come I have to—that's the question. Where's th' Lord when you need 'im is what I'd like to know."

The hot coffee cup warmed his cold hands. "Right here with us, believe it or not."

"You're a preacher. That's easy for you to say."

"Not really. I have times of doubt. I stumble around . . ."

"All that schoolin' you had makes a difference."

"Schooling doesn't count for much in the end. What counts is our personal relationship with God. Period. Bottom line."

"I prayed about this."

"You'll get an answer."

"This ain't any kind of answer."

"I have to tell you that He always answers. And He always shoots straight."

"Well, He's done shot and missed, if you ask me."

The rector looked around at the dark, dismal basement. "Somebody said the brightest diamonds grow in the darkest cavities of the earth . . ."

"Meanin'?"

"In Isaiah, God said, 'I will give you the treasures of darkness, riches stored in secret places, so that you may know that I am the Lord . . .' Times of darkness can be some of the best times."

"My daddy told me for a fact th' Lord helped him start this business. Why would th' Lord be throwin' me out?"

"He may have something different for you now. Something terrific, actually. Maybe it's time, Percy, to look at other options . . ."

"Bein' out of a job at age sixty, with your wife doin' piecework at the glove factory—buddyroe, that ain't an option. Cuttin' and haulin' wood and sellin' it door to door ain't an option either, not with my back. And I can tell you right now that pumpin' gas at Lew Boyd's ain't an option, not now or in the dadgum future. So . . . I ain't got any options."

"Right. Maybe you don't."

Faint rays of daylight shone through the small window that faced the sidewalk on Main Street.

"But maybe God does," the rector said. "Look here. When God takes away the good, He replaces it with something better. Didn't Jesus tell the disciples, 'It's for your good that I'm going away'? And do you think they went for it? No, it plunged them into despair—they felt orphaned and desolate, probably angry into the bargain."

Percy stared at the furnace.

"But when the Holy Spirit came, the disciples had more than Christ in their *midst*—now He was in their hearts." Yes! He felt encouraged just talking about it. He clapped his hand on his friend's shoulder.

"So, Percy—screw up your faith and get ready for something better."

Percy stood and glared at him. "We better screw something up, all right, and get these boxes packed. Start with th' sauerkraut on that top shelf and work down to the pork an' beans. We won't mess with th' jukebox 'til th' college boys get here."

At noon, Mack Stroupe dropped in with a sack of hot dogs all the way, and Winnie Ivey brought a dozen cream horns and napoleons. The Collar Button donated a case of Classic Coke, Coot Hendrick brought a pie his mother had baked, the police chief dropped in with a sack of apples, and Joe Ivey stuck a bottle of brandy under his belt, buttoned his jacket, and walked to the Grill where he passed the bottle around to whoever wanted a taste.

Joe eyed the rector. "If I was you, I wouldn't let your boy cut your hair."

"Dooley?"

"He's made a mess of th' sides," said Joe. "You want a little nip?"

"Thank you, but I pass. I'm a sherry man."

"You can get stumblin' drunk on sherry," Joe told him.

"Man!" said Mule. "This is killer kraut. This is the third box I've heaved up th' steps. Who eats this stuff, anyway?"

"Nobody," said the rector. "That's why he's got a surplus."

Mule looked up as J.C. came down the stairs, wearing his Nikon on a strap around his neck. "I thought you were puttin' out the paper."

"I've said all I've got to say."

"We haven't packed all we've got to pack, so hop to it. Here's a box. There's the stewed okra." Mule kicked an empty box into the light of a sixty-watt bulb.

"I hate stewed okra."

"You don't have to like it to pack it."

"No way, Jose. I did my time. I'll just sit and watch you boys." J.C. scratched himself and sat down on a step.

Fancy appeared at the hatch door, wearing a form-fitting cashmere sweater, pink tights, and white boots with spike heels. "Yoo hoo, Mule honey, Coot's back with the truck. Do y'all have another load ready? If not, we need him to help us clean these floors."

"It'll be awhile, yet."

"Super. Oh, Father, I didn't say one word to Joe Ivey about how you've switched over to me."

He'd switched over?

"I'm about wore out," said Percy. "I wish I dipped or chewed or smoked—somethin'."

"Joe offered you a taste of brandy," said Mule. "You ought to have had a little shooter."

"No sir," said Percy, looking mournful, "I've gone sixty years without it, and I don't intend to start now."

"Liquor gets your kidneys," J.C. announced. "Not to mention dries out your skin, ruins the veins in your nose, gives you palsy, and wrecks your coordination. I've heard that people on gin start walkin' sideways, like crabs."

Mule scratched his head. "They drink an awful lot of gin at the country club, but I never saw anybody walk sideways."

Fancy's spike heels clicked above them like castanets.

"How you 'uns comin'?" Uncle Billy stuck his head in the hatch door and peered into the gloom.

"We need a joke!" said the rector. They had packed seventy-two boxes, all told, not a few of which were breakables that had already been broken.

"How about if I stand right here t' tell it," said Uncle Billy. "Arthur won't let me come down steps, don't you know." Activity subsided as the old man reared back to deliver his contribution to moving day.

"Did you 'uns hear about th' feller lookin' for a good church?"

"No!" chorused his audience.

"Well sir, he searched around and found a little fellowship where th' preacher and th' congregation were readin' out loud. They were sayin', 'We have left undone those things which we ought to have done, and we have done those things which we ought not to have done.'

"Th' feller dropped into th' pew with a big sigh of relief. 'Hallelujah,' he said to hisself, 'I've found my crowd at last.' "

The rector laughed heartily. "It's about time you worked our bunch into your repertoire."

"Hit us again, Uncle Billy," said Mule.

"This feller, he went t' th' doctor and told 'im what all was wrong, so th' doctor give 'im a big load of advice about how to git well. Th' feller started to leave, don't you know, when th' doctor said, 'Hold up. You ain't paid me for my advice.' 'That's right,' th' feller said, 'because I ain't goin' t' take it.' "

"I'll print that one," said J.C., scribbling in his pocket notebook.

"Well, I'll be pushin' off. It's a shame what's happenin' here t' two good friends. Me and Rose, we think th' world of you 'uns. Try not t' take it too hard."

Uncle Billy vanished from the hatch door, and they returned wearily to their work.

Fancy appeared on the top step, where she leaned over and whispered, "Percy, Velma's cryin' again."

"What do you want me to do about it?" Percy snapped. His arms were wrapped around a tub of Crisco.

"Let her cry," said the rector. "It helps."

J.C. cocked his head and listened. "Run for th' hills. It's Lucrezia Borgia."

Mule furrowed his brow. "Who?"

"I'll just duck behind the furnace," said the rector.

Edith Mallory appeared at the hatch door. "Who's down there?" she demanded.

"Mule Skinner, Percy Mosely, and J.C. Hogan," said Mule, peering up the stairs.

"When will you be finished?"

"Before tomorrow."

"What time before tomorrow?"

"We don't have a clue."

"I suggest it be no later than midnight, as agreed. Is Father Tim down there?"

"I don't see him."

"Where do you think he might be?"

"Heaven knows."

"Remember, Mr. Mosely, that the booths come out also. I see they're still attached to the wall. And you'll recall that the stools must be out, as well."

Percy clenched his fists.

"Mr. Coffey will meet their truck in Wesley tomorrow morning. He'll lead the way and they'll proceed. They'll occupy the premises at eight o'clock sharp." Edith stomped away from the hatch door.

"You can come out now," Mule said in the direction of the furnace.

They heaved the last of the boxes up the steps, too weary to speak.

"Give me a flashlight," said the rector. "I'll look around, one last time."

He couldn't remember feeling such exhaustion and soreness of spirit. All he wanted to do was go home and go to bed. Yet, they didn't want to leave behind any valuable items that Percy might be able to turn into cash. The Collar Button man had offered five hundred dollars for the jukebox, if Percy would also let him have the records that included "Sixty-Minute Man," "One Mint Julep," and "Chattanooga Shoeshine Boy." Percy was thinking about it.

Mule had swept the concrete floor and stood the broom in a corner. Strange that nothing but a worn-down broom was left of a family's fifty-two-year history.

He shone the light throughout the eerie space, which had grown colder and damper with nightfall. He had smelled all the sour earth he could stomach and decided that plans for cleaning his own basement could wait a few years.

He pointed the flashlight under the floor joists where raw dirt left only a few feet of interval space. Maybe some of those old advertising signs had been stored in there—the Collar Button man's excitement indicated they were valuable.

That was when he saw it.

CHAPTER SEVENTEEN

Broken Rules

Ron Malcolm whistled.

"The joists are rotten from front to back, but it looks like the worst is smack under the rear booth."

All he could see were Ron's feet sticking out where he'd crawled between the floor joists and the bank of earth.

"For goodness sake, tell Percy to stop jumping around up there."

"Percy!" the rector shouted up the stairs.

"What?"

"Hold it down a minute." He hadn't told Percy what he had seen. Instead, he said he thought Ron Malcolm, being a former builder, might like to see the interesting way the building was supported.

"How fast can you get here?" he said from the phone booth in front of Happy Endings, and Ron had hit the floor beside his bed running.

Ron wriggled out of the space. "After forty years in the construction business, I sure as heck don't want to be crushed under a pile of rubble."

"That bad?"

"You wouldn't believe it. Southern pine, plenty old, and rotten to the core. I've seen it a hundred times. It's a miracle we haven't all been dumped in the basement. Especially the rear booth—it's a real hot seat."

"The new tenants come in tomorrow morning."

"Not in here, they don't. When the town inspector gets a look at this . . ."

"Could we call him, get him to take a look at it . . . now?"

"Now?"

"Edith Mallory needs to hear this, but she probably needs to hear it from a town authority."

"It's eleven o'clock at night . . ."

"How long could it take for repairs?"

Ron looked up and around. "Two months, six months. There's a lot of hidden stuff in a setup like this. Who knows? Minimum, maybe two months. You got to rip out the joists from front to back . . . lay a new floor. . . . Maybe we could salvage some of the old floor. I don't know. I saw this same thing happen in a church once—a few more Sundays and the entire gospel side could have been swallowed up.

"They'll want to check the stairwell that goes to J.C.'s press room, too. That whole area is pretty bouncy, as I recall."

"Let's think this through," said the rector, sitting down on the bottom step.

Edith Mallory looked as if she'd dressed for a bridge luncheon, although it was nearly midnight. She drummed her fingers on the surface of her breakfast counter where they sat on stools. A cigarette smoldered in the ashtray.

"Rotten," said the rector.

"Clear through," said the former builder. "I plan to report it to the town inspector first thing in the morning, because it's a hazardous situation. Somebody could get killed in there."

The muscles in her face appeared to tighten, which made her enormous eyes seem larger. "I have a moving van arriving in Wesley at seven o'clock in the morning."

"When the inspector sees the problem, chances are he'll condemn it." She uttered an oath.

"It'll take a couple of months, maybe more, to make repairs. Worst case, other problems could be lurking in the structure, as well."

She put the smoldering cigarette out. "I'm flying to Spain day after tomorrow." She sat immobile, frozen. "I don't suppose this is some cooked-up ruse to keep your friend from leaving . . ."

"Keep him from leaving?" said Father Tim. "He's already gone. Midnight, remember?"

She stared at the wall clock, a nerve twitching under her left eye.

"How long will you be in Spain?"

"Three months," she snapped. "Then on a world cruise."

"You said the dress shop would have to go elsewhere if they couldn't occupy tomorrow, is that correct?"

"That," she said, turning on him with a kind of seething fury, "is precisely what I said and precisely what they will be forced to do." She drew one of her brown cigarettes out of the package. "That odious place has never been anything but trouble to me."

"Perhaps the space will be attractive to another of your connections . . ."

"I wanted it finalized before I leave." She got up and paced the kitchen floor. "I suppose you think I have time to recruit tenants before Wednesday?"

"I have a tenant for you."

She looked at him condescendingly. "Really?"

"The same tenant who occupied it for thirty-four years."

She sniffed.

"I hear you'll be spending more of your time in your Florida home."

"You heard correctly."

"Sign a lease with Percy and make your repairs. This would put the place in good hands, with no running back and forth to pacify a high-rent lessee. You'd have no fancy carpeting to pay for, no walls and ceilings to restore and paint, no upgraded toilet to install." He paused and plunged ahead. "A five-year-lease with a twenty percent rent increase."

She glared at him. "You must be kidding."

"Five and twenty," he said evenly.

The nerve under her left eye twitched again. "One year at forty percent."

"Five and twenty, and you replace the awning. We'll scrape and paint the front of the building."

"Right," said Ron.

She stood in the middle of the floor, rigid. "One and thirty. Bottom line."

The rector got off the stool. "Have a good trip, Edith." Ron followed him to the door.

He was turning the knob when she came into the foyer behind them. "All right, then. Five and twenty."

He turned around to face her cold rage. Edith hissed a bitter curse, which, for all its foulness, didn't surprise him in the least.

"Not one bit of skin off Percy's nose," said Emma. "He had to move out, anyway, for all that work to get done. Plus, it was in the nick of time, before the whole thing caved in and people raised a stink."

It hadn't been what the scripture from Isaiah had meant, exactly, but God had given Percy a treasure in the darkness. There in that dim basement were the rotten joists—which, oddly, had been worth their weight in gold.

"It's wonderful," said Cynthia. "You're the man of the hour!"

He'd never been the man of any hour. He discovered that he felt taller, even thinner. How that was possible, he had no idea. However, he didn't want to get carried away with such nonsense. And he also didn't want to gloss over the most important of his feelings, which was joy.

A comfortable way of life was being changed—but then, it would soon be restored. Percy would not die, Velma would not cry, he could get a bowl of soup somewhere other than his own kitchen, and life would go on.

He walked to the church and knelt down and prayed, having a good laugh with the Lord as he confessed he had no idea that he'd wind up playing hardball with Edith Mallory—and win.

He would have to do something about Meg Patrick, but he didn't know what.

Also, he needed to contact a few more schools and meet with at least two of Dooley's teachers for the hoped-for recommendations.

Most important, Mitford School would be out in June, which was next month, so he'd better get cracking and have a talk with Dooley Barlowe.

June! he thought, sitting uneasily at his desk. The month in which a tutor would have to be brought in, Puny would be getting married and going away for two weeks, Hoppy and Olivia would be married at Lord's Chapel and feted at Fernbank, and, last but not least, the bishop would come to perform the annual confirmation service—one in which both Dooley and Cynthia would be welcomed into the church. This time, Martha would come with the bishop, and he felt compelled to entertain them.

It seemed that something else was going on in June, but he was relieved that he couldn't remember what.

He took a break and drove to the country to see Brother Greer.

They sat on the porch of the store that looked out to a pasture across the road and slugged down a couple of Cheerwines from the drink box.

Barnabas slept with his head on the old pastor's foot.

"That little handful still needs a preacher," he told Absalom.

"I laid it before the Lord and let it winter over."

"And?"

"I'll do it."

"Splendid! Wonderful!" He felt invigorated by the cheerful light in his friend's eyes.

"How do I get in there and all?"

"Rodney Underwood, our police chief. He said he'd have you picked up and escorted every Wednesday at six o'clock. It's hard to find your way along the creek, and it's rough territory into the bargain. Are you sure you want to do it?"

"The Lord spoke to my heart about what to preach, so I'm set on doing it. 'Behold, now is the accepted time; behold, now is the day of salvation.'

"Lots of folks plan to get around to the Lord tomorrow, but tomorrow never comes. I'm to go on from there with something else Paul said to the Corinthians, 'Therefore, if any man be in Christ, he is a new creation; old things are passed away; behold, all things are become new.' "

"Amen!" said the rector.

"Will you drop in on us now and again?"

"Consider it done," he said, warmed by the old man's fire.

Buck Leeper shouted an oath into the phone and merely said, "Get up here. Now."

He had driven to the office this morning, because it was Saturday and he needed to run errands, but it never occurred to him to drive to the job site. Leaving the office unlocked, he raced up Old Church Lane and headed right on Church Hill, glad for the running shoes he'd worn.

There was something in Buck Leeper's voice that told him everything and nothing. Something was horribly wrong; he could feel it.

His heart pounded as he raced over the brow of the hill and onto the Hope House property. From the direction of the hospital, the shrill whine of the ambulance pierced the air.

He ran toward the group of men standing by a pile of lumber and saw what appeared to be a boy lying on the ground.

Dear God! he prayed, his heart bursting, don't let it be Dooley!

It wasn't Dooley.

"It's Tommy," said Dooley, his face a shocking mask of fear. He was shaking uncontrollably as the rector clasped him to his side.

Buck Leeper loomed over him, cursing so vehemently that he drew back. "Didn't I tell you to keep these kids off my job? I hope to God you like what you see."

What he saw was the boy, lying unconscious on his back. A terrible bruise colored his temple, and his bleeding right leg was gashed from the calf to the thigh, exposing the bone. He had seen this very sight before, in a dream about Buck Leeper. The strangeness of the coincidence was unspeakable.

He instinctively stepped toward Tommy.

"Don't touch him," growled Leeper.

Dooley was sobbing. "We was playin' on that pile of lumber. It started rollin' and Tommy fell down in it. He went on down and hit th' ground. When it started rollin', I jumped off." A deep moan came from Dooley.

The men stood by, shaken, helpless. "We wasn't workin' today. We just drove up to check . . . ," somebody murmured. Then, the ambulance attendants were among them, and the quiet, wounded boy was laid on a gurney and the doors slammed shut and the ambulance was gone up the hill, and they were left there, stunned.

Buck Leeper's presence seemed to consume the very air, so that the rector gasped for breath. He had seen the man angry, but this was something else, something more frightening than anger.

He instinctively looked around for his car, but of course, it wasn't there, and Buck Leeper had turned and headed toward his red pickup.

He looked helplessly to the men.

"Let's go!" They sprinted toward a truck parked at the trailer.

"It's the head I'm worried about, not the leg," said Hoppy.

"Wilson's giving the leg a pressure dressing, and we're taking him to Wesley immediately. Must have been a nail—as he fell, the nail kept ripping. It just missed the femoral artery. I could see the artery and the nerve right beside it. Another quarter of an inch and he could have bled to death before we got to him.

"They'll do a CAT scan in Wesley. I've got a call in to Dr. Hadleigh. Good man. Neurosurgeon. There could be blood between the skull and the swelling, a hematoma. He'll need watching."

"Is he still unconscious?"

"Big time. What about his parents?"

"Can't reach them. Got an answering machine."

"Listen," said Hoppy, his face troubled, "I'm praying about this— for whatever it's worth."

"It's worth more than we know," said the rector, who could not stop shaking inside.

They sped to Wesley, trying to keep the ambulance in sight.

He burned with shame and guilt. In all his life, he couldn't remember feeling this terrible nausea of the spirit; he had wounded Tommy by his own hand, by an act of senseless, unforgivable neglect.

He glanced at Dooley, whose face remained a mask of white. The responsibility for Dooley was not only real, it was constant—twenty-four hours a day. He had failed, he had let down, he had only been pulling halftime, when overtime was clearly required.

Five miles out of Mitford, Buck Leeper's truck passed them and held the lead.

He had never felt so worthless, so frightened, and so desperately out of control.

Tommy's stricken parents arrived, responding to the rector's answering-machine message to call him on the third floor at Wesley Hospital.

He wanted nothing more than to say, "I'm sorry, it's all my fault," but could not speak when they came in. A clergyman who couldn't speak in someone's time of need? He felt miserably impotent.

Buck Leeper paced in and out of the smoking room, hovering on the fringes.

"No hematoma," said Dr. Hadleigh, who had just read the X rays. "We don't know how long he'll be unconscious. It could be hours or days. Actually, it could be weeks, but we're hoping against that."

Tommy's mother looked at him and held out her hand. "Go in with us, Father." It was something in her voice, perhaps, but he felt forgiven. He began to weep, unable to control it, and they walked into Tommy's room together.

"I puked," said Dooley, wiping his mouth and getting in the car.

"Good."

"I been wantin' to. Is he goin' to die?"

"No."

"It was my fault," said Dooley, suffering.

"Why?"

"It was my idea. Tommy said we better not go up there n'more. Mr. Leeper told us not to."

He drove in silence. It was nine p.m. They had stayed through the operation that mended the hideous gap in the boy's leg. He felt exhausted, he felt angry, he felt unutterably sad, he felt too much at once.

"Are you mad?" asked Dooley quietly.

"Yes," he said, meaning it.

There was a long pause. "I'm sorry," Dooley whispered.

"Are you?"

"Yeah."

"It seems to me you're in a big hurry lately to mess up your life."

Dooley stared ahead.

"You get thrown out of school and a friend nearly gets killed, all because of breaking the rules. You could have been killed yourself. What is it with you? Talk to me about this."

"I just done it, is all."

"Tell me why you did it."

"It was fun."

"What was fun?"

"Smokin', playin' on 'at ol' lumber pile, messin' around."

"I didn't see you having fun when smoking got you stuck in the house for ten days. How much fun have you had today?"

"I don't know."

"The accident happened about eleven o'clock. How long had you been playing on the lumber?"

"We jis' started. About ten minutes."

"You swapped ten hours of agony for ten minutes of fun."

Dooley was silent.

"Think about it. You're smart enough to know that's stupid."

Sending him off to school could now seem a punishment instead of a privilege. But that's the way it was and no turning back.

"For Tommy, the agony will last more than ten hours. It'll be ten weeks, three months, maybe six months 'til that leg heals up. And when he gets off crutches, he could walk with a limp."

He didn't mention that the boy could lie for weeks in a coma or that serious complications could result from the head injury.

Maybe what Dooley Barlowe needed wasn't talk but a good hiding. Frankly, he couldn't manage giving him one, but perhaps that's why they were in this predicament.

Dooley didn't speak again until they turned into the garage. "Yeah," he said slowly. "It was stupid."

He sat at his kitchen table with Cynthia, having a bowl of her leek soup and talking about what had happened.

He heard the guest room door open. If Meg Patrick came down his stairs and along his hall and into his kitchen where he was trying to sit peacefully with his neighbor, he would dump her in the street, bathrobe and all, followed by her suitcases that approximated the weight of a pair of 1937 Packard sedans.

His cousin must have read his mind, because he heard the door close firmly.

"Nobody's perfect," Cynthia said.

"To roughly paraphrase Paul, why do I do what I don't want to do and don't do what I want to do? I find it one of the most compelling questions in Scripture."

She nodded.

"Why can't I get it right, Cynthia? Right with you, right with Dooley? Blast it, a man's life has to count for more than getting it right in the pulpit once in a blue moon.

"Speaking of which, my sermon for tomorrow is as rough as a cob. I'm going to toss it and ask the Holy Spirit to take over—start to finish. After what I've seen today, it makes the whole thing seem . . . insipid."

He stood up and paced the kitchen. "I'm sick of preaching, anyway."

"Timothy! You can't mean it."

"Oh, but I do mean it. I'm sick of boundaries and twenty-minute sermons and man-made rigmarole. I meant it when I said I want the Holy Spirit to be in control. I don't want to go into the pulpit with anything in my hands . . . 'in my hands no typewritten pages I bring, simply to Thy cross I cling.'

"I'm tired of trying to hold on to the reins and go in this direction or that direction because that's where the propers are leading me, or the congregation is pulling me, or the signs of the times are yanking me. Tomorrow, I'm going to talk about rules—and about breaking them—and what it costs when we choose any means at all to satisfy our own shallow and insatiable longings."

She gazed at him steadily.

"I'm glad you're here," he said, feeling suddenly weak and exhausted.

She came and put her arms around him and held him and patted him gently on the back, and he realized something he hadn't realized before:

Cynthia Coppersmith was his friend.

He wasn't going to wait any longer. He was going to catch up and stay caught up.

After the second service, he would talk with Tommy's parents and confess his neglect in warning Dooley, then commit his help throughout the long ordeal ahead.

Next, he would talk with Dooley and lay out the school proposition. Maybe the time wasn't right, but waiting for the right time had caused this whole tragic episode in the first place.

Finally, he owed an apology to Buck Leeper, plain and simple.

He went into the first service fired with an energy and conviction that lasted through the second, and he delivered a message that made his scalp tingle.

He had prayed for years to find the spiritual gall, the faith, to let go completely of his notes. That prayer had been answered, he knew it. He felt some oppressive weight fly off him.

Tommy's mother said, "Nobody's perfect."

"But if I had come down on Dooley, reinforced the rules . . ."

"It might have worked—we can't be sure. What's done is done, Father. It's hard being a parent."

Truer words were never spoken.

He stood by the bed of the still-unconscious boy and held hands with his parents and prayed. Dooley sat in the waiting room and stared out the window.

"Let him go in for a moment," he implored the nurse. "They're best friends."

When Dooley left Tommy's room, the rector searched the boy's face for information. A place the boy had long and fiercely guarded in himself had somehow been broken into. A process that might have taken years had instead taken minutes.

He sat on Dooley's bed. "There's something you need to know."

Dooley looked up from the veterinary book. "What's 'at?"

"I love you," he said.

He laid it all out, exactly as it was, and told him why going away to school was important and that he believed in him and in his special skills and abilities and so did Miss Sadie and his teachers.

"It's going to be a busy summer. You'll need some tutoring, we'll make a couple of trips to visit schools—and you'll want to spend time with Tommy. He's going to have a tough time adjusting."

He spoke his heart to the boy and waited for the script he had worked out in his mind to be executed: Dooley would say he wasn't going to do it, and a battle of wills would ensue.

Dooley stared at the book in his lap.

Perhaps he might do a little more selling, treat it as a real campaign, but no, he had made it plain and simple and he rested his case.

He leaned over and gave the boy a hug. He didn't flinch or move away.

He went to the house in the woods, finding it at the end of a rough lane, and saw Buck Leeper's truck sitting in the yard.

Except for trips along the creekbank to see Homeless Hobbes, he seldom ventured off the beaten path. He stood for a moment in the yard, looking into the woods and hearing birdsong.

The smell of sour ashes in a cold fireplace carried through the screened door as he stepped onto the porch and knocked.

Buck came down the hallway carrying a glass in his hand. He didn't walk to the door but stopped in the middle of the room. He swayed slightly on his feet. "What do you want?"

"I want to talk to you."

He stood, blocking the light from the other end of the hall, a dark, featureless apparition whose face the rector couldn't read. He swirled the liquid in his glass and swallowed it down. "It's open."

Father Tim opened the door and stepped inside. He still couldn't see Buck's face. "I'd like to apologize."

There was a pause. "Help yourself."

"You asked me to keep the boy off the job site, and I didn't speak to him about it. I meant to, but I didn't. I'm sorry for the turmoil it brought to all concerned. I regret it deeply."

" 'The road to hell is paved with good intentions.' Isn't that the saying? You ought to know."

Buck flicked his cigarette into the fireplace. "Sit down," he said, moving into the light from the windows.

He might have sat in the chair near the door but instinctively walked to the sofa, going deeper into the private territory of a private man. Buck left the room and came back with a bottle, then took a chair opposite him and poured a glass of vodka. He sat hunched over, his elbows on his knees, holding the bottle. "You came to talk? Talk."

He hadn't come to talk; he had come to apologize. "I looked for you at the hospital this afternoon."

Buck drank from the glass. "I was there this morning."

"Right."

There was a long silence. The sour smell of the fireplace ashes permeated the room.

"Drink?" said Buck, tipping the neck of the bottle toward him.

"No, thanks."

"Put hair on your chest." When Buck Leeper laughed, it growled up from him like something boiling on a stove. "Why don't preachers give a crap when it gets down to where the rubber hits the road?"

"What do you mean?"

"You preach eternal life but don't give a crap about this life."

"I do care about this life," he said.

"Not enough to watch out for a couple of stupid kids who're lookin' to get killed." His eyes narrowed. "You should have been all over their butts about it."

"Have you ever meant to do something right and failed?"

Buck drained the glass and cursed.

"Have you? You talk to me."

Buck got up and walked to the windows. Keeping his back to the rector, he looked out into the woods. The silence lasted a long time, then he said, "I got a kid killed."

Through the windows, the rector saw a squirrel leap from one branch to another. He didn't speak.

"It was my first construction job. I was seventeen. I was crazy about those machines. The power in them, even the colors, excited me. My old man turned me loose with a back hoe. He said if I didn't do good, he'd kick my butt all the way to the Mississippi." Buck set his glass on the windowsill and lit a cigarette, cursing his father.

"Then I took th' kid out on the job one night and put him in th' cab, and showed him the hole I'd been digging, and let him dig a bucketful. It had rained for a week, and the ground was mush. I'd pulled the hoe too close to the edge of the hole and when we raised the boom with the dirt on it, the dirt caved away under the stabilizer."

He took a long drag on the cigarette.

"The machine pitched into the hole, and I jumped out. But it . . .

knocked the kid off and pinned him under. When we got the hoe off, he was . . ."

Buck wheeled around from the window and slung the bottle at the fireplace chimney, where it smashed against the rock. Shards of glass rained to the floor and rattled across the hardwood.

Tears coursed down his face. "That kid," Buck said hoarsely, "was my brother."

The violent storm of weeping and cursing went on around him for hours, as he sat it out with the man who had nowhere left to go with his pain.

At one point, Buck picked up a wooden chair and hurled that, too, at the stone of the fireplace, smashing it apart. The rector flinched as a leg careened over the floor and landed at his feet. Any fool, he thought, would run from this violent place, but he could not run.

The bile of bitterness and suffering and impotence and hatred poured from a man who was fighting for his life, as he cursed God, his father, and then, himself.

Yet, as the venom spewed out of Leeper, a deep peace entered into the rector. He didn't try to understand what was happening, and he didn't try to speak. He only sat, praying silently, and went through it with him.

It was ten o'clock when he left Buck Leeper sleeping on the sofa where he had fallen, and went out the door and down the steps to his car.

"You won't believe this," said Emma. "Three guesses what Velma and Percy are goin' to do."

Emma had two infernally favorite games: Three Guesses and Last Go Trade. He despised both.

"Do I have to?"

"Yes," she said, sounding final.

"They're ah . . ." He had never been good at this sort of thing. "They're going to Hawaii!" he said with abandon.

She looked shocked. "How did you guess?"

"You mean they are? Good heavens! I simply picked the most far-fetched thing I could think of."

"That's exactly where they're goin'. You must have ESP. Their kids passed th' hat and collected enough money for a cruise. Velma called me last night. Does that beat all? Velma Mosely has never been outside the county, as far as I know, except to visit her cousin—and then she got carsick."

Percy and Velma in Hawaii? That did, indeed, beat all.

Emma answered the phone.

"Hold on a minute, Evie."

Emma held the receiver against her bosom. "Do you want to talk to Evie?" she whispered.

No, he didn't want to talk to Evie. What could he possibly do? Go by after lunch and watch Miss Pattie stare out the window? Hold Evie's hand and pray, once again? He didn't think he could bear to see any more suffering. No, he didn't want to talk to Evie.

He reached for the phone. "Hello, Evie."

"Hello, Father! For a change, I'm not calling to ask you for anything . . ."

"That's all right," he said, hearing an odd lightness in her voice. "Ask me for something."

"I just wanted to say that Mother had a lucid moment this morning and wanted me to call and give you a message."

"She did?"

"She wanted me to call," said Evie, choking up, "and say that she loves you."

He felt as if he were punched in the chest. "Please tell her I love her, too." He did, of course. He'd merely forgotten it for a moment. "Tell her I'll come by after lunch and give her a hug."

He hung up the phone, beaming.

"What's Miss Pattie done now?" asked Emma.

Percy called to report how lease negotiations had gone with Edith's lawyer. Apparently, the town inspector hadn't found much to be concerned about, outside the rotten joists and flooring. Minor repair was needed to correct the roof leak, and the washroom plumbing would have to be replaced. Bottom line, the Grill was set to reoccupy the premises on August 15.

"I'll bring you one of them wild shirts," said Percy.

"Father?" It was Tommy's mother. "Tommy is trying to talk."

He ran with Barnabas from the office and met Dooley coming out of school alone with his book bag. He thought he had never seen him look so desolate.

"Tommy's trying to talk," he said, swallowing hard.

Dooley's face was transformed. If the rector had never witnessed pure joy, he had now.

With Barnabas straining ahead of them on the leash, they ran all the way home.

CHAPTER EIGHTEEN

The Ceiling

On a scale of one to ten, his energy level was hovering around two and a half.

Age, blast it, and diabetes. And no chocolate cake when a man would give his eyeteeth for a slice.

He thought of taking Cynthia to Wesley for a decent dinner in that place with the green tablecloths, but recalled Edith Mallory's brown cigarette smoldering in the ashtray and didn't think he could stomach it.

Every day after school, he was driving Dooley to the hospital, where Tommy's recovery was brutally slow.

Tommy was stringing words together now, but when he arrived at the end of a sentence, he had forgotten what he said. Blinding headaches accompanied all the repercussions of his accident and the surgery.

The rector sat at his desk in the office, staring through the high windows at the trees. Maybe he should take vitamins.

"Miss Sadie," he said when she answered the phone, "I'm feeling an old, worn-out clergyman. May I walk up and hear the story of the ballroom ceiling? I'll bring lunch."

"Don't bring pizza," she said, "it gives me heartburn!" Apparently, even Miss Sadie had tried the new drive-through pizza franchise on the highway. "Let's have something plain, like sandwiches on white bread—you bring the filling."

An hour later, carrying a sack from The Local, he climbed the hill to Fernbank and delivered a bag containing sliced turkey, sliced ham, and a jar of honey mustard into the hands of his hostess.

"We forgot to tell you, Father—we don't like olive loaf." She peered into the bag suspiciously. "Is this olive loaf?"

"No, indeed."

"Good! I said, 'What if he brings olive loaf?' and Louella said, 'We'll eat it anyway. It's the right thing to do!' "

Throughout lunch, they clinked the ice in their tea glasses, laughed over nothing at all, and Louella called him "honey."

During dessert, which was a plate of Fig Newtons, he told them how well they were looking, and they, in turn, commented on his jacket and his good color and his trim size, and before he knew it, he wasn't feeling like an old clergyman anymore; he was feeling like a boy.

Miss Sadie pushed open the door to the ballroom with her cane.

"It's the first day I haven't had workmen in here, and I can't tell you how glad I am for the peace.

"I don't know how we're making it through all the uproar, except by the grace of God. Have you ever had your house torn up, Father?"

"I've had a washing machine flood the kitchen."

"Poshtosh! You've led a sheltered life."

She took his arm as they stood and surveyed the scene.

"Sadie Baxter's folly, that's what it is. But it's going to be more beautiful than it was the evening President Wilson danced right over there with my lovely mother."

He felt the sense of new life, of renovation, that permeated the vast room. There was freshness to it, and hope. "Has Olivia seen what's going on?"

"Oh, no! And she won't, until the day of the reception. I pray she'll think she's stepped into heaven itself. Oh, Father, in all my life, I've never wanted something to be so perfect! What do you think?"

"I think your prayers are being answered," he said, looking at the freshly restored windows that ran from ceiling to floor and the scaffolding built to lift workmen to the water damage on the ceiling and walls.

A film of sanding dust clung to everything, including the white canvas over the floor and the furniture, so that the whole room was a dreamlike shade of ivory in the early-afternoon light. The only color was on the ceiling, where robed angels burst from clouds and swept among the cherubim with blazing authority.

"Tell me what I can do to help," he said. Somehow, offering to bake a ham didn't seem right.

"Not one thing. The caterer from Charlotte is doing it all—food, flowers, music, chairs. And the cost? Through the ceiling, no pun intended. I just closed my eyes and jumped in."

"I suppose you'll be having a splendid new gown?"

"Certainly not! I'm too old for new gowns. There's not enough time left to wear them out, you see."

He put his arm around her shoulder.

"Let's go to my bedroom, so we can relax while we talk. But first, I want you to take a look at something."

"Yes, ma'am," he said.

She pointed her cane toward the ceiling. "See the angel just over there? That one with the smile—not all angels smile, you know."

"On the far right . . . with the rose in her hand?"

"It's the only single rose on the ceiling. All the other roses are in garlands or swags. Now look how her robe flows behind her—and see her feet peeping out? Aren't they beautiful?"

"Exquisite! In fact, she's my hands-down favorite."

"What do you think of the wings?" she asked.

"One might feel the very air moving through them."

"Carry that in your mind's eye," she said, taking his arm.

Pleased at the prospect of a good story, they went up the stairs as contented as children.

"See down there, Father?"

They peered through her bedroom window, into grounds leading to the orchard.

"That's the old wash house. Our home wasn't even near to being finished when we came to this hill, so we all moved into the wash house like a troop of gypsies.

"China Mae had the room on the back, about the size of the hall cupboard at Lord's Chapel—and not one floorboard was there in any square inch of that little place! Just bare dirt, swept clean and hard as tile.

"It was close living, Father, like sardines in a can, but it was the happiest time I ever knew. After a long day at the lumberyard, Papa would draw up to that big fireplace, and Mama would sit and do her sewing, and I would be making doll clothes as hard as I could go."

She laughed gently and took his arm. "Let's sit down before we fall down."

They sat in the old wing chairs, facing each other, where she had confided so many painful secrets.

"Oh, the smell of cooking that China Mae could stir up in that wash house! If anything ever smelled better than chicken and dumplings, I don't know what it is—unless it's cornbread baked in an iron skillet—or a deep-dish apple pie!"

"Don't even start, Miss Sadie . . ."

"China Mae's little room didn't have a thing but a wood stove and our pots and pans and her cot—there was a Bible, too, even though she couldn't read—and a peg for her clothes and a tin washtub hanging on the wall. We all used the same outhouse—at different times, of course!

"I think living that way got on Mama's nerves something awful, but when our house was finished and we moved in, I cried. I did. I could have gone right on living in the wash house for the rest of my life.

"I remember Papa started talking about his master plan.

"He said the first thing to do was get the orchards planted.

"The second thing to do was get the ballroom ceiling painted.

"And the third thing was have Mr. Woodrow Wilson come for a visit. He didn't want any cabinet members or senators, and nobody from Congress—he wanted the president!"

"Good thinking!"

"When the orchards were under way, Papa started sending letters to Italy. He was writing off for someone to come and paint the ballroom ceiling, you see.

"A man in Asheville wanted to paint it, but Papa saw his drawings and didn't like them at all. He kept saying, 'The artist must be *Italian*.'

"In case someone really came from Italy, I learned three words out of a book. I had no idea what they meant, but I was very proud and made China Mae say them too. *'Tempo è denaro!'* Do you know what that means, Father?"

"I don't have a clue," he said, smiling.

"Good! You'll find out later. Well, now, to make a long story short . . ."

"Don't do that," he said.

She laughed. "All this was a long time ago, and I was too young to pay attention to details. I just know that Papa wrote a lot of letters and got a lot of sample drawings in envelopes with strange stamps. Then he had scaffolding built in the ballroom—just like what's down there now, except it was wood.

"One day two strangers showed up on the porch—a short, dark man with a happy face, and a thin, dark boy with a sad face.

"It was Michelangelo and his son, Leonardo! 'My goodness,' said Mama, 'You send for Italian artists and look who you get!'

"Their last name was Francesca, and they were from Florence. I went around for weeks shouting, 'Michelangelo and Leonardo Francesca from Florence!' I had never heard such words in my life!

"Papa introduced us and I curtsied and said, *'Tempo è denaro!'* And Angelo laughed and laughed, so we had a wonderful start-up, but they could hardly speak a word of English.

"Mama took them to their room down the hall, and China Mae cooked them a wonderful meal, and they rolled up their pants and went right to work.

"Wouldn't you think an artist would roll up his sleeves? But these two always rolled up their pants. I'll never forget it.

"Angelo and Leon did fresco painting. It's like watercolor, but it's done on wet plaster. And you must paint very fast, because when the plaster dries, it won't take color. So they would mix what they might paint in a day, and if any plaster dried before they could paint it, they cut it away.

"I remember they began with the border around the ceiling. They must have worked on that for eight or nine months, every single day except Sunday. On Sunday, they disappeared into their room or packed a knapsack and went walking in the country and sketched in their books.

"I loved to peep into their room, for each had a beautiful cross over his bed, and they always left their room so neat, I could hardly believe my eyes.

"That's where Leon did his studies every evening. Angelo was Leon's tutor, and he was very good at carrying through with his lessons. In the meantime, Mama was teaching Leon English every day after lunch.

"It turned out Leon was sad because his mother had died, and Angelo was always laughing to try and cheer him up. Leon was only twelve years old, but he looked much older because of his sorrow. Dooley reminds me of Leon more than you know, Father.

"Anyway, my mother's gentle way was good for him, and before you know it, he could say, 'I like garden peas!' Or, 'The day is very warm.'

"I know my Mama didn't teach him this, but one day he said, 'Sadie, you are beautiful, *bella.*'

"Can you imagine? I thought I was ugly as a mud fence. But I could tell he meant it. You should have seen his face when he said it."

"Those Italians!" said the rector, grinning.

"Aren't they something, Father? But good gracious, I was only ten and still playing with dolls!

"When they were through with the border, Papa pronounced it excellent. That was high praise from Papa. You had to work like a beaver to get such laurels from him.

"Then the work began on the ceiling itself. Oh, Papa was fussy. He would come home from the lumberyard and stand in the middle of the floor, looking up 'til his neck got a crick in it. He knew just where the angels were to be placed and how the roses were to spill from their hands.

"Slowly but surely, the angels began to fly on the ceiling, and behind them, Leon made the rose-colored clouds appear and painted their robes and their hair. Only twelve years old, Father, and *painting* like an angel!

"They worked so hard that Mama took it on herself to give them a special day off. 'Just go!' she said, 'and I'll deal with Mr. Baxter when he comes home.'

" 'May I go?' I said.

" 'No, they need their rest,' Mama told me, but Angelo said, 'Please!' and for a moment looked so mournful, himself, that I got permission and went!

" 'Til my dying day I'll never forgot the happiness of roaming over the fields and hills with Angelo and Leon. Why, it was one of the loveliest days of my life, until that awful thing happened.

"You can't imagine what was in their knapsack! Colored pencils and sketch pads and a book of verse, not to mention olive oil from Italy and apples and cheese and bread and chicken—and a handful of new potatoes from our garden. They dug a hole in the meadow and built a fire and roasted those little potatoes to a turn, and we broke them open and put coarse salt inside and a bit of the olive oil and—oh, my goodness!"

"Miss Sadie, I can't imagine how Swanson's Chicken Pie ever got to first base with you!"

She laughed. "Nothing ever tastes as good as it did in childhood, does it, Father?"

"Nothing!"

"Even colors were more intense. I remember the purple and aquamarine Leon used to paint some of the robes. I've never seen anything like it again. But it wasn't the tubes of color, Father. It was my childhood eyes—how fresh it all was, what a gift!"

He nodded. Miss Sadie was preaching him a fine sermon without even knowing it. It was splendid to have the shoe on the other foot for a change.

"After we ate, Angelo wanted to lie down in the grass and sleep, and he told Leon to watch after Sadie. Leon always did what his father told him, and so we ran down the hill lickety-split and what did we find? An old orchard!

"I had never seen an old orchard before. Our trees were very small and new, and our orchard floor was raked as clean as a parlor.

"On this orchard floor, there were apples everywhere, a whole carpet of apples, and butterflies by the dozens—you could hardly see the grass! And the smell, Father! It was a perfume I've never forgotten."

She shook her head slowly. "I forget what sweet memories come flooding out if only we open the tap."

He kicked off his loafers, contented.

"Leon chased after a butterfly, and a little further down the hill, I spied an old tree just hanging full of red apples. They were different from those in the orchard, and they looked much redder and sweeter.

"I took off running toward that tree—then, all of a sudden, I started falling and everything went black as ink.

"I had stepped into an old well—the boards over it were rotten and soft as marrow. One minute, I was in an orchard with the sun shining and my heart beating for joy, and the next minute . . ."

"Very much like life in general," he said.

"I was stuffed in there like pimento in an olive. I fell with one leg down and one knee bent against my chest, and there was so much pain I thought I would die. I must have passed out, and when I came to, I was cold. Even though the sun was shining, I was freezing cold.

"I tried to call Leon, but my knee was so tight against my chest, and the pain was so horrible, I could only whisper. Whisper! Who could hear a whisper in a great big orchard on a great big hill?

"I heard Leon calling me. 'Sadie! Sadie!' There was real desperation in his voice because he couldn't find the English words he needed. He called for a long time and finally shouted, 'I like garden peas! Sadie, I like garden peas!'

"Oh, Father, I was so miserable. I wanted to die and get it over with. In a while, I heard Angelo calling too. Their voices would come close, then go far away, and I couldn't move. My arms had gone numb, one leg was completely numb, and I felt like a cube of ice.

"Then the voices stopped, and I felt so alone, and it started raining.

"Believe me, *The Book of Common Prayer* was just words on a page 'til I fell in that hole. You've heard of foxhole religion? I got well-hole religion, and I thank the Lord for it, to this day.

"I'd said 'Now I lay me down to sleep' and 'Our Father who art in Heaven' and 'Give us this day our daily bread' a thousand times. But I'd never once prayed a prayer of my own until then.

"I believe that's when God first started speaking to my heart—the very day I started speaking to His!

"It rained and rained and rained some more. Over the years, the hole had filled with dirt and runoff, but it was still a long way to the bottom. I was stuck about six feet down, and if something didn't happen soon, I knew I'd be six feet under.

"I remember hearing Papa call me, over and over. I would go to sleep, I think, and wake up crying. It was so hard to breathe. It was so horrible I can never express it to you.

"I found out later that the rain had washed away my scent, and the dogs from town couldn't track me. They let them loose, but they just ran every which way and came back to where they started and lay down.

"They searched into the night, Mama said. Leon went to bed about two o'clock in the morning and he couldn't sleep. And he was staring out the window, praying to the Virgin Mother, when he saw a light.

"It was in the air, he said, and it kept growing brighter, but it didn't hurt his eyes. It was a soft light, very soothing. When he told the story later, Mama was able to translate enough to know the light was gentle and loving and reminded him of his mother.

"The light, he said, became an angel, a very beautiful angel like something from the Sistine ceiling. She was dressed in the most beautiful blue robes trimmed with gold, and she was smiling. She beckoned to him through the window, and very fast, he put on his pants and shoes and woke Angelo, and they ran out into the night.

"Angelo never saw the angel, but he believed his son, and he ran with him. And Leon said the angel did not touch the ground but flew above them, slightly in front of them, and the light gleamed from her, showing the way.

"It hadn't occurred to them to bring a lantern, but you see, they didn't need one, for the angel hovered over us, giving light, and Angelo lay down near the hole and stationed his foot behind a big rock and held Leon by the ankles.

"Leon crawled into the hole toward me, and very gently began prying my shoulders up and away from the sides of the well, and slowly but surely he was able to lift me a little.

"The pain just flooded into me, but I remember what a relief it was to be in a different position.

"I could hear Angelo praying very loudly the entire time. I felt we were covered with prayer and with light, just bathed in it.

"Well, Father, somehow they got me up and out, and Angelo was weeping with joy, and he picked me up and they carried me home, and this lovely light covered us all the way."

He was mesmerized.

"I declare," she said, "I'm dry as a bone from that ham. Could you step in my bathroom and get me some water? There's a glass on the sink."

His mind had gone so far away on this celestial ramble that his concerns seemed remote and his heart set free. He returned with the glass of water, proud to have been sent on a mission for Miss Sadie.

She raised the glass with a steady hand and took a sip. "Good, pure well water! Thank you!

"Just think, Father. From the age of four, Leon was taken to the museums and cathedrals of Florence where he saw the work of the Italian masters and was trained to go home and draw the images from memory!

"Angelo said Leon drew and painted the face of the Madonna of the Rock nearly four hundred times before he came to Fernbank. So you see, it's hardly any wonder that he attracted an angel who was properly dressed. You hear a lot about angels these days, but have you noticed how they're usually wearing business suits?"

"A sign of the times," he said, marveling.

"I was awfully bruised and sore and scratched up, but not one thing was broken except two ribs where my knee had cracked against my chest so hard.

"Papa wanted to be angry with Leon for letting me out of his sight and angry with Mama for letting me go off with them. But I preached Papa a sermon, and he changed his mind! I think he did something special for Angelo, but I don't know what.

"Things went on as usual after that. Angelo painted angels and cherubim, and Leon painted clouds and robes and helped with the roses.

"Then something wonderful happened.

"Angelo came to Papa and said in his broken English, 'I know my son was to assist me only with borders and backgrounds and such, but I believe he's ready to paint an angel. Will you trust us, Mr. Baxter? If it doesn't work, we will cut it away and begin again and make up the time on Sunday.'

"For Angelo to offer to work on the Sabbath was shocking. Anyway, what could Papa say? There was Angelo with his happy, expectant face and Leon with his sad, longing face. Papa spoke his first word of Italian. He said, *'Bellisimo!'*

"And so, on the day he turned thirteen, Leon began painting the angel I showed you. He painted the angel who led them to the well in the middle of the night—the only angel on the ceiling who's smiling.

"He wanted to paint the rose in her hand as a tribute to me, but though I was only eleven then, I had enough sense to say he must paint the rose for his mother.

"And so he did."

He sat for a time, silent, as one sits in a movie theater after a film that has stunned the senses. "Words fail me, Miss Sadie."

"That's not one of my handicaps, Father."

They laughed gently, not wishing to break the spell.

"Leon's sorrow went away as he painted the angel. He was done with grieving, somehow, and became the brightest, sweetest boy out of heaven. It broke my heart when they left. I grew to love them so. You don't know how many times I've thought of Leon and yearned to see him again. But he was two years older and must be ancient by now . . . ninety-two, if he's a day."

She closed her eyes and sighed. "Memories give a lot, but they take a lot, too. I'm limp as a dishrag."

"I should have brought you a bag of doughnut holes from Winnie's."

"You could go down to the kitchen for some tea. We've got plenty of unsweetened for you, but I want the sweet!"

"Consider it done," he said happily.

Back at the office, he called the operator and got information on how to do it—including what the time difference was and when the rates were cheaper.

After all, he had never called Italy before.

Tommy had laughed today. It wasn't downright hilarity, by any means, but it had been reviving to hear.

The psalmist had said, "Laughter doeth good like a medicine." Clearly, that was true for the one who heard it, as well as for the one doing the laughing.

He wanted to hear Tommy laugh again and again and see Dooley Barlowe laughing with him.

If he really put his mind to it, perhaps he could think of something funny to do.

Cynthia! There was a brilliant thought. She was funny without even trying to be. He would ask her what to do.

They had walked up the Grill side of Main Street in the balmy spring evening, come back down the post office side, then crossed the street and cut through his backyard to a bench in Baxter Park.

"I think you should wear a gorilla suit," she said.

"Now, Cynthia, be reasonable."

"Timothy, being funny and being reasonable have nothing to do with each other."

"A gorilla suit?"

"I'm serious."

He exploded with laughter. "I can't even imagine such a thing."

"That's the problem," she said, looking cool. "*I* would do it. In fact, I've always wanted to do it."

"Would you do it, then?"

"Certainly not. You're the one who wants to be funny, and I won't be your henchwoman."

He thought she had the most mischievous look in her eye.

"Isn't there something else I could do?"

"Oh, hundreds of things, I'm sure. But wearing a gorilla suit is the best thing of all, so why discuss the others?"

"I wish I hadn't asked, " he said, defeated.

She smiled, looking a trifle superior.

"Will you go with me to the reception at Fernbank for Hoppy and Olivia? In June?"

"Ummm," she said.

"Well?"

"Well, then, yes. I'd love to go."

He was suddenly aware they'd never been out together, officially. This would be something new and different; and it went without saying that everyone would talk.

He felt reckless and expansive and put his arm around her.

"If you were ever . . . ," he began and paused. "That is to say, if you . . ." He thought for a moment. "To put it another way . . ."

"Spit it out," she said.

"Well, then, suppose you actually lived with a clergyman . . ." He thought the pounding of his heart might be heard all the way to the monument.

"*Lived* with a clergyman?"

"You know . . ."

"In *sin?*"

"Certainly not," he said.

"Do you mean, what if I were *married* to a clergyman?"

"Well, yes. If you were ever *that,* what would you do? That is, what sort of . . . how would you spend your time? Just asking, of course." He felt a light perspiration on his forehead. What had happened, anyway? He hadn't meant to stumble into such a conversation.

"I already have a full-time job, as you know. And a clergyman would be another."

"Puny has said that very thing."

"I can't play the piano or the organ."

"Most churches pay someone to do that."

"I can't carry a tune in a bucket."

"Most churches have a full choir, already."

She furrowed her brow and looked at him darkly. "I definitely wouldn't do spaghetti dinners or pancake suppers."

"Good thinking!"

"And I couldn't be bleaching and washing and ironing altar linens."

"There's usually a horde signed up for Altar Guild."

"But," she said, "I can teach Sunday school!"

He saw the warm light in her eyes and the irrepressible hope in her smile.

". . . with a blackboard and colored chalk—the stories of the Bible, illustrated! In fact, I'd like nothing better."

"You're hired!" he said, caught up in the excitement.

"And I can give a tea once a year, with layer cakes and tarts and sorbets and all that. But only once a year, mind you, for it's killing to do it."

"The entire parish will come running." He felt his heart fairly bursting with pride.

"So there," she said "That's it. That's all I'm good for, save an occasional fill-in at lay reading. Oh, and no banners and no needlepoint kneelers."

"Deal," he said, putting his arms around her and kissing her cheek. He liked a woman who knew what she wanted—and didn't want.

"Wait a minute," she said, pulling away, "we're talking what if, not real life, remember?"

"Why, yes," he said, coloring. "Of course we were. I knew that."

The phone rang as he was walking across his bedroom to turn off the light.

"Hey," she said.

"Hey, yourself."

"I've been thinking."

"Umm."

"We were only playing when we talked about being a clergyman's wife . . . right?"

"Oh, yes. Just . . . idle abstraction."

"Well, then, I've something to add to it . . . since we're just playing."

"Do!"

"Yes, I have my own work and I love it and want to continue it, but if I were a clergyman's wife and I truly loved the clergyman, I'd want to do something I failed to mention tonight. More important than teas and teaching, I'd want to take the tenderest care of the clergyman himself."

She was silent for a moment. "That's all," she said softly. "That's all I wanted to say. Good night, Timothy."

After turning off the bedroom light, he went to the alcove window and looked down at the little yellow house with the glow of a lamp burning under the eaves.

"Good night," he whispered, his breath making a vapor on the glass.

"Come home," said Puny, breathless.

"What is it?"

"Come quick as you can," she said.

He went.

CHAPTER NINETEEN

Hasta la Vista

Puny met him at the kitchen door.

"You won't believe this," she said.

"What? What is it?"

She marched down the hall to the stairs. "I've never seen anything to beat it."

He raced behind her up the steps. "What happened?"

"The most disgustin' thing in th' world is what it is."

"What's going on?"

She stopped at the guest room. "I've lived on this earth thirty-four years, and I've never . . . see this little rug? She must of thought she was puttin' th' key in her pocket, and it fell on th' rug, where I found it."

She turned the knob and threw open the door.

Puny was right. He couldn't believe it.

From the unmade bed to the bags of garbage that littered the floor, the room was in complete chaos. Nothing had escaped the disorder—even the pictures hung wildly crooked on the walls.

"Smell that?" demanded his house help. "Nothin' in here's been washed or cleaned for two months. You could get arrested for livin' like this."

He walked slowly into the room.

He saw his books scattered about, many of them open and lying face down. Everywhere, garbage bags spilled forth their contents: KitKat wrappers, old newspapers, scribbled notes, soda bottles, crumpled dinner napkins, tin foil, drink cans.

Clothing lay in a soiled heap in the corner.

"A pigsty!" said Puny, clearly enraged. "And look at this bed." Full of crumbs, he saw. The remains of a sandwich lay on the pillow, and an open bag of potato chips had been shoved under the blanket.

The typewriter sat in the only cleared space on the floor, a sheet of paper rolled into the carriage. What he presumed to be a manuscript lay in sections around the room, the bulk of it scattered across the foot of the bed.

He picked up a page and scanned it. His face burned.

"Good Lord!" This was definitely not about the Potato Famine.

"I read one of them pages, and it shamed me t' death. Her writin' must come straight off th' walls of a public rest room. We ought t' jis' heave it into sacks and burn th' lot of it." Puny was trembling with anger. "And what do you think about that?"

She pointed to an empty milk carton on the dressing table.

No, she was pointing to what lay beside it:

The brooch.

"I found it on the landing," said Meg Patrick, white with fury. "I was going to give it to you, but I forgot. It was right there on the dressing table, in your own house, in plain view—it wasn't as if I'd stolen it, for heaven's sake. And what were you doing in my room? I should think you would respect my privacy as I have unfailingly respected yours."

She stood in the hallway outside the guest room, her hands shoved into the pockets of the belted trench coat, glaring at him.

"I considered asking that you merely clean your room, but I realize that isn't what I want to say, after all."

"What do you want to say, then?" He saw that her magnified pupils had dilated alarmingly.

"I want to say that I'll drive you to the airport in Holding or the bus station in Wesley, whichever you prefer, and we'll leave here this evening at eight o'clock sharp. I'll thank you to pick up my books and stack them properly and take that manuscript out of here before I dispose of it personally."

She didn't slam the door until she had cursed his paternal line all the way back to his great-grandfather.

He lugged the suitcases down the stairs and loaded them in the trunk. His cousin had asked to be dropped at the bus station in Wesley.

"I don't have any money," she said, glowering. "I had thought the heart of a cousin would be generously disposed to a relative who has has traveled all the way from the home country.

"Further, I believed that my needs would be considered as graciously as yours were considered in Sligo, while you lapped up our hospitality like a stoat."

He choked down a retaliation, which would have been futile, and peeled two bills off the money he'd got from the bank only this morning. He handed them to her without a word.

Dooley came along, so they could pay a surprise visit to Tommy.

His houseguest of two months rode to the station without speaking and disappeared into the terminal without a word of good-bye.

"Gross," said Dooley.

His sentiments exactly.

Before Percy let the jukebox go to the Collar Button man, he discovered it was worth more than five hundred dollars—a lot more. Then, before he could run a classified ad in the Wesley paper, Esther Cunningham talked him out of it for the museum, along with a stack of early advertising signs for Camel cigarettes, Dr. Pepper, and Sunbeam bread.

"Just think of the tax deductions," she said, peering at him over a sausage biscuit from Hardee's. "And think of seein' your name on a little sign on the wall next to that jukebox. How about 'Early Wurlitzer, a gift of Percy and Velma Mosely, proprietors of the Main Street Grill, established World War II.' How's that?"

On Wednesday, the mayor called an informal meeting of intimates at her home, hastening to add that Ray would be cooking barbecue with all the trimmings.

The subject was a festival to celebrate the opening of the first room of the museum and the installation of the Willard Porter statue on the lawn.

"Mayor," said the rector, who arrived early with a six-pack of Diet Sprite, "you are hopelessly prone to festivals."

"There's worse things mayors are prone to," she said. The red splotches had appeared on her face and neck, indicating her special enthusiasm for this project.

She stationed him in the family room where he could watch Ray finish making coleslaw. "Take a load off your feet," she said. "I've got to call the hospital an' see if th' new grandbaby is comin' anytime soon."

"Another grandbaby?" he said to Ray with astonishment.

"Number twenty-four!" Ray said, stirring the homemade dressing into the grated cabbage. "Esther likes to be there when it happens, but this one has been hemmin' and hawin' for better than a week."

"Doesn't want to come out here and face the music, I suppose. And no wonder."

Ray shook his head over the vagaries of modern life.

"Can I give you a hand?"

"You can put th' ice in th' glasses. There'll be six of us. Table's set, chairs are pulled to th' table, cornbread's bakin'. We're on go."

"Oh, well," said Esther, blowing into the room, "not a peep. I guess nobody told it that Cunninghams like to jump out and hop to it."

After dinner, the mayor occupied a velveteen swivel rocker in her family room and opened the meeting for discussion.

"I think we ought to have a band for when we unveil the statue," she said. "Do you think the Presbyterians who play the Advent Walk would do it for nothin'—or charge an arm and a leg?"

"I'll call," said Ernestine Ivory, making notes.

"And I think we ought to have the jukebox fixed so we can play it as a demonstration. But it's going to cost money."

"What doesn't?" said Linder Hayes, a local attorney and councilman. "How much?"

"A hundred bucks."

"Are we goin' to charge admission?"

"I should say so! Two dollars a head—man, woman, or child—and no discounts for any faction."

"What are our other expenses?"

"That depends on what we come up with at this meeting. Ernestine, tell them our ideas."

"Well, you see," said the secretary, blushing deeply as all eyes turned to her, "we came up with this list of fun things to do. We'd start the bidding at a certain dollar figure and auction each one to the highest bidder."

"Give us an example," said the rector.

"Well, we thought we could have somebody kiss a pig. We figured the bidding for that ought to start at a hundred dollars."

"If Esther will do it, I'll personally give you a hundred on the spot," said the rector.

The mayor rose to the challenge. "You can't scare me. I like pigs. Put me down for kissin' the pig."

"On the mouth?" inquired Ernestine, her pen poised.

"Make it a hundred and fifty," said Esther.

"Make it five hundred," said Ray. "Think big! After all, it's for a good cause."

"Five hundred," said Ernestine, writing.

"Who in the dickens," said Linder, "can lay out five hundred dollars to see somebody kiss a pig?"

"You've got it all wrong, Linder, honey, which wouldn't be the first time. The money is not to see somebody kiss a pig. It's to help renovate the second room in our one-and-only town museum, which will reflect the culture of this unique place and the history of its people, not to mention provide a valuable document for all time."

"But . . ."

"Kissing a pig is a mere . . ." Esther searched for a word.

"Adornment!" said Ernestine.

Ray attended the meeting from the kitchen, where he had gone to clean up. "By th' time we renovate twenty-two rooms, th' Porter place will be historic all over again."

"Get Percy to do the hula," said Joe Ivey. "That ought to be worth somethin'."

"Write that down," said Esther. "Fifty dollars. If he played a ukulele, we could get seventy-five."

Ray walked into the room carrying a pot and a drying towel. "Tell 'im to wear a grass skirt," he said. "That'll be a crowd pleaser. And another thing. Somebody could push a peanut down Main Street with their nose. I've seen that done. You could get a bundle for that."

"Depends on who you get to push it," said the rector. "For example, Esther doing it might bring five hundred, whereas Coot Hendrick, not being a town bigwig, would bring less."

"Why don't we put you down for that one?" said Esther, peering intently at the rector.

"I pass."

"Eatin' Miss Rose's cookin'—that would be a good one," said Joe Ivey.

"There ain't enough money in the world to get *me* to do that," said Ray, who threw the towel over his shoulder and went back to the kitchen.

"Has any consideration been given to a fund-raiser with more dignity?" asked Linder.

"Dignity?" sniffed the mayor. "You can't raise cash money with dignity. It's hard enough to sell history, much less dignity."

"Just asking," said Linder.

"The peanut deal will definitely draw a crowd," said Ray, not wanting the idea to lose momentum.

"Do you think they ought to push it all th' way down Main Street?" asked Joe. "Lord have mercy, that's a long way. How about from th' bookstore to th' bakery?"

"Fine," said the mayor. "Write that down."

Ernestine raised her hand. "I've got one," she said, coloring furiously. "You could do a demonstration of how the father's dog reacts to Scripture. Nobody's ever seen a thing like that. You could maybe get a hundred."

The rector sighed. "I sincerely hope all this isn't happening in June."

"June twenty-fourth," replied the mayor, looking at the table where Ray was setting out a homemade apple crisp.

On an afternoon jog that took him across Main Street, he met J.C. Hogan.

"Where are you taking nourishment?" he asked, panting from the run.

"On a hot plate. Mule and Fancy gave it to me. I've burned more than I've consumed."

"Come by the rectory one evening, and Dooley and I will set you up to a hamburger."

"How's your cousin? Haven't seen her around."

He wiped his forehead on his sleeve. "Gone. Vamoose. Outta here." He was unable to control the grin that spread across his face.

J.C. emitted one of his rare laughs. *"Hasta la vista?"*

"Right-o. I hear they've started on the Grill."

"I can't think clear enough to write a complete sentence for all the racket goin' on down there."

"Use stringers. I'm sure Hessie Mayhew would fill up a page or two."

"Ha, ha. Have you seen Percy?"

"They're leaving June the tenth. Are you going to publicize the museum festival?"

"What museum festival?"

"Hotfoot it over to the mayor. She'll tell you everything."

J.C. set off at a trot, headed north; the rector sprinted in a southerly direction.

He drove Miss Sadie to see the progress on Hope House. They got out of the car, where she leaned on her cane and gazed across the construction site to the blue swell of mountains.

He looked down at her with affection. "Big things come in little packages, Miss Sadie."

"What do you mean?"

"I mean you," he said, putting his arm around her shoulder.

Buck Leeper left a machine operator and walked over to them.

"Buck Leeper, Miss Sadie Baxter, the generous lady responsible for Hope House."

Buck removed his hard hat. He sheepishly extended his hand, then withdrew it. "Dirt," he said.

"Nothing wrong with dirt," she said brightly.

"Pleased to meet you, Miss Baxter."

"Well, I'm pleased to meet you, Mr. Leeper. I hear wonderful things about your abilities, and I'm proud to have you on this job."

"Thank you," he said, clearing his throat.

He was not imagining it at all. There was something different in Buck Leeper's face, something very different.

"See you at the hospital," he told the rector. Making what was clearly an involuntary bow to Miss Sadie, he said, "Ma'am," then turned and hurried away.

"Shy," she pronounced, looking after the superintendent.

"Twenty-four hundred dollars!" said Cynthia, sitting at his kitchen table, drinking tea.

"Amazing."

"What do you think he'll do with it?"

"I don't know. Stuff it between the matress and box spring, I suppose."

"I wish he wouldn't do that! Life is too short to stuff your money between the matress and box spring."

"Agreed."

"Five of his drawings will appear in the fall. Hardcover. Coffee-table edition! With other art, of course."

"A grand display for the museum." Uncle Billy Watson would be a local celebrity, at the very least.

"Found a tutor yet?"

"Seems there's a Louise Appleshaw around these parts. Spinster. Terribly good at English, but stern."

"Stern. Oh, dear."

"When it comes to English, Dooley Barlowe needs stern. She'd come in the afternoons, three days a week, and take the evening meal with us."

"Always heating up the oven for somebody or other. Not missing your cousin, are you?" She leaned her head to one side and grinned.

"You mean my attractive, terribly good-looking cousin?"

"The same."

"Whatever possessed you to call her good-looking?"

"Oh, but she really is, don't you think? So tall and thin . . . for those of us who're short and dumpy, she seemed . . ."

"You aren't short and dumpy. Short yes, but dumpy, no."

"Thank you," she said sweetly. "I'm not searching for a compliment, I promise, but not only do I feel short and dumpy, I feel vastly old . . ."

"You're a mere child, for heaven's sake. In heart and spirit, quite my junior. Exceedingly my junior."

"Well . . ." she said, gazing at him.

"You look wonderful. Everyone says so."

"They do?"

"Absolutely."

"Who is everyone?"

"Uncle Billy thinks you're a dish. And Mule Skinner still talks about your legs—it's shocking."

"Really? I love this."

"Be glad we're not playing Emma's favorite game, Last Go Trade."

"What's that?"

"I tell you something wonderful I've heard about you, and you, having the last go, had better be prepared to top it. It is a very taxing game."

"I can play that," she said.

"Remember I've just told you some pretty terrific stuff."

"Ha, I can top it all."

"Fire away, then."

"You're sexy, witty, and fun to be with."

"Who said so?"

"I said so."

"It has to be something someone else has said."

She looked blank. "Oh."

"See there? Nobody has said anything worth repeating."

"Avis Packard said you were a good cook."

"That's scraping the bottom of the barrel."

"And Puny once told me you're not hard on shirts."

"Ah. Lovely."

"Let's see . . ." She furrowed her brow in mock concentration.

"Well, enough of that game. I knew I didn't like it." He sipped his tea. "So, I'm all those things you said?"

"What did I say? I forgot."

"You know. Sexy, witty, fun to be with."

"You have your moments. You're not all those things across the board, of course."

"Of course."

She laughed. "I love it when you loosen up."

"What don't you love?" he asked, looking at her intently.

She gazed back at him. "Oh, soggy mittens, chocolate without nuts, and a man who can't find it in himself to hold your hand when it's sticking right out there in plain view."

He took her hand that was resting on the table. "What else?" he said.

"Never being asked out to dinner, not even once."

He got up, still holding her hand. "I have just the place!"

Edith Mallory's smoldering cigarette never entered his mind. He thought only of the soft green walls, the intimate, no-smoking corner table he'd admired, the smiling maitre d', and the menu that, apart from the elk, bison, and reindeer, offered fresh mountain trout.

"You've got something the color of hyacinths . . ." he said.

"I'll wear it! If you'll wear the blue jacket."

"Deal," he said, excited as a boy.

"I think the world of Dooley!" said Miss Pearson, his music teacher. He had crept into her little house like a sneak thief, thinking he'd rather be horse-whipped than spotted by Myra Hayes, who lived only a block away.

"Yes, but he's gotten in a lot of trouble, lately."

"I know," she said, looking forlorn. "But he's working so hard and he's so talented. I believe in him, you see. It would be grand if he could go away to a fine school and have all the privileges."

"Mitford School is itself a privilege, but if we can . . . it will be for the best. Would you write a letter to whom it may concern?"

"Without question," she said, immediately picking up her pen. "I'll do it this minute. And Father . . . ?"

"Yes?"

"Please don't tell Miss Hayes I did this."

"Mum's the word," he said.

Louise Appleshaw would appear at the rectory the first Wednesday after school closed, and tutoring would begin at once.

He had talked with her on the phone, and though she certainly lived up to her reputation for being stern, he put his head down and pushed along.

She was the best, they all said, and he'd better snap her up at once or make do with leftovers.

He wrote a check covering the first three afternoons of tutelage and the books she required, mailed it, and put the whole thing out of his mind, greatly relieved.

Ever since he returned from Ireland, he'd been tripping over the sack of family records in his walk-in closet.

Who else would trip over a sack for better than nine months? The habit of procrastination was something he roundly despised, yet he was, as Coot Hendrick might say, "eat up" with it.

He dragged the sack to the foot of his bed and sat on the floor and opened it.

Postcards, old family letters trustingly lent by Erin Donovan, photographs given him by that dear old neighbor of Erin's whose grandfather had known his . . .

He pored over the dim image of his grandfather as a young man, standing upright and unsmiling in the midst of a field, with a hunting dog at his heels. Was his own face forecast in the face that looked out at him?

He set it aside to show Dooley and Cynthia.

He rifled through the bag, glad to be in touch with all that he'd felt and learned in Sligo, the love that had poured in, and the kindnesses he'd been shown. He caught himself wondering if he'd done the right thing by Meg Patrick, but refused to wonder. Of course he had.

Who had she stayed with in Massachusetts? Riley Kavanagh? He'd always wanted to call Riley, who once sent him a book at Christmas.

Where was the bound document with the family names and addresses in it? At the bottom, of course. He pulled it out and looked up Kavanagh, then looked at his watch. The rates were just going down. Perfect.

He sat on the side of the bed and dialed.

"Hullo?"

"Hello, is this Riley Kavanagh?"

"Speaking."

He introduced himself and reminded his cousin of the Christmas book, and they set off talking at a pace. He gave him the full details of the tea at Erin Donovan's, trying to recall as many names as he could to satisfy Riley's excited curiosity.

"And then of course, Cousin Meg has been here for . . . an extended visit."

Riley let out a whoop of laughter that nearly deafened him, then shouted: "He's got Cousin Meg! He's got Cousin Meg!"

Hysterical laughter erupted in the background. He had never heard such uncontrolled hooting.

"Riley!" he yelled into the phone.

"Oh, heaven help us!" said Riley, gasping for breath. "You do mean the Cousin Meg who eats like a trencherman?"

"The same."

"Room like a pigsty? Eyes like a barn owl?"

"I'm afraid so."

"How long have you had her?"

"Well, I . . . she's just left. Two months."

"Two months!" Riley shouted into the background. "He's had 'er for two months!"

More raucous, knee-slapping laughter, then he heard someone say, "Poor soul. How's 'is blood pressure?"

"Riley . . ."

"Forgive us, Tim. If laughter heals as they say it does, I'm a well man for life. You don't know about Cousin Meg?" Riley blew his nose roundly.

"What's to know?"

"What's to know, he wants to know!" A veritable throng of eavesdroppers broke into convulsions. No wonder Cynthia Coppersmith had developed the habit of hanging up on people. They could be a blasted nuisance.

"God help us!" Riley said, returning at last to the conversation. "Where shall I begin?"

"At the beginning," he said, tersely.

"Cousin Meg is a bloody fraud! She's not even a cousin."

"No!"

"Yes, indeed. Has a hookup with somebody in Sligo who lets her know which poor cousins have been stumbling around the local graveyards looking for their roots, and from all I can gather, she goes from so-called cousin to cousin without a bloody dime in her pocket. She's a professional Irish cousin, you might say. But that's not the worst."

He was afraid to ask. "What's the worst?"

"He wants to know what's the worst!" Riley exploded with laughter yet again, which set off another earsplitting clamor in the background.

He tapped his foot, waiting, his face growing redder and his collar growing tighter. What the deuce . . .

"The worst of it," said Riley, "is she's not even Irish!"

"Not even Irish?"

Something began to bubble up in him. It was the strangest mixture of feelings. What in heaven's name was it? It finally emerged and revealed itself.

It was laughter.

"Never set foot in Ireland, as far as we can learn," said Riley. "Her hookup in Sligo mails those letters that say she's coming, from over the pond. She made the rounds with four of us for seven months. You got off light."

Once he started laughing, he couldn't stop. In fact, he was rolling on the floor, clasping the telephone to his ear, and trying to find the breath to apologize—though, come to think of it, why should he?

CHAPTER TWENTY

June

June.

When he turned the page of the desk calendar and saw that four-letter word emblazoned across the top of the overleaf, he took a deep breath.

Hold on to your hat, he warned himself.

"Jis' say yes," said Puny, beaming.

"Yes," he said, beaming back. "I'll be honored to do it. But must I give you away entirely?"

"I keep tellin' you I'm comin' back!"

"I keep needing reassurance."

"You're a big baby."

He supposed she was right, as usual.

He took the brooch to Wesley for cleaning and repairs.

He waited until the rates went down and called Tiffany's, ordering two wedding gifts and taking the news of the total cost like a man.

He bought a rubber mask of a duck and hid it in his bureau

drawer. As soon as Tommy's headaches subsided, he had every intention of making him laugh like a hyena.

He tried to correct his tendency to procrastinate by jotting down a dinner menu for the bishop and Martha on the evening of the fourteenth, which would follow Puny's afternoon wedding and precede the confirmation service and the bishop's brunch—for which he'd recklessly promised to bake a ham.

He searched for free dates among the jumble of entries on his calendar, then called two schools and arranged visits. It was putting the cart before the horse, since Dooley hadn't done the SATs, but there was no time to waste. He knew the boy could make the cut in math and had to believe the tutoring would bring him around in verbal skills. Getting him in the right school by fall was a seat-of-the-pants, wing-and-a-prayer deal, no two ways about it.

Finally, he apprised Dooley of some social obligations.

"We'll be going to Puny and Joe Joe's wedding and also to the Harper wedding and reception."

"Mush."

"In fact, we're buying you a new jacket this very day. A navy blazer!" he said with pride. "You'll look . . ." He recalled the word the Collar Button man had used to sell him last year's sport coat. ". . . *stunning.*"

"Double mush!" said Dooley.

He was on his way to the Grill for lunch when he remembered there was no Grill.

He fled his office anyway.

At the door of the Oxford Antique Shop, Andrew Gregory was sitting on an early-eighteenth-century bench next to a late-nineteenth-century urn from Sussex.

"Father! Turn in and visit."

"And add another antique to the jumble?"

The handsome Andrew threw back his head and laughed. "I've been waiting for you to come along. I have a glorious art book you'd like to see."

"I'd do well to replace lunch with a feast for the eyes."

"You're looking terrific, actually. In fact, I hear that . . ." Andrew paused discreetly.

"Yes?"

". . . you and your neighbor may be getting married."

"I've heard that very rumor myself. You know how small towns are."

"I'm afraid I do. In any case, if it were true, I wanted to say you're a very lucky man."

He smiled and nodded. "If it were true, I'd have to agree."

"Have a cup of minestrone with me. I fumbled around and made it from a family recipe. You can sit by the window at my prize Georgian dining table and have a go at the book."

How could he refuse?

As the warm June sunlight streamed through the windows of the Oxford, he sat at the mahogany table, contentedly turning the pages of a book on early religious art, unmindful of time.

It was another volume, however, that captured his attention. In a stack of books on one of the dining chairs, he found it.

It was a glorious celebration of the chambered nautilus, from medieval times to the turn of the century. Brilliant scientific drawings and artists' renderings sought to capture the mysterious beauty of the handsomest denizen of the mollusk kingdom.

Excited, he paid Andrew and went on his way, refreshed.

Sixty dollars for lunch! Ah well, he thought, *tempo è denaro,* whatever that meant.

Tommy would be home from the hospital around the time Louise Appleshaw began her afternoon tutoring sessions. That would relieve them of the drive to Wesley and allow Dooley a quick visit to Tommy's house between Miss Appleshaw and dinner.

Dooley felt called to minister to his friend, cheer him on, and tough it out by his side. He was even giving a hand with some light schoolwork. Seeing Tommy's alarming brush with death and feeling the guilt of helping it happen had made Dooley more reflective, less hostile.

Clearly, Tommy's leg was good for Dooley's heart.

He had to miss Louise Appleshaw's first visit because of a three o'clock funeral. Thankfully, her first visit did not stipulate dinner.

When he came home, he found the boy sitting at the study desk, facing a tangle of books and papers and looking disconsolate.

"How'd it go?"

"I'm about t' gag," said Dooley.

"Well, hang in there."

"Have you seen 'er?"

"Who?"

"That ol' teacher that come in here t'day and messed up my mind."

"I have not seen her. We spoke on the phone."

"Here's her picture," said Dooley, who grabbed a felt-tipped pen and angrily drew a long face, a pointed nose, a furrowed brow, and a slash for a mouth.

"That looks like a witch," he said, laughing.

"You got that right."

"Dooley, for Pete's sake, loosen up and learn something new. If you're going to get ahead in this world, you've got to speak and write the King's English. It's that simple." Blast it, he'd already fought this battle.

"I don't want t' go t' that ol' school, no way."

"Anyway! And stop making up your mind ahead of the facts. We're going next week to visit Elmhurst, right after Puny's wedding."

"I don't want t' go t' no mushy weddin', either."

"Go see Tommy," he snapped, "and get back in time for dinner. While you're at it, work on your attitude."

He watched Dooley walk across the backyard and through the hedge to Baxter Park. The little creep, he thought. I love him better every day.

It was amazing. Louise Appleshaw looked exactly like Dooley's drawing. He would have recognized her anywhere.

She looked so stern he thought he'd warm up the introduction. "Louise . . ." he said, extending his hand.

"I don't believe you should call me by my Christian name."

"Of course . . ."

"We wouldn't want your parishioners to talk, since we're both unmarried and thrown together in the intimacy of the home environment."

He felt a positive wrench in his stomach. What was worse, he had to make dinner for this person.

"I got a stomach cramp," said Dooley, whose eyes looked bloodshot.

"Me, too," said the rector. They were still sitting in the kitchen, unable to move since Louise Appleshaw had risen from the table and insisted on seeing herself to the door.

"I hate 'at ol' bat."

"Let me ask you something," he said wearily. "Can you say 'I hate that old bat'? Try it, just like I said it."

"I hate that old bat."

"Well done. Who needs a tutor?"

Dooley looked mournful.

"Tell me you're not going to the hardware store."

"I ain't goin' to th' hardware store."

"Wrong."

"I'm not going to the hardware store," said Dooley.

"Right."

"Why don't you teach me?"

"You don't need teaching as much as you need to shape up and get conscious of the problem. Think before you speak, and you can improve yourself."

"Lots of people say ain't."

"Never mind." He was exhausted. And since Louise Appleshaw was allergic to anything with barley, oats, raisins, nuts, pineapple, white flour, sugar, cow's milk, carob, chocolate, dates, leeks, cabbage, lima beans, beef, pork, and tomatoes, what in the name of heaven was he going to do about dinner on Friday?

He had a word of wisdom so full of meaning that he called the boy on the phone.

"Think of it this way. If you put your head down and give it all you've got, it'll be over before you know it. If you let it get to you, you'll suffer, I'll suffer, Barnabas will suffer. What's the point?"

Dooley was silent, thinking. He had learned when his silences were thoughtful, when they were hostile, and when they were mindless.

"This hurts me worse than it hurts you, pal. I've got to do the cooking. What should we feed her tonight?"

"Rat tonsils, snake bellies, and frog puke."

"OK, that's her menu. What about ours?"

Dooley laughed. Bingo! "Hamburgers all the way and french fries."

"Deal," he said.

No, there was not another English tutor around, except for a student at Wesley college, who, according to one report, was tattooed all over.

He might as well swallow his own advice:

Put your head down, Timothy, and give it all you've got.

The wedding gifts arrived, wrapped in the signature blue paper and simple white ribbon. One detail down and two hundred to go, he thought, taking his dark suit from the closet. He'd lost so much weight since those heedless days before the big D . . .

He tried the suit on and stood before the mirror. Not bad. Slap a boutonniere on the lapel, and it would look good as new.

He went to the alcove window and saw the glow of her bedroom lamp under the eaves.

He wished she were here, sitting in the wing chair. She would know whether the suit needed taking in or whether it would get by with a pressing. Besides, he wanted to show her the picture of his grandfather and ask if she saw any resemblance.

It meant something to him to resemble somebody. He hadn't looked like his mother, who was beautiful, or his father, who was handsome. "Woodpile kid," some unkind neighbor had once been heard to say.

In any case, why did he suddenly need someone to help him make the sort of simple decision he'd made quite alone all his life?

The truth was, he didn't *need* someone to do it; he *wanted* someone do it.

He received that truth as a minor revelation.

"Dooley!" He stood at his bedroom door and called across the hall. The guest room door stood open, thanks be to God, and was not only empty of his fraudulent cousin but clean as a pin. He hoped Puny Bradshaw was not lying in the emergency room at Wesley Hospital from having tackled the nastiest job since the Boer War. He had given her an extra twenty-five dollars, which had made her eyes light up, but only feebly.

"What?" said Dooley, coming into the hall.

"Please step in here a minute. I'd like your advice."

Dooley walked in, glowering.

"What the dickens are you glowering about?"

"You ought t' see th' homework she give me."

"She *what* you?"

"*Gave* me!" said Dooley, raising his voice.

"You don't need to raise your voice to speak proper English," he said grumpily. "What about this suit? Is it too baggy?"

Dooley walked around him as if he were the Willard Porter statue on the lawn of the town museum. "You look huge."

"Huge? Are you sure?"

"You look huge in the waist."

Rats! The last place anyone wanted to look huge. "All right, I'll take it in for alterations. Let me see you again in your blazer."

Dooley didn't waste a minute stepping across the hall to put the new blazer over his striped pajamas.

"Cool," said the rector. "Here's the tie I'm giving you to go with it."

"Tie? I have to wear a tie?"

"You have to wear a tie."

"Gag."

"Gag all you want. You're wearing a tie."

"Puke."

"Gag and puke. What a vocabulary."

"I'm going to bed," said Dooley.

"Good riddance," said the rector, "and say your prayers."

Homeless greeted him at the door.

"Come in! Come in! You must have a nose like a beagle—the' coffee's just perked."

Barnabas bounded into the small room on the red leash, his own nose to the floor. "He's looking for Barkless!" said the rector.

"Over yonder on 'is pallet." Homeless pointed to the short-haired, spotted dog who blinked at them. "He cain't bark, but he can blink. See there—blink, blink, blink. That's how he barks at ol' Barnabas, here."

Barnabas barked back. Then he went to the spotted dog and sniffed it. Barkless didn't flinch.

"Chippy, ain't he?"

"I'll say!" The rector moved to the stove. Though it was a warm day, the fire Homeless had built to perk the coffee was nonetheless inviting. "I'm glad to see you, my friend. It feels like I've come home when I visit the creek."

"You're welcome as th' flowers in May—day or night, hard times or fair."

"I thank you. Tell me how your crowd is taking to Pastor Greer."

"Well, sir, they love 'im, they do. He's one of them. He once fought th' Lord just like they're doin', and so they connect. He's preachin' on th' big stump every Wednesday, and we're drawin' 'em in pretty good."

"How's the soup pot holding out?"

"Now and again, somethin' leaks in. The Baptists sent a hundred last week, and out it went for five pairs of shoes.

"Th' Presbyterians put in fifty back in February. That went for medicine for two sick young 'uns. As for th' Methodists, I've not heard."

"You'll be hearing soon, is my guess. The summer crowd is back. Here's ours." He handed over an envelope.

"I like a preacher that makes house calls," said Homeless, stuffing the envelope under his mattress, "and I thank you mightily. Now, set."

He folded a blanket for his guest and put it in the nearly bottomless ladder-back chair. "M' chair's gettin' bottomless to go with m' dog named Barkless."

Laughing, the rector sat down. As he did, the spotted dog sailed through the air and landed in his lap. He nearly tipped over backward.

"I like a dog with timing!" he exclaimed. Barnabas looked up and growled.

"Hold off, now." Homeless stooped down to give the big dog a good scratching behind the ears. "How're things comin' with your lady friend?"

The rector sighed. Then he smiled. Then he sighed again.

"That's a good place to begin," said Homeless, going to the stove to pour two strong cups of coffee.

He had never before given away a bride.

That the bride was Puny Bradshaw supplied one of the great joys of his life.

He walked down the aisle of First Baptist Church as if on air and could not take his eyes off the lovely creature at his side. Every freckle sparkled, and under the little hat she wore, every curl of red hair seemed to glow.

As he stepped away from her at the altar, he briefly took her hand and felt the shocking roughness of it. This hand had mopped his floors, scrubbed his toilets, ironed his shirts, made his beds, cooked his meals, paired his socks, and fed his dog. He might have sunk to his knees on the spot and kissed it.

"Now we're related!" Esther Cunningham said, loud enough to be heard to the monument.

"Mayor," he said, "we've always been related. Philosophically."

When Puny marched into the reception in her enchanting dress, he had to gulp down his emotions. She flew to where he was standing with the Baptist minister and hugged him warmly.

"Father!" she said.

Father! He heard the name in a way he'd never heard it before.

I may have missed the boat in that department, he thought, but not, thank God, altogether.

When he arrived home from the wedding, Cynthia had everything under control.

The roast was coming along nicely, as were the potatoes. The fresh asparagus was washed and lying in the steamer. The butter was set out to soften, the rolls had risen, the salad greens were clean, the raw vegetables were chopped, the salad dressing was concocted, the Camembert was ripe, and the merlot was open and breathing.

As he came in the back door, she turned around from the stove and smiled.

Good Lord, what had she done to herself? She looked so positively breathtaking that he was stopped in his tracks.

"It's the apron," she said, reading his mind. "Men like seeing women in aprons."

He kissed her tenderly. "Please!" she murmured against his cheek. "One mustn't put dessert first."

"Cynthia, Cynthia." He caressed her shoulders. "What is this happiness?"

"You've been to a wedding," she informed him. "You've seen someone with the bald courage to make a commitment. It's invigorating!"

"Turn around," he said.

"What for?"

"I'm checking you for hair curlers."

They laughed hysterically. Hadn't he taken her to visit the bishop last year, with a maverick curler banging around in her hair? She'd been gravely disinclined to forgive him for not bringing it to her attention—though heaven knows he'd tried.

At dinner, Dooley Barlowe looked a fashion plate, used his manners to a fault, and said 'ain't' only once.

Cynthia Coppersmith made the bishop laugh and caused Martha to exclaim, and as for himself, he was hard-pressed to do anything more than pour the wine, compliment the cook, admire Martha's dress, and ask the blessing. "I'm giving you a break," he told Stuart, who appreciated it.

After Stuart and Martha went up to bed in the scrubbed, polished, disinfected, and thoroughly set-to-rights guest room, he put the blue velvet pouch in his pocket and led Cynthia into the study.

"I've already given you this once, so you don't have to thank me again."

"Good! I'm too tired to enthuse over anything more than the complete success of your dinner party."

"Our dinner party."

She sighed happily. "Whatever."

They sat on the sofa, and he handed her the brooch.

"Thank you," she said, sniffing. "It means more than you know."

"Are you going to cry?"

"Certainly not!"

"Excellent!" He held her hand. "Will you wear it tomorrow?"

"With my bedroom shoes!" she said. He smiled, thinking of the time she met him in the street before church, absentmindedly wearing her embroidered scuffs.

He put his arm around her and looked into her eyes.

"In the morning, the bishop will be confirming you. But you confirm something for me every day."

"What, for heaven's sake?"

"That love is a divine gift and should not be held back. Thank you for not holding back."

She put her head against his chest and he stroked her temple.

The Lord's Chapel bells were chiming eleven o'clock when he discovered she had fallen asleep in his arms.

He felt a great swelling in his heart as he watched them come toward the altar.

His thoughts flashed back to the first time he'd seen Dooley Barlowe—barefoot, unwashed, looking for a place to "take a dump."

Today, he was seeing more than a boy wearing a new blazer and an uncontrollable grin. He was seeing a miracle.

Cynthia came behind Dooley, beaming, wearing the pearl and amethyst brooch. Cynthia! Another miracle in his life.

The candidates for confirmation were presented to the bishop by Hal and Marge Owen, who stood with them throughout the ceremony.

The sight of Stuart Cullen laying his hands on their heads, and praying the centuries-old prayer for God's defense, spoke to him more deeply than he expected.

In fact, the only thing that kept him from bawling like a baby was the sudden realization that he'd forgotten to bring the platter for the ham.

Esther Bolick rang the bell for silence in the parish hall.

"I'm glad," said Stuart Cullen, "that Lord's Chapel hasn't grown too big for us to hold hands around the table."

The excited throng formed a circle, as someone fetched Rebecca Jane Owen from under a folding chair and rescued five-year-old Amy Larkin from the hot pursuit of a mechanical toy run amok from the nursery.

"Give us grateful hearts, our Father, for all thy mercies, and make us mindful of the needs of others; through Jesus Christ our Lord."

"Amen!"

Father Tim joined Stuart and Martha at the head of the buffet line, so the Cullens could eat and get on the road to yet another sermon, a ground breaking, and the installation of a deacon.

"Timothy," Martha said as she helped herself to the string beans, "are you going to marry that lovely woman?"

"Why, yes. Olivia asked me some time ago if I'd officiate."

"Not Olivia! Cynthia!"

He laughed. "Now, Martha . . ."

"Don't 'now Martha' me. Time is running out, dear. I can see she's doing her part. Are you doing yours?"

Martha Cullen was a carbon copy of Katherine when it came to meddling.

"We can't do it all, Timothy. The men must do *something*. When Stuart finally understood that, things fell into place. By the way, is that famous orange marmalade cake here today?"

"I'll have a look," he said, bounding from his place in line, never to return.

He spied Emma Newland, who hadn't darkened the doors of a worship service since she married Harold and "went back to bein' a Baptist."

He saw Miss Sadie, Louella, Hoppy, and Olivia gabbing a mile a minute by the piano.

Dooley and Cynthia were in line with the Owens, and as far as he could tell, the orange marmalade cake had not made it to the reception.

He sliced a piece of homemade coconut, instead, and carried it to Martha's place at the table, fetched the bishop a cup of coffee, picked up Amy Larkin and admired her patent-leather shoes, removed a stuffed bear from the floor, kissed two old parishioners, hugged several of all ages, sat down with Rebecca Jane who bit his nose and chewed on his lapel, fielded an enthusiastic round of congratulations upon Dooley's confirmation, rummaged in the kitchen and found extra flatware for a table of eight who didn't get any, pitched in to serve coffee for the frazzled ECW, and checked the ham to determine its popularity, which, considering the bare bone he found on the tray, was immense.

He packed Stuart and Martha out the side door, waved them off, and went back to join Dooley, Cynthia, the Owens, and Rebecca Jane for the last hoarded pieces of Esther Bolick's coconut cake, served with a pretty good joke from Uncle Billy Watson.

Tommy was asking for Buck Leeper, who had visited the hospital faithfully but hadn't been seen since Tommy came home.

The rector supposed Buck Leeper was far too private a man to invade someone's home. The impersonal ground of the hospital had been a different matter.

Breaking a light sweat, he jogged up the hill to the construction site with the book under his arm. It wasn't every day he could kill two birds with one stone.

Buck Leeper was sitting at the desk with his back to the door.

"Buck?"

The chair creaked as his heavy frame swiveled around to face the door. The superintendent merely nodded.

"Two things . . ."

"Number one," said Buck, stubbing out his cigarette.

"Tommy is asking for you, misses seeing you. I'd be glad to tell you how to find his house, if you'd like to pay a visit."

Buck cleared his throat. "Number two."

"I found something I wanted to give you."

Buck stood up as he handed the book over. He looked at it for a moment before taking it in his hand.

The rector shrugged. "I thought you might like it."

Buck studied the cover silently, drawing a cigarette out of the pack of Lucky Strikes in his shirt pocket. He held it, unlighted, as he laid the book on the desk and opened it. Then he bent over the book and slowly turned a few pages.

The rector wiped his forehead with his sleeve.

The superintendent stayed bent over the book so long, the rector thought he'd forgotten anyone was in the room.

Buck turned, finally, and looked at him. "Thanks."

"You're welcome. Well, I won't keep you."

"Where's th' kid's house?"

He told him, pointing this way and that.

As he was leaving, Buck said, "Something I ought to say to you."

"What's that?"

"Nobody around here knows what I told you the other day."

"Nobody will hear it from me."

Buck lit the cigarette. "I'll go see the boy."

"Good. He'll like that."

Jogging down the hill definitely felt better than going up.

It was a long push to Elmhurst, but if they hustled, they could make it in a day, arriving back home at midnight. His jam-packed calendar wouldn't permit dawdling.

But Dooley Barlowe did not like Elmhurst, which was only one day away from dismissing for the summer.

He did not like the grim look of the brick buildings, he did not like the cool demeanor of the headmaster, he did not like any of the teachers or even one of the boys, he hated the drab, ill-fitting school uniforms, and he refused to eat a bite in the dining room that was morbidly silent.

The boy had judgment, you could say that for him. They were in such a hurry to get out of there that the Buick nosed into the garage an hour and a half ahead of schedule.

As Olivia Davenport walked down the aisle on the arm of Dr. Leo Baldwin, the wedding guests gawked as shamelessly as tourists at a scenic overlook.

No one had ever seen anything like it in Mitford—a successful heart-transplant recipient who looked like a movie star, a famous heart surgeon from Boston, Massachusetts, and a wedding gown that would be the talk of the village for months, even years, to come.

This wedding, as someone rightly said, was "big doings."

If the wedding of Dr. Walter Harper and Olivia Davenport was big doings, the doings that followed at Fernbank were bigger still.

People turned out merely to see the long procession of cars snaking along Main Street and up Old Church Lane.

"Is it a weddin' or a funeral?" Hattie Cloer, who owned Cloer's Market on the highway, was being taken for a Sunday-afternoon drive by her son. Her Chihuahua, Darlene, sat on Hattie's shoulder, with her head stuck out the window.

"Looks like a funeral," said her son. "I seen a long, black deal parked in th' church driveway."

"Oh, law," said Hattie, "I hope it's not old Sadie Baxter who's keeled over. This is her church, you know."

"I hear she had a United States president at her house one time."

"President Jackson, I think it was, or maybe Roosevelt," said Hattie.

Entering Fernbank's ballroom was like entering another world.

No one stepped across the threshold who didn't gasp with amazement or joy or disbelief, so that the reception line was backed up on the porch and down the steps and across the circle drive. No one minded standing on the lawn, some with their heels sinking into the turf, for they'd heard that a marvelous spectacle awaited inside.

Quite a few had never been on the lawn at Fernbank and had only seen the rooftop over the trees. They'd heard for years the place was falling to ruin, but all they saw was some peeling paint here and there, hardly worse than what they had at home.

Not a soul was untouched by the enchantment of it, and the skirted tables on the lawn, and the young, attractive strangers in black bow ties who smiled and poured champagne and served lime-green punch and made them feel like royalty.

Enormous baskets of tuberoses and stephanotis and country roses and stock flanked the porch steps, pouring out their fragrance. And through the open windows, strains of music—Mozart, someone said—declared itself, sweetening the air all the way to the orchards.

Uncle Billy Watson stood near the end of the line and straightened his tie. "Lord have mercy!" he said, deeply moved by the occasion. He gave Miss Rose a final check and discovered he'd missed the label that was turned out of her collar. He turned it in.

Absalom Greer felt an odd beating of his heart. Where had more than sixty years gone since his feet came down those steps and he drove away with Sadie Baxter in her father's town car, believing with all his heart that she would be his bride?

Hessie Mayhew did not wait in line. She marched up the steps and across the porch and slipped in and found a chair and claimed her territory by dumping her pocketbook in it.

Then she took out her notepad and pen. After all, she was not here to have a good time; she was here to work. She had finally talked J.C. Hogan into letting her do something besides the gardening column.

The reception line alone had been an emotional experience for the rector. When he met her, Olivia Davenport had been dying, and he had, with his own eyes, witnessed her agonizing brush with death. Now, to see her beauty and to feel her joy . . . it was another miracle in a string of miracles.

Hoppy Harper clasped his hand and held it for a long moment. Working as a team, they had pitched in and prayed for Olivia, and it would bind them together for life.

But perhaps what he was feeling most deeply of all was this strange, new sense of family as he moved through the line with Cynthia and Dooley. He felt a connection that was beyond his understanding, as if the three of them were bound together like the links of a chain.

It was a new feeling, and he was intoxicated by it even before he got to the champagne.

Esther Bolick had made the wedding cake, which was displayed on a round table, skirted to the floor with ivory tulle and ornamented with calla lilies.

"A masterpiece!" he said, meaning it.

Esther was literally wringing her hands, looking at it. "I declare, I've never done anything this complicated. I was up 'til all hours. Three different cakes, three layers each—it looks like the Empire State Buildin' on that stand the caterers brought."

"What do you think of the other masterpiece in the room?"

"Law, I haven't had a minute to look around. Where?"

"Up there."

Esther looked up and gasped. "Who painted that?"

"Leonardo and Michelangelo."

"You don't mean it!"

"I do mean it!" he said.

Once again, he went to the windows that faced the circle drive and looked out. Planes were always late, weren't they?

And then he saw the taxi coming up the drive, and he went out quickly and hurried down the steps and was there to greet the tall, dark, gentle man who was Leonardo Francesca's grandson.

Sadie Baxter came off the dance floor in her emerald-green dress, on the arm of Leo Baldwin. Leo retrieved her cane and gave it to her as she turned and saw the man walking into the ballroom.

There was an astonished look on her face, and the rector went to her at once, wondering if the shock might . . .

But Miss Sadie regained her composure and held out her hand to the young man and said, wonderingly, "Leonardo?"

Roberto took her hand and kissed it. "I am Roberto, Leonardo's grandson. My grandfather salutes your beauty and grace and deeply regrets that he could not come himself. He has made me the emissary of a very special message to his childhood friend."

The rector was enthralled with the look on her face, as she waited eagerly to hear the message that had come thousands of miles, across nearly eighty years.

"My grandfather has asked me to say—*Tempo è denaro!*"

Roberto smiled and bowed.

No one had ever seen Sadie Baxter laugh like this; it was a regular fit of laughter. People drew round, feeling yet another pulse of excitement in a day of wondrous excitements.

"Does he," she said, wiping her eyes with a lace handkerchief, "still like garden peas?"

"Immensely!" said Roberto.

Miss Sadie reached again for Roberto's hand. "Let's sit down before we fall down. I want to hear everything!"

"Miss Sadie," said the rector, "before you go . . . what does *tempo è denaro* mean, anyway?"

"Didn't I tell you? It means 'time is money'!"

"Is this heaven?" asked Cynthia as they danced.

"Heaven's gates, at the very least."

"Everyone loves you so."

"Everyone?"

"Yes," she whispered against his cheek. "Everyone."

"That's a tough act to follow," he said, his heart hammering.

"You were the one who brought Roberto here."

"Yes. I didn't say anything to you because I wanted to . . . I wasn't sure we could pull it off. I called Florence for his grandfather, who answered but had forgotten all his English. He handed the phone to his son, who knew a bit of English—and then Roberto, whose English is flawless, called me back.

"I said, 'Please, if you could do it, it would give great joy.' And Roberto said, 'My grandfather's life has been spent in giving joy. I will come.'

"I had tickets waiting at the airline counter in Florence, and here, thanks be to God, is Roberto."

"It's the loveliest gift imaginable."

"Miss Sadie is so often on the giving end . . ."

"How long will he be with us?"

"Only a few days. We'll have Andrew step in for a glass of sherry while he's here. They can rattle away in Italian, and we'll do something special for Miss Sadie and Louella. Roberto will occupy my popular guest room. Of course, there's no Puny to give a hand, but we'll manage."

"I'll help you," she said.

He pressed her hand in his. "You always help me."

As the eight-piece orchestra played on, he saw the room revolve around them in a glorious panorama, bathed with afternoon light.

He saw Absalom Greer laughing with Roberto and Miss Sadie.

He saw Andrew Gregory raise a toast to the newlyweds, and Miss Rose standing stiffly with a smiling Uncle Billy, wearing her black suit and a cocktail hat and proper shoes.

He saw Buck Leeper standing awkwardly in the doorway, holding a glass of champagne in his rough hand, and Ron and Wilma Malcolm trying to lure him into the room.

There was Emma wearing a hat, and Harold looking shy, and Esther Bolick sitting down and fanning herself with relief, and Dooley Barlowe walking toward Miss Sadie, who was beaming in his direction.

He saw Winnie Ivey taking something fancy off a passing tray, her cheeks pink with excitement, while J.C. Hogan conferred with Hessie Mayhew next to a potted palm.

And there was Louella, in a handsome dress that brought out the warmth of her coffee-colored skin, dancing with Hal Owen.

The faces of the people in the sun-bathed panorama were suddenly more beautiful to him than heavenly faces on a ceiling could ever be. Let the hosts swarm overhead, shouting hosannas. He wanted to be planted exactly where he was, enveloped in this mist of wisteria.

"Man," said Dooley, as they came toward him off the dance floor, "you were sure dancin' *close*."

"Not nearly close enough," said Cynthia, looking mischievous.

"Dooley, why don't you dance with Cynthia?" Dooley, who was unable to imagine such a thing, paused blankly. Seizing the moment, Cynthia grabbed Dooley and dragged him at once into the happy maelstrom on the dance floor.

He who hesitates is lost! thought the rector, grinning.

"Mrs. Walter Harper?"

"The very same!"

"May I kiss the bride?"

"I'll be crushed if you don't."

He kissed her on both cheeks and stood holding her hands, fairly smitten with the light in her violet eyes. "You're a great beauty, Mrs. Harper. But there's even greater beauty inside. I won't say that Hoppy is a lucky man, for I don't believe in luck, but grace. May God bless you both with the deepest happiness, always."

"Thank you. May I kiss my priest and friend?"

"I'll be crushed if you don't."

She kissed him on both cheeks, and they laughed. "I've never been so blessed and happy in all my life. A wonderful husband, a loving and doting aunt . . . and this glorious room that I know was done just for us. How can one bear such happiness?"

"Drink deeply. It's richly deserved."

"I hope you'll soon be doing this yourself, Father."

"This?"

"Getting married, sharing your life."

"I don't know if I could . . ."

She looked at him, smiling, but serious. "Don't you remember? Philippians four-thirteen, for Pete's sake!"

CHAPTER TWENTY-ONE

Knowing

Dooley's homeroom teacher wrote in a neat, confined hand:

> *To Whom It May Concern: When it comes to math,*
> *Dooley Barlowe is a genius.*

He felt fortified. Now if Louise Appleshaw could pull off a miracle . . .

He said as much. "Miss Appleshaw, I confess I'm expecting a miracle."

"Rector, one does not *expect* miracles. A miracle is, at least partly by definition, something quite *un*expected." She looked down her nose at him.

He became a worm and crawled from the room.

Andrew Gregory stopped in for a glass of Italian wine before meeting friends for dinner at the club.

Roberto had put on the rector's favorite apron, tucked his tie into his shirt front, and was busy creating the most seductive aromas in the rectory's history.

"Osso buco!" Roberto announced, taking the pot lid off with one hand and waving a wooden spoon with the other.

"Ummmm!" cried Cynthia, coming through the back door with an armful of flowers. "Ravishing!"

"Man!" exclaimed Dooley, lured downstairs.

"Oh, my gracious!" gasped Miss Sadie, who arrived with her usual hostess gift of Swanson's Chicken Pie and a Sara Lee pound cake for his freezer.

Louella sniffed the air, appreciatively. "That ain't no collards and pigs' feet!"

The toasts flew as thick as snowflakes during last year's blizzard.

To Leonardo, who lay crippled with rheumatism in Florence.

To Roberto's happiness in Mitford!

To Miss Sadie's good health!

To Louella's quick recovery from an impending knee operation.

To Dooley's prospects for a new school.

To the hospitality of the host!

To the charm and beauty of the hostess!

To Olivia and Hoppy at Brown's Hotel in London!

Avis Packard called to find out if everything was going all right, thrilled with having cut veal for a real Italian who knew what was what.

Roberto showed photos of his wife and three beautiful children, of his grandfather's work in the homes and churches of Florence, and of Leonardo himself, wearing the same boyish smile Miss Sadie remembered from his long-ago visit to Fernbank.

The rector had never seen so much toasting and cooking and pouring of olive oil and peeling of garlic, nor heard so much laughing and joking.

It was as if Roberto were one of their very own and had come home to them all, at last.

Bingo.

Dooley liked the second school they visited. And why not? Cynthia went with them on the journey and kept them laughing all the way.

Better still, she never once let the admissions director believe he was interviewing them but that it was definitely the other way around.

Though the boys were away for the summer and they couldn't tell much about the tone of the place, Dooley warmed up to the affable headmaster who dropped in from his home next door, dressed in khakis, loafers, and a sweatshirt, to give them an enthusiastic tour.

He also liked the science lab with the brain in a jar, and the gym, the track, the football field, and the horse stables where the groom put him on his personal steed and slapped its rump and sent Dooley flying around the ring, barely clinging on.

"Needs polish," said the groom.

The dorm rooms did not measure up.

"Gag," said Dooley.

"Spoiled," said the rector.

"No problem," said Cynthia, who rattled on about paint and curtains.

In all, a satisfying trip, which brought them home at two o'clock in the morning, reeling with exhaustion.

The statue of Captain Willard Porter was definitely the centerpiece of the first—and soon to be annual—Mitford Museum Festival.

It stood on the freshly groomed lawn of the Porter place, mysteriously draped with a tarpaulin and encircled by booths.

Over by the lilac bushes, Joe Ivey had set up a barbering chair and a table displaying the tools of his trade, from tins of talc and bottles of Sea Breeze to a neck brush and a battery-operated shaver. Shaves were three dollars, haircuts were six, and all proceeds would go to the museum.

Across the circle, as far as she could possibly remove herself from the competition, was Fancy Skinner, dressed to the teeth in lime-green pedal pushers and a V-necked sweater. When someone wondered about the shocking departure from her favorite color, she said she was "trying to cut through the clutter and stand out in the crowd, which, as anyone ought to know, is what business is all about."

Fancy was offering manicures for five dollars and lip waxings and pedicures for ten (behind a sheet that was hung on a wire). The only problem with her assigned location, as she later pointed out in a letter to the town council, was that Mack Stroupe was boiling hot dogs right next to her booth, which created both a clamor and a smell that were entirely inappropriate for beauty treatments.

Winnie Ivey manned the Sweet Stuff doughnut stand, which was staked out under the elm tree, in conjunction with her cousin who had made thirty pimento cheese sandwiches, thirty sliced ham and cheese, and forty chicken salad, which she was keeping on ice in a cooler.

On the opposite side of the elm tree, two llamas stood patiently in the shade gazing at the crowd. *Pet the Llamas Fifty Cents,* read the sign tacked to the tree.

"Fifty cents is way too much to pet a llama!" said a young mother, who decided to invest in doughnuts. Her brood of three stood howling at the mere sight of a llama.

There were cakes baked by Esther Bolick, who complained that the Harper wedding and museum festival were far too close together. Her cakes, however, were selling fast, with her prize two-layer orange marmalade waiting to be auctioned to the highest bidder at noon. It sat on review under an open tent, as Percy and Velma Mosely's youngest grandchild waved a fly swatter over it.

Free lemonade was available on the porch, which was the only concession the town council had made in the area of hospitality—except, of course, for the Porta John that leaned alarmingly to the right on a bank next to the cellar door.

Dora Pugh offered a miniature garden shop under a tent, with a box of newly hatched biddies to entertain the children. Ten percent of Dora's sales would go to the museum, while Andrew Gregory was donating all proceeds from the sale of his English Lemon Furniture Wax, which he displayed on an eighteenth-century teak garden bench under the redbud tree.

"Law!" said J.C. Hogan, wiping his face with his handkerchief, "this is a whopper." He had shot four rolls of film in only one hour since the festival officially opened, one of which featured Mayor Cunningham standing on the steps of the Porter place, flanked by Miss Rose and Uncle Billy.

According to Uncle Billy, Miss Rose started the day in one of the worst moods he had ever witnessed and completely refused his offer of help with her wardrobe.

She had turned up at one of the most important events ever staged in Mitford, wearing a cracked-leather bomber jacket from World War II, a black cocktail hat with a mashed-flat silk peony that had come loose and slipped down over one ear, a pair of saddle oxfords, and a flowered dress that had belonged to her mother. She had chosen to carry a handbag made from the cork circles that once appeared in the caps of Pepsi-Cola bottles.

Uncle Billy had been able to make only one inroad on the discouraging situation—his wife had let him tie the laces of her shoes.

As the brass band marched around the lawn playing special selections, the crowd increased. Also, it was the first time anyone could remember the street being roped off, which clearly added to the general excitement.

A list of the day's activities was handwritten on a blackboard, which stood teetering on an easel at the sidewalk facing Lilac Road.

Included in the long list were:

> *See someone you know push*
> *a peanut with their NOSE!*
> *Watch Percy Mosely do the*
> *HULA DANCE in a grass skirt!*

"I ain't doin' any hula dance," said Percy, who had come home from Hawaii with a tan. "I told 'er that plain as day, but Esther Cunningham don't take no for an answer, and now she's got false advertisin' on her hands."

"Aw, Percy," someone cajoled, "go ahead and do it. It's for a good cause."

The band passed by, drowning out Percy's list of indignations.

"I declare," said Chief Rodney Underwood, who was eating a hot dog and talking to the rector, "we go along thinkin' we're a small town. Then we get big doin's like this, and first thing you know, we look like New York City."

Esther Cunningham drew alongside them, wearing a new red linen suit. "Th' tourists are swarmin' over this place like flies," she said with disgust. "You'd think they'd let us alone for five bloomin' minutes."

Rodney wiped the chili off his hand. "It's June, Esther. We always get tourists in June."

She looked down at her jacket. "I hate linen. Would you look at this suit? It's got more wrinkles than Carter has liver pills. I'm packin' up and goin' to Colorado as soon as this thing's over."

She stomped off to get a doughnut.

"I thought this was a festival," said Mule Skinner, arriving fresh from a round of golf, "but it looks like a circus to me."

"Big crowd," said the rector.

"Next year, they better bring in barbecue and sweet-potato pie. Hot dogs won't cut it."

"We'll get Percy to set up a booth."

"When do the events begin, the pig kissin' and all?"

"One o'clock, if there's a soul left alive to watch," said the rector.

"Mack Stroupe?"

The rector nodded, laughing. Two dogs streaked by them, chasing a squirrel. Rodney ran after somebody whose shopping bag had lost its bottom and was spilling a trail of tea towels and bran muffins bought at the Library Ladies booth.

"Are you on for the Scripture Dog act?" said Mule.

"That's me," sighed the rector. "It was that or push a blasted peanut . . ."

"Esther Cunningham makes my army sergeant look like Mother Teresa."

They looked up to see Hattie Cloer charging toward them with Darlene on a leash.

"Duck," hissed Mule, but it was too late.

"Father," said Hattie, "how far gone do you have to be to get last rites?"

"Pretty far," said Mule, helping out with the conversation.

Darlene bared her teeth and growled at the rector.

"I was thinkin' last night of askin' Clyde to call you," said Hattie. "I was layin' there 'til way up in th' morning with somethin' I thought was gas. Oh, law, I was so distended! But it had a worse pain to it than gas, you know. It was something really serious, I could just tell. So I said, 'Clyde, honey, wake up and feel this.' And he rolled over and felt of it and sat straight up and called the ambulance, but he dialed the wrong number and got Charlie's Tavern on the highway. And by the time he was through talkin', I was feelin' better and got up and cooked a pot of string beans that just came in down at th' store. And knowin' how you like string beans, you might want to come over and get you a pound or two. They'll freeze. You know I give a quarter off for clergy. But anyway, it did cause me to wonder about maybe needin' you to come over . . ."

"Call me anytime," he told Hattie, who dragged Darlene away, still growling.

"I'd get an unlisted number if I was you," said Mule.

At one o'clock sharp, the mayor stood on the front porch steps as the brass band played "God Bless America," and everyone crossed their hearts.

The Rotary had loaned a small sea of folding chairs to the festival, which were neatly placed about the lawn in rows near the steps.

Miss Sadie, Louella, Roberto, Father Tim, Cynthia, Dooley, and Andrew Gregory occupied the front row.

The rector glanced anxiously at Miss Sadie. How would she react to seeing the statue of the man she had loved for so many years? She didn't care for public display, to say the least.

The mayor thanked everyone for turning out, reminded them of the free lemonade, and launched into a prepared speech that was ghost-written, as far as he could tell, by Hessie Mayhew.

She thanked Miss Rose and Uncle Billy for their civic generosity in letting their home be overtaken by a museum, and everyone applauded.

Miss Rose stood and bowed, sending her mashed-flat silk peony into the grass.

Then the mayor went on at some length about Willard Porter, his deep roots in Mitford, his fondly remembered generosity to the Presbyterian church, his brilliant contributions to the pharmaceutical profession, and the noble architecture of the house, which, for nearly seventy years, had been the centerpiece of the village. His death in France, she said in closing, had been to the glory of God and America.

Ernestine Ivory stood by the statue, holding the tarpaulin.

Esther Cunningham signaled the band, which struck up at once.

Then she signaled Ernestine, who, blushing furiously, ripped the cover from the statue.

A gasp went up.

Silence ensued.

Then everyone stood and applauded and whistled and cheered. It was the first statue ever erected in Mitford, and public opinion was unanimous—it was a sight to behold.

Willard Porter stood looking toward the blue mountains that swelled beyond the village, his eyes fixed on freedom, his hand over his heart. Nobility was expressed in every feature of his handsome face, in every detail of his officer's uniform. A bed of flowers sprung up at his feet.

"Oh, my," said Miss Sadie, using her handkerchief.

Roberto nodded approvingly.

"Man!" said Dooley.

Some people were still clapping, as the band began to march around the statue.

He thought he had never seen Miss Rose look so wonderful— standing by Uncle Billy, saluting the statue of her brother, and keeping time to the music with her foot.

"Th' deal," announced the mayor from the steps, "is that anytime th' father's dog gets out of hand, all th' father has to do is quote Scripture and his dog . . ."

"Barnabas," said the rector.

"Barnabas . . . shapes up and lies down."

The crowd laughed.

"I'm askin' for fifty dollars for a demonstration," she announced, peering around.

Silence. Birdsong.

"Not twenty-five, so don't even think about it. Fifty! A small price to pay to see somethin' you can't even see on TV! And think what that fifty will do—help add yet another room to this fine museum, the likes of which you'll not see across the whole length of the state . . ."

A hand went up in the back row. "Thirty-five!"

"Get over it!" said Esther. "I'm lookin' for fifty or we move on to th' pig kissin'."

"Fifty!" shouted a voice from the vicinity of the llamas.

"Do I hear fifty-five?"

Silence.

Esther signaled the band, which struck up a drumroll as the rector led Barnabas to the foot of the steps.

He didn't know whether to laugh or cry. How he had ever been talked into this was beyond all understanding.

"One thing you need to know," said Esther. "We do not mean to poke fun at the Word of the good Lord.

"We intend to demonstrate to each and every member present what we should all do when we hear his Word . . . which is to let it have its way with our hearts."

"Amen!" somebody said.

J.C. sank to his knees in the grass and looked through the lens of his camera. Something interesting was bound to happen with this deal.

At that moment, Cynthia Coppersmith rose from her front-row seat, holding what appeared to be a large handbag. As she held it aloft for all to see, Violet's white head emerged. Violet perched there, staring coolly at the crowd.

"That cat is in books at the library," someone said.

Keeping a safe distance, Cynthia turned around and let Barnabas have a look. Violet peered down at him with stunning disdain.

Barnabas nearly toppled the rector as he lunged toward the offending handbag, which Cynthia handed off to Dooley.

His booming bark carried beyond the monument, all the way to Lew Boyd's Esso, and the force of his indignation communicated to every expectant onlooker.

The rector spoke with his full pulpit voice. " 'For brethren, ye have been called unto liberty, only use not liberty for an occasion to the flesh.' "

Barnabas hesitated. His ears stood straight up. He relaxed on the leash.

" '. . . but by love serve one another.' "

The black dog sighed and sprawled on the grass.

" 'For all the law is fulfilled in one word: Thou shalt love thy neighbor as thyself.' "

Barnabas didn't move but raised his eyes and looked dolefully at the front row. Not knowing what else to do, the rector bowed. The crowd applauded heartily.

"A fine passage from Galatians five-thirteen and fourteen!" said the jolly new preacher from First Baptist.

"That was *worth* fifty," said Mule Skinner, pleased to know the dog personally.

As Dooley hurried to take Violet back to her sunny window seat at home, Esther resumed her place on the steps and looked around.

"Ponder that in your hearts," she said.

Somebody heard the pig squeal behind a column on the porch, which encouraged more applause.

Linder Hayes strolled to the foot of the steps and stretched to his full height of six feet, four and a half inches. His courtroom demeanor brought a hush over the assembly.

"Ladies and gentlemen, on this distinguished and momentous occasion, we will now open the bidding that will permit everyone here—with their own eyes—to see a unique and historic event, to see, in other words, the mayor of this fine village . . . kiss . . . a pig."

They gasped. Esther Cunningham would kiss a pig? A great clamor ran through the booths and among the crowd. Coot Hendrick, maybe, but Esther Cunningham?

"Twenty-five dollars!" someone shouted.

Linder held up his hand for silence.

"Surely you jest," he said in the deep baritone that he had honed to reach the hearts of a jury. "This penultimate event will not go for so crass a sum as twenty-five dollars. In fact, no amount of money could fully compensate the priceless act of sacrifice and civic responsibility that . . ."

"Hurry up, dadgum it," hissed Esther.

"The bidding, my friends, will begin at five hundred dollars."

The stunned silence changed into an uproar.

Linder pulled at his chin and looked thoughtful. Esther broke out in a rash.

Someone standing under the elm tree shouted: "Five hundred!"

Linder held up his hand. "Do I hear five twenty-five?"

Silence.

"Going, going, gone for five hundred."

"And dern lucky t' get it, if you ask me," said Percy, who stood under the elm in a shirt printed with chartreuse palm leaves and red monkeys.

"Will someone please bring down the pig?"

A great expectancy hung over the gathering. What kind of pig would it be? A sow? A shoat? What difference did it make?

Ray came down the steps with the pig in his arms. He held it while Esther kissed it.

The crowd cheered as J.C.'s flash went off.

"One more time!" said J.C. "Th' pig moved!"

Esther did it again. More hollering and whistling.

Esther turned to the crowd, who, she knew, would deliver a strong Cunningham vote next election, and raised both arms in triumph.

"I'm about half shot," said Winnie Ivey. "Up at four in th' mornin' to cook all these doughnuts, and here it is way up in the day, and all I've had is half a pimento cheese sandwich."

"Only one more event to go," he said, trying to locate Cynthia in the swirling crowd. "I'll get you some lemonade."

There was Cynthia—trying to pin the errant peony on Miss Rose's bomber jacket. He liked spotting her in the crowd, seeing the blond of her hair and the apple green of her dress. She was wearing tennis shoes, as high heels would only have sunk in the lawn, and looking very much like a girl.

He saw Dooley and Jenny peering at the llamas. Lovely, he thought. And there by Andrew's garden bench was Roberto. Both men gestured happily—speaking Italian, no doubt.

"Father! You're positively radiant!" It was Miss Pearson, Dooley's music teacher, hand in hand with her mother.

Radiance, he was soon to learn, can be exceedingly short-lived.

"I've had about all the fun I can stand, ain't you?" said Uncle Billy.

"One more event," he said, wishing he could rent a hammock and lie down in it.

"I ain't even heard th' jukebox."

"Me, either."

Uncle Billy sighed. "They hooked it up in th' front room. I sure hope it don't cut on in th' middle of th' night and go t' playin'."

He happened to look toward the alley behind the Porter place and saw a red truck slowly driving through. Buck Leeper peered out the window at the throng on the lawn, at their laughter and air of anticipation.

He waved. "Buck!"

Buck threw up his hand and nodded and was gone.

"Dadgum if he didn't wave back," said Mule, who was passing by with lemonade for Fancy. "What's got into him?"

The rector believed it was what had gotten out of him.

Esther was back on the porch steps. If she didn't have laryngitis from the long day's events, it would be a miracle.

"How many of you have ever seen anybody push a peanut down the street with their nose?"

Heads turned. People shrugged. Clearly, no one had ever seen such a thing. Some didn't want to. A few didn't care one way or the other.

"I've seen a sack race!" yelled one of Dooley's classmates.

"That's not the same," snorted the mayor. "This is a hundred times better. That's why we're going to start the bidding high."

The crowd groaned. Some people walked away. Two senior citizens went to sleep sitting up in folding chairs near the lilac bushes.

"To see our brand-new Baptist preacher push a peanut from th' bookstore to th' bakery . . . the bidding will start at five hundred dollars!"

"Not again!" shouted an irate observer.

"That's a dadgum car payment!"

"Lord have mercy, what do you *drive?*

A total stranger stepped forward. As everyone could plainly see, it was a tourist. He was wearing sunglasses, a navy blazer over khakis, and no socks with his loafers.

"I would *not* give five hundred dollars to see only one member of your local clergy fulfill this unique fund-raising proposition . . ."

Several people looked at each other. Not only was this person a tourist, he was a Yankee.

"However, I would most gladly put five hundred into your town coffers to see all your clergy do it—as a team."

"You better jump on that," Linder whispered to the mayor.

The rector could feel Esther, who had eyes like a hawk, boring a hole in him all the way to where he stood with Uncle Billy.

The mayor took a deep breath and bellowed. "Do I hear five hundred to see Reverend Sprouse push the peanut?"

Heads wagged furiously in the negative.

"It's fish or cut bait," hissed Ray.

"Where's th' father?" said Esther, knowing perfectly well where he was. He might have dived under a chair.

"Right here!" hollered Mule.

"Where's Pastor Trollinger from th' Methodists?"

"Over here!" cried the pastor's wife, who couldn't wait to see her husband push a peanut with his nose.

Esther's eyes searched the throng. "That leaves Doctor Browning from over at th' Presbyterians."

"He's not here," said the band leader. "He's doin' a funeral today."

"Where at?" asked Ray.

"Ash Grove."

"Ernestine," said the mayor, "run over there—it's just two miles—and tell 'im to come right after he throws th' dirt in."

"Right," said Ray. "Five hundred bucks is five hundred bucks."

He dragged home at four o'clock, weary of the world.

Dooley and Cynthia trooped down Main Street behind him, laughing like hyenas all the way to the rectory.

"Now, that," declared Cynthia, "was the spirit of ecumenism in a nutshell."

He refused even to crack a smile, though Cynthia, of course, found her odious pun hysterical.

Dooley closed his English book. "I'm not goin' to that school," he said.

"Really?" He wouldn't have uttered another word if his life depended on it. He wasn't fighting battles tonight; he was sitting on his sofa reading his newspaper.

Total silence reigned for some time.

"That ol' brain in that jar—whose do you reckon it is?"

"No idea."

"Th' head guy said they go to Washington on bus trips and all."

"Aha."

"He was cool."

"Umm."

"That groom person said I could ride 'is horse all I wanted to, if I'd help take care of it."

"Sounds like work."

"I wonder what th' football uniforms look like."

"Beats me."

"I like th' school colors."

"Black and gray."

"You got it wrong. Purple and orange."

"Oh."

"We could paint my room and then put posters up. Cynthia has a purple bedspread she'll give me."

Why was he always knocking himself out to convince the boy of something? From now on, maybe he'd keep his mouth shut and let Dooley convince himself.

When the box of monogrammed stationery rolled in from Walter, he realized the worst:

Tomorrow was his birthday.

He had just had a birthday—it seemed only weeks ago. And how old was he, anyway? He could never remember. He had once added a year to his age by mistake, which appalled his friends. Take a couple off, maybe, but *add?*

He did some quick figuring on a piece of paper.

Sixty-two.

Rats.

But what was there to worry about, after all?

At the age of eighty-nine, Arthur Rubinstein had given one of his most enthralling recitals, in Carnegie Hall.

At eighty-two, Chruchill wrote *A History of the English-Speaking People*—in four volumes, no less.

And hadn't Eamon de Valera served as president of Ireland when he was ninety-one? Not to mention Grandma Moses, who was still painting—and getting paid for it—at the age of one hundred.

He stood up from the desk and sucked in his stomach.

"Happy birthday, Father! Ron and I have to go out of town this afternoon, and we didn't want to leave without wishing you the best year ever!"

After Wilma called, so did Evie, who had carefully rehearsed Miss Pattie to say the thing herself. He heard Evie whispering in the background, "Say it, Mama!" "What was it I was supposed to say?" "Happy birthday!" There was a pause, and Miss Pattie spoke into the phone, "I hope you win the lottery!"

He roared with laughter.

Evie grabbed the phone. "She wouldn't say it! I declare, I worked and worked with her . . ."

"Evie," he implored, "don't be disappointed. I loved what Miss Pattie said. It was very original—head and shoulders above the usual greeting."

"Well . . ." He heard the smile creep into her voice.

He didn't think he would ever again have those yearnings to be a milk-truck driver. If he couldn't say another thing about himself, he could say he loved his work.

What Cynthia and Dooley might be plotting, he couldn't imagine.

Roberto had flown home, Andrew Gregory had houseguests, Miss Sadie and Louella were frazzled from all the gaiety and would hardly answer the phone, Esther had carried out her threat and gone fishing with Ray . . .

Then again, maybe Cynthia and Dooley weren't plotting anything at all. Maybe they'd forgotten. Hadn't he forgotten Dooley's birthday? And when was Cynthia's? He felt a moment of panic.

Wait, there was the date—written on the wall next to his desk, his only graffiti since grade school. July 20. He breathed a sigh of relief.

He was convinced they'd forgotten.

At lunch, he saw Cynthia in her backyard, idly pruning a bush. And when he called home at three-thirty to see if Dooley was prepared for Miss Appleshaw, there was nothing in his voice that hinted at anything unusual.

He went home early, carrying the bundle of cards he'd received from the ECW, the Sunday school, Walter and Katherine, Winnie Ivey, Emma, Miss Sadie and Louella, and a dozen others.

As he went in the back door, he saw Cynthia going up her steps with something bulky under her jacket, glancing furtively toward the rectory. When she saw him, she averted her gaze as if he didn't exist.

Had he hurt her feelings after that blasted peanut business, when she laughed at him and he didn't laugh with her? He'd been pretty huffy about it, but why not? He'd gone nonstop for days on end and was flatly exhausted. Run here, run there, do this, do that, and then . . . crawling down the middle of Main Street on his hands and knees into the bargain.

He pricked his finger. He checked his urine. Then he put on his jogging suit and headed across Baxter Park.

Panting, he sat on the old stone wall beyond the Hope House site, at the highest elevation in Mitford. How long had it been since he overlooked this green valley, the Land of Counterpane?

Since he came into the world, he'd seen a lot of changes, but the sight that lay before him had changed little. Over there, a river gleaming in the sunlight. There, a curving road once hewn out for wagons. And there, scattered among the trees, church steeples poking up to be counted.

He heard a distant whistle and saw the little train moving through the valley. Train whistles, crowing roosters, the sound of rain on a tin roof—such simple music had nearly vanished in his life, and he missed it.

But then, life was full of valuable things that somehow managed to vanish.

He was startled to remember the green and sapphire marble that, at the age of twelve, he thought was the most beautiful object he had ever seen.

He had kept it in his pocket, showing it only to his mother, and of course to Tommy Noles, who crossed his heart three times and hoped to die if he ever mentioned its existence to another soul.

Showing it around would have been a violation, somehow. He kept it, instead, a private thing, never using it in a game. But he grew careless with it, he began to take it for granted, and where he had lost or misplaced it, he never knew.

He had grieved over that marble, in a way. Not over the thing itself, but over the loss of its private and remarkable beauty.

Hadn't Cynthia been like that to him? He had enjoyed the warmth and rarity of her nature, but he had never cherished her enough. Over and over, he had carelessly let her go, and only by the grace of God, she had not been taken from him altogether.

He remembered the times she had shut herself away from him, guarding her heart. The loss of her ravishing openness had left him cold as a stone, as if a great cloud had gone over the sun.

What if she were to shut herself away from him, once and for all? He stood up and paced beside the low stone wall, forgetting the scene in the valley.

He'd never understood much about his feelings toward Cynthia, but he knew and understood this:

He didn't want to keep teetering on the edge, afraid to step forward, terrified to turn back.

He felt the weight on his chest, the same weight he'd felt so often since she came into his life and he'd been unable to love her completely.

Perhaps he would always have such a weight; perhaps there was no true liberation in love. And certainly he could not ask her to accept him as he was—flawed and frightened, not knowing.

He turned and looked up and drew in his breath.

A glorious sunset was beginning to spread over the valley, and across the dome of heaven, stars were coming out. He had stood on this hill, wrapped in his selfish fears, while this wondrous thing was shaking the very air around him.

He felt tears on his face and realized the weight had flown off his heart. Every cloud over the valley was infused with a rose-colored light, and great streaks of lavender shot across the upland meadows.

Dear God! he thought if only Cynthia were here.

But Cynthia was there—in the little house just down the hill and through the park. She was there, not in New York or some far-flung corner, but there, sitting on her love seat, or feeding Violet, or putting her hair in those blasted curlers.

The recognition of her closeness to the very spot on which he stood was somehow breathtaking. He remembered the long, cold months of the dark house next door and the strained phone calls and the longing, and then she had come home at last.

The very sight of her had sent him reeling—yet once again, he had closed down his deepest feelings and managed to keep his distance from the only woman, the only human being he had ever known, who would eat the drumstick.

He was amazed to find that he was running; there was nothing but his beating heart and pounding feet. He felt only a great, burning haste to find her and see her face and let her know what he was only beginning to know and could no longer contain.

"There comes a time when there is no turning back," Walter had said.

He pounded on, feeling the motion of his legs and the breeze on his skin, and the hammering in his temples, feeling as if he might somehow implode, all of it combusting into a sharp, inner flame, a durable fire, a thousand hosannas.

Streaming with sweat, he ran past the cool arbors of Old Church Lane and across Baxter Park, desperate to see some sign of life in the little yellow house, to know she was there, waiting, and not gone away from him in her heart.

Her house was dark, but his own was aglow with light in every window, as if some wonderful thing might be happening.

He bounded through the hedge and into his yard and saw her standing at his door. She opened the door for him and held it wide as he came up the steps, and for one fleeting moment suspended in time, he sensed he had come at last to a destination he'd been running toward all his life.

Before the eleven o'clock service began, many of the Lord's Chapel congregation opened their pew bulletins and read the announcements.

There would be a regional Youth Choir performance in the church gardens on August 1. The Men's Prayer Breakfast would begin meeting at seven instead of seven-thirty on Thursdays, and would those who brought dishes to the bishop's brunch please collect their pans and platters from the kitchen.

Directly beneath the names of those who were bequeathing today's memorial flowers, they read the following:

I publish the banns of marriage between
Cynthia Clary Coppersmith
of the parish of the Chapel of Our Lord and Savior
and Father Timothy Andrew Kavanagh,
rector of this parish.
If any of you know just cause
why they may not be joined together in Holy Matrimony,
you are bidden to declare it.